The
COINCIDENCE

I0639825

Lauran Chilton

Editing, design, typesetting and publishing by UK Book Publishing

www.ukbookpublishing.com

ISBN: 978-1-918077-00-1

Preface

Love isn't always candlelit dinners and grand gestures. Sometimes, it's tripping over your own feet in front of your crush or accidentally sending a very inappropriate text – to the wrong person. This story is about romance in all its awkward, hilarious, and heartwarming glory. So buckle up for a journey filled with unexpected twists, laugh-out-loud moments, and just the right amount of chaos. Because when it comes to love, perfection is overrated – messy is way more fun.

Playlist

Lizzy McAlpine – *Ceilings*

Roses – *Imanbek, SAINt JHN*

Lika Morgan – *Go with the flow*

Moving On – *Porsche Love*

360 – *Charli cxc*

Lauve – *There's no Way*

Chapters

Aimee

NEW YORK, 9PM

Sitting on a cold, brass, unforgiving evening in a small diner on New York's busy Park Avenue nursing my coffee which I have been staring at for what seems like weeks, going through old photos of my mother and wondering what she would be saying to me and the mess I have gotten myself into.

I always seem to gravitate to this spot, I pick the same place, the same booth and I am here at the same time after I finish selling my soul for a lousy, less than adequate wage. I stare. I stare at people out the window who are laughing, going shopping and just, in general, going on with their lives. For myself though, I feel stuck. Stuck in a time warp, stuck in a never-ending cycle and life just seems to pass me by.

Wondering constantly why my 32-year old self finds myself in these predicaments. The waitresses keep looking over and I can tell from the disdain on their faces that they are annoyed, I haven't shown any kind of typical human social skills since I parked my backside on this seat. I live three blocks away from here so it's easy to come here and it's close by to my retail job which I loathe. I have been applying for jobs every day for five months and no nibbles, no interest – my love life is the same: *super ironic*. I lost my mother five years ago and I haven't been the same since, every day is a constant struggle and I keep feeling the sense of pure unwavering heaviness, it's paralysing, crippling and destroying me. I have lasted this long though, as my very few, selected friends tell me. Not that I get to see them very often as I am constantly running low on my social battery, another part of myself I am trying to work on; however, my mind keeps reverting to its old paranoid ways. As I reach in my tattered black bag to put away the photos of my mom, my phone vibrates. My long life friend Sacha blows up my screen:

1

> **Sacha:** Hey, hope you're doing good! I haven't seen you in what feels like forever, me and the girls are heading out to see a movie in a couple of hours if you fancy it?.

> **Me:** Hey, I'm not up to going out tonight, been a crazy day at work! Next time though! <3.

I sigh, take a deep breath, knowing I don't have the patience or, yet again, the social battery to attend their night out.

I await a reply; however, it never comes – they are probably irate at the fact they have asked me to go out three times this month and every single time, I say next time and it doesn't happen. Deciding to head back to my small apartment, I get up slowly whilst the eyes of the waitresses are burning holes in the back of my skull, I set out a larger tip as I know my vibe today is off. Heading out onto the sidewalk I wrap up warm, and zip my coat so far up my torso it's covering my mouth. Hearing people laugh and the different smells of the various food stalls has my stomach doing gymnastics. I throw in my headphones and decide to turn the volume up so high, I'm sure this amount of decibels is not recommended. The air is cold, but it's a welcome addition to wake up my tired eyes. The pavements are bustling with feet, and the yellow cabs are constantly beeping their horns. My long brown hair keeps getting tangled in my scarf so I just throw it up in a messy bun so it's out of my face and away from causing any passers by a face full of hair.

As I slowly approach my apartment building, I am so relieved; my apartment is small but it's the home I have made my own. I use the key fob on my keys to activate the door mechanism to open, my room is three flights up so it's not a crazy amount of stairs and you still get an acceptable view from the vast windows in the apartment. My door is number 33 and as soon as I turn the key, I can feel my battery slowly beginning to increase. My home is gorgeous here, the walls are lined with thick wood that gives it the old cottage vibe, long light fittings hang from the ceiling, they aren't too bright but just enough for them to make an impact. Numerous rugs adorn the different rooms which tie in with the cosy vibe in here too, I would say personally eighty-five percent, *no*, a solid ninety-five percent if I was to be smug about it. This place was desolate when I first moved in, I have put my finishing touches to it – or tried to. It's my sanctuary now, my favourite place to be. The high walls, and delicate structure offer such a kind aesthetic. Photos of my mom stare back at me; she always had the kindest eyes. My day job is crippling me at present, I am overworked, undervalued and most importantly, underpaid. *Don't you just love capitalism?* As I summon all the energy to thrust myself off the sofa, I take my phone out of my bag and put it on charge. As I bend down to plug in the cable, I notice my aunty Clara trying to call. I ignore it, I will call her back later once I have showered and once my brain stops spiralling. I walk slowly to my TV and turn it on for background music and sway along the oak stained floors. My bathroom is very minimalist, white décor with hanging plants that embellish the style and serenity that I wanted to achieve in my home. As I slide into the shower, the steam flowing through my nostrils automatically makes me relax, I take five deep, deep breaths and feel so much lighter, I feel elevated. The bubbles from the shower soap feel so soothing on my skin. I can hear the traffic outside and all the commotion of the city. As much as I enjoy living here, I have been thinking about changing my life up a bit, perhaps a new location? New job? Might even try and put myself back out there on the dating scene, since that aspect of my life has been pretty lifeless too. Deciding that my shower is finished, I grab the nearest towel from my tall, slim towel stand and wrap it around myself. I then suddenly catch, at the corner of my eye, my phone screen blowing up. I run to it and see a text from my ex-boyfriend Sebastian, *Urgh, what the fuck does he want?*

I slide open the text message notification, I look at the screen bewildered.

> **Sebastian:** Hey, I know we haven't spoken in a few months but do you fancy meeting up for a drink? I would like to talk to you about something. S X

> **Me:** Sebastian, Can I ask what is so important? Its late and I can not be involved in your BS!

> **Sebastian:** Look, I know things between us went south, I'm really sorry. Please can we just talk? I'm literally 6 blocks away, there's a small bar near you; I can meet you there in 30?

> **Me:** Look, I will meet you for 30 minutes, I have had one hell of a day, don't know what is so important that you couldn't just text me! I will be at Uno's in 25.

> **Sebastian:** Look forward to seeing you Amz 😊

> **Me:** *Thumbs Up*

"What an absolute hindrance he is!" I say to myself as I scramble through my clothes to try and make myself look presentable. I know, I know I should be more nonchalant about making myself look presentable; however, I guess my petty side is rearing its ugly head, and considering the reason we broke up was because of him wanting his cake and eating it! Too. As I storm around the apartment, my feet slapping the floor like a penguin on steroids, huffing and puffing for the inconvenience that this is, thank god tomorrow is Saturday and I am off work. I stare at myself in the mirror, being very overcritical I might add. I wear some baggy ripped jeans, a black polo neck sweater and throw my hair in a classy bun; I style my hair so I have two strands dangling on either side of my face. A very light dusting of make-up and I am ready to go! I take the phone off charge, pick up my keys that stay in a small basket on top of the long oak table in my hallway and head into the night.

As I bounce down the stairs in my apartment block – not because I'm excited, I feel angered and irked, to know I'm going to see my ex whose actions showed me the most disrespectful thing that someone can do – I take deep breaths, trying to compose myself. He must not see the vulnerable side of me, he has seen it before and it has done me no favours. Pressing the large green exit button by the door I join the footpath with so many other New Yorkers, I am cold, nervous – *Why on earth am I nervous?* I see Sebastian from the other side of the sidewalk. He's just as I remember him. Tall, thick black hair, tattoo sleeves on both his arms, Antarctic blue eyes, and a smile that would break a heart… it has. He approaches me, I appear standoffish. I stand in one place and just look at his face, take it all in and I remember the trauma that came with it. He pulls me in for an embrace; however, I keep my arms to my sides, I don't reciprocate the affection. *Why would I?*

"You look beautiful, you really do," is the first thing that comes out of that mouth as he smiles, showing his pearly whites at me.

I smile and say thanks. "Should we head in? I'm pretty cold out here," I retort to have him move us inside where I can have an alcoholic beverage.

Walking into UNOs is the typical Italian bar: dim lights, candles, booths and those emerald green leather seats; the atmosphere is so welcoming here as we usher ourselves to the booth at the back of the bar, the waitress guiding us through the Friday night crowd. Taking our seats and sitting opposite each other we have that stare, the stare where you look into each other's eyes and wonder where it all went wrong. We aren't saying a word to each other, just an awkward silence… *It's so awkward.*

Sebastian coughs. "So, how have you been? You're looking well." Smiling at me.

I take a deep breath. "Yeah, I'm good thanks, just working a lot and getting the apartment sorted; how is everything with you?" I pause, wanting to get to the bottom of this rendezvous. "What's this about, the reason for wanting to see me?"

He gives me the puppy dog eyes, the same puppy dog eyes he gave me when I found texts on his phone that day. We were so fucking happy, and he went and ruined it. He takes a moment to compose himself. "I needed to see you because I have been thinking a lot about you the past few weeks, daily actually."

My eyes start to roll, having a feeling of what's coming. "Why have you been thinking about me? We haven't seen each other in nearly ten months, Sebastian?" I say, staring into his eyes with a look of total confusion and frustration.

He answers back almost instantly, "Look, I know what happened hurt you in the most unforgiving way, we had something so spe–"

I cut him off with a look of pure venom. "Special? Yeah, I thought we were, I thought I was. Your actions proved otherwise."

He tenses his fists and starts rubbing them together in an awkward attempt to overlook how forward I am being. "Aimee, I have learned so much about myself the past few months and where I went wrong, I miss you, I miss what we had."

I swallow the Cabernet wine in my large glass and force my hand to grip the stem on the glass, surprised it doesn't break by the brute force. He notices and takes my hands into his. "Sebastian, what you don't seem to realise is: I will never be able to trust you again, it's done. Ten months done! Why come to me now and say all of this? It's not exactly warranted, is it?" Tears start to form in my eyes because he does this, he seeps underneath my skin like an acid, my skin burns and I feel myself reaching breaking point. *How fucking dare he!*

The waitress glides over wearing a smile, bringing Sebastian some more bottled beers. I take a menu and nearly slam it in my face, wanting to avoid any eye contact with her at all. She gives him the beverages and leaves our table. Very reluctant to move the menu away from my face, I slowly lower the menu away and look at him gulping the beer down his throat: he's nervous. *Good.*

"Why are we here really?" I snap.

He moves to be closer to me, he grabs my hands again. "I want us to try us again, Aimiee, I am so sorry about what happened, I was totally blind sighted, it was a mistake; I don't know what you want me to say."

I give him eyes that resemble daggers. "You texted me, don't act like this is something I can go through again, I can't. What you done took the air out my lungs for so long, it's never going to work, the one thing that could get us through any argument, you broke. Don't put this on me, to force a bond that I didn't break in the first place."

He's gesturing his head in his hands – I need to give this meeting an early exit. This is not doing me nor him any good.

"I need to go, Sebastian, this is not helping. I appreciate you trying to do this, but it's a no from me, you broke me." I stand up to go and he tries to stop me, I force his hand away from me, pull out my purse and pay for my wine – I may be pissed off but I'm still courteous. I slam the $30 on the table and walk out, the room is spinning around me and I feel like I can't breathe. I bust through the door and take the deepest intake of air to my lungs; the walls were closing in on me in there. I pull out my phone and scroll down to Sacha's number in the phonebook and call her. I need another drink but not with him; the sensible thing to do would be to head home, but I don't want to go home now, I need to just be.

The connection tone blasts through my ears and she answers "Hello?" in her innocent voice.

"Hey, where are you?" I ask, hoping she hasn't gone home and that she's still out, checking my back to see if Sebastian follows – he doesn't.

"I'm still out, just left the movies actually, why what's up, you sound upset?"

If only she knew, if only I could tell her what's happened. I find a quiet alleyway in the city and sit down to collect my thoughts. "Do you fancy going to Black Lounge? I need a drink, something's happened and I need someone to talk to." A sombre cry erupts in my chest; my heart is breaking. Part of me wants to run back to him and forget everything, but...the stubborn side of me will not let this happen.

"Aimee?" she questions as I have stopped talking. "Meet me at the Black Lounge in fifteen minutes?" she shouts, concerned.

"Okay," I reply and we disconnect from each other.

I rejoin the sidewalk and walk over to my next venue of the evening. *Here's me thinking tonight was gonna be pretty chilled!* I try and speed up my walking as I can feel the tears building up in the back of my eyes, the pressure is amplifying. I'm ready to let loose now, fuck it. Alcohol is never the answer, my Aunt Clara always used to tell me, in my young days after high school that the answers to life's issues are not at the bottom of a wine bottle; well, tonight they are; and I'm ready to hunt for them. Approaching the Black Lounge I scan the faces of the people drinking and I see her.

Sacha jumps up. "AIMEE!" waving her hands as if she has been trapped at sea.

I run. Run to the only person who I genuinely can trust at the moment. As we embrace each other I muffle words into her shoulder, she's hugging me so tight she can't hear what I'm saying. She's concerned, her eyes are bulging out of her sockets almost. She pulls my head to face hers and asks, "What on god's green earth has happened? You were going home after the diner, weren't you?"

I gulp, knowing I need to tell her what actually happened. The waiter brings us a bottle of wine and we sit, the partygoers looking at me, feeling their stares burn into my psyche. I need to just bite the bullet and tell her, I force myself to compose my heart thrashing in my chest. "I was in the shower and Sebastian texted me."

She raises one eyebrow, a look of disdain and a 'go on' motion with her head.

"He wanted to meet up as he needed to tell me something, cut a long story short he apologised for what he done, I wanted to believe it."

She pulls herself closer to me, shielding me; as she always has done. "What has his sorry ass got to say then, what's it been now? Eight, nine months?"

I reply to her, "Ten months now."

She continues to listen, and she asks, "So, how are you feeling? What's made you react this way? I thought you were past this?"

I think, I continue to think, piece together what has happened in my mind to answer her question. "I don't know, part of me wanted to take him back, but I could never trust him again."

She looks and replies, "Do you want my honest opinion?" I gulp and start to shake as I feel like she's going to rip me to shreds. She looks down at her shoes and then faces me. "I think you need to leave New York, get away; even if it's for a few months, you need to regroup. There's too many demons here for you; pack a bag, start from scratch and see what happens."

I'm shocked by her reply, I was expecting something warm and fuzzy, but being told to leave New York and start a new life; I mean, she doesn't mean permanently, does she? *No, she can't mean that.* I give her a look of confusion and the waiter comes and hands us the bill. We have been here for over an hour now and they are closing.

"Let's go back to yours, I will stay the night if that's okay?" she asks me.

I nod my head and we place our chairs under the tables and head to my apartment. Linking arms, we take in the sights, the skyscrapers are other worldly.

This city is mind-blowing at night, it's electric. We are five minutes from my apartment and we aren't talking, tonight has been very overwhelming for myself personally, *what an absolute headache this is.* Sacha has been my oldest friend, we met in Kindergarten and we have been inseparable since; she knew my mom, more importantly she knows me, in such a deep way. She's a tall, blonde, bubbly bombshell and the love I have for her holds no bounds. I will always have time for her, always.

We reach my apartment and walk up the stairs, dragging our feet. Using all the effort in our bodies to put one foot in front of the other. We finally get to the door; our sore feet and the throbbing sensation takes over our bodies. I open the door and turn my keys anticlockwise, the mechanism clicks into place and we walk into the apartment; the scent of vanilla and rosebud fills both of our nostrils. We both collapse on the sofa and inhale long sighs. We stare into each other's eyes, no words are said, it's almost like we can communicate telepathically. I lean over to peak through my bag and pull out my phone. I expel a slight groan: it's Sebastian.

Is this guy joking? I have no energy to fight this anymore, I'm empty. I pass the phone over to Sacha, she snatches it from my hands in lightning speed and glares down back at the screen, then turns to me.

"Aimee, you know I love you, you need to seriously consider the advice I gave you before, I can take care of this place, give yourself six months and try to regroup your mind."

I stare back at her with my bloodshot eyes, my eyelids struggling to keep themselves open. I start to type.

> **Sebastian:** I left UNO's and started looking for you, you really didn't need to storm out, I was being honest Aimee, I still love you; please can we not sort this?

> **Me:** Look, I cant do this. Please delete my number. I have been doing some thinking and I'm going to leave town for a while, I wish you all the best in what you do. But I need to leave, you hurt me so fucking much and I don't think I will even forgive you. Just stay safe please.

I wait a couple of moments, which feel like centuries, for a reply and no reply comes. I glance over at Sacha and she's typing a million miles an hour on her phone.

"What's up?" I ask quietly.

She has a demented look on her face, I can see her fingers and thumbs on her phone exiting apps and reopening new ones in lightning speed, she's also writing numerous texts. She sets her phone down on the side of the sofa and turns to face me. "My aunt owns her own bridal shop in Boston, her assistant manager just quit out of the blue a couple of days ago, she said with your experience you would be a great fit, no interview needed; you wanna take it?"

My eyes bulge, I press down on the bottoms of my eye as I feel like I am in a Catch 22 situation. *What do I do?* I respond with, "I love how you just drop news like that on me, especially after the night I have had." I try and smirk to bring a lightness to the conversation, however it falls flat.

She starts to fidget, this is a bad sign, she only fidgets when she's annoyed. "It's not news, Aimee, it's a choice. You don't have a lot of them flying around in your life at the moment so I just wanted to help you. What do you wanna do?"

I decide to remove myself form the situation momentarily. I am not the most confrontational of people, this is for the best.

I walk over slowly to my balcony and stare at the skyline outside my window, I need to make a decision. I turn my back to see Sacha has gotten up and is making us a cup of hot chocolate, she knows my kitchen inside and out. It hits me like a truck that my Aunt Clara did try and call me this evening; it's two am now, she won't be awake, *Will she?* I pull out my phone and text my aunt...

> **Me:** Aunt C! How are you doing? SOOOOOOOOOOO Sorry I missed your call tonight, its been a crazy one!! Give me a call back in the morning please ☺ love ya xxxx

To my absolute surprise I see the three small dots writing back. I glare at the screen, she's never up this early, late, early – whatever.

> **Aunt C:** Yes! I tried to call you! What's happened? I'm just out with a few friends at the moment honey. Do you need me to swing by? Aunt C <3

> **Me:** No it's fine, I met up with Sebastian, Look I'm wanting to potentially take a new job in Boston... I wanted you advice on the subject... Sacha has kindly said she would stay at my place for 6 months until I sort my head out. xxx

Incoming Call: *Aunt Clara... Compose yourself, Aimee, Here we go.*

"Good Morning, Aimee, what's all this about? I am growing ever so slightly worried," she exclaims. Aunt Clara is sounding more inquisitive than normal.

I take a quick intake of oxygen and just let my mouth get carried away. "Sorry to disturb you so late, I need your advice on something," I say quietly.

"Go on," she drags out.

"Sacha's aunt has her own bridal store in Boston, and she feels I would be a good fit for the job, so I was thinking of accepting the job, going to Boston for six months and see what happens, leave my future totally in the hands of fate." A cheeky grin arrives on my face at the prospect of something new.

"Aimee darling, I have always promised after we lost your mum to be your cheerleader in anything you do, you make me so proud every day, sweetheart, The important question is do you want to go?"

I stop in my tracks, staring at the twinkling lights of New York beneath my feet, trying to weigh up the pros and cons in my head before I give her a definite answer. "Yes," I say. I stand back to check on Sacha to see if she heard me answer the question; she didn't. She's asleep and the hot chocolate she made has gone cold. I can tell as the steam from the cream and marshmallows has disappeared. I sit back down, still on the phone to my aunt Clara.

"You need to go, sweetheart, if it doesn't work out then your apartment will be here in New York and you can just carry on as normal, the only issue will be your retail job. However, I'm sure I can find you something, being a lady of business."

She's right, she knows some pretty high profile people. My aunt Clara was more into adding education and research to her life instead of having kids. I do ask her sometimes if she regretted it and her answer is always the same: "me and your mum shared you, your father was never in the picture so I took on the father duties – which I was more than happy to do as I fell in love with you when you were born". I think when my mum had passed my aunty took it upon herself to be in my back pocket most of the time; however, now she hasn't taken her place as sorts, but she's accepting the responsibility to be there, which I will be forever grateful for.

"Look, let me know when your flights are and keep me updated with everything! And remember, I'm only a phone call away!"

I smile, knowing that whatever happens with me, she will always be there. She really is my guardian, in another aspect she's my guardian angel. We end the phone call, and I notice Sacha doesn't have a blanket. I walk over to her, mostly tiptoeing trying not to make noise and I reach over to my other sofa and pull a warm, dark orange throw over her to keep her warm. Once that was done, I dragged my feet to my bedroom. Tonight has been a whirlwind for me, so many emotions and so many thoughts ricocheting from the sides of my brain. I take off my clothes and starfish in my fresh Egyptian cotton sheets, my head falls into the duck feather pillows and they swallow my head. Within minutes I am out.

Sam

I am woken by the incessant sound of my alarm, another day, another dollar as they say. I have my own apartment, I work in a small antique store outside of town which is a nightmare to get too; however, I go in every day – antiques are my passion and the people I meet along the way are an added bonus! I swing my whole body clockwise and my feet slam on the floor. No point in checking my phone as I have been under the radar recently, I think my friends have just stopped asking me how I am since work has been pretty hectic. I step into my bathroom and look in the mirror – my thick brown hair seriously needs a trim. I work out twice a week. I have recently been checking out some tattoo designs; however, not sure I have the balls to go through with it. The shower takes up the majority of the bathroom, a long rectangular shape of glass, pristine white tiles with black accessories. I have done well, my parents are high end realtor agents, so money has never been an issue for me growing up. Dad wanted me to go into the family business but instead of being obsessed with houses, I was obsessed with the objects that went in them, the objects that create memories. It was a hesitant time at the dinner table at home when I told Mum and Dad that I wanted to go off on my own and build my own life – they didn't like that; but it happened anyway.

I slam the shower door behind me and start my showering routine, I use the shower gel slowly over my abs and make sure to give my hair the wash it needs. Most women think a guy having thick hair is a blessing; to the guy, it's a curse. The scent of Oak, Cedar and Oud fills the room and it smells delectable. The steam swallowing my whole body and relaxing my muscles as they tense, thinking of the day ahead. I hop out of the shower and open my Bradwell Oak wardrobe, the shirts are snow white, crisp and ironed to perfection. I always dress smart for work, image is confidence and when you are selling items that cost over $2,000 a piece, you need to look your best. I quickly use the hairdryer through my thick hair to make sure I can style it as needed. Before I leave my three-bedroom apartment in Devonshire Street, I give myself a quick glance in the body length mirror in the apartment, I wear a gentlemen's coat to top of my signature look, with a grey scarf. I scarper down the halls, passing different residences and I wave to my neighbours on the way out. I walk toward my car, a Jaguar I – Pace, jet black; this car is one of my most prized possessions. I got a pretty decent bonus a few months back from my job so decided to splash out on a new car.

My phone automatically connects to the car when I am a certain distance away. It alerts me to look on at the screen – I stare at the screen, a text has come through from one of my best friends.

> **Duncan:** Dude! What's happening with you recently? We never hear from you now! Look, if we aren't too much of peasants for you, we are going to Offsuit tonight for 7, if you wanna tag along??? Let me know ASAP

I speak to my car as it writes the reply on command.

> **Me:** Hey, I'm really good! Just focusing on work! And yeah, be good to catch up with you guys! I will be there for 7.30. See you all then!

18

That ought to shut them up for the remainder of the day. To be fair, I'm being harsh, it's nice to have friends who actually check in and give a shit.

My workplace is around a forty-five minute drive out of the city, a beautiful drive on a summer's day. Passing landmarks like Fenway Park *GO SOX!* And the public garden, it really is good for the soul and makes me appreciate the city with every bated breath. The antique shop is small; however it houses insane artefacts – we tend to not get the general public in here, it's more of the high clientele clients, celebrities and such like, people who have more money than sense, quite happy to spend a month's wage on a small trinket box; well, because they can. The warm Boston air running through my hair, I have my music almost on full volume as I pull up to the store, cars are already in the parking lot waiting for us to open. The building is nestled in plants, bushes and all kinds of shrubbery, we have a groundskeeper who keeps it well maintained; in the winter – not so much. I walk over the gravel outside, my shoes making a crunching noise with every step I take, take a deep breath and my day begins.

Aimee

NEW YORK, 7AM

I stir in my sleep, I feel like I have been hit by a juggernaut, my head hurts, my stomach is in knots, my feet hurt, and my head is banging like I have a full bandstand of drums banging in my head. I force both my eyes to open, the sun blinding through my curtains in my bedroom, I sprint up wanting to talk to Sacha and get the wheels in motion for my new adventure. I roll on my front and throw myself up, jumping to the door I pull my dressing gown off the hook and wrap it around my curves. My door makes a long creaking sound as I tiptoe down the hallway to wake Sacha; her long blonde hair covers her face and I can't tell if she's still dead to the world or wide awake. I stand over her and touch her shoulder ever so slightly, I push her shoulder using the most minimum force.

"Hey! Good morning" I whisper. My eyes watching her stretch and try to gather her thoughts.

"Oh my days! How long have I been asleep for?" she asks. "I went asleep around 3am, as soon as my head hit the pillow I was done."

I smile.

Sacha moves her body so that she's facing me, adjusting herself and wrapping the blanket around her frame. "So how are you feeling? Have you thought about what I suggested?" she asks.

I stare at her and smile. "Yeah, I spoke to my Aunt Clara last night and she's all for it."

"How do you feel about it though? Don't do it for the feeling of being forced, do it because you want to," she says.

"I know, I need to do something, I need to hit the reset button I think, who knows, I might end up really enjoying this venture," I say in an excited tone.

She stands up abruptly and grabs her phone, starts typing and she stops, looks at me and a cheeky grin swallows her face. "Well, you are now officially a Bridal Store assistant manager! You start in four days." She shows her phone to my face, and her aunt has provided all the necessary information. I go quiet. *I can't believe I'm actually doing this. Am I doing the right thing?*

As I sit down next to her, I pull my laptop from under my sofa with a groan; I flip over the screen and start looking to book flights, the nervousness in my mental state starting to set in. I take a deep breath and select a one-way ticket, *Should I? Or to be safe shall I just buy the return ticket?* My eyes are scanning the different options, my eyes making the fast movement from one option to the other. I look over at Sacha; she stares at me with her left brow uplifted.

"I know, I'm stalling, aren't I?" I ask in a sheepish manner.

She exclaims in her own typical fashion, "Yes. Yes you are; do you want me to get them for you?"

I feel disappointment in myself: *how can I not even do this part right with no support?* I check my diary and make a note of the dates and start writing a list of loose ends I need to tie up before I leave. *This is really happening.* I hear the banking app on my iPhone make a noise – the money has been debited from my account, the flight has been paid for, JFK – BOS in four days, it's there in black and white now.

As Sacha Sachays away into the kitchen, still with the blanket wrapped around her frame, I hear a loud pop in my kitchen. I gasp at the noise, turning around, throwing myself off my sofa. I see Sacha standing there with a champagne bottle and two champagne flutes.

"You done it, my girl! I am so proud you're going on this journey."

I walk over to her, dragging my feet, tears starting to form. *Have I made the right choice? I'm actually going to do this…by myself.* The doubt seeps in through my veins like a poison, slow and insidious, clouding my mind with whispers of uncertainty. I get to my best friend, and she wraps her arms around my frame; I repay the favour by hugging her back. *Silence.* We don't say anything, time stops, stands still, refuses to move forward; a very sombre emotion fills us both. I'm only an hour and twenty minutes away from her, but it's still something to contend with. We look at each other, a couple of minutes go by, we both smile; it sinks in: I'm leaving New York in a matter of days.

She cranks the radio and turns the music up, we both dance around my kitchen island like a pair of uncontrollable monkeys, moving our arms and hips to the beat, grabbing each other's hands and swinging each other around.

"You're going to Boston, baby girl," she screams. "Oh my days, there is so much to sort out before you go."

After our fun of acting like teenagers ends, we both sit on the small balcony. I have my small notepad with me, I start to write down notes. My main focus is to leave my current job, *thank heavens, I never thought I would get out of there.* The apartment is fine as Sacha will be staying here, her boyfriend will just keep an eye on their place. Beyond work and the logistics, I have a more personal set of things to wrap up. I need to say a proper goodbye to friends and family, making sure to meet up with those I haven't seen in a while. The thought of leaving my support network behind is bittersweet, but I am eager to embrace the challenges and opportunities that await me in Boston before continuing my journey to New York. With each passing day, my to-do list seems to grow, but I am determined to leave no stone unturned as I am stepping into the future I have always dreamed of.

Sam

BOSTON, 5PM

I have been on my feet all day, surrounded by the scent of aged wood and leather in the small antique store I work in. It had been a typical hectic Saturday, with customers browsing for hours, some searching for rare treasures while others simply enjoyed the atmosphere of the place. I love the charm of the store, but by the end of the day, my mind is drained, my feet are sore from pacing the floors. The shop is a maze of quirky furniture, vintage jewellery, and dusty books, and I've spent most of the afternoon carefully wrapping fragile items, negotiating with potential buyers, and making sure everything was in its proper place. The work was fulfilling, but it was also exhausting.

I stare at the large grandfather clock in the store and I was finally able to close up, take a deep breath, and change into something a little more relaxed. I normally don't look forward to seeing my friends as much as I have today, we have gotten into the rut of families, girlfriends, fiancées; well not me, not speaking for myself on that one. I just haven't had: one, the time; or two, no one special enough has caught my eye; takes a lot for a woman to appreciate I enjoy my work – finding a guy who talks about his job can put some broads off. The day has been long, but the thought of unwinding with a cold pint at the local bar has kept me going. I've never been one for wild nights out, but I do enjoy these low-key evenings with my friends, talking about everything and nothing over pints of ale. It is the perfect antidote to the relentless pace of my workday, and as I step out into the crisp evening air, I feel a sense of relief wash over me, ready to relax and enjoy the night ahead.

I step into the bar with my mates, the heavy wooden door creaking behind us as we shuffle inside. The warm buzz of conversation and clinking glasses hits me right away, and I can feel the energy of the place wash over me. The dim lighting casts a comfortable glow, and I notice a few regulars gathered at the bar, chatting with the bartender. The smell of fried food and beer is thick in the air, a familiar scent that always seems to bring a smile to my face. My friends are already joking and laughing, making their way towards a booth near the back. I follow close behind, scanning the room, soaking in the low hum of Boston's nightlife. The place has a gritty charm to it, the kind of bar that has seen its fair share of good times and bad. There's something about it, though – something real – that makes me feel at home. I slide into the booth next to one of my mates, giving the waitress a nod as she approaches.

We order a round of drinks, the conversation flowing as easily as the pints. I can hear snippets of the talk around us, a mix of sports chatter and old stories, and it reminds me why I love this city. The camaraderie here is like no other, and I realise that moments like this, with good friends in a familiar spot, are what make life feel grounded. As the night wears on, the laughter gets louder, and I can't help but think this is exactly where I'm meant to be. We throw a couple of jokes around the table, as young guys our age do, the waitress brings us a full round of Samuel Adams beer steins, we all take a sip and the conversation starts rolling.

"So how are you guys then? Been a few months since we all caught up like this?" Robert exclaims. He is just recently married; dad of one, so the chances he gets to let his hair down are few and far between; he looks more rugged than usual.

Josh answers his question as if instantaneously: "not too bad, obviously me and Rachel split a few weeks ago; so it's been a bit rough".

There's silence across the table. *How come none of us were told about this?* We all glance at each other with a look of bewilderment on our faces.

"What?" I shout to him. "When did this happen, how, why?"

He starts to look down at his drink, picks it up by the bottom and start to swirl it around using his fingers; indicating he's nervous. He takes a long gulp of his beverage and slowly starts to revert his eyes back to us all, he takes a long breath and exclaims, "We just weren't working, families didn't get along in the first place, I loved her; I guess sometimes it's not meant to be." His tone lowers an octave.

We all take a deep sigh for him.

"I can't believe you never told anyone about this, dude, it's not something you keep to yourself, times like that you needed us."

A nonchalant look appears on his face. "I still do, I'm devastated; you guys all have busy lives, I didn't wanna ruin the dynamic of that," he expresses, his face falling back to his beer.

I pipe up and say hastily, "You still should have told us, man, what are friends for? Doesn't matter what's going on in our lives, we are always there for each other." I hold my hands out to gesture his response; nothing comes.

Steven quickly ushers the conversation in a different direction. "So, Sam? How have you been? Anyone on the scene for you yet?"

I smirk, "nope" very suddenly.

They all tut their heads, I face them all and stare into their eyes. "There isn't, haven't been looking, to be honest. My mom keeps asking the same thing. I'm pretty happy with how my life is at the moment." I shrug off his question in a typical fashion for myself. I can see their eyes examining me and my body language to see if they can sense a flicker of deception. I hope I don't give anything away. Truth is, a part of me does want to get on the dating scene, I just can't physically stomach the awkward first date stages, where you're constantly putting your best face forward, to hope someone will like you; not my thing. The waitress arrives at the table with another round of drinks; I can see a bottle of Jägermeister in the front of her apron. She picks the bottle by the lid and pushes it on the table as my eyes begin to water. *Knew this night would end up on the crazy side.*

As the hours go by, the liquor turns to shots, more steins, and some bad decisions from the rest of the boys. A couple of them have started loitering on the dance floor; Steven and myself decide it's a smart idea to try and finish the bottle, looking on at our friends making absolute fools of themselves trying to attract the opposite sex. *It's quite entertaining.* We both start to combust into a frenzy of sheer giggles. The hours ahead don't disappoint. It's coming up to 10.30pm now, I would be lying if I said I never had my try on the dance floor, I dance appallingly. We took photos, made idiotic videos, before I know it the night is over and we are standing outside finishing our conversation and saying goodbyes, no doubt tomorrow our group chat will be buzzing. Little did I know, in three days, my life was going to change forever.

Aimee

NEW YORK, 10AM, THREE DAYS TO GO...

As I step out onto the bustling streets of New York, the hum of the city vibrating through my shoes as I make my way down the crowded sidewalk, the constant chorus of honking taxis, the chatter of hurried pedestrians, and the distant rumble of the subway underneath adds to the cacophony that is uniquely New York. The wind carries the sharp smell of hot dog carts and street food, but I barely notice it as I weave in and out of people, making my way towards the nearest corner shop.

Inside the small store, the familiar ding of the door chime rings out, followed by the soft shuffle of people moving about the aisles. The fluorescent lights buzz overhead, casting a harsh glow on the shelves lined with snacks, toiletries, and all sorts of last-minute essentials. The faint sound of music plays from an old radio behind the counter, a mix of pop hits and local advertisements that drift in and out of focus. I hear the crinkle of plastic bags as others grab their items, the clink of coins in the register, and the occasional murmur of someone asking the cashier about the nearest subway.

As I grab the last few things on my list, I can't help but notice how the city's noise seems to follow me, even inside the quiet corners of a shop like this. The sounds of footsteps on the pavement, the low chatter from the street outside, and the occasional burst of laughter from the people in the aisles create this constant rhythm that feels like the heartbeat of the city. I take a deep breath, feeling the energy of New York around me as I head for the checkout, ready to face whatever the day holds next.

My phone starts beeping as the group chat myself and the girls are in goes haywire.

> **Sal:** Okay girls, what we thinking for @Aimees leaving party?
> I was thinking of cocktails in SoHo and maybe a horse and cart ride through Central Park

Sally questions.

> **Isabella:** GIR£, there ain't no carriage big enough for all 7 of us 😮😮😮

Isabella exclaims.

Hope chimes in

> **Hope:** "TBF @Sally is at least thinking of something. I was just gunna show up for drinks and see where the night takes us LOL"

I smile at the discussion; some of the girls are super organised, then the most of them are free spirits. I wait for Sacha's response, nothing comes through directly, then I see the three dots appearing on my screen. She then enters the chat:

> **Sacha:** Girls, it's all planned, and BTW, the woman who we are doing this for is in the chat! Come on now! I surely have taught you guys better than this! No more will be spoken on the subject

She's such a boss!

> **Sal:** 😵

> **Isabella:** 👻?

A small giggle leaves my throat. My girls have always had my back! Through losing my mom, the whole Sebastian situation, and now I get to embark on this journey with them not by my side; but I know in spirit they are with me. I will be forever grateful for them always. My leaving party is happening tomorrow night, I have tonight by myself in my sanctuary. I need to regroup and get back into the journaling side of things, I have a lot of thoughts and feelings that need to be extracted from my head. I used to always carry my journal with me, but I have let it slide the past few months. I need to keep my demons at bay, they are starting to surface again.

Before I lost my mom I was diagnosed with an disorder. I wouldn't wish it upon my worst enemy, it's such a complex state of mind to explain to anyone who doesn't experience it themselves; it was a huge issue in mine and Sebastian's relationship; a huge life drain, we were at each other's throats, he was fighting with my disorder; I was fighting with my head, none of our arguments were directly at each other. It sometimes felt like there were three people in our relationship, well there was because he cheated; however, if I say four, myself, Sebastian, my anxiety and his side chick. I would be lying to you if I didn't think my anxiety played a part in him feeling the need to do that.

Anxiety often feels like an ever-present weight pressing down on my chest, making it hard to breathe or think clearly. It creeps in at the most unexpected times, a sudden rush of dread that I can't shake off, no matter how hard I try. Sometimes, it's the simple things – leaving the house, making a phone call, or even just getting through the day without feeling overwhelmed. My mind races with a thousand thoughts, each one worse than the last, convincing me that something terrible is about to happen. It's exhausting, this constant battle, trying to keep it all together while feeling like I'm on the edge of losing control. Even when I know there's no real danger, my body reacts as if there is, and it's hard to convince myself that I'll be okay. When I was with Sebastian a few days ago, it was so difficult to leave as a part of me felt the reason our relationship broke down was because of my mind, my ever so damaged, hurt and confused mind.

I walk through my apartment door and smell the rosemary candles that I must have forgotten to blow out before I left; I glance around the living room/ kitchen to see the packages of new clothes, considering I will be in Boston till the autumn, then depending how the job goes and if I find my footing, I will hopefully be in New York for November time. I have treated myself to some Victorian style dresses, some of them come with the most cutest hats. It's only right I dress the part – I can't really be in charge of a stunning bridal shop in Boston and turn up in drab clothes. I turn on the TV for background noise and I start the preparation. My new boss kindly sent an email detailing all the plans for when I am in Boston. I look at the photos of my new apartment; it's on Brookline Avenue and looks so cosy and decadent. The street is right in the middle of the city; which is ideal for me. I have so much sightseeing planned as soon as I touch down.

Looking over at my bright blue suitcase, I start to pack some of my essentials; I have the other essentials arriving via mail. Sacha has been kind enough to agree to do this for me. Feeling very excitable and a dash overwhelmed, I throw myself from the sofa to the bathroom, time to take a long soak, read a good book and to relax before the mayhem with the girls tomorrow.

Sam

BOSTON 10.30 AM

I wake up slowly, disoriented by the soft light streaming through the floor-to-ceiling windows. The room feels too warm, too still, and my head is pounding like it's got its own rhythm. I sit up, squinting as I glance around the space, realising I'm not in my usual place. The apartment is stunning – everything sleek and modern, with glossy surfaces and soft, ambient lighting. The city skyline stretches out beyond the glass, but I can't quite focus on it yet. My body feels sluggish, as if it's still recovering from whatever was consumed last night.

As I swing my legs over the side of the bed, I immediately regret the movement. The world spins for a moment, my stomach churns, and my dry mouth reminds me of the half-empty wine glass I'd left on the coffee table last night. I rub my temples, trying to summon any memory of how I ended up here. The faint scent of aftershave still lingers in the air, and I wonder briefly if I'd even locked the front door. It's strange to feel so out of place in such a luxurious setting, like I'm a guest in someone else's life.

I pull myself up, walking cautiously across the polished floor towards the kitchen. There's something comforting about the space – a mix of expensive yet inviting. The espresso machine hums to life as I press the button, hoping the coffee might make this unbearable headache subside. The bright morning light reflecting off the marble countertops only adds to the surreal feeling that today is somehow both new and a continuation of yesterday's chaos. A quick glance at the clock tells me I've overslept. The day is already well underway, and yet I feel stuck in a haze, as if time itself has slowed down just for me.

The coffee is strong and bitter, and I sip it slowly, leaning against the cool granite. The high-end kitchen, with its immaculate surfaces and state-of-the-art appliances, only heightens the feeling of detachment. I don't belong here, I tell myself. My clothes from last night are scattered on the couch – nothing about this place feels familiar. Yet, as I try to piece together the fragmented moments of the evening, I realise that nothing is truly out of reach. I could almost see myself living this life... if only I could remember how I got here.

Steven pokes his head out of the bathroom. "Oh wow, good morning, was beginning to think you weren't gonna wake up today." He smiles at me and begins to walk towards me; I strain my eyes to match his.

"Hey, how on earth did I end up here? I thought we all got separate cabs home?" I ask him, confused about last evening's antics.

"Yeah, we did; I hopped in your cab very last minute, you then decided to crash here," he answers my question subtly.

I decide to finish off this coffee and head to the room I stayed in.

I groggily pull on my clothes from the night before, hoping I haven't spilled anything down myself, and make my way to the bathroom. The mirror reflects a face I almost don't recognise – hair a bit of a mess. I splash my face with cold water, attempting to shake off the grogginess, but it's clear I'll need more than just a quick rinse to get back to full functioning. My friend's house is quiet, he's probably still recovering in the kitchen from last night's chaos.

After a quick breakfast of whatever's in the kitchen – bread, a quick spread of jam, nothing too fancy – I gather my things, checking the pockets of my jacket for my wallet and keys. It's strange, I'm not entirely sure what time it is, but I've got a feeling it's later than I should have let it. I take one last look around the living room, where we were all sitting and laughing just hours ago, now looking eerily quiet. A few half-empty glasses, shoes strewn about, and the odd jacket left behind. I need to leave and plant myself on my sofa, with junk food and bad horror movies. So, with a half-hearted wave and a quiet "see you soon", I grab my bag and head out the door, ready to finally make my way home.

The cab ride through Boston feels like a slow return to reality. The streets are quieter now, the early morning fog still lingering over the city, as if it hasn't quite woken up yet. I lean back against the seat, the hum of the engine filling the silence, while the occasional bump in the road reminds me that my head's not exactly at its sharpest. The driver's focused on the road, glancing at me in the rearview mirror every now and then, probably wondering where I've come from – or more likely, if I'll make it through the journey without passing out. I glance out the window, watching the city go by, feeling like an outsider in my own town. The streets I usually walk with ease now seem foreign, as though I've just stepped out of some strange dream.

As we pass the Commons, the trees are bare, their skeletal branches reaching up like twisted fingers. There's a certain stillness to the place in the morning, almost peaceful, but I can't help but feel the weight of the night still pressing on me. My mind is flicking between fragments of last night – laughter, a few too many drinks, faces I'll probably never see again – but it all feels distant now. Boston's skyline looms in the distance, its towering buildings catching the early light, and I realise I'm almost home. The familiar streets bring a sense of comfort, but my body is craving the quiet of my apartment. I'm so close, I can practically taste it.

The cab pulls up to my building, and I hand the driver more than I probably should, still feeling a bit dazed. He gives me a nod, and I climb out, grateful to have finally made it. I shuffle through the lobby, the smell of old wood and faint disinfectant welcoming me back. As I walk up the stairs to my apartment, the last remnants of last night slip away with every step. The door clicks open, and I'm hit by the familiar scent of my place – coffee, fresh linens, and that odd mix of comfort that always makes me feel at ease. I toss my bag on the couch, kick off my shoes, and collapse onto the bed, finally letting myself exhale. Home at last.

My home is my safe place, my mom and dad come and visit me once a month. I am grateful for the visits of course; however, all I get asked is "have you found a girlfriend yet?" from my mom. My dad will then pipe up "Can't believe a dashing guy like you isn't snapped up", the inevitable eye rolls will be in full force. I quickly run to my kitchen and check the calendar, thank all my lucky stars there isn't a visit coming up in the not so distant future. I start slowly undressing, my clothes hitting the floor as I walk along my hallway to the bathroom, I need a shower. Once the shower is finished, I will be reacquainting myself with the sofa.

As the hot water hits my skin, and I let out a relieved sigh, as if it's washing away the remnants of the night – both the exhaustion and the memories I'm not ready to deal with just yet. I stand there for what feels like ages, letting the steam fill the bathroom, the pressure of the water soothing the tightness in my muscles. It's like I'm stepping into a different world, where everything can be put on hold for a moment. The shower gel smells familiar, a simple scent of lavender and something fresh, and I take my time, scrubbing away the grime and the fatigue. The warmth wraps around me, and for the first time today, I feel like I can breathe, like I'm getting a second wind. It's one of those small luxuries that make everything feel a little bit more manageable.

Aimee

As I slowly stir from my slumber, staring at the ceiling with endless possibilities proceeding through my skull, I can't shake off the constant feeling of the unknown. I don't know if this my anxiety playing its old tricks again; sucking the joy out of any pleasant experience I have encountered in my life, turning things into disasters. I honestly feel like this is a curse, it's not like the tablets the doctor has prescribed me help, it's just a never ending cycle. I turn over and look at my phone: 8.15am; tonight is the big night where me and the girls are hitting the town! Worst of all, I have no idea what's planned, the girls were about to spill the plans a couple of days ago, however Sacha stopped them before they did. *I actually don't know what they have planned – should I be excited? Concerned?*

My bags are packed, and it's official, tomorrow will be my last day in New York before I descend into the unknown. I am excited, nervous but more importantly; I'm stepping out of my routine and that can only be a good thing.

I glance at the clock, realising I was running out of time. The girls would be here in a couple of hours, and I still had a mountain of things to do before the big night out. It was supposed to be a celebration, but with everything going on, it felt a little surreal. I was about to leave New York for Boston, and the thought of saying goodbye to everything I knew was starting to hit me.

I shove the last of the laundry into the washing machine and started to tidy up the kitchen, wiping down surfaces and throwing away empty bottles. The apartment looks like a bomb has gone off – typical me when I am stressed. I am used to chaos, but not on a night like this.

As I pick up a few bits from the counter, I catch sight of the packed boxes stacked by the door. A weird mixture of excitement and dread bubbles up inside me. I haven't really let myself think about it – about leaving my life here behind – but now, with everything suddenly so real, it feels like I am suffocating under the weight of it all.

I quickly push the thoughts aside, taking a deep breath and reminding myself this is supposed to be fun. A night with the girls. A farewell to New York, not a goodbye. I need to pull myself together.

I select some music to drown out the silence, the upbeat rhythm filling the apartment, and get to work on tidying the living room. I arrange the cushions, set out some snacks on the coffee table, and light a couple of candles. Nothing over the top, just enough to make it feel like a proper send-off.

Once that is done, I dig through my wardrobe to find something to wear. I have no idea what the night holds in store, but I know I have to look my best – one last hurrah before leaving for a new chapter in a new city. I try on three different outfits, none of them feeling quite right, before settling on a simple red dress. Classic, elegant, and just the right amount of effort.

The doorbell rings, snapping me back to reality. The girls are here. I take a final look around the apartment, mentally noting the last few things I need to grab before I leave, then pick up my phone and keys.

"Right," I mutter to myself. "Let's do this."

I open the door to their eager faces, and for a moment, everything feels normal again. Tonight isn't about goodbyes. It is about celebrating the adventure ahead. I sprint up wearing a knee length red dress which has no straps, my hair is pinned up like a Hollywood starlet in the 60s, my make up is effortless but chic, red lipstick adorns my face and it sets off the whole ensemble. I stare at myself in the long mirror in the hallway *I must say, I do scrub up well, if I don't say so myself.* The doorbell rings again, not just one ring, four rings and this did indeed declare the girls' impatience. I snap back into the real world with a force that rivals being dropped from space, with a thud;

my eyes refocus on my blurry reflection and I turn around and throw my arm to the front door and flick the latch off the mechanism, the door then flings open, there they are: my girls.

They come running towards me, open arms and smiles, Sally and Hope have tears in their eyes, avoiding eye contact with them as that will get the evening off to a not so good start. They walk past me one by one, giving warm hugs as they move into the living room. Sacha opens a large bottle of rose Moet champagne and you hear the pop all through the apartment. As the cork hits the ceiling, we all look to find where it has landed, already on our feet we all start to giggle in unison. I glance back to see Sacha filling one champagne flute up to the brim, then she takes a gulp from the bottle herself. *She always has been greedy.* She begins to shout, "Come on, ladies, your drinks are served." Banging her hands on the countertops and being her loud usual self. We all scarper to the island in the kitchen and stand around it, we grab the glasses in our hands ready to toast.

Sacha pipes up again and raises her glass. "We are all gathered here to cordially bid farewell to our missing piece in our friendship group. She's moving to Boston in a matter of days and yet it's not goodbye, it's just a see you later." Her voice croaks. "We will miss you, and let's make tonight a night to remember, oh, and don't forget to text us when you land." A smirk lifts on her face.

Tears are forming in my eyes already and I look at all their faces, I am so blessed to have these girls in my life, they are the reason I am still here. My head faces down to avoid contact again and I can feel their eyes burning at my forehead, I lift my head up ever so slightly, they are smiling at me. I cough to try and make my voice less hoarse, I plaster a smile on my face, and face the music. "Thank you, ladies." I stop, take a deep breath, well a couple of deep breaths, I focus on my drink, trying not to become emotional at their wide eyes.

"You girls have honestly been my saviours the past few years… you are so amazing and I can't thank you enough for all the love you have given me, especially when I made it hard to love myself. I am so thankful for you all and I can't wait to come back and spill all the goss to you all."

Hope has tears crashing down her cheeks. "OMG, you haven't even gone yet." She walks over to me and cuddles me, she lets out a sob. I return the cuddle...and the sob. I whisper into her shoulder "thank you for everything" and she pulls me in closer so our bodies have nearly collided into one. "It is my pleasure, and it always will be." We start to make sniffling noises.

Sally comes over and rubs both our shoulders. "We have only been here forty minutes and you guys are crying already."

Sacha jumps in and announces, "Come on, ladies, let's wrap this up and leave, we have lots of sights to see for this one." That warning gives us a shake and not to waste anymore of our time together being sad, I have hours left with them at best, and I intend to cherish it.

We all make mini movements to each other with our high heels making a clip clopping noise along the floor, we all end the last night at my apartment with a group hug. This only lasts three minutes, but it's long enough as I can feel the emotions are running high tonight. It's about time we all head out into the New York night.

The city is alive, buzzing with energy as we step out into the crisp New York night. The lights of Times Square are blinding, almost overwhelming, but in the best way possible. It feels like the world is watching us. We have no particular plan, just a vague idea to wander, take in the sights, and let the night unfold as it would. We laugh, as usual, at how completely unprepared we are, but that's what makes it all the more exciting.

We stroll down Broadway, dodging the crowds of tourists snapping photos and street vendors shouting their wares. My best friends and I have a habit of making ridiculous jokes, even about the most mundane things, and tonight is no different. Each corner we turn brings us a new source of amusement, from the outrageous costumes of the street performers to the random strangers we end up chatting with. We are loud, giddy, and completely carefree, as if nothing else matters but this perfect moment.

Around the corner from a quirky little café, we come across a rooftop bar. We hadn't planned on it, but we are drawn in by the twinkling fairy lights and the hum of conversation. The view is breathtaking – just the right balance of towering skyscrapers and the distant glow of the Empire State Building. We grab a round of cocktails, the conversation flowing almost as smoothly as the drinks, and just soak in the view. The city stretches out before us, the skyline lit up like a dream. "This is it," I think, "this is what New York nights are made of."

As the night wears on, we decide to venture over to Greenwich Village, where the streets feel a little quieter but still alive with energy. The charm of the old brownstones, the soft jazz music spilling from bars, and the late-night buzz of people walking with purpose makes it feel like something out of a movie. We end up in a cosy little dive bar, the kind you'd miss if you weren't looking closely enough. It is intimate, warm, and has the best jukebox tunes playing in the background. We sit in a corner booth, laughing until our sides hurt, recounting ridiculous stories from our college days, and joking about what the future might hold.

I can't help but feel this immense sense of contentment. Here we are, five girls in one of the most vibrant cities in the world, living in the moment without a care. The worries about work, life, and everything else seem so far away in this instant. We are just friends, enjoying each other's company, celebrating the freedom of being young and alive. Every time one of us speaks, we end up in fits of laughter, clinking our glasses together in cheers, feeling on top of the world.

By the time we make our way to a late-night diner for a greasy slice of pizza, I am absolutely exhausted, my feet are swollen from all the steps I've taken, I am tired but it is the good kind of tired – the kind that comes from a night well spent with the people you love. We've seen the sights, experienced the energy of New York, and filled our hearts with memories to last a lifetime. As we all sit there, the city outside still pulsing with life, I realise this is exactly how I'd imagined a night out in New York would be: spontaneous, full of laughter, and completely unforgettable.

We gather our things and head outside to the cold breeze of the subway entrance, Hope, Isabelle and Sally fall into a yellow cab; they live in the same district and if my memory serves me correctly, they live within streets of each other. We bid our farewells, hugs, tears and well wishes. Sacha stays back and cuddles me so tight it restricts my breathing. "You're hurting me," I say in a exaggerated breath.

She steps back and lets go, nearly falling backward in her heels. "Sorry, I just can't believe this is it."

I try and gather my thoughts, and I stare into those huge blue eyes of hers. "I get it, trust me, thank you so much for helping me with this, you have done me a real solid here."

She smiles nonchalantly. "My aunt will keep me up to date, don't worry, and remember, I'm only a phone call away, only a few hours' drive away if need be! I will 100% come over and visit sometime."

We spend the next five minutes in silence, staring at each other, New York time travels as normal, taxis pull up, pick their guests up and drive off. We just stand there not wanting to say the word goodbye.

I take a leap, I rush in for a quick goodbye embrace, then I hail a cab, my emotions are starting to get out of control now, it hurts to leave her, my heart is aching. The night went so beautifully and now it feels like I have been hit with a juggernaut and now I see things for how they are: I'm leaving her behind. I need to get into this cab and Leave. Her. Behind. *I can't do this anymore,* I whisper under my breath as I turn my back to her and open the cab door. I stop.

"Yes, you can!" she shouts, smiling, giving me an encouraging smile and a small wave with her right hand. "Stop doubting yourself and go, get in the cab and call me when you land. You got this, Aimee."

My heart is now doing summersaults in my chest and I feel a sob working its way up from my core. "Thank you," I mouth to her. I make the I love you sign, and finally get into the cab; tears are now steamrolling down my cheeks. I'm leaning forward on the backseat, sobbing into a tissue so I don't draw attention to myself. I turn my head to look out the back window and she is standing on the sidewalk, waving her goodbyes to me.

The cab drives through New York, the twinkling lights and skyscrapers towering over each other, it's like they have been built in comparison. Small sobs still echo throughout the back of the cab. Luckily my cab driver isn't the most talkative – I couldn't stomach trying to make small talk the way my heart is aching. I can't help but feel I am making the wrong decision. *I surely don't need to do this? Do I? If I'm happy with my life here, why am I leaving?* The doubt settles in again, here we go. Sitting in silence now and having an invisible argument with my head, trying to push the voices out of my mind and to try and calm myself down.

It takes around thirty minutes before the yellow cab is pulling up outside my apartment, I put the $20 plus a tip through the small gap of the glass in the cab for the driver. I exit slowly, I turn around and say "Thank you" to the cab driver and slam the door. Before I walk through the main doors to my apartment building, I stand on one leg and take off my heel on my left foot, then I switch to the right; the instant relief that flows over my feet, to the tip of my toes is instantaneous. I check my handbag and forage for my keys, I reach the steps outside and I feel eyes burning at the back of my head. I go to slowly turn my head and I hear a voice: "Hey Stranger". I see the eyes that are an Atlantic blue; *this can't be happening to me, not tonight.* He smiles and his posture is leaning on a nearby tree outside my building. It's Sebastian.

My shoulders tense up, the stare on my face reflects my disdain for him. I stagger forward and meet his gaze. "What are you doing here, Sebastian?" I ask him in a quick tempered manner. His mouth marks his face with a smirk, his cheekbones rise.

"I just wanted to come and see you before you left for Boston."

A confused look on my face appears. "Who told you?" I spit out.

He begins to slowly snake his way towards me, slow movements to try and get me flustered. "I had a conversation with your aunt Clara yesterday, I just happened to spot her in the department store and she told me you're leaving."

Why on earth would she tell him where I am going?

"The important question here, Aimee, is why didn't you tell me?"

"Because you don't need to know, it's after 2am, why are you outside my apartment?" I ask him, demanding answers. This is giving me chills – how long has he been waiting here?

He points to the main door of my apartment building with his hand. "Should we take this inside please, I don't want to argue on the street with you."

I step up to him, toe to toe, ready to battle this out on the sidewalk if needed, I'm ready for war after all the emotion that has been cooped upside my veins, they are ready to burst like a dam. "You have no hope in hell of stepping over that threshold, just go, Sebastian," as I mirror his actions.

We go silent for a few moments, he steps forward to me and puts his hands on my waist. I don't stop him, which is all the more confusing. He's holding me, I glance up to his face and see tears pouring down those cheekbones. I try to avert my gaze and turn around to leave, he's not letting go. I can feel his fingers tightening around my waist; my throat closes up as I find myself being pulled towards closer to him, a magnetic force.

He knows me, he knows me too well. He thrives in my darkness, he knows he can take a peek in the darkness that is me anytime, he knows my buttons. I feel like I'm being hunted, when I saw him outside the apartment block, I thought I was the hunter, turns out I'm the prey. Before I know it, our noses are practically touching, his hand has moved to my head, I can hear his breathing quicken, mine does too, he is scanning every ounce of my face, taking it all in. Before I know it he moves his lips towards mine, I let them, I start to close my eyes, I haven't felt like this in a long time, I would be lying if I said I didn't miss him. I get ready for the kiss, but as if by magic, my phone starts to vibrate and it snaps me out of his spell. I look at him and whisper, "I need to get that, please let me get it." He smiles and he lets me pull my head away, I check my phone and see a text from the airline about the flight. It's now giving me the option to check in. That one text really pushes me into the present moment. I exit my app and try and deal with the situation at hand.

"Sebastian, you need to leave, please." I am defeated by this point. I need sleep and I need to rest, I need to summon all the strength I have in the world.

"Aimee, I can make this right," he exclaims.

"No, you can't, look, I have one day left here, I need you to leave and face the fact that nothing will be the same, if you love me as you say you do, please go."

His face goes from God like, to Demon in a flash. His pupils grow larger, his lips thin. "I'm not leaving, Aimee, until I get what I want."

I turn my head to face him, a scowl overcomes my face, and he knows he has gone too far, my brows furrow into my face. "I want sleep, I need rest. Leave. Me. Alone." Eye contact at its strongest, my voice hoarse, and sick of his bull crap. I make another power move, I simply turn and walk away towards my door, I get prepared by sliding the key between my fingers in case he tries to force himself on me, or to get past me. *The joys of being a woman.* I'm ready for a fight now, the adrenaline is coursing through my veins and my senses are kicking in even more so than before. I take this moment to quickly activate the fob on the door; I flick my head over my shoulders, he looks ready to pounce. I still stare at him while I hear the beep and open the door. As the door opens, I don't take my eyes off him, I physically can't.

I quickly dash into the building, and slam the door with such force that I did for one moment think that the glass would shatter into a thousand pieces. I am safe though, that's all that matters. I run to the elevator and he's still standing outside, pressing the button to my floor in a manic movement, over and over and then the door finally shuts. It's now after 3am and I need to get home, lock my doors and check out of the window to see if he is still there. If he is I need to call the police. The chime operates when the doors open sideways, and I scarper to the apartment door, my hands shaking; *come on, get it together* I think to myself. I force the key into the lock, and turn clockwise, and the familiar smell hits my nostrils. I slap the door behind me, I barricade myself in by using the four locks and panting for breath. I throw my bag on the floor and stamp towards the window. I peek my eyes over the window ledge to see if I can see him, I feel like I'm a spy. My heart drops to the floor. He's gone. *Where are you?* I mutter under my breath. Checking all the windows and locks on the doors, I scale the apartment for ways that he could potentially trespass. I go into my bedroom and open the app that is linked with security on the door, I advise them of what's happened this evening; and that I must not be disturbed by anyone.

As I walk towards my nightstand, I pause at the photo that's staring right back at me. My mom; I know she would want this for me. I open the drawer to retrieve some pyjamas. A deep sigh of relief leaves my core and causes me to fall back onto the bed, with such a clatter. I stare at the ceiling, I know I need to shower, my head is telling me to try and sleep. I turn on my side and before I know it; my eyelids are closing before me, I have no control, no power. Nothing.

Sam

BOSTON

In the early hours on a Monday morning, I stir out of restlessness in my bed, I toss and turn, the moonlight disappearing above the clouds. I take a moment to rise from my sheets and I sit on the side of the bed, taking in the city's aura; this place is truly breathtaking. It's not silent by any means; however, you can certainly tell when the working men and women of the city are arising and another work week begins.

I pick up my phone and check the time: it's 5.45am, my alarm is due to go off in fifteen minutes so I make the decision to get up and shower to start my day. It's still dark outside, and I can hear the faint patter of rain against the window. I stretch and yawn, taking a moment to gather myself before dragging myself off the bed. I always wish I could just stay under the covers for a bit longer, but I know that if I don't get up now, I'll be rushing later. Slowly, I make my way to the bathroom, blinking against the harsh bathroom light, and splash cold water on my face to wake myself up.

The first thing I do is get into the shower. The hot water is a relief against the cold morning air. I take my time, letting the steam fill the bathroom as I scrub away the sleep from my body. I can't say I enjoy the early mornings, but there's something satisfying about that moment when you step out of the shower and feel awake, refreshed, and ready to take on the day. After a quick towel dry, I pull on my robe and slide back to my bedroom to get dressed.

I've already laid out my clothes the night before, so getting dressed is a relatively easy task. It's usually a simple choice: something comfortable but professional enough for work. Today, I opt for a pair of tailored trousers and a smart shirt. I quickly iron the shirt to avoid any creases, which is a step I always seem to leave to the last minute. Once I'm satisfied with my outfit, I take a moment to check myself in the mirror. It's an odd routine – trying to make sure I look put together enough for the day ahead, even though it's barely light out.

Once I've dressed, I move to the kitchen to make breakfast. The ritual of brewing my coffee is one of the few things that truly wakes me up and gets me in the right mindset for the day. I throw some oats into a bowl and microwave them while I wait for my coffee to brew. I like the quiet of the morning – no one else is awake yet, so it's just me and the sound of the kettle clicking off, the microwave buzzing, and the faint drip of coffee into the pot. I pour myself a cup and sit at the kitchen table to eat, scrolling through my phone to catch up on the news or check any emails.

After breakfast, I gather my things for the day: wallet, phone, keys. I check the weather one more time to make sure I'm dressed appropriately, and then it's time to leave. My bag's already packed with everything I need, and I make sure to grab my coat, as the forecast predicts more rain. I head out the door, locking up behind me, and stand outside for a moment to take a breath. It's still dark, the air crisp, but there's a certain quietness to the world before the rush of the day begins.

I walk out to my car. It's a bit of a routine at this point, and though I'm still tired, I'm starting to feel a sense of purpose. The day ahead holds its usual tasks and challenges, but for now, I have this brief moment of peace before the workday truly begins. It's funny how I've grown to find comfort in this early morning routine, even if it feels like a struggle some days. But as I sip my coffee and watch the world go by, I know that I'm ready to face whatever comes next.

I take the usual journey, and my phone automatically connects to my Spotify account. The sky today is cloudy. I drive past the countless coffee shops starting to fill with customers about to start their working day. I do love my job and the journey to work just outside the city is a delight for the senses. Because it's a Monday, today is the day we get the new pieces. Some are gorgeous quality;

however, some I can take them or leave them. I indicate to take the turning off the interstate, I follow a small road down to the shop, it's in a very private location; however, we do have an array of exclusive buyers, it's best for them to be able to browse in peace and quiet. We do also have appointment schedules where they can call ahead and we can give them our undivided attention. As I approach the building, I drive my car over the gravel and park up outside in my designated space. The parking spaces are surrounded by an old limestone wall which adorns a colourful clematis.

Working in the antique shop is a strange mix of tranquillity and excitement. The shop itself is quiet, the sort of place where time seems to slow down as soon as you step through the door. I'm surrounded by pieces of history – every corner of the shop is filled with furniture, paintings, porcelain, and trinkets from different eras. It's fascinating how each item has a story to tell, and while I may not know all the details, I can't help but wonder about the lives they've touched. I find myself constantly moving between admiration for the beauty of the pieces and a sense of awe at how they've lasted through generations.

Most of the customers who walk through the door are serious collectors, looking for something special to add to their collection, or they're enthusiasts with a keen eye for craftsmanship. I can usually tell when someone is genuinely interested in a piece versus when they're just browsing. There's a certain reverence that comes with handling something so old, and I've learned to pick up on it. I make sure to greet them warmly, always offering a bit of background on whatever they're looking at – whether it's an exquisite Victorian chair or a delicate Georgian vase. I've grown to recognise many of the regulars, and it's always a pleasure to chat with them about new arrivals or the history of a particular item.

When customers are truly intrigued by something, I can see the spark in their eyes as they get closer, inspecting the details. It's at these moments that I feel most connected to the work I do. Sharing my knowledge with them, watching their faces light up when they uncover something special, makes every long shift worthwhile. Sometimes, they ask questions I don't have an immediate answer to, and I find myself diving into research later, eager to learn more about the piece. It's a constant learning experience, which keeps the job interesting and challenging. There's always more to know, and that's one of the things I love about working in such a unique environment.

The most satisfying moments, however, are when I can help someone find exactly what they're looking for. It's not always about the most expensive item or the rarest find, but about connecting a person with something that will resonate with them. Whether it's a particular style of clock, a set of antique silver, or a painting that captures their imagination, there's a quiet sense of accomplishment when you can tell they're happy with their purchase. It's like finding the perfect match, like being part of a story that will continue long after the transaction is complete.

It's also incredible to see how many customers are surprised at how much they learn from simply spending time in the shop. Some come in with little knowledge about antiques, but after chatting about different periods, artists, or the craftsmanship involved, they leave with a newfound appreciation for the value of the pieces. There's a certain joy in helping people understand why these objects are worth preserving, why they matter beyond their monetary value. It's not just about selling, but about fostering a deeper connection to the history embedded in each piece.

After the shop closes, I often spend a bit more time with the items that didn't sell that day. I love taking the time to appreciate the finer details – the wear of an old leather-bound book, the delicate inlay work on a wooden chest, or the faded gold leaf on an old mirror. There's something humbling about being surrounded by so much history, and I can't help but feel like I'm a part of it, even if just for a brief moment. It's the sort of work that's easy to get lost in, and I find myself looking forward to each new day, eager to see who will walk through the door and what story we'll share next.

Aimee

LAST DAY IN NYC

I wake up to the sharp, unforgiving ring of my alarm, my head pounding as if it's being squeezed in a vice. I squint at the clock – 9:30 am. My first thought is that I should be up, should be packing, should be doing something, but the overwhelming nausea and the haze surrounding me tell me otherwise. I roll over, pressing my face into the pillow, trying to hold onto whatever sleep I can still grasp. The room is spinning slightly, and for a moment, I wonder if I'm still dreaming. I can't quite make sense of anything, but I know I'm not feeling like myself at all.

Then it all comes rushing back. Last night. The bar, the laughter, the endless drinks, but mostly, Sebastian. I can't quite piece together the details yet, but I know something happened. I can feel the weight of it pressing on me, a heavy, uncomfortable sensation that lingers in my chest. I try to sit up, but the world tilts, and I grip the bedframe to steady myself. My throat feels dry, my mouth tasting bitter. I can't even remember how I managed to sleep after what happened, I felt like a prisoner in my own home, that has never happened before.

My fingers tremble as I reach for my phone. I dread looking at the screen, knowing there are messages from friends asking if I'm okay. But what I really dread is seeing something from Sebastian. I don't know what I expect, but when I scroll through my messages, there's nothing. Not a single word. He's not the type to just disappear, to leave things hanging like this. My stomach churns at the thought. What did I do? What did he do? I can't grasp the fragments of the night, and it frustrates me, leaving me with an unsettling feeling that I can't shake.

I force myself out of bed, the air around me thick with the remnants of last night. My clothes are lying across the floor, a reminder of how little control I had over my actions. The overwhelming scent of alcohol clings to my skin, and I can almost taste it as I move to the bathroom. I splash cold water on my face, trying to clear the fog in my mind, but the more I try to piece together the events, the more I realise how little I actually remember. What was supposed to be a fun last night in New York has somehow turned into a blurry mess, and I can't help but feel a sense of dread creeping in.

I sit on the edge of the bathtub, trying to steady my thoughts. This was meant to be my goodbye, my final night in a city that has been both exhilarating and exhausting. But now, I'm left wondering what's left in the wake of whatever happened between Sebastian and me. I never imagined this would be how I'd say goodbye to New York. But the more I think about it, the more I realise I don't know if I want to find out what he's done or if I can even face it. My last day here, and I feel more lost than ever.

I need to speak to someone about this, so I call the only person I can, Sacha.

I hear the dialling tone as I wait anxiously to speak to her. The line goes quiet, "Hello?" she whispers.

"Oh, sorry, have I woke you?" I apologise.

"No, you're fine, you feeling delicate today? I know I am!"

I bite my lip knowing I just need to come out with it and bite the bullet asap. "Something happened last night," I blurt out, disrupting her mid-sentence.

"Oh?" She pauses for a couple of seconds. "Go on."

I stand up from the side of the bathtub, waiting for the water to warm up. "Sebastian," I say. I wait.

"Oh no, you didn't…"

I'm confused by what she means by that – does she honestly think I would go there again? "Nothing like that, Sacha, come on – I was drunk but not totally off the planet. He was outside when I pulled up in the cab, he wanted to come in and I said no; he then turned absolutely psycho."

I can hear her stumbling to her feet on the phone. "So what happened? What did you do?"

I exhale a long breath. "All I remember is, we had a moment, I said no and turned to leave. He wouldn't let me go, Sacha, I had to glare at him for him to let me go. He said he wasn't going to leave until he got what he wanted. After that I just came inside and barricaded myself in the apartment." The phoneline goes deathly silent, I even ask her if she's still there. "Hello? Are you okay?" I shout, my bath now being ready.

"Yeah, I'm just confused, what did he want? Does he know where you are going? Did you call the police or not?"

Why did I know she was gonna ask me that? "I didn't, no, I got into my apartment, went to the window and I checked outside, he was gone; obviously if he was still there I would have," I retort. I can hear her coffee machine in the background firing up, so I know after she has her morning brew, she will be reeling.

"I can't believe he done that, you should have called me, Aimee, that could have been a very dangerous situation," she snaps at me.

"I know Sebastian, he wouldn't do anything like that, not in public. He did want to come inside but luckily the airline texted me my 24-hour check in information so that brought me back to reality. When I came in I literally passed out on my bed, I woke up wearing some of the clothes I was wearing last night, so I'm just running a bath now."

I do feel slightly better; however, I do feel a lecture coming on.

She pipes up, "That is so scary, I wish you had've called me, I would have came over. Look, how are you feeling? What time is your flight tomorrow?"

I like how the subject has changed, maybe for the better. "I am up at 4am for the flight, I have a few days in Boston to get settled before I start the new job so that's cool."

She laughs. "OMG, what if you meet someone when you're there, this might–"

I cut her off in less than a millisecond. "Doubt it, my days are going to be working and saving. Can't see my Prince Charming in Boston, can you?"

She giggles over the phone. "Hey, you never know. And please do not become a recluse, you need to make your way in the city, join some friendship groups online where you can meet other women and see what happens; the last thing you wanna do is get into a routine of work, eat, sleep and repeat. Trust me, I know how a mundane existence like that will affect you – not in a good way either."

I huff and puff because she is 100% right, she can read me like a book. "I know, I know; I will certainly give it my all – you know this. You still looking after the apartment when I'm away?"

She also starts huffing and puffing. "Yes, Aimee, it has been agreed, I am going to spend four nights a week at your apartment – scattered obviously. I will keep the place ticking over until your six months is up; who knows, you might wanna stay there longer. You literally do not know what is around the corner."

A smile lifts on my face. "Anyways, Sacha, I'm gonna head off and have this bath now. I will text you later."

She sighs. "Okay, just message or call if you need me, if you don't wanna be alone on your last night, I get it."

"It's fine, I love you, okay?" The phone disconnects.

I trail my fingers along the water ever so softly, the ripples barely show on the surface. The water is lukewarm now, I decide to just brave it and throw myself in. As I lower myself further down into the tub, the stress seems to evaporate from my bones, I take a large breath in and let the water consume me. For a moment, everything is quiet, the only sounds that I can hear ring in my ears, feels like static. I feel free, like I'm floating in a vacuum and succumbing to whatever has a hold of me. This is the most peaceful state my mind has felt in a long time; it's addictive. I stay still under the water, letting the motion keep me wading in the sense of tranquillity in which my whole being is in. I open my eyes in shock under the water, and bolt upright, gasping, nearly choking on saliva, the tears streaming down my face, a snap back to reality. I glance at my towel on the floor and glare at the clock, it's already 7.30pm and my flight is early tomorrow morning, as I try to compose myself by taking slow inhales and exhales, trying to force my mind to slow down, to not be racing one hundred miles an hour. Fifteen minutes goes by, my heart rate has slowed down, I decide it's time to vacate the tub and get my shit together. I turn and look at my hands, they look ten years older, more lines, rough to the touch.

I use all my strength to defy the gravity pulling me down and climb out of the tub, not very graceful by no means; however I have done it. Steam from the condensation fills the room, I wrap the towel around me and make my way to the long mirror in the bathroom and wipe the condensation away so I can see my face; I look tired, gaunt. I decide to stop criticising myself in the mirror and throw on my pyjamas. Making sure the bathroom is clean for when Sacha comes to stay, I walk along the hallway, trailing my fingertips over the photo frames hanging along the walls, so many memories in New York; sad to leave them behind. As I come out of the hallway into the open plan kitchen/ living room, I spy my bags already packed by the door and let out a morbid sigh. My flight is early in the morning, documentation has been checked and I'm officially packed, I wander slowly to the fridge and pour myself a glass of wine. Once the wine is poured in the glass, I sit on the balcony, listening to the chaos of the city and taking in the skyscrapers. Once I finish my wine, I decide to take a walk and watch the sunset over the city, give myself some fresh air. The sunsets here are always magical nature experiences.

The evening air in New York feels cooler than usual, a welcome breeze brushing against my skin as I walk through the quiet streets. The sun is low now, casting long shadows between the towering skyscrapers that seem to stretch endlessly toward the sky. My brown dress sways gently with each step, the fabric soft against my legs, while my red heels, scuffed from city life, tap lightly against the pavement. There's something serene in the way the city moves at this hour – still bustling but more subdued, as though the buildings are taking a collective breath before the night falls.

I'm walking toward the pier, the promise of the water offering me a kind of escape that only a city like New York can give. The crowds seem to thin out as I get closer, and soon the only sound is the rhythmic clapping of waves against the dock. The sun, now just a golden disc on the horizon, casts a warm, orange glow across the water. It feels like the city is holding its breath, waiting for the final moments of daylight to unfold. The reflections of the skyscrapers shimmer on the surface of the water, as though the city itself is merging with the sea in one final dance of light.

As I get closer to the edge of the pier, a deep sense of nostalgia washes over me. It's not just the beauty of the sunset, though that certainly plays a part, but the overwhelming awareness that I'm leaving soon. The thought of leaving this city that's held so much of my life in its towering arms stirs a bittersweet ache in my chest. I've walked these streets a thousand times, but this time feels different. There's a finality to it, and it's hard not to feel the weight of that final walk down to the water, as if I'm walking away from something precious.

I close my eyes for a moment, allowing myself to just feel the cool breeze, the warmth of the setting sun still lingering on my skin. It's a gentle reminder of all the moments I've lived in this place – the laughter, the late nights, the unexpected encounters that made this city feel like home. And yet, as the sun dips lower, I feel the stirrings of something new on the horizon. There's a quiet excitement mixed with the sadness of departure. A new chapter awaits, but it's hard not to mourn the end of this one.

The skyscrapers around me, bathed in the golden light, stand as silent witnesses to my departure. They shimmer, their glass windows reflecting the last light of day, casting long, dramatic shadows that stretch far beyond the pier. It's as if they're saying goodbye too, their gleaming facades fading slowly into the night.

I've always admired the way the city seems to transform at sunset, as if it's shedding the harshness of the day in favour of something more vulnerable, more beautiful.

A soft sigh escapes my lips as I take in the scene one last time. The pier feels quieter now, the hum of the city in the distance almost like a lullaby. My heart aches with a mix of love for this place and fear of what comes next. But even in the sadness, there's a sense of peace in knowing that I'm leaving at a time when the city is showing me its most tender side. The sunset is like a gift – a reminder that everything changes, but there's beauty in that change.

As the last traces of daylight fade into the horizon, I stand there for a moment longer, watching as the city begins to glow with the lights of the evening. My brown dress clings to my skin a little more now, the coolness of the night settling in. The pier feels empty now, except for me, and I know it's time to go. But as I turn and walk back toward the streets, there's a sense of quiet resolve within me. I'll carry the memory of this sunset with me wherever I go, and maybe, just maybe, I'll return one day to watch the sun set on this city once again.

Sam

BOSTON

The workday finally winds down, and the feeling of freedom is palpable as I gather my things and head out. It's been a long week, and I'm more than ready to let off some steam. I meet up with the group of other antique merchants just outside the office, the city's energy still buzzing around us as we make our way to the bar. There's something about these after-work meetups that I always look forward to – the shift from the monotony of meetings and deadlines to the laughter and easy-going chatter of friends. It feels like a reset.

As we walk in, the dim lighting and the low hum of conversation immediately take me to that familiar place of comfort. I spot Steven and Robert already at the bar, nursing their drinks. Steven flashes a grin and waves, his usual energy lighting up the room. Robert, on the other hand, is more reserved but gives me a nod as I slide into the seat next to him. The bartender comes over with a knowing smile – she always remembers what I like – and I order my usual, letting the weight of the workday begin to melt away.

We chat for a few minutes, catching up on the mundane things that fill our lives – what's going on at work, the latest gossip, random thoughts that pop into our heads. It's comforting in a way, this rhythm we've all fallen into. Robert begins talking about work, as he often does. He's the serious one of the group, the one who always has something on his mind about projects, deadlines, and the latest office drama. His voice is steady as he goes on about his latest challenges at the office. I listen, nodding along, half in tune with what he's saying but mostly just appreciating the familiarity of it all.

Josh, of course, is doing what Josh does best – telling jokes. He's always got some ridiculous quip or comment ready to lighten the mood, his voice rising and falling with his own comedic timing. I can't help but chuckle, even when his jokes are the kind of corny that makes me roll my eyes. But that's the thing about Josh – he knows exactly how to get under my skin and make me laugh at the same time. There's a warmth in his humour that just makes everything feel lighter, even if the jokes are utterly absurd.

But then, as always, they ask me about my dating life. It's become a kind of ritual at this point.

"So, how's the love life?" Steven asks, his voice teasing but kind.

Robert glances over, eyebrows raised, curious but cautious.

I take a slow sip of my drink before answering, already knowing what's coming. "Same as last time," I say, trying to keep my tone light, not giving away how much the question kind of stings. "Nothing new."

Josh grins mischievously, leaning forward. "Oh, come on, you can't still be 'taking a break', right?" He laughs, clearly not convinced. I shake my head, giving him the same answer I've given a hundred times before. "Nope, not much to report. It's been quiet." They look at me, a mix of concern and amusement in their eyes, but I don't elaborate. There's a certain finality in my answer, one I've perfected over the years, and yet, I can see that they're not fully satisfied.

Robert shifts in his seat, clearly not content to leave it at that. "I mean, you're out here, right? We go out and you haven't met anyone? There has to be something going on." His voice is softer than usual, like he's genuinely trying to connect, but I don't have much to offer.

"I'm just enjoying the peace for now," I reply, hoping that will end the conversation. But it's always the same. They just don't let it go.

"Seriously?" Steven asks, his eyebrows furrowing. "It's been a while since you've gone out with anyone. You're not talking to anyone?"

I feel the familiar pressure in my chest, the weight of expectations that I should have a different answer. But I keep it simple, keep it light. "Nothing serious, guys. Just living my life." It's a cop-out, I know, but it's easier than getting into the complexities of why my dating life feels stagnant, or why I haven't felt like pursuing anything lately. The truth is, it's a little more complicated than I care to admit, and I've never been good at explaining that part of myself.

Josh laughs, trying to break the tension. "You're just waiting for Mrs Right, huh?" His tone is playful, but I can tell he means well.

I force a smile, shrugging. "Maybe. Or maybe I'm just not in any rush."

The conversation shifts again, as it always does, but I feel that familiar, nagging sense of discomfort linger in the back of my mind. It's not that I don't appreciate their concern – I know they care about me – but sometimes it feels like they're pushing for answers I'm not ready to give.

The night continues to unfold with laughter and light-hearted banter, and the earlier question fades into the background as I sip my drink and enjoy the company of my friends. But even as the conversation moves on, I can't shake the feeling of being a little out of sync with where they think I should be. It's not their fault. I know they just want the best for me. Still, there's a part of me that wishes they'd stop asking about something I'm not sure I have an answer for yet.

I'm not going to lie, it's not that I haven't wanted to start dating, just haven't met the right person yet. I spend most of my time at work, if I'm lucky I get to catch up with my friends; if I have a lot of time on my hands, I would normally go and visit family, or vice versa. My friends seem to have moved on in their lives, I feel I'm stuck. I am happy, but I feel stuck in a concept of time, it feels like I'm watching montages of my friends' lives; at the end, I haven't moved. Maybe I'm not trying as hard as I should be to move on to the next chapter of my life.

As the night progresses on, the drinks keep flowing and time just seems to be gliding through. I check my phone and there is one message from Mom. I click into the app store; I hover over a couple of dating apps, my thumb is dangling over the install button, but nothing materialises. Before I know it, I click off the screen and exit the app store entirely. "This isn't for me," I whisper under my breath.

I stagger out of my seat in the bar and fling open the double doors into the fresh air. I didn't think that I was drunk; however, the air seems to have amplified the volume of alcohol in my system. I feel too impatient to wait for a cab, so I stagger home, my feet struggling to hold my weight.

The streets feel oddly familiar and distant at the same time as I stumble home, the cool night air hitting my face in short bursts. The alcohol still burns in my veins, making everything seem a little slower, a little hazier. My steps are uneven, and I can feel the ground shifting beneath me, as if it's not quite sure where it wants to be. I try to focus on the streetlights, their soft glow flickering ahead of me, but the light seems to dance just out of reach, like it's mocking my attempt to keep it together.

As I pass by a cluster of partygoers, their laughter and chatter almost feels like it's part of the soundtrack to my unsteady journey. Some are laughing too loudly, others are hugging too tightly, and a few are stumbling just like me. I try not to make eye contact with any of them – don't want to get caught in their energy, not when I'm already feeling a little too much of my own. They look like they're having the time of their lives, but I'm just trying to get to my damn door without falling flat on my face.

The smell of takeout hits me next. It's the kind of greasy, comforting scent that wraps itself around you and pulls you in even when you're not hungry. I catch a whiff of fried chicken, soy sauce, and something that smells like warm dough, all blending together in the humid air. The little shops along the street are alive with the chatter of the cooks and the hum of delivery bikes waiting for their next orders. I pause for a moment, tempted to stop in and grab something to soak up the booze, but I know it won't help. It'll just make me feel more bloated, more sluggish, and I have enough of that already.

I keep moving, my feet dragging as I make my way past the corner where the neon lights flicker from the convenience store. It's so close to home, but it feels like miles away tonight. The world around me is a blur of lights and shadows, the occasional honk of a car, the distant music from a club. Everything is louder and sharper than usual, but it all feels muffled, like I'm looking at the world from behind a thick glass. I just need to get inside, shut the door behind me, and let the world quieten down.

Finally, I reach my apartment building, the familiar steps leading me up to the door. I fumble for my keys, laughing at myself when I almost drop them, but the thought of being inside is all I need to straighten up. I finally get the door open, and the cool air inside is a relief. The night's noise fades away as I step inside, leaving the street, the party, and the smell of takeout behind me. The silence here is comforting, and as I lock the door, I take a long breath, ready to face whatever tomorrow brings.

Aimee

THE DAY TO VACATE NEW YORK – 2AM

I wake to the gruelling sound of my alarm clock. I spring into action knowing what today is going to bring. I make a beeline for the shower to give myself a quick body wash before leaving my sanctuary. I walk into every room checking everything is in place, trying to make a mental note of it before I leave.

I am standing in my living room, my hands wrapped around my suitcase, I struggle to put one foot in front of the other, my anxiety is setting in, that annoying voice in my head that tells me I can't do it, that the journey is too much and that I will fall flat on my face. Before I get a chance to argue back at the voice, an alert comes up on my phone that my cab has arrived. My phone jilts me out of my trance and I am snapped back into reality. I look down at the screen and my lips thin together in a tight smile. As I wheel my suitcases to the door, I turn the handle and stare back over my right shoulder. I walk out the door with my bags, one last check that I have my passport, and documents of my new accommodation, it's all been accounted for.

The morning is quiet, too quiet for a city that's always alive, but it feels fitting. The sun hasn't fully risen, and the streets of New York are empty, save for the occasional cab passing by. I can feel the weight of everything as I step out of my apartment, the reality of leaving starting to settle in. I drag my suitcase behind me, the wheels rolling slowly over the pavement, and it feels like I'm walking through a dream – like I'm not really here. But I am. The day has come. I'm finally leaving New York.

The cab ride to the airport feels longer than it should, the city still shrouded in the early morning haze, lights casting a soft glow on the buildings that seem to go on forever. It's surreal, really. I've lived here for so long, and now I'm on my way out, not sure when or if I'll return. The driver's casual chatter barely registers as I stare out the window, lost in thought. Every landmark, every familiar street I pass feels like a memory I'm saying goodbye to. I don't know if I'm ready for this, but I know it's happening, and there's no turning back.

Arriving at the airport feels almost like another world, a sterile, quiet space in contrast to the chaos of the city outside. The hustle and bustle of travellers is just starting to pick up, and the lights of the terminal flicker overhead, harsh and cold. I stand in line, feeling strangely out of place, as if I'm not sure how to fit into this routine. There's a mix of anxiety and excitement running through me. I'm about to board a plane that will take me to an entirely new life, but the idea of leaving this city behind still stings in ways I didn't expect.

When I finally reach the check-in counter, the attendant greets me with a practised smile, one that I can tell has been repeated a hundred times before. I give her my name, and she types it into the system without looking up, her fingers moving quickly over the keyboard. "Window seat, all set for you," she says with a glance up, handing me my boarding pass. It's such a small moment, but it's the final step in this transition. I take the ticket in my hand, feeling the weight of it, knowing that this is the last time I'll be at this counter in New York.

The security line is long, stretching out in front of me as I shuffle along with the rest of the crowd. Everyone is in their own world, a mix of people all headed somewhere, each carrying their own story. I try not to think about the fact that I'm one of them now – just another person heading off to somewhere else. The routine of security, the process of emptying my pockets, taking off my shoes, walking through the metal detector, feels oddly comforting. It's something that doesn't change, no matter where I'm going. I'm a little nervous, but the routine almost eases it, like I'm already halfway through the journey, even though I'm still standing in the terminal.

As I make it through security, I gather my things and head toward the gate, still feeling a little disoriented by how quickly everything is happening. I find a seat near the windows, the massive glass panels giving me a view of the runway where planes are already lined up, ready for take-off. The sun is finally starting to rise now, and the sky is painted in soft shades of pink and orange. For a moment, I just sit there, staring out at the planes, trying to soak it all in. This is it. This is the beginning of something new, but the finality of leaving New York still hangs heavy in the air.

I glance around the terminal, watching people come and go, all of them with their own destinations, their own paths. It's strange how impersonal airports can feel, even though they bring people together from all corners of the world. I feel like a small piece of this larger puzzle, just one of many, but the journey ahead still feels like something uniquely mine. I take a deep breath, trying to calm the swirling emotions inside of me. There's excitement, yes, but there's also a sense of loss I can't quite shake.

The announcements start blaring overhead, the voice of the gate attendant calling for passengers to begin boarding. I feel a little rush of adrenaline, but also a deep sense of exhaustion, like the weight of the last few days is catching up with me. I stand up, stretch, and gather my things, making my way to the gate with everyone else. The process is mechanical now, each person moving toward their plane, eager to settle in and start the flight. There's no fanfare, just the quiet shuffle of people in a shared moment of transition.

I make it onto the plane, find my seat by the window, and settle in. As the plane begins to taxi down the runway, I look out at the city one last time. New York is still there, sprawling out beneath me, but it's already becoming smaller, fading into the distance. The realisation hits me then – this is it. I'm leaving. And even though I know it's time, it doesn't make the goodbyes any easier. The city that I've known so well is slipping away, and I'm headed toward an unknown future.

The flight attendants go through their usual spiel as the plane ascends, but I'm not really listening. My thoughts are somewhere else, drifting between the memories of New York and the uncertainty of what comes next. The noise of the plane, the hum of the engines, becomes background noise as I sit back in my seat and let my mind wander. The city below is a distant memory now, and I realise that even though I'm leaving, a part of me will always carry it with me. As I play my Spotify song Moving On by Porsche Love in my ears, it really resonates with everything that has happened the past few months.

I close my eyes for a moment, feeling the weight of everything settle in my chest. There's a mixture of relief and sadness, of excitement and fear. The future is wide open, but that doesn't make it any less daunting. The only thing I know for sure is that the day has come – I've left New York behind, and I'm on my way to something new. I don't know exactly what that is yet, but for the first time in a long while, I'm okay with not knowing. It's the beginning of the rest of my life, and that's enough.

Sam

4AM, BOSTON

As I turn over in my bed and try and find a glass of water that I normally have on my night stand, I make slight jerking motions to try and find it in the darkness, I try and rack my brains to see if I had actually poured myself a drink before bed, I can't remember anything at all. I can't remember getting home, I can't even remember walking through the door. I must have just come home and come straight to bed. With great hesitation I take a deep breath and use all the force I can to lift myself from my pillow and drag my feet to the bathroom, with every movement I can feel my throat closing up due to being so thirsty. *I don't know why I do this to myself,* I whisper in my mind. Gliding along the floor to the bathroom I turn on the cold faucet and force my head in the sink to make sure my mouth can reach the faucet, I gulp like I haven't drank anything in weeks, like water is somewhat going out of fashion. I rest my head on the side of the sink as the water is still running, my thick black hair getting caught in the flow of the water. I place my hands on the side and give my head a literal shake.

I glance into my bedroom with water on my face and try to scan the room for the alarm clock to check the time. Nothing is on my bedside table, everything I could have possibly needed this morning apparently is not in reach. I take a towel from the rack, run it through my hair to try and wipe the remnants of liquid out of my hair. Once my hair has dried, I slowly make my way back to bed; the sheets are cold to the touch and I drift back off within minutes. Knowing I'm off work tomorrow helps, I have the full day planned of getting some fitness goals in, which I keep putting off due to my busy schedule.

The sun is already up when I finally stir, the morning light creeping through the blinds. My head feels heavy, like someone's been hammering away at it all night. I squint at the clock on my phone – 11:30 am. I must've really needed the sleep. Last night's drinks, the laughter, and the good times with friends all seem like distant memories now, fading as the hangover starts to settle in. My mouth is dry, my muscles sore, and my brain is fuzzy, but I don't feel like getting up just yet. The bed feels too cosy, too warm, like it's holding me in place. I pull the covers tighter around me, letting myself drift in and out of consciousness.

Eventually, I manage to peel myself out of bed, each movement slow and deliberate, like I'm navigating through thick fog. My body protests every step I take, but I push through. I shuffle to the bathroom, grimacing at my reflection in the mirror. My hair is a mess, my eyes are bloodshot, and I look like I've aged ten years overnight. A quick splash of cold water to the face does little to wake me up, but I'm desperate to feel at least somewhat human again. I know I need to shower, to wash off the remnants of last night's fun, but all I can think about is getting something to eat first.

After a quick and somewhat unenthusiastic breakfast, I head into the shower. The hot water feels good as it hits my skin, washing away the remnants of sleep and alcohol. I stand under the stream for a while, letting the heat and the rhythm of the water do their magic. The shower is my moment of clarity, the only time I can truly clear my head and breathe. My body relaxes as I scrub away the lingering fog, and slowly, my mind starts to catch up with the rest of me. It's not much, but it's enough to give me the energy to keep going, to face the day.

I towel off and get dressed, not really in the mood for anything too complicated. A simple pair of shorts and a t-shirt will do. The room feels quieter now, less disorienting, and I finally sit down at my desk to catch up on the world. I open the Boston Globe and scroll through the headlines, trying to shake off the remnants of my hangover while reading about local events, politics, and whatever else is happening in the world. The stories blur together a bit – nothing too gripping in the moment – but the act of reading gives me something to focus on, something to ground me after a night of chaos.

I skim through some articles, my attention flickering between the words on the page and the quiet hum of the apartment around me. It's peaceful in here, despite the low throb in my head. The city outside seems to be waking up in its own rhythm – cars honking, people rushing by – but it all feels distant now, like I'm in my own little bubble. I'm glad to have the morning to myself, even if it's a little slower than I'd like. My body needs this time to recover, to reset, and for now, that's all I can give it.

After a while, I grab my phone and scroll through my messages, checking in with friends, replying to a few things that had come through overnight. That's when I see a FaceTime call from Mom. I smile, realizing I haven't spoken to her in a few days. She's been calling more often lately, checking in on me, asking about my life, how I'm adjusting to everything. I tap the screen to answer, and her face lights up as soon as she sees me.

"Hey, kiddo!" Mom says with her usual warmth, her voice a comforting balm. "How are you feeling? You look like you had a good time last night." *How does she know that?* I think to myself.

I laugh, rubbing my temple. "Yeah, I had fun, but I think I had a little too much fun. Woke up with a bit of a headache this morning." I glance at the coffee cup on the table. "But I'm surviving."

She raises an eyebrow, clearly amused. "You're not getting any younger, you know. Maybe you should slow down a bit."

I chuckle, knowing she's right. She's always the first to remind me that I can't party like I used to, but that's part of the charm of Mom, always looking out for me, even when I'm hundreds of miles away. We chat for a few minutes, asking each other about the usual – how work is going, any updates on the family, random little details that make me feel connected to home.

After a while, Dad's face pops into the frame next to hers. "How's my favourite kid doing?" he asks with a grin, making me laugh.

"Better now," I say. "Just needed to sleep it off."

"Well, you look better than you did last time I saw you," he teases. "You sure you're not out there partying too hard?"

I roll my eyes but can't help the smile tugging at my lips. "I'm not partying too hard, Dad. But I might've overdone it just a little."

They both laugh, and we talk for a while longer, catching up on everything and nothing at all. But then, Mom surprises me with a bit of news.

"We've been thinking," she says, exchanging a glance with Dad. "We're coming to visit you in a couple of weeks."

I blink, caught off guard. "Really? That's awesome! When exactly?"

Dad chimes in, "We'll be there for a long weekend. It's been too long since we've seen you, and we're ready for a little getaway. We'll stay with you, if that's okay?"

My heart warms at the thought of having them here, of showing them around Boston, of making new memories together. It's been a while since we had a chance to just hang out without the pressures of daily life, and I'm looking forward to it more than I care to admit. "Of course, I'd love that. It's been way too long since I've had you guys around."

Mom smiles. "We thought you could use some family time. We'll book the flight soon."

I feel a rush of gratitude and excitement. It's a small thing, but it means so much. It's the kind of comfort I didn't realise I needed until just now. We wrap up the call with promises to talk again soon, and after I hang up, I sit back in my chair, letting the warmth of their words linger. The day may have started off slow, but suddenly, it feels a little brighter. I might be nursing a hangover, but the thought of seeing Mom and Dad soon fills me with a sense of joy that cuts through the haze.

A couple of messages from Josh and Steven come through regarding last night's antics – apparently one of them was locked out of the house by his wife and had to knock on their next door neighbour for him to spend the night there, I chuckle at the thought of him being on someone's doorstep at that time in the early hours of the morning. I try to call Josh, it goes straight to answerphone. I decide this is my time to get the day started.

I head down the hallway to my bedroom and open my closet and pick out a pair of shorts and a t-shirt; I have it ingrained in my head that I need to go for a run. I decide to take this opportunity to head to the Boston Public Garden – it's a stunning collection of architecture and different types of shrubbery, plants and wildlife. I throw on my running trainers and check the weather on my iPhone before heading out.

The air outside is crisp, a slight chill that cut through the layers of my shirt but feels refreshing all the same. I look around my apartment one last time before closing the door, making sure I haven't forgotten anything. I wasn't planning to be gone long, just a quick jog to clear my head and get some fresh air. As I lock the door behind me, the sound of the bolt clicking into place signalled that I was officially stepping into the world outside, leaving the comfort of home behind.

I step onto the stairs and begin my descent, the familiar creak of the steps underneath my feet grounding me. It's strange how such a small thing can be so comforting. The building has always felt like a second home to me, and as I walk down the hallway and out the front door, I realise how much I've grown attached to this place. But today, the open road calls me, and I can already feel my muscles warming up as I approach the sidewalk.

The city is quieter than usual, with just a few cars passing by, and the sound of birds chirping high above the streets. The early morning sun bathes everything in a golden light, casting long shadows that stretch out like fingers reaching for the horizon. I take in a deep breath of the fresh air, letting it fill my lungs. There is something about the rhythm of the world in the early morning that makes everything feel like it is in perfect harmony. I smile to myself and begin jogging slowly, my feet hitting the pavement with a steady beat.

I let my mind wander as I run, each step carrying me farther away from my apartment and deeper into the stillness of the morning. The city is waking up around me, but I am in my own little world, a world where nothing matters except the sound of my breathing and the rhythm of my steps. Running always has a way of putting everything into perspective, making all the stress and distractions of life seem so distant. It is just me and the road ahead, with no pressure, no obligations, just freedom.

As I push on, my pace picks up, and I feel the endorphins start to kick in. I have no destination in mind, no set route, just a vague sense of heading toward something better. The streets blur together as I lose myself in the movement, the joy of just being outside and doing something for myself. For those few moments, nothing else matters. It was just the run, my thoughts, and the open road, and in that simplicity, I find peace.

Aimee

Well, I arrived safe and sound early this morning, the Boston air feels different when I step out of the airport from arrivals, the time is around 5.30am when I landed. I am not too tired considering, the adrenaline is coursing through my veins at this point. It is still dark outside but the most magical moment is walking out of the airport and seeing the buildings with my own eyes, there's a certain aura about them, I can understand why a lot of people call this place home. As I am wheeling my case on the concrete outside I pull out my confirmation for the apartment from my bag and show the cab driver, The address says "Brookline Avenue", the keys have been left in a key box on the outside of the building, the code has been sent via SMS.

The cab ride to my new apartment in Boston feels surreal, especially in the quiet of the early morning hours. The city seems asleep, with the streets reflecting the faint glow of streetlights. The soft hum of the car engine and the occasional whoosh of tyres on wet pavement are the only sounds breaking the silence. It is still dark outside, and I can see the first hints of dawn creeping over the horizon, as if the world is waking up with me. The excitement mixes with the exhaustion from the short journey, but there is a strange comfort in the stillness of the city at this hour, as if I am beginning a new chapter all on my own.

As the cab rolls down the last stretch of road, I can feel the anticipation building. I haven't seen the apartment in person before, only in photos and through a few emails, but now it is real. The cab pulls up to the building, and I pay the driver, my hands a little unsteady from the anticipation. Stepping out, I grab my bags from the trunk. The cool Boston air nips at my skin, making me shiver briefly before I adjust to it. The bags feel heavier than expected, filled with everything I have brought with me – clothes, books, and all the little things that feel like home, even if they are far from it right now.

I walk through the entrance of the building, the soft clink of the keys in my hand echoing through the empty hallway. There is something calming about the silence of the space, as if it has been waiting for someone to fill it with life. The elevator ride is short, and as the doors open to my floor, I step out and find the door to my new apartment. A deep breath, then I unlock it and push the door open. The space that greets me is simple, yet exactly what I need.

The apartment has large windows that let in the soft glow of early morning light, and the floors are made of polished hardwood, smooth under my feet. The walls are a soft neutral colour, and the place has an airy, open feel. The living area is small but cosy, with just enough room for a couch and a coffee table. It isn't much, but it is all mine. The kitchen area is compact, with sleek, modern appliances and plenty of counter space. A small dining nook sits next to the windows, offering a view of the quiet city streets below. There is a calmness to the place, a sense of peace that makes me feel like I can breathe easier already.

The bedroom is simple too, with a comfortable-looking bed that has a dark blue duvet and a few pillows stacked neatly. A dresser sits against one wall, with a few empty shelves just waiting to be filled with books and mementos. The bathroom, though small, is exactly what I need. It has a glass shower stall with shiny tiles and chrome fixtures, and the mirror above the sink seems to stretch up forever. There is something about the clean lines and minimalistic design that makes it feel welcoming, like it is ready for me to settle in.

I place my bags down on the living room floor and wander into the bathroom, the coolness of the tiles beneath my bare feet grounding me in the moment. I turn on the shower, letting the warm water pour down over me as I stand there for a few moments, letting the tension of the journey slip away. The steam fills the room, and I close my eyes, appreciating the solitude and the feeling of being in my own space at last. It is a small comfort, but after the long travel and the uncertainty, it feels like exactly what I need.

After a long shower, I step out, wrapping myself in a fluffy towel. I feel cleaner, lighter somehow, like I can finally start afresh. I dry off, then go into the bedroom to grab some comfortable clothes from my suitcase. The morning light is brighter now, and the apartment has an entirely different feel to it. The dark, quiet hours are gone, replaced by the warmth of a new day. I let myself smile at the thought of what is to come. This is a new beginning.

The process of unpacking feels like a ritual, something to help me settle in, to transform the bare apartment into a home. I open the first suitcase and begin hanging clothes in the closet, organising shoes, folding shirts and pants neatly. There is a certain satisfaction in seeing everything in its place. I unpack the rest of my things, finding spots for everything. The kitchen now had a few mugs, plates, and utensils; the bathroom is stocked with toiletries; and my books and photographs find homes on the shelves. Little by little, the apartment is becoming my space.

As I put the last of my things away, I stand back and survey the apartment. It is still bare, but it feels more like mine now. The walls aren't so empty anymore, and there is a sense of familiarity in the air. I sit down on the couch, exhausted but content. The city outside is beginning to wake up, the streets now filled with the sounds of early morning commuters and the bustle of people starting their day. I feel a sense of belonging, even in this unfamiliar place. This is my new life.

I sit there for a while, just soaking it all in – the quiet of the apartment, the sense of peace that has settled over me. There is still so much to do, so much to explore in this new city, but for now, I am content. I have arrived, and for the first time in a long time, I can take a breath and begin to build my life here, in this new apartment, in this new city. It is the beginning of something, and that is enough.

I decide it's time to go to bed and try and get some sleep, I send the girls a text in our group chat we have, to let them know I have arrived. They will all be asleep; however, it will be a nice message for them to open when they awake from their slumbers.

> **Aimee:** Hey Girls, Just to let you all know I have landed and I am slowly making progress in the apartment – time for sleep now <3 A xxx

I decide to go for a walk, I head to the public garden, I hear it's a stunning garden, filled with so much wildlife and endangered plants. I head to my suitcase and pull out my leggings and a baggy t shirt, adorned with a cap where I could feather my ponytail through the back, I still have a couple of days off before I start my new job so it's time to get acquainted with my new city. I have downloaded the City Mapper type of app so I can find my way around.

I have barely finished unpacking when I decide to take a break. The apartment feels almost complete – everything is where it should be, or at least in its temporary place. The books are stacked neatly on the shelves, the clothes hung in the closet, and the kitchen is stocked, even if the counter is still a little bare. I wander around the apartment a few times, admiring the way it has come together. There is a stillness to it now, and though it isn't yet home in the way I envisioned, it is getting there.

I grab my jacket from the bedroom, and as I put it on, I feel a pull to get out, to explore the city I am now calling home. The early afternoon light outside beckons, and I know the Public Garden, just a short walk away, is the perfect spot for a little adventure. I step outside, locking the door behind me, and take a deep breath of the crisp Boston air. The city feels fresh and alive, even though it is still relatively quiet. There is something comforting about the buildings lining the streets, their old brick facades contrasting with the modernity of the new constructions.

As I walk down the sidewalk, I notice the first few people on the streets, bundled up in coats and scarves, going about their day. There is a quiet, friendly energy in the air. People smile as they pass, a mix of locals and a few tourists, all sharing the same sense of quiet excitement about being out in the world. I smile back at a couple walking their dog, the dog wagging its tail happily as it bounds ahead. It is the kind of simple interaction that makes me feel like I could belong here, that this city has a kind of warmth, even in the chill of February.

The further I walk, the more I notice the little details – the sound of the subway rumbling beneath the streets, the distant hum of cars, and the occasional beep of a crosswalk signal. There is something about being on foot in a city that allows me to take in the nuances of my surroundings. As I near the Public Garden, the streets become more open, and I can see the trees and pathways of the park in the distance, still bare of leaves but full of promise. It is peaceful here, a slice of nature amidst the bustle of the city, and I can't wait to see it up close.

Turning onto the street that leads into the park, I pass by more people walking leisurely, some alone and others in small groups. A jogger runs past me with a steady pace, his breath visible in the cold air, and I step aside to let him pass. As I approach the entrance to the garden, I notice a couple sitting on a bench, sharing a thermos of coffee, laughing at something only they know. Their warmth and ease are contagious, and I find myself smiling at the sight of them. It is the kind of casual moment that makes me feel a little less like a stranger in a new place.

I enter the park and take a deep breath, feeling the calmness of the space wash over me. The trees stretch high above, bare branches crisscrossing against the sky, but their quiet beauty is striking. I wander along the paved paths, the crunch of frost beneath my boots the only sound breaking the stillness. The air feels fresh here, the kind of crispness that makes you feel awake and alive. The park is more serene than I expected, even though it is right in the heart of the city, and it feels like a place where you can truly breathe.

As I walk deeper into the park, I notice more people – an elderly man feeding the birds near a pond, a young woman sketching in a notebook while sitting on a bench, and a group of friends laughing as they throw snowballs at each other. It is an unspoken sense of community, a collection of moments that, though small, make the city feel welcoming. I pass by a man playing his guitar, the soft strumming drifting through the air. His music feels like a natural addition to the peaceful surroundings, blending with the hum of life in the park.

I take my time walking, enjoying the simple pleasure of just being outside, surrounded by nature, and letting the quiet moments of the park ground me in the newness of it all. The contrast between the serenity of the Public Garden and the vibrancy of the city around it is striking, and it feels like the perfect reflection of Boston itself – a city that balances its history and its modernity, a place that is both calm and full of energy. The more I walk, the more I can feel the city's rhythm, like a gentle pulse that is steady and inviting.

Eventually, I find a bench overlooking the pond and sit down to take it all in. The sun has risen higher now, casting a warm glow over the scene, and the reflections on the water shimmer like diamonds. I pull my jacket tighter around me as I sit and let the world go on around me. There is something comforting in the way people interact with the park – there is no rush, no urgency. The city is alive, but here, in this moment, time seems to slow down.

As I sit on the bench, I realise how much I need this quiet time. The unpacking, the move, all of it has felt a little overwhelming, but now, as I breathe in the fresh air and watch people go about their peaceful routines, it feels like everything is falling into place. I feel more grounded, more present in the city I have just arrived in. It isn't home yet, but it could be. And for the first time since I arrived, I truly believe I could make a life here. As I'm sitting on the bench, I happen to see a tall, dark gent in his running ensemble, he looks very focused, you can tell he works out often; he has a rugby player's build and the run he's taking part in doesn't seem to be affecting him at all.

Sam

I allow my mind to wander, letting the rhythm of my feet on the pavement become a calming backdrop to the world around me. The trees are bare, but their gnarled branches create intricate patterns against the pale sky, and the park has a quiet stillness that makes it feel like a world of its own, separate from the city that buzzes just beyond it.

The sound of my breath and the steady pounding of my feet are the only things breaking the silence. The park isn't too crowded this early, just a few joggers here and there, a dog walker with a cheerful golden retriever, and an elderly couple strolling slowly along the lake. But as I round a corner of the path, I notice her. She is sitting alone on a bench by the water, her eyes focused on the distant skyline, seemingly lost in thought.

She has long brown hair tied back in a ponytail, the kind of natural movement in her hair that makes it clear she didn't try too hard. She wears a simple black cap, which pulls the focus to her face. I can't help but glance her way as I run past. She is stunning in an effortless way, like she has just woken up and already looks perfect. Her features are delicate, soft, but there is an undeniable strength to her expression, like she has an inner peace that I envy. I can't say what it is exactly, but there is something about her that feels magnetic.

For a split second, I nearly stop in my tracks. Her beauty catches me off guard, and I feel my pace falter. I try to look away quickly, but my eyes linger just a moment too long. She is real, sitting there so casually, yet in that moment, she feels like she is part of the landscape, as if she belongs to the park itself. I can tell she is different – she doesn't belong to this routine of runners and dog walkers. There is an unfamiliar energy about her, a quiet grace that makes me wonder if she is a visitor, someone passing through, or if she lives here, in this city, like I am trying to.

I keep my pace steady, but my thoughts begin to race. Have I seen her before? I run this route often, but she doesn't look like someone I would forget. I try to shake off the curiosity, focusing instead on the rhythm of my breathing and the sound of my footsteps. But every time I glance back, she is still there, sitting on the bench, the silhouette of the city in the background. It feels like she is part of the scene, a piece of the morning puzzle, and yet something about her makes me feel like she doesn't quite belong. She stands out, in the best possible way.

I think about turning around, maybe jogging back past her, but that feels too obvious, too forward. Instead, I let my feet keep moving, pushing me further along the path, knowing I probably won't see her again. It isn't like I can just walk up to her and start a conversation. I am not that kind of guy, not to mention the awkwardness of it all. But there is something about her, a quiet allure, that leaves a mark on me.

The more I run, the more I realise how fleeting the encounter has been. It is one of those moments that could have easily slipped away unnoticed, but it hasn't. I feel that lingering pull, the feeling that I have just brushed past something important, something significant. I'd only caught a glimpse, but it is enough to stir something inside me. I start to question why I hadn't stopped, why I hadn't said something, but the moment is gone, and I am left with only the memory of her presence.

I try to push her out of my mind, focusing on the path ahead, the turn of my legs, the steady thump of my heart. The park is beautiful, and I am grateful to be running in such a peaceful space, but it feels a little less complete now, with her out of sight. I hadn't expected this, not from a simple jog, not from a park bench. But life has a way of surprising you like that, bringing a brief spark of something unexpected into your routine.

By the time I complete my loop around the park, I feel more restless than usual. I slow my pace as I near the entrance again, looking for her, but the bench is empty. For a brief moment, I wonder if I had imagined it all, if she had ever been there at all. But I knew I hadn't. The image of her sitting there, lost in thought, is too vivid. The way the light had caught her face, how she'd seemed so serene, so comfortable in her own skin – no, I hadn't imagined it.

I stop for a moment by the entrance, catching my breath, scanning the area one last time. The park seems quieter now, the sunlight beginning to filter through the trees, casting long shadows on the ground. The day has started to unfold, and with it, so have my thoughts. I'd let the moment slip by, and maybe that was for the best. But something tells me that if I stay in Boston long enough, if I run this route enough times, our paths might cross again. And if they do, I'll be ready. For now, though, I turn and walk away, the city's pulse beneath my feet, the memory of her still lingering like an echo in the back of my mind. As I slowly walk to my apartment, I keep picturing her in my mind – *why didn't you go and speak to her? Have I missed my chance to even introduce myself with her?* I feel like such an idiot, literally would have taken me a few minutes and now I won't be able to get her out of my mind. I head to the nearest Starbucks to try and catch my luck and see if I can casually bump into her again; it is to no avail – she isn't there.

The barista greets me with a smile as I place my order. I am still thinking about her – the way her long brown hair moved with the breeze, the calm, contemplative look she wore on her face, like she didn't have a care in the world. She was probably just someone passing through, but there is something about her that feels different. It wasn't just the beauty, though that definitely struck me. It was the way she seemed to belong in that space, how natural and at ease she looked sitting there, like she was a part of the park itself.

I take my cup when it is ready, the warm ceramic comforting in my hands. The caffeine will help, but I still feel a lingering curiosity, an itch to know who she is and what brought her there. As I walk out of the Starbucks and back onto the street, I pull out my phone, scrolling through my contacts until I land on Josh's name. He always knows how to talk me through things, especially when I have a little too much going on in my head. He is one of my closest friends, and I need to tell someone about the encounter.

"Hey man, you're not going to believe what happened this morning," I say when he picks up. I can already hear the background noise of his place – probably still lounging around, still in bed.

"What happened? You still running, or did you bail on your workout?" Josh's voice is lazy but curious, like he knows something is up.

"I was running in the Public Garden, and I saw this girl sitting on a bench. I've never seen her before, and I don't know why, but she just kind of stopped me in my tracks. She was just sitting there, looking out at the skyline, wearing a black cap and this long ponytail. I don't know, man, it sounds dumb, but it was like, this moment that I couldn't shake. I didn't even say anything to her. Just ran right by."

Josh is quiet for a moment. "Dude, you're telling me you didn't even say hi?" He sounds incredulous. "You're killing me. You don't see a girl like that every day."

"I know, I know," I sigh, a little embarrassed by my own hesitation. "I don't know what it was. She had this calm about her, like she just belonged there, you know? I don't know if I've seen her before, or if I just imagined it, but I swear, there was something different about her. It's like she's from a different world or something."

Josh laughs lightly, the sound of him shuffling around in his bed on the other end. "Sounds like you're falling for her without even knowing her name. Classic Sam move. I mean, come on, dude, what's the worst that could happen if you just said something?"

"I don't know. I guess I was just... caught off guard," I say, trying to justify it. "I've got enough going on right now with settling in and all. I didn't want to complicate things."

"Well, if it's meant to be, you'll see her again. Just don't let the next girl slip by like that, okay?" Josh says, his voice turning serious for a second. "You've got to take chances, man. Otherwise, what's the point?"

I think about it for a moment. "Yeah, you're right. I just don't know if I'm ready for anything right now. But we'll see. Who knows? Maybe I'll run into her again."

"Alright, man, keep me posted. I want to hear the rest of the story if you do."

We wrap up the call, and as I hang up, I feel a bit lighter. Talking it out with Josh always helps. I still can't shake the image of her face from my mind, but there is something comforting about sharing the experience, even if it is just a fleeting moment. I look up at the sky for a second, trying to let it go and move on.

When I get back to my apartment, I set the coffee down on the kitchen counter and make my way to the bathroom. The phone call has helped, but I still need to shake off the lingering feelings. A hot shower would be the perfect reset. I turn on the water, the steam filling the room as I step under the spray. The hot water hits my skin, soothing my muscles from the run. My mind wanders again, this time back to the quiet calm of the Public Garden, and I can't help but replay the scene in my head.

I stand under the water for a while, letting the heat relax me, letting my thoughts drift. I don't think too much about the girl anymore; the park and the run are just memories, moments that would fade. But for some reason, this one feels different. It isn't like any other fleeting encounter I'd had in a long time. Maybe it is the unpredictability of it all. Maybe it is just the beauty of the moment. Either way, I know I will be thinking about it for a while.

When I finally step out of the shower, I wrap myself in a towel, feeling the warmth from the water still lingering on my skin. I take a deep breath, the air in the apartment feeling cool after the heat of the shower. I don't need to rush into anything; the apartment is quiet, still. I decide to take it easy for the rest of the afternoon. There is no rush to unpack more or to figure out the next step. I lean against the kitchen counter, sipping my coffee slowly, letting the steam curl up into the air.

The apartment feels a little more calmer, and though the mystery of the girl in the park still floats around in my mind, I feel content. I open the blinds and let the sunlight flood in, illuminating the bare walls and polished floors. I still haven't decided on a specific direction for the day, but I am not in any hurry. I could just exist here, in the calm of the apartment, and let the city outside unfold at its own pace.

I spend the next few hours just chilling around, not doing much. I flip through a few books I have had sitting on the shelf for months, skim some articles online, and let the thoughts of the morning's encounter drift in and out of my mind. Maybe she'll cross my path again. Or maybe she won't. Either way, life would go on, and for now, I am okay with that. I can just enjoy the simplicity of the moment – no pressure, no expectations – letting the day unfold naturally.

Aimee

It's been a couple of days now in my new apartment, and I'm starting to feel like it's a little more mine. The boxes are mostly unpacked, though there are still random piles of things that don't seem to have a place. The kitchen looks like it might be a nice place to cook, once I get the hang of it. There's an old window above the sink, and every time I stand there, I find myself gazing out at the city beyond. It's all still so unfamiliar. The street noise, the busy rhythm of life happening just outside the window – it's a bit of a contrast to the quiet suburbs I grew up in. But I'm starting to like it, little by little.

The apartment is cosy, small enough to be manageable but big enough that I don't feel like I'm trapped. It has its quirks, though. The floor creaks in strange places, and the radiator hisses whenever it kicks on, making me feel like I'm living in an old novel. It's charming, in its own way. I think I'm going to like it here. But there's something else that's been lingering in the back of my mind, something I can't shake. The man I saw in the park.

I keep replaying the scene over and over in my head. I was just sitting on the bench admiring the pond, the kind of aimless wandering you do when you're new to a place. It was late afternoon, and the park was quiet, a few people scattered around, enjoying the calm before evening. And then, I saw him. He just came jogging past, out of nowhere, his hair dark and thick but his posture still strong. There was something magnetic about him, a presence that made the world around him seem to pause for just a moment. I don't even know why I noticed him, but I did, and ever since, I can't stop thinking about it.

I try not to overthink things, to let my mind drift into a sea of what-ifs, but every time I close my eyes, I see him standing there.

There was something comforting in his stillness, something in the way he blended into the surroundings so effortlessly. I never talked to him, never even got close enough to say hello. But I keep wondering who he was, what his life was like. It's a strange feeling, this lingering curiosity.

After leaving the park, I decided to keep walking, maybe shake off some of these thoughts. Boston is a city full of surprises, and it didn't take long before I found myself wandering down unfamiliar streets, admiring the old architecture, and trying to get a feel for the place. There's a sense of history here that I haven't felt anywhere else. The cobblestone streets, the buildings that seem to have stories embedded in their walls. It felt like every corner I turned had a new little treasure waiting to be discovered.

As I walked, I found myself gravitating toward the old bookshops. They were tucked away in quiet corners of the city, each one with its own distinct personality. Some of the stores were small, cluttered with books spilling over shelves, while others had a more polished feel, with neat displays of leather-bound classics. I wandered into one that smelled like dust and old paper, the air thick with the scent of stories long since read. The shelves seemed endless, and I felt a sense of comfort there, as if the words on the pages could wrap around me like a blanket and shield me from all the unknowns.

I lost track of time in those bookshops, flipping through pages of books I'd never heard of and marvelling at the covers of editions that seemed ancient. It was easy to get lost in there, in the quiet corners of the city and in the comfort of all those stories. But, in the back of my mind, the image of that man in the park kept returning. His presence was a strange comfort, like he belonged there in the park, watching life go by without ever needing to be a part of it. Maybe that's what I was missing – that kind of calm.

After a while, I decided to take a break from my wandering and sit down at a café. It wasn't far from where I'd been walking, just on the edge of a small square. The coffee was good, strong and warm, just what I needed to clear my head. I kept watching the people around me, trying to figure out if anyone was like me, someone who was still figuring out their place here in the city. I couldn't help but feel like an outsider, though everyone around me seemed so comfortable in their routines. I hadn't yet made any real connections here, and the idea of putting myself out there seemed intimidating.

I spent the rest of the afternoon exploring more of the city, walking through neighbourhoods and peeking into random shops. It felt like the more I explored, the more I realised how much there was still to see. Boston is one of those cities that never feels fully explored, no matter how much you walk. Every corner holds something new. But even as I wandered through the unfamiliar streets, my mind kept returning to that man. Who was he? Why had I noticed him at all?

As the evening came, I found myself drawn to the notice boards scattered around the city. They were full of announcements for local events, classes, and gatherings. I started reading them, looking for something that might help me meet new people, something to help me feel a little less alone in this big city. There were book clubs, meetups for writers, art classes, and a whole list of community events. I wasn't sure what I was looking for exactly, but the idea of making connections with others felt necessary, like something I had to do to make this place feel more like home.

There was a posting for a local book club that caught my eye. It was small, just a handful of people, and they met once a month to discuss novels they all read together. I thought about signing up for a moment, the thought of joining something new feeling both exciting and terrifying. But it felt like a step in the right direction, so I made a note of the date and location, planning to show up when the time came. Maybe this would be the thing that finally helped me settle in.

The idea of meeting new people is always a bit daunting, though. It's one thing to walk around and look at bookshops, but it's another to actually try to make a connection with someone. But I know it's something I have to do. It's just that nagging feeling of wanting to be a part of something, to find a place where I truly belong. I can feel myself starting to miss that sense of connection I used to have, the comfort of knowing where I fit in. But this is all part of the process, I guess. Starting afresh in a new place means starting over in many ways, and that's both thrilling and terrifying.

As the sun dipped below the horizon, I found myself wandering back to the apartment, my head full of thoughts. There was a part of me that still couldn't shake the image of that man in the park. It felt like he was a symbol of something I was striving for – that calm, that stillness, that ability to be at peace with the world without needing to constantly be in motion. Maybe I'm not quite there yet, but I think I'm starting to understand that it's okay to not have everything figured out immediately. Maybe it's enough to just keep moving forward, to keep exploring, and to see what happens next.

When I finally got back to the apartment, I sat on the couch for a while, the quiet of the room surrounding me. It's still a bit strange here, the place where I sleep but don't yet truly live. There's something in the air that still feels unfamiliar. But I think it's just a matter of time. Each day brings something new, and slowly, I'm learning how to navigate it all. I don't know if I'll ever stop thinking about the man in the park, but I do know that I'll keep moving forward, finding new paths to walk, new spaces to fill, and maybe, just maybe, new people to meet along the way.

As I take my notepad and write down some of the classes I would be interested in taking, I hear my phone start to buzz; it's the girls.

"So, Aimee, how's Boston been treating you so far? I can't believe it's already been a couple of days! Have you had a chance to explore yet? Or are you still figuring things out?" Hope asks.

I reply to her, matching her energy. "It's been... interesting, honestly. I've been walking around, trying to get the lay of the land. It's kind of overwhelming, you know? But also kind of magical. I went to this park today, and I saw this guy jogging in the park, he just went right past me. He had this sort of quiet energy about him, like he belonged there. It was strange... like he didn't have to do anything but just be. It stuck with me for some reason."

I hear Sacha take a deep breath before she chimes in. "Ooh, that's intriguing! Was he doing anything? Or just...getting your attention on purpose?"

I knew I would get this reception; I retort to her: "Exactly! He wasn't doing much of anything, just jogging, and the way he was so confident... I don't know. It was like he was part of the park itself. I felt like I could watch him forever, like he knew something I didn't. I don't know why it stuck with me, but it did. I keep thinking about him."

I can hear Isabella trying to get a word in edgeways and it doesn't work, the chat goes silent and then she says, "That's so mysterious. It's funny how certain people can leave an imprint on you, even without saying a word. Did he look... sad? Or peaceful? There's something about moments like that – when someone is just existing – that can feel really profound." I mutter back them at all. "He was peaceful. Almost like he was in his own world, not needing anything from anyone. I don't know, it just made me wonder who he was, what his life was like... Why did I notice him out of all the people there? It felt like there was something there, but I couldn't quite place it."

Hope goes on… "That's so interesting. Sometimes, you meet people who just feel different, even from afar. Maybe he's someone you'll run into again. You never know how small the world can be. Or maybe it's just the city itself, making you notice the little things."

The girls make jokes and we giggle for a while until Sacha being her normal self just as sharp as she is shouts, "You should have just asked for his number, you need to be more confident, girl."

A smile lifts my cheekbones as I know what she means; however, it's not my style to come out right at someone for something so personal, especially when we only looked at each other for a moment.

Hope questions her as she always has done. "Sacha, you can't be serious? Were you not told about stranger danger when you were small?"

Sacha has a laugh that erupts from her chest. "Come on, I said she could have gotten his number, a number isn't going to hurt."

They have their moment of bickering and disagreements, I miss this about them. I miss the different points of views they all have. I glance over at the clock and it's getting late, we say our goodbyes and before I know it it's back to silence in the apartment.

I take the decision to go and lie in bed, try out one of the books I bought at the bookshop today. I start my new job in two days so I am excited to go and do some more exploring tomorrow.

Sam

BOSTON

The evening before another workday at the antique shop, I feel an odd mix of excitement and nervousness. I wasn't exactly sure what to expect, but there was this undercurrent of anticipation. I spend the evening preparing, picking out what I would wear – something that felt professional but still had a touch of my personality. I wanted to be comfortable but make a good impression. I settle on a simple shirt paired with slacks, something I could move in but still look put together.

I try to wind down early, knowing I need a good night's sleep to face the day ahead. But my mind is racing with thoughts of the shop, the people I would meet, and everything else I am trying to adjust to. It is harder to fall asleep than I had hoped. I keep tossing and turning, my mind replaying all the little details. Her. Eventually, though, exhaustion takes over, and I drift off into a restless sleep, not fully at ease, but knowing I had to get some rest.

I wake up to the soft light filtering through the window, the morning sun just beginning to rise. The city outside is already coming to life, the noise of traffic faintly drifting in through the crack in the window. I turn over and glance at the clock. It is earlier than I needed to get up, but I decide to stay awake and let the day unfold. There is something about the stillness of the morning that makes everything feel a little more manageable. I have time to collect my thoughts before the rush of the day begins.

I move through my morning routine slowly, trying not to rush. I make coffee and stare out of the window for a moment, letting the warmth of the cup seep into my hands. The smell of the coffee is comforting, grounding me for what lies ahead. I thought about how much has changed in just a few days – how unfamiliar everything still feels and yet, how much it has already started to feel like home. Even so, I know today will be another new experience. I dress quickly, grab my bag, and am out the door, making my way to the antique shop.

The drive to work is a little longer than I had anticipated, but it gives me the chance to clear my mind and get used to the rhythm of the city. The streets are busy, the usual bustle of people rushing to work, and the sound of footsteps mixed with the hum of traffic. I drive with a purpose, trying to keep my focus on the task at hand. There is a slight chill in the air, but the day promises to warm up. As I make my way through the city, I can't help but notice the little details that have begun to make the city feel more familiar – the scent of fresh bread wafting from a bakery, the old brick buildings with their ivy-covered walls, the vibrant street art that adds colour to the grey urban landscape.

When I arrive at the antique shop, I feel a jolt of nervous energy. The shop is tucked away on a quieter street, the kind of place you might miss if you weren't looking for it. The windows are lined with old furniture and trinkets, and the scent of aged wood and leather hits me as I step inside. When I first started there, it was exactly how I imagined it – warm, inviting, but filled with the weight of history. The shop was smaller than I had expected, but every inch of space seemed to be filled with something interesting, something with a story.

The owner, a woman named Eleanor, greets me warmly when I walk in. She has a kind face, and her eyes sparkle with the kind of knowledge that only comes from years of working in this world of antiques. She has been a fantastic tutor to me from the moment I applied for the job and managed to secure the job offer within three days of the interview. She is a fantastic boss and this makes me want to work harder as she has been a guide for me in my new career.

As the day progresses, there is Samuel, the shop's resident expert on vintage books, who has a gentle, thoughtful manner. He is passionate about the history behind each book and could go on for hours about their origins. Then there is Clarice, a woman in her late twenties who has a no-nonsense attitude and was quick to teach me the ropes when I first stepped through the door. She was efficient and always seemed to know what needed to be done. Her confidence was contagious, and I found myself learning from her every time we spoke.

As the day wears on, I find myself becoming more comfortable with the rhythm of the shop on that particular day. I begin to understand the regular customers' preferences, know where to find certain items, and start to feel like I am becoming a part of something here. The constant hum of the shop, the quiet conversations, and the delicate handling of old items feels oddly calming. There is a certain reverence to the work, a sense that the objects in the shop are more than just things – they are pieces of history, carrying the stories of the past with them.

The hours pass quickly, and before I know it, it is time to close the shop for the day. I feel a quiet sense of accomplishment, though there is still so much to learn. As I say goodbye to everyone and step out into the street, I can't help but feel that familiar sense of peace that comes with the end of a long, productive day. The drive back to my apartment is quieter than the drive in, and I feel the weight of the day settling in my bones. But it is a good kind of tired, the kind that comes from doing something meaningful, even if it is just the beginning.

By the time I get home, the city feels even more familiar, even if only by a little. I decide to message the guys to see if they fancy a couple of quiet drinks.

Sam: Boys! Fancy meeting at the bar in 45 minutes for a couple of "quiet ones"

Josh: Sure Bud! I will head over soon!

Steven: Is it wrong that I'm already here? ƐＯＬ

I chuckle at Steven's response; this is very him. He likes to finish work and just have a couple of drinks by himself.

I quickly dash home and change into more comfortable clothes and I'm back out the door again, walking the streets of Boston. I can already sense the anticipation in the air, people are already flooding through the bars as I can hear laughter echo throughout the main street. As I open the door to the bar I see Steven and Josh in our usual booth, I head over and I can see they have already gotten the round in. I smile and take my seat.

The conversation takes place almost instantly,

Steven kicks off the questions as I pull the bottle towards my mouth to take a gulp of the beer. "So, Sam, you've been talking about this woman in the park for a few days now. Did you ever go up and ask her out, or at least see her again? I mean, it sounds like there was some kind of spark. Or are you just going to let it slip away?"

I laugh. "Oh, come on, man. You know me better than that. I'm not just going to randomly ask someone out. She was sitting there, staring into space, completely lost in her world. I didn't want to interrupt her. And honestly, I don't even know if I should've said anything. It just felt like one of those moments that was too perfect to mess up by speaking."

Josh, the ladies' man, gives me his point of view. "I get that. Sometimes it feels better to just leave things as they are, like they're meant to stay that way, y'know? But I also know that if I were in your shoes, I'd probably regret not saying anything. What if she's still out there, reading, and you just missed the chance to talk to her?"

The sarcastic part in me wants to correct him – I hope she isn't sat in the park at nighttime by herself. I know this already; however, I just can't shake the image of her.

Steven exclaims, "That's the risk, man. You're overthinking it. I'm sure she's not just out there waiting for someone to ask her out, right? It's not like you're her destiny or anything. But I get it. Sometimes you see someone, and it feels like the universe is handing you this perfect moment, and you don't want to let it go."

I take a deep sigh. "Yeah, that's the thing. I keep thinking about it. But what if she was just... I don't know, someone who likes the park and reads books? Not everyone is looking for something. And besides, I've got enough on my plate with everything else going on."

Josh groans and puts his head in his hands. "Tell me about it. I can't even remember the last time I had a quiet moment to myself. Between work and everything at home, I'm just drained. My place is chaos. My wife and I are constantly at odds. She's frustrated because I'm always working late, and when I am home, I'm not present. It's a mess, man. I barely have time to think, let alone meet some stranger in a park."

I flick a look over to him over my shoulder as I do feel like I am being mocked. I do try to play devil's advocate with this one. "I hear you, Josh. I can't even imagine the stress you're under. It sounds like you're being pulled in a million directions, and none of them are the right one for you right now. But hey, have you and Sarah talked about it, really talked? You know, sat down and had an honest conversation about how both of you are feeling?"

He pauses. "Yeah, we've tried, but it always turns into this huge argument. She feels like I'm distant, and I don't know how to tell her that I'm just trying to keep things together, you know? I want to make her happy, but I'm so tired of all the tension. She wants me to be more involved, but I don't know how to fix it. She doesn't get how much pressure there is at work right now. I feel like I'm losing my grip on everything."

I can see Steven watching us, he's taking everything in "Man, that's tough. And I get it. Having a family is a lot of work. I'm learning that firsthand. I've got a baby at home now, and I feel like I'm always running on empty. I mean, you can never really prepare for it, right? You think you know what being a dad will be like, but when the baby's up all night crying, and you're both exhausted, it's easy to feel like you're drowning. And then you've got the added pressure of trying to balance work and home life. It's crazy."

Josh lets out an over-exasperated laugh. "Right? I was just thinking, when's the last time I even saw my wife for who she is, and not just as the woman I'm arguing with over laundry or bills? It feels like I'm failing her. And now, with the way things are going at work... I don't know how to turn it around."

I don't know what they are going through personally but I try to offer the best advice I can. "I think, sometimes, we just get so caught up in our heads, you know? We think we're failing because we're not being perfect, but honestly, none of us are perfect. And I think that's where you guys are – trying to juggle all this stuff, trying to be the best version of yourself for everyone. But it's okay to not have all the answers, to be exhausted, to even have a bad day."

I have never heard Steven say I'm right; however, there's always a day for everything. "Sam's right. It's like, you're constantly giving pieces of yourself to other people, and then you don't have anything left for yourself. I don't even remember the last time I had a moment to just sit down and breathe, let alone go out and meet someone in the park like I should. But we'll figure it out. It's a lot of pressure, but we can't carry everything by ourselves."

Josh retorts, "I want to believe that, but sometimes it just feels like I'm on the edge of it all crumbling down. I'm just trying to keep everything intact, but every day it gets harder."

Steven starts to rub his face and I can see his face turning a bright shade of maroon. "I get it, man. I've been there. It's overwhelming. But think about this – being a father, for example, doesn't come with a handbook. Every day is figuring it out as you go. Same with relationships. Same with work. It's about doing your best, not about being perfect."

As the night goes on we throw a few more jokes in each other's way, it's now getting late and I am concerned that I am at work tomorrow, so I decide to bid the boys goodbye. As I walk out the double doors to the bar and walk home, as I step outside the air sends my thoughts spiralling. With every step I take, I can hear the heel of my boot hitting the pavement, my foot movements are getting faster. I need to get some shut eye, I have an early start and I need to be on top form; the shop is open to the general public tomorrow so my mind needs to be sharp.

As I finally make my way home and I unlock the door to my apartment building, I give a swift nod to the security on the door, and he greets me with a pleasant smile. I press the large silver button to the lift and I wait patiently for the lift to come. I hear the mechanisms click into place and hear the lift starting to move. Once the lift arrives, I step in and no one is sharing this ride with me – makes a change, this apartment block is busy. I enjoy the silence. Once I have arrived at my floor, the noise from the elevator dings and I wait for the doors to part, I step out and stagger to my door.

I lock the door behind me, the familiar click of the deadbolt making the apartment feel secure and quiet. The soft hum of the refrigerator is the only sound I hear as I take my shoes off. The stillness feels peaceful, almost like I'm the only person awake in the world. I toss my keys in the bowl on the hallway table and wander toward the bathroom, already thinking about the shower I'm about to take. The day is behind me now, and I'm looking forward to washing off any remnants of the night out.

The hot water feels like a relief when I step into the shower, steam quickly filling the small space. I let it pour over me, the warmth a contrast to the cool air I left outside. I lean my head back, letting the water cascade down, as if it can wash away the last bit of the day. There's something soothing about this routine, the quiet time spent under the water, my mind finally starting to slow down. The scent of soap and shampoo fills the air, and for a moment, it's just me and the rhythm of the water.

I take my time, letting the steam settle around me, feeling the tension of the evening melt away. The quiet hum of the water and the gentle sound of it splashing on the tiles are all I need to relax. As the water cools, I reach for the towel and wrap it around myself, grateful for the warmth it provides. The bathroom mirror is fogged up, but I don't mind. I quickly dry off, and my movements are automatic at this point – slow, deliberate, nothing to rush.

When I finally step into my bedroom, it feels like the world is at a quiet standstill. The dim light from the lamp on the nightstand gives the room a soft, warm glow, and I can already feel the heaviness of sleep pulling at me. I strip down to my pyjamas and pull the covers back, the bed inviting me to finally relax. The soft sheets feel like a comfort after being out in the world for a few hours. I slide in, sinking into the mattress, letting out a soft sigh of relief. It's nice to be back in my own space, away from everything.

As I close my eyes, my body slowly unwinds, the gentle weight of the blanket grounding me. My thoughts are soft, fleeting, as I sink deeper into the warmth of my bed. The quiet of the night is calming, and the stillness is enough to ease me into sleep. There's no rush, no noise, just the peaceful rhythm of breathing in and out. I let go of the night, of the little bits of conversation, the walk, the laughter – everything that isn't here in this moment. And before I know it, I'm drifting off, the world outside becoming a distant echo.

Aimee

BOSTON

The morning light seeps through the curtains, casting a soft glow across the room. I wake up with a slight stretch, the coolness of the sheets still clinging to my skin. It's still early, but the quiet of the apartment invites me to rise. A brief glance at the clock tells me it's just past seven. I sigh, not quite ready to leave the comfort of the bed but knowing I should get up if I want to make the most of the day. I swing my legs over the edge of the mattress, my feet hitting the cool hardwood floor. The familiar chill of the morning air wraps around me as I stand up, but it's refreshing. It's the kind of day that promises the freedom of exploration.

I make my way into the kitchen, the creaky floorboards beneath my feet echoing in the otherwise silent apartment. My bare feet pad across the tiles as I reach the fridge and pull out the ingredients for breakfast. I've always been a simple breakfast kind of person – just a bowl of cereal and a cup of coffee. Nothing fancy, but it's enough to get me started. I pour the cereal into the bowl, the sound of the crunchy flakes filling the kitchen. The coffee machine hums softly as it brews, filling the room with a comforting aroma.

While I wait for the coffee, I take a seat at the small kitchen table by the window, looking out at the street below. The world feels so still in the morning, as if it's holding its breath before everything picks up. A few people pass by, already on their way to work, but the pace is slow, almost like the city is still waking up too. I take a slow sip of my coffee, savouring the warmth as it spreads through me. It's the perfect start to the day. After a moment of quiet contemplation, I finish my breakfast and clean up quickly. There's something about mornings like this that makes me feel like anything is possible.

I grab my jacket from the coat rack and slip it on, knowing I'm going to do some more exploring today. There's something about wandering through the city that feels freeing. The sidewalks are full of promise, with so many corners to turn and shops to discover. I'm in no rush to get anywhere in particular, just enjoying the process of seeing new places and breathing in the city's rhythm. I head for the door, a small thrill of excitement bubbling up inside me. Every day feels like a new adventure here.

As I step outside, the crisp morning air greets me, filling my lungs with freshness. I pull the collar of my jacket up, trying to ward off the chill as I begin walking down the sidewalk. The streets are still relatively quiet, the early morning commuters starting to find their rhythm. I follow the familiar route, past the small cafes and local shops, the occasional burst of conversation drifting out into the air. There's something so comforting about the way the city moves, its pulse steady and unhurried. I let myself get lost in the details, the sound of footsteps, the breeze through the trees, the soft hum of life around me.

As I walk, I spot a sign leaning against the sidewalk, partially hidden behind a row of flowerpots outside a small, quiet street. I stop for a moment, curiosity piqued. The sign is old and weathered, the text faded but still legible: Antique Shop – Rare Finds and Hidden Treasures. My eyebrows lift slightly, the idea of a hidden antique shop catching my attention immediately. I've always loved places like that – filled with old objects and history, stories waiting to be discovered. I wonder what kinds of treasures might be tucked away in a place like that.

I pull out my phone, checking the map to see just how far outside the city this antique shop might be. The location isn't far at all, just a short bus ride away. I make the quick decision that this is exactly what I need today. A quiet stroll through the shop, maybe picking up something unique, could be the perfect way to spend the morning. The thought of discovering something old and beautiful is enough to spark my curiosity.

I turn back toward the bus stop, scanning the street for the right line. The sun has begun to rise higher now, casting a warm golden glow over the buildings. I can feel the city waking up, and the air is filled with the hum of activity as more people join the sidewalks, heading to their destinations. I catch the bus within a few minutes, the soft rumble of its engine lulling me into a quiet calm as it pulls away from the stop. The ride is peaceful, the streets passing by in a blur of everyday life. It's a short journey, and before long, I find myself at the stop closest to the antique shop.

I step off the bus and look around, the area outside the city feeling quieter, less hurried. The buildings are spaced farther apart, and the streets are lined with trees and greenery, giving it a more peaceful, almost rustic vibe. I walk a little further down the road, following the signs that lead me to the antique shop. The shop is tucked away behind a small garden, the old brick building standing out with its rustic charm. The windows are filled with all sorts of trinkets and curiosities, a little glimpse of the treasures waiting inside. I glance at the cars that are already parked there, some looking very expensive. This place looks like something out of a fairy tale, it looks like a small cottage tucked in the middle of woodland, the flower beds are starting to spring into life and the building almost has a pull to it. I walk slowly to the door; the building looks dark. I place my flat hand over my forehead and lean against the glass to see if the shop is open. I can see people inside so I take a deep breath and push the door open; the bell above the door signals my arrival.

I pause for a moment, taking in the shop's exterior. There's a certain allure to places like this – places that feel timeless, like stepping into a different era. The smell of aged wood and dust hits me immediately, a comforting scent that reminds me of old libraries and vintage bookstores. Inside, the shop is crammed with shelves full of antiques – old furniture, delicate China, vintage books, and strange little objects that tell stories I can only guess at.

I wander through the aisles, running my fingers lightly over the edges of a beautifully carved chair, admiring the craftsmanship. The shop is full of hidden gems, and I can already tell I could spend hours here, just soaking in the history that fills every corner. I'm lost in the quiet of the place when I suddenly spot someone in the corner of the room, standing by a large mirror and speaking to another gentleman. At first, I think I'm imagining it, but then I realise – it's him.

The man I saw in the park a day or so ago. The one with the easy smile and the casual, yet mysterious aura. He hasn't noticed me yet, absorbed in examining the mirror with someone, he looks in deep conversation about it. I take a moment to watch him, wondering what he's doing in a place like this, just as I had decided to explore it. He looks different in this setting, somehow more at ease among all the antique objects, his posture relaxed as he examines the reflection in the mirror.

It's strange seeing him again, but there's something comforting about it. I'm not sure why, but I feel a little more grounded in this quiet space now that he's here. Maybe this explains the pull after all, the magnetic force that I felt had drawn me to the shop. He looks different, he looks put together, smart and agile. After a few more moments, I decide to approach, not wanting to stare at him for too long. As I walk over, he looks up and catches my eye, a brief flicker of recognition crossing his face. He smiles, that same easy smile, and I can't help but smile back. The connection from the park feels strange, but it's nice to see a familiar face in such an unexpected place.

"Fancy seeing you here," I say, a little surprised at how casual my voice sounds despite the unexpected encounter.

He chuckles softly, his eyes warm with amusement. "It seems the city has a way of bringing people together in the most random of places." He steps aside from the mirror, making room for me to look at it too. It's an ornate piece, the glass slightly cloudy with age, but still beautiful. We stand there for a moment in comfortable silence, both of us absorbed in the simple beauty of the object.

"So," I begin, breaking the silence, "what brings you here? I didn't expect to run into you."

He glances at me with a raised eyebrow, a little mischievous. "I work here, I work and appraise antiques. More to the point, what are you doing here?" He pauses, looking around the room as if noticing the place for the first time. "Seems like there's always something new to discover."

I nod, feeling the same sense of wonder in the air. "Exactly. There's something about these places. It's like they have stories to tell. I just moved to the city from New York so I am doing some exploring before I start my new job in a couple of days."

His eyebrows rise and he takes out his hand and shakes mine. "I'm Sam, by the way, it's nice to meet you…"

I stand there dumbfounded, I don't think I have ever shaken anyone's hand, especially not in New York. I stare at his hand and realise I could be coming across as being rude, so I snap out of this trance and take his hand; an electric force zips through my torso. "I'm Aimee, sorry about that, Boston people are very friendly; it's taking some getting used to."

He laughs, and I can feel my face turning bright pink, my cheeks are heated and a little smile lifts my face and I stare into his kind eyes. He begins to speak. "I see you found one of my favourite spots in the city?" he questions me.

I answer him wide eyed. "Yeah, I love to go for walks and the public garden is stunning, I was amazed with the beauty it held. I left not long after you ran past me."

"So, you new to the city?" he asks.

I glance at him, surprised by the question. I'd thought about the move, sure, but I didn't expect someone to ask about it so directly. "Well," I start, a small laugh escaping my lips as I try to organise my thoughts. "It wasn't exactly a whim, but I guess it was planned to the minute."

He nods, clearly listening intently, his eyes never leaving me as I speak. It's like he's genuinely interested in the story behind the words. "I get that. The city definitely has a pulse, doesn't it? I can imagine it's a pretty big shift coming from somewhere larger."

"It is," I agree, my voice softening as I think about the change. "I like it, though. It feels like there's always something happening, but there's still room to breathe. I like being able to walk around and just get lost. I've only been here a few days, but it already feels like home."

He smiles, and I feel a sense of understanding in the gesture. "That's pretty amazing, actually. It's rare to find a place that clicks like that, you know? A place that feels right."

I smile back, grateful for the way he's listening, like he's hearing the unspoken parts of my words too. "Yeah, it feels like a fresh start. And I needed that." I pause, shifting my weight slightly as I study the items on the shelf in front of us. "How about you, Sam? You don't seem like you're from here either. What brought you to Boston?"

Sam's expression softens a bit, and for a moment, I notice a flicker of something in his eyes – maybe nostalgia, or something deeper that he's not quite ready to share. He shifts his position too, leaning against a nearby shelf with his arms crossed. "You're right," he says, his voice low. "I'm not from here. Originally from a small town in the Midwest. Decided to move out here a couple of years ago. For work, mostly. But I've stayed because I've found a rhythm here, too. It's different from home, but there's something about Boston – about the energy – that keeps pulling me back, you know?"

I nod, feeling the weight of his words. There's a hint of melancholy in his voice, but it's not heavy. He's not complaining, more like reflecting on a decision that had its reasons, but didn't come without its challenges. I can relate to that. "I can see that. It's easy to get swept up in everything here, but I imagine it's not always easy to leave the places you know."

He looks at me then, and for a moment, it feels like the space between us narrows. "Yeah. It's not. But sometimes, you have to leave to see what's really out there. And in a way, you have to leave behind a lot of things you thought you knew, to let something new in."

I swallow, his words resonating with me more than I expected. He's speaking from experience, and I can tell there's more behind them, but he's not pushing me to ask. I decide to leave it, for now. There's something calming about this exchange, about the way he doesn't rush or force things to go deeper. The conversation has a natural rhythm, and I don't want to break it. "So, do you like it here?" I ask, my curiosity about him returning. "Boston, I mean. Beyond work, is it a place you actually enjoy?"

He smiles, a little wryly. "It's complicated. But yeah, I like it. It's definitely not home, but there's a sense of adventure here that I don't think I'd find anywhere else. It's a good place to discover things – about the city, and maybe even about yourself."

I chuckle softly. "That's a bit deep for a random antique shop, don't you think?"

He laughs, the sound easy and warm. "Maybe. But sometimes the best conversations happen in the most unexpected places. Like right now, for instance."

I feel the smile tugging at the corners of my mouth again. "I'll give you that," I say, taking a step back toward the shelves, pretending to look at an old set of teacups, though I can't quite shake the feeling that the conversation isn't finished just yet. I glance over at him, and he's still watching me with that steady, almost thoughtful expression.

"I didn't mean to be forward," Sam says suddenly, his voice quieter now, a little more hesitant than before. "But, well, I was wondering if... if you might want to grab a drink sometime. I know we just met, but you seem like you could have someone show you around the city?"

I blink, taken aback for a moment. His question catches me off guard, but it's not the awkward kind of surprise – it's the kind that makes me pause, makes me consider what I want. I can feel the warmth of the shop around me, the low hum of activity, and in that moment, it feels like everything slows down. He's asking me, and there's something genuine in his tone that makes me hesitate before responding. I look up at him, meeting his gaze, and the words come more easily than I expected. "I'd like that," I say, smiling a little. "I think a drink sounds nice and will be nice to see the city after dark, I tend to be in the apartment after 6pm most nights."

He seems to relax at my response, a soft smile curling on his lips. "Good. I wasn't sure if I was being too forward, but I thought I'd take the chance." He shifts his weight, glancing around the shop. His face is turning red, and I feel like a schoolgirl who has been asked to prom, I can't hide my smile, he has a genuine aura about him.

"Well then," Sam says with a playful grin, "I guess it's a date, then."

Instead of looking around as I wanted to do, I decide to turn on my heel and leave, we exchange numbers and I leave the store with my tail in-between my legs. I can sense him staring as I leave the shop but I am too scared to turn around to validate that for myself. As I leave the store, I inhale a momentous breath, I pull out my phone straight away and call Sacha – she will not believe what has happened.

The phone rings a couple of times before Sacha picks up. Her voice is chipper, like I knew it would be.

"Aimee! What's up? How was your day? Are you up to anything fun?"

I can hear the excitement in her voice and it makes me grin. She's been asking about Sam (the guy at the park) non-stop since I mentioned him yesterday. I'm not sure how to even start this conversation, but I can't hold back anymore. "Sacha, you're not going to believe this," I say, my voice almost bubbling over with excitement. "I met him. I finally met him! Sam. The guy from the park."

There's a pause on the other end, and then Sacha's voice jumps up in pitch, her excitement mirroring mine. "Wait, wait, WAIT. You met him? Like, you actually talked to him? How did it happen??"

I can practically hear her leaning forward, hanging on to every word.

"Yeah, we... we ran into each other at this antique shop," I say, still in awe of how everything unfolded. "I mean, I wasn't expecting it at all. But there he was. Just standing there. In the same antique shop I was exploring. It was crazy, Sacha."

Sacha lets out a loud gasp. "No way! That's literally insane! So, what happened? What did you say?"

I can't help but laugh, because the excitement is contagious. "Well, I walked over and he looked up, and he recognised me right away. He smiled, and we started talking. He was so... I don't know, easy to talk to? It was like we'd known each other for longer than just meeting in the park. It was kind of surreal. And then, Sacha – get this – he actually asked me if I wanted to grab a drink with him!"

"Shut. Up!" Sacha exclaims, her voice practically bouncing through the phone. "No way. He asked you out? And you said yes, right?"

I can't stop smiling, even though I'm on the phone. "I said yes! I can't believe it, but I actually said yes. We're going for drinks tomorrow night. I gave him my number, and now we have plans. It's happening, Sacha! I'm going for drinks with Sam!"

"Oh my god, Aimee, I'm so excited for you! This is what happens in those corny movies. I can't believe you actually went for it. I thought you were going to chicken out or something!"

I laugh again, feeling the warmth of her support. "I almost did! But I don't know, there was something about him. The way he was listening, the way he looked at me – everything just felt... natural. Like it was meant to happen, you know? I never expected to actually run into him again, and definitely not in an antique shop of all places!"

Sacha's laugh rings out, and I can picture her grinning from ear to ear. "Of course it was an antique shop! Where else would a romantic encounter happen but somewhere full of history and old things? That's so you, Aimee. But seriously, I can't believe you went to where he works! That's such a bold move. I'm proud of you."

I roll my eyes, still feeling a little embarrassed but mostly excited. "Yeah, well, I didn't exactly mean to go to where he works, but once I walked in and I was browsing, I saw him. I guess it worked out," I add, a little sheepish but still thrilled by how things turned out. "I can't believe I actually went to his workplace, though. What if he thought I was weird or something?"

"No way! That's actually super cute. You didn't know where he worked though! This has kismet written all over it! OMG I can't wait to tell the girls!" She pauses for a second, then teases, "Just don't go all stalker mode on him, okay? One visit is enough for now!"

I chuckle, her teasing making me feel lighter. "Yeah, no more stalking, I promise. I just... I don't know, I had a feeling. And now here we are. I'm going for drinks with him tomorrow night!" There's a beat of silence before Sacha speaks again, her voice softening with excitement. "Aimee, this is huge. You've been talking about this guy for what feels like forever. And now you're actually going out with him? I can't believe it. I'm so happy for you."

"Me too," I admit, my voice quieter now. "It feels surreal. I never thought anything would come of it when I saw him at the park as we only looked at each other, and the next day I walk right into his workplace, but here we are. It's crazy."

Sacha sighs dreamily on the other end. "Well, you deserve it. Seriously, Aimee. You've been so open to new experiences lately, and it's about time someone like Sam stepped into your life. I just have one question – how is he? Like, in person?"

I smile at the thought of him, my heart doing a little flip. "He's... amazing, Sacha. He's charming, but not in that over-the-top way. He's genuine, you know? He listens, really listens. And I don't know, I feel like I could talk to him for hours. It's just easy with him."

Sacha's voice takes on a dreamy quality as she coos, "Aimee, you are so smitten. I can hear it in your voice! I am dying to hear how the drinks go tomorrow. This is the start of something epic, I just know it."

I grin, feeling my cheeks warm a little. "Yeah, I think it could be. I'm just... so excited, Sacha. I can't believe it's actually happening. It feels like a dream."

"Well, enjoy it, girl. You deserve this. And I want all the details tomorrow. Every little thing, got it?"

"Got it," I laugh. "I'll let you know how it goes, promise. Thanks for being so excited for me."

"Are you kidding? I'm living vicariously through you right now. Go get your man, Aimee! And have fun!"

"Will do; however, he isn't my man, we have just met. Talk to you soon!"

We hang up, and I just sit there for a moment, letting everything sink in. I'm actually going for drinks with Sam. The guy I've been thinking about since that day in the park. I can't believe it. As I disconnect the call, I decide to walk for the bus back into the city. I don't have to wait long until the rundown bus comes chugging along the road, still not being able to comprehend what has just happened, my palms are sweaty and I can't help but think of the coincidence, the chances of myself finding that poster on the Main Street, the chances of seeing Sam there, this feels strange, very unusual; however, welcoming at the same time. Apart from feeling like I'm walking on air and that nothing can stop me, right on cue I feel the thoughts from my anxiety creeping in: *Maybe this will be another Sebastian?, maybe this will be another relationship you fail through, I don't know why you are bothering.* These voices have been in my mind for so long, I have become accustomed to them, that's the unfortunate thing, life is hard enough and then your mind decides to make these voices in your head scream louder the harder you try and numb them or push them out.

Sam

After Aimee leaves the store, I need to go out back and compose myself, I feel like I have won an award – she not only found me, she literally walked into my place of work, as if being presented to her by the gods themselves. I can't fathom the coincidence of the events of today, can't reckon it in my mind. I decide on my lunch break to call Steven, I pull out my phone, my hands still shaking in anticipation, I select Steven from my contacts, the dialling tone commences.

Steven answers in his normal cheerful self. "Hey, what's up, Sam? Thought you were on lunch break."

The news is too much to hold in, it's like a caged animal banging on my ribcage "Oh man, you're not gonna believe this! I just saw her again. The woman from the park the other day!"

Steven was in the middle of doing something, I hear something smash on his side of the phone. "Wait – hold on. You mean the one you were practically daydreaming about? You saw her again? Where?" He asked inquisitively.

I can't believe my luck. "Yes! She came into the antique shop." I chuckle. "Can you believe it? I've been telling you, I had a feeling she was close by!"

Steven's voice rises an octave. "No way! You're serious? So, what happened? Did you talk to her?"

I reply to him sounding like a schoolboy. "Absolutely! I couldn't just let her slip by again. I asked her about the old mirror she was eyeing, and we got to chatting. And guess what – her name's Aimee. Aimee! And get this, she just moved to Boston from New York."

Steven starts to laugh and asks more questions about the woman I saw for just a few moments who has not been off my mind since. "Aimee, huh? That's a nice name. Boston, you say? Sounds like she's making a fresh start. What else did you find out?"

"Oh, I learned all sorts of things. She's actually got a pretty cool job – she's starting a new job as a bridal shop manager in the next couple of days, which makes sense. She loves art, old furniture, and the whole vintage vibe. That's why she was so interested in the shop."

I can hear the cogs in Steven's mind turning, he comes right out and asks the inevitable: "Oh, nice! That's actually pretty awesome. So, what's next? You're just going to leave it at that?"

I roll my eyes at the suggestion – does he honestly think I would not want to see her again, does he honestly think I would let her walk out of the store without speaking to her? "No way! I asked her out for a couple of drinks. We're meeting up tomorrow after work. I mean, she was so down-to-earth, and we hit it off immediately. It just felt like the right thing to do, you know?"

Steven pauses and sighs for a moment. "Woah, woah, woah, Sam… You're jumping in pretty fast, huh?"

I begin to think and decide that I'm not jumping the gun, how else was I going to be able to get to know her? "Nah, I mean, I didn't want to wait too long. It felt like the moment. Besides, I can't let this opportunity slip away," I retort.

He pauses. "Look, I get it. I really do. But don't go getting ahead of yourself, alright? It's just drinks, Sam. Keep it light. You don't want to put all this pressure on it. You're still just getting to know her."

I do try and make light of the situation and add a slightly lighter vibe to the conversation. "Come on, Steven! It's just a couple of drinks, not a wedding proposal. I'm not that crazy. But yeah, I guess I'm just excited. She's so cool and I felt like there was some real chemistry, y'know?"

Another sigh expels from Steven and I'm feeling more uncomfortable as the discussion goes on. He says, "I get it, I get it. I just don't want you to set yourself up for disappointment if things don't go the way you're imagining them. It's early days, man. Take it slow, alright?"

I begin to roll my eyes, why do I feel I am having a conversation with my father? "You're right. I should probably calm down a little bit. Just, when you meet someone who seems like they could be a good match, you get a little carried away." I add, he has to understand that this is a huge deal for me, for months my friends have been trying to get me on dating apps and set up blind dates, instead of giving in to their ideas, I decided if I was going to meet someone, it would be on my own accord. I know Steven is just looking out for me, I know that, we have been friends for years and he knows me as well as I know myself.

"Oh, trust me, I know. I've been there. But hey, if things go well, then awesome. Just don't get your hopes too high. You don't want to be crushed if things don't work out," he replies.

As I walk around the parking lot, my shoes making the gravel move and creating friction underneath my feet, I decide to wrap up the conversation. A couple of black cars pull into the lot. I think I need to finish my lunch break to help out in there. The general public being allowed in the store always works out well, people love to be curious. I say to Steven, "I promise I won't. Alright, I got to get back to the shop, but I'll catch up with you soon. Thanks for the advice!"

We say our goodbyes and he disconnects the phone and the beeping noise runs through my ears, letting me know that we have disconnected.

I hang up the phone with Steven, still feeling a rush from our conversation. I could barely concentrate on what he was saying because my mind kept going back to Aimee. Around twenty minutes ago, she had walked into the antique shop, and my heart skipped a beat. That had to be the universe giving me a sign, right? She was so much more than I expected. She was kind, intelligent, and had this warmth about her that made everything else fade into the background. I knew I shouldn't get ahead of myself, but I couldn't help it. She felt like someone worth getting to know.

The bell above the door jingles, pulling me out of my daydreams. A customer has entered, and I quickly put on my best "store assistant" face. It wasn't that I didn't enjoy talking to customers – it was just hard to focus when Aimee kept floating through my mind like a constant, lovely distraction. But I have a job to do, so I straighten up and approach the couple that have just walked in.

"Hi there! Can I help you with anything?" I greet them, flashing my usual friendly smile.

They look at me for a moment, glancing around the shop. The man, a little older, steps forward. "Actually, yes," he says. "We're looking for an old clock for our living room. Something that has character, you know?"

I nod, feeling a bit of relief at the change of subject. It is easier to talk about clocks than it is to talk about Aimee. I lead them over to the far wall where we have a collection of antique timepieces. "This one here is from the 1920s," I explain, pointing to a brass clock that is ornately designed. "It's got that timeless elegance. Some people really love the patina it's developed over the years."

The couple seem impressed, but their conversation quickly shifts to whether it would fit in their living room and match their furniture. I show them a few more options, but honestly, my mind is still elsewhere. I could see the time ticking away, and the thought of my date with Aimee the next day keeps creeping back in. What was I going to do? Where would we go? Was she the type to enjoy a quiet bar or something more lively?

I help the couple make their decision – nothing too extravagant, just a small but charming wall clock – and ring them up. I make small talk as I wrap their purchase, but all the while, I am trying to come up with some sort of plan for tomorrow night. I don't want to overthink it, but I can't help myself.

After they leave, I turn back to the counter and look out the shop window. The day had been moving at its usual pace, the store buzzing with the occasional customer. The more I thought about Aimee, the more I realise that I have no idea what to expect. I had asked her out, sure, but now what? What do you do on a first "date" with someone you feel so drawn to but don't actually know all that well? I didn't want to make her feel uncomfortable by suggesting something too intimate, but I also didn't want to come across as boring. I try to focus on the customers coming and going, but it isn't easy. Aimee had sparked something in me that I hadn't felt in a long time – this blend of excitement and nervousness. It felt fresh and new, and part of me just wanted to make sure everything went perfectly. The thought of planning something memorable for her gnawed at me.

By the time the last customer leaves, the clock is showing five o'clock, and the shop is closing up. I lock the door behind them, letting out a sigh of relief. The day has been long, but it feels like the universe is pushing me toward something bigger. I grab my things, put my jacket on, and head out into the cool evening air. It is time to go home.

When I get back to my apartment, I drop my bag on the couch and walk straight to the bathroom. A long, hot shower is just what I need to clear my head. The steam seems to wash away the stress of the day, and for a few moments, I could just let go of everything that was making me anxious. Aimee was constantly in my thoughts, but I knew I had to focus if I wanted tomorrow to go smoothly.

Stepping out of the shower, I wrap myself in a towel and stand in front of the mirror, staring at my reflection. I didn't know what I was doing. It wasn't like I had a ton of experience with this sort of thing. I had been on dates before, sure, but there was something about Aimee that felt different. I wanted to make it special, but I didn't know where to start. What would she like? I didn't even know what kind of places she enjoyed.

I dry off quickly and pull on some comfortable clothes, then sit down at my desk. I open up my laptop, thinking maybe I could get some inspiration from the internet. I scroll through a few local restaurants, bars, and other spots in the city, but nothing feels right. It is hard to gauge Aimee's style based on the brief conversation we've had at the shop. Would she like something cosy and intimate, or is she into something a little more adventurous?

After a while, I give up on the online research and decide to go with my gut. I could take her to one of those quaint little spots I've always loved – somewhere quiet, where we could actually talk and get to know each other better. That seemed like a safe bet. I didn't want to overwhelm her, but I also didn't want to make it feel like an awkward coffee shop hangout.

I stare at my phone, my thumb hovering over Aimee's number. I have the urge to text her and confirm the details. I can already feel my heart racing, just from thinking about it. Would she think I was too forward if I reached out before the date? Would she even want to hear from me, or had I already messed things up by asking too quickly? Finally, I take a deep breath and type out a quick message:

> **Sam:** "Hey, Aimee. Just wanted to check in and see if you're still up for drinks tomorrow. I'm really looking forward to it! 😊

I stare at the screen for a moment, feeling a rush of uncertainty. But then I hit send. I couldn't back out now, and if she was as interested as I was, she'd probably appreciate the little gesture.

I lean back in my chair, letting the tension drain out of me. There was no turning back now. I'd done all I could for the night. The rest is up to Aimee.

Aimee

The sun has started its descent onto the Boston skyline, she really does look beautiful. The city of Boston.

My Aunt Clara called shortly after I had spoken to Sacha. It was just the standard catch up small talk, nothing exciting or remotely interesting was mentioned. I'm relaxing on my sofa when my phone vibrates, I glance over and see it's from Sam; strange how after today, I can finally put a face to the name. I swipe up the phone and respond.

> **Aimee:** Hey Sam! I am 100% still up for drinks tomorrow! Where would you like to meet? ☺

> **Sam:** That's great! Do you know where Beacon Hill is? If you don't I can come and pick you up? ☺

> **Aimee:** Sorry Sam, I'm still pretty new to Boston so I don't? If you could collect me from the end of Brookline Avenue? ☺

I wait eagerly as I hope my previous text has not come across as bad mannered to Sam, I just wouldn't want to go on a wild goose chase in a city I'm not 100% comfortable travelling on my own. I see the three dots appearing in my messaging app . . .

> **Sam:** That's not a problem, I will call you tomorrow when I am 5 minutes away. I am really excited. BTW bring comfortable shoes as well. ☺

> **Aimee:** Oh wow! You have something different planned then? I will try my best to accommodate! I'm heading to bed soon, will message you tomorrow. Sweet dreams ☺

He seems like a gentle soul. My last day off tomorrow before my new job. I have called the hairdressers for my blowout, and I have my outfit planned to the smallest detail. I climb into bed with a warm, light feeling in my stomach, I feel excited for the first time in what feels like forever. I can't describe this feeling, I only hope my mind can let me enjoy this, I am somewhat nervous, my mental health has always been an obstacle in my relationships, I don't ask for the voices, they are there regardless. My pillow moulds itself to the shape of my head and I slowly lose the battle of keeping my eyelids open, they slowly close and before I know it, the night is over.

I tossed and turned a bit as sleep took over, my mind racing with thoughts of Sam. I hadn't expected our conversation in the antique shop to leave such an impression on me, but it has. There was something about him – his energy, the way he made me feel so comfortable, like we'd known each other for much longer than a few minutes. I found myself smiling in my sleep, dreaming of what tomorrow would bring. Drinks with Sam and finding out all of his quirks. I had never imagined a simple invitation for a drink could stir up such excitement, but I could hardly wait.

When I finally wake up, sunlight is spilling through my bedroom window. I groggily reach over to check the time on my phone. It is still early, but I know I am not going to be able to go back to sleep. My mind is already buzzing with thoughts of the evening ahead. Sam. The man I met in the shop. What did he think of me? Was he as excited about the drinks as I was? I smile to myself, almost giddy at the thought of seeing him again.

I throw the covers off and hop out of bed, still feeling the excitement bubbling up inside me. I take a deep breath, trying to calm myself down. It is just drinks, right? Nothing too serious. Yet, I can't help but feel like there is something more to this. Something worth exploring. I make my way into the kitchen, my stomach rumbling in anticipation of breakfast. I need to start the day right, feeling energised and ready for anything.

After a quick scan of the fridge, I settle on making a simple breakfast – avocado toast with a fried egg on top. Nothing fancy, but satisfying. As I sip my coffee, my mind drifts back to Sam again. The way he had asked me out, so casually yet with genuine interest.

I had felt the connection too, though I wasn't sure if it was the kind of thing you could build on so quickly. Still, something about him makes me feel like it could be worth exploring.

Finishing up my breakfast, I make a quick mental note of the things I still have to do before the evening. I was getting drinks with Sam, but I also have a few errands to run, starting with my hair. I need to look put together – not overdone, but still presentable. I grab my purse and head out the door, excitement practically bubbling over as I make my way to the hairdresser's.

When I arrive at the salon, the familiar smell of shampoo and styling products fill the air. It is a place that was recommended.

"Morning, Aimee! Ready for the blowout?" she asks, smiling brightly as she leads me to my chair.

"Yep, just a trim," I say, settling into the seat. "Nothing too dramatic today, but I want it to look nice. I'm meeting someone later."

"Oh?" She raises an eyebrow, her interest piqued. "Someone special?"

I smile, a bit of a blush creeping up on my cheeks. "Maybe. We'll see."

She doesn't press me for details, and I am thankful for that. The last thing I want is to get into the whole 'dating scene' conversation. I just want to focus on making myself feel good today. The stylist snips away, her hands moving expertly through my hair, and I find myself staring at my reflection in the mirror, imagining how I might look when I meet Sam later that night. Would he think I looked good? Would he notice if I'd done something different?

After a few minutes, she finishes trimming the ends and styles my hair in loose waves. I look at myself in the mirror and smile. Perfect. I hadn't wanted anything too flashy, just something easy and natural, but it still makes me feel a little more polished. I feel a little lighter, like I am ready for whatever the evening has in store.

I pay for my appointment, leave the salon, and head back home. As I walk into my apartment, I feel that familiar pre-date nervous energy creeping back in. The kind of fluttering feeling in your stomach that you can't quite shake, no matter how much you try to calm down. I need to get ready for the night, but I also have one more thing to do: sort out my outfit for tomorrow. I am starting a new job, and the last thing I want is to be scrambling to figure out what to wear last minute. The last time I had a date with anyone would have been with Sebastian, Those memories are etched in my mind like an unforgettable memory.

I rifle through my closet, scanning the rows of clothes that I'd accumulated over the years. I want to look professional for my first day, but I also don't want to feel stiff or uncomfortable. Finally, I decide on a black pencil skirt and a fitted blouse – something simple yet elegant. I want to feel confident, but not like I am trying too hard. I pair it with classic black heels and a subtle gold necklace. It feels like the right balance between polished and approachable. As I lay out the outfit on my bed, I can't help but feel a little proud of myself. A new job, a new city, a potential new connection with Sam. It feels like I am moving forward in ways I hadn't expected when I first arrived in Boston. I am stepping into this new chapter of my life, one I have been both nervous and excited about. I take a moment to breathe, running my fingers over the fabric of the blouse and letting the excitement of both the new job and the drinks tonight sink in. Tomorrow, I'll be starting something fresh and challenging. But tonight – tonight is for Sam. I wasn't going to overthink it. I was going to enjoy the evening, let myself relax, and see where it went.

After making sure everything is ready for tomorrow, I glance at the clock. It is still a few hours before my date with Sam, but the anticipation is building. I decide to take a few moments to unwind – maybe watch a show or listen to some music to calm my nerves before I have to think about what to wear for tonight. I grab a blanket, curl up on the couch, and flick through my streaming service. Even as I watch the TV show, my mind wanders back to Sam. I wonder what he is doing right now. Is he nervous too? Is he thinking about me the way I am thinking about him? It seems silly to feel this way so soon, but the connection we'd shared during our brief time together felt special. It wasn't something I experienced every day.

Eventually, I snap out of my thoughts and glance at the clock again. It is time to start getting ready. I stand up, grab the clothes I'd picked out earlier, and head to the bathroom. I want to make sure I am perfect without overdoing it, and I still have a few hours to go before meeting Sam.

As I run my fingers through my hair one last time, I think back to that moment in the shop when Sam asked me out. It had felt so effortless. I don't know what the night will bring, but I am ready for it. I am ready to see Sam again, to get to know him better, and maybe even – who knows – see if this spark between us could turn into something more.

As the time draws nearer, I decide there's no time like the present to start and make myself look human. I raid my wardrobe and choose a burgundy jumper with a black skirt with tights. It looks smart but it's not too much, not an outfit that is in your face. I really don't want him getting the wrong impression. The saving grace is that my hair is already done; since my hair is long and thick, this would have taken a good two-hour session to do by myself. The make-up look I have gone for is natural, I don't want him to be disheartened, he has already seen me in the park with no make-up on so there's no need to overdo that part. The butterflies in my stomach are fleeting, it's a bittersweet feeling. I haven't been excited about any event in the past six months compared to what I feel for tonight. *Don't get your hopes up, the voice echoes in my head,* unwanted and undeserved. I shove the words to the back of my head, trying to ignore them, they have no purpose to be in my mind.

I walk into the kitchen for some Dutch courage and throw back a shot of bourbon. I can feel the liquid cascading down my throat, it's bitter and it causes me to take a deep inhale. I gather my things for the evening, my keys, lipstick, my normal shoes as per Sam's instruction and my mobile phone with my cash. My handbag is black with speckles of gold glitter which glow in the sunset that peaks through my window. I rush to take my phone off charge and I see a text from Sam…

> **Sam:** Hey Aimee, I am outside.
> See you soon x

A smile takes over my fresh face as I run to the window like a child, I look out the window and see his car, *that's a really nice car, didn't realise working in antiques was so well paid,* I think in my mind. I stare out the window and wave at him, he waves back, I give him the universal "two minutes" sign with my fingers and turn around to run to the door, throwing my handbag over my shoulder. I can't believe I have been in the city a matter of days and the universe has presented him in my wake. As I run down the stairs, missing one step, then missing two I bust through the main doors of my apartment, not look graceful at all, we share a look together, he's laughing at me, I compose myself, straightening my outfit and fixing my hair as I walk to his car. I step inside.

"Hello, how have you been? Thank you for coming to get me."

He smiles. "It's not a problem, honestly. You look stunning by the way."

As the last words leave his lips, I feel my cheeks start to blush. I begin to display a cheeky grin, I start to feel myself shrinking into my seat. "You're too kind. How has your day been then? Anything exciting?" I ask him.

Our eyes meet; his eyes are the most suspenseful colour imaginable, dark and wonderous. We have pulled away from the apartment and are now heading to the Charles River Esplanade.

"It's been good, I have had a busy day, sold a few things and made more contacts which is great. I love my job, still can't believe it when you walked in yesterday," he says to me, his eyes looking to his right at me in the passenger seat.

"It's a gorgeous store where you work, so many interesting things, how did you get into that sort of business, if you don't mind me asking?"

He smirks before he replies, "My mom and dad have a real estate business, they wanted me to carry on the family business but I have always been interested in the different origins of items and the history behind them. It wasn't welcome news for them; however, over time they accepted it. They are actually coming to visit soon, be nice to see them. Where do you work again?" he asks me.

The more he talks, the more I think I have found a kindred spirit, he is so gentle, so wise and I'm happy he had the guts to pursue what he loves instead of just going with the easy path of what his parents wanted. I cough, and reply to his question. "I actually start my new job tomorrow, I'm the assistant manager of a Bridal store, totally different sector to what I have done previously but my best friend's aunty owns the store. I needed to leave New York, so it was just something for the time being, until I go back."

I see his eyebrow rise on one side. "So you're going back to New York then, you aren't staying here permanently?"

I realise now he's probably thinking what's the point in getting to know this woman, if in six months she's going to leave anyway. I try and save myself from rejection before I even get started. "The plan is to go back, but I'm not ruling anything out. If I enjoy it here there's nothing stopping me from making Boston my permanent residence. Time will be the decider, I think."

As we pull up to the cobbled streets of Boston's Charles River, it looks like something from a movie, beautiful flowers adorn the window sills, the bars are full of customers sitting outside, it's still chilly outside but the people of Boston are tough, they are wrapped up and having a great time. Conversations and laughter fill the atmosphere. We are walking side by side and I can see he keeps glancing over at me. It makes me feel something I haven't felt in a long time. We decide to grab some food before we go for a nice stroll along the river. The restaurant is full of other couples; as we take our seat we are staring at each other. The waitress wanders over, she hands us both the menu.

Sam then pipes up, "Can we order a bottle of red Merlot for the table please?" He looks at me. "Is that okay with you?"

I smile and nod. As she walks off we dive deep into conversation.

I ask, "So how long have you lived in Boston then?"

He leans back in his seat and tells me, "I have lived here for a few years now, a couple of my friends moved here with me, the small town where we come from we just wanted a change of scenery. I love it though, it's a beautiful place, people are nice and there's always something to do. Why did you leave New York?"

Here it is, do I tell him? I'm not sure, I don't want to be too heavy on a first date. I pluck up the courage and just decide to throw all my cards on the table. I take a long breath. "I decided to come here to just get away from the fast moving city life. I had some issues with an ex and it was just an indicator that I needed to move and try something new. We have been split for ages so it's nothing to worry about. My best friend suggested I just leave and see if I can get a break of a different city, try and find myself I guess..."

There's a pause and I am honestly petrified, I feel he's going to leave – who wouldn't? I just wanted to be honest. Looking back, I perhaps should have waited till like the fifth date or something to go into the domestics of why I have come here. I look at him and give him an awkward smile as my lips thin.

He's looking at me, but he begins to say, "Seems a lot, sometimes you do need to escape to be able to gather your thoughts. I'm not judging you though, I'm glad you are being honest with me." A smile takes over his face.

The waitress then brings the wine, *thank the lord!* He takes our two glasses and pours mine for me; we decide to look at the menu and it looks delicious.

The restaurant is warm and intimate, the kind of place where the candlelight flickers just right, making everything feel softer, more inviting. Sam has been the perfect gentleman all evening, holding doors open, pulling out my chair, and making sure my glass of Merlot was never empty. But I can feel the weight of my confession still lingering in the air between us – I finally told him why I left New York. He listened, his dark eyes filled with understanding, never interrupting, just letting me speak. It felt good to say it out loud. He reached across the table, his fingers brushing against mine for just a second before he pulled back, giving me space. "I get it," he said simply. And somehow, those three words meant everything. We had gone through almost two full bottles of Merlot by then, and my head felt light, but not in a way that made me unsteady – just warm, content. The restaurant hummed around us, filled with the quiet murmur of other diners, but in that moment, it felt like we were in our own little world.

As we step outside, the night air wraps around me, cool and refreshing.

"You okay?" Sam asks, his voice gentle.

I nod, slipping off my heels. "Hold on," I say, digging into my bag for the flats I packed. He chuckles but doesn't tease me about it. Instead, he waits patiently as I switch my shoes. It is a small thing, but it makes me smile. We start walking along the river, the path bathed in silver light from the full moon above. The water shimmers, reflecting the glow of street lamps in long, rippling streaks. The scent of flowers drifts on the breeze – sweet and delicate, mingling with the crisp night air. Everything feels calm, peaceful, like the city itself has taken a deep breath and exhaled.

Sam walks beside me, hands tucked into his pockets, his pace matching mine effortlessly. "So, do you miss it?" he asks after a while. "New York?"

I think about it for a moment, staring out at the water. "Sometimes," I admit. "But I don't regret leaving." I glance at him, catching the way he is watching me, his expression unreadable. I do remind him I have only been here a week.

"I think you were brave," he says finally. "Leaving something behind like that? Not everyone could do it."

His words surprise me, sending a warmth through my chest that has nothing to do with the wine. I had spent a few days wondering if I had made the right decision, but hearing him say that – it makes me feel lighter. We keep walking, the sound of our footsteps soft against the pavement. The world around us feels hushed, like it is giving us this moment, just the two of us. The scent of jasmine is stronger here, carried by the wind, and I breathe it in, letting it settle something deep inside me. Sam slows his pace, and I do the same, turning to face him. The moonlight highlights the sharp angles of his face, but his eyes are soft, searching.

"I'm glad you're here," he says quietly. It is such a simple statement, but it makes my heart stutter.

I smile, looking down at my shoes for a second before meeting his gaze again. "Me too." And in that moment, with the river beside us and the night stretching ahead, I knew I had made the right choice – not just about New York, but about being here, with him. He is such a kind soul, I would never normally go for those types; however, the evening has proved to be a huge success. Sam would be off work tomorrow as he needs to come for his car in the morning, since we have drunk two bottles of Merlot.

As we walk back to the main street, we head over to the taxi rank, our fingertips touching as our arms are by our sides; we keep giving each other small but meaningful glances. The whole evening I have had goosebumps and I can honestly say, I have loved this evening; it has been one of the best nights I have ever had; just being able to find out more about him, get to know the man behind the facade of the antique store. He is so endearing, soulful and special.

As we approach the stand, he says, "I hope you have had a lovely evening, Aimee, it's been lovely getting to know you. We will get you dropped off first – how does that sound?" He stares down at me.

"Yes, that's lovely, Sam, thank you. I really have had a lovely evening – I would like to do it again if you want–" but before I even finish the sentence, like a gravitational pull, we are interlocked between each other, his lips are touching mine and I feel like I am walking on air, he smells divine and I never want to come down from this high that he makes me feel. It's crazy, one night and I feel like I have known him my whole life; I need to slow down and not get ahead of myself. I never want to let go of him, I feel whole.

"You guys need a cab?" the cab driver shouts as he winds his window down, disrupting our moment. We both are pulled out of our trances and we exclaim a soft giggle once we both look at him.

"Sure, that would be great!" Sam exclaims. He moves his hands to the bottom of my back and guides me into the cab. As we are both on the back seat we sit in silence for the start of the journey. "When do you want to go out again? You can pick what we do next time, no pressure!" Sam exclaims.

I let out a cheeky giggle. "I will certainly try and keep it on par with this evening, Sam, it's been great".

As we are pulling up to my apartment, we turn to each other. It's now 11.25 and I am up early for work tomorrow; I am dreading the early morning alarm. As I look into those gentle eyes, the butterflies are still going hell for leather in my stomach. "Text me when you get home, Sam, thank you for tonight again. I will see you soon."

He smiles and kisses my forehead. "Enjoy your first day at work. I will message when I'm back home, I have loved tonight, thank you for letting me take you out."

I smile; and as I exit the cab, I turn back – there he is on my side of the cab looking at me through the window. I give a little wave with my shaking hands and turn on my heel, walk up the stairs to my apartment. As the cab pulls away my heart sinks: the evening is officially over.

Walking towards the elevator I send the girls a message to let them know how my evening has gone.

Aimee: OMG girls, just arrived home from my date with Sam, it was amazing! He is so lovely! I have a good feeling about him.

Sally: NO WAY! Don't get yourself carried away! Take this one slow Amz. I am so happy you had a good night though, when do you start your new job btw?

Sacha: YESSSSS GIRL! Was he a gentlemen I hope? Where did you go? What did you do? I hope whatever this is you are happy! Give me a call tomorrow after work....

Hope: I hope he is the prince charming you have been looking for! Keep us updated, when are you seeing him again?

Aimee: I will facetime you all tomorrow night after work, say 7ish. Will you all be ready?

As the girls respond with thumbs up emojis, the elevator takes me higher onto the different floors until I reach my floor. I drag my tired feet along the carpeted hallway. I step into my apartment, closing the door behind me with a quiet click. The space still feels unfamiliar, even though I have been here for a week now. The furniture was in place, the shelves half-filled with books, but it lacked something – maybe warmth, maybe memories? It still feels like a transition rather than a home. I slip off my flats by the door, stretching my toes against the cool wooden floor. The evening with Sam has been perfect, but now, alone in the quiet, I feel the contrast. I walk through the apartment, flicking on a few lamps to chase away the dimness. My outfit still smells faintly of jasmine and the night air. I smile to myself, remembering the way Sam had looked at me by the river. I shake my head, pushing the thoughts aside as I gather my things for a shower. Tomorrow is my first day at the bridal boutique, and I need to be well-rested, not lost in my head over a man I have only just started seeing. The bathroom fills with steam as I step into the hot water, letting it wash away the lingering traces of the evening. My body feels relaxed from the wine, my skin still warm from the cool night air outside. As I massage shampoo into my hair, I think about how different my life is now compared to just a week ago. No more crowded subways, no more rushing to beat city traffic, no more feeling like I am constantly running toward something without knowing what it was. Here, things feel slower, more intentional.

After my shower, I wrap myself in a plush towel and pad into the bedroom. My phone buzzes softly on the nightstand, and I reach for it, already knowing who it would be. But instead, I hesitated for a moment and decide to text first.

> **Me:** Thank you again for tonight Sam. I had such a wonderful time. x

A minute later, my phone vibrates.

Sam: I have just gotten home, Best of luck for tomorrow, I had an awesome time too. I will text you tomorrow, sweet dreams x

Simple, but enough to make my stomach do a little flip.

I set my phone down with a smile and made my way to the kitchen, craving something warm before bed. The apartment is quiet except for the faint hum of the fridge as I reach for the cocoa powder and milk. There is something comforting about the ritual of making hot chocolate – the gentle heat of the stove, the rich smell of chocolate melting, the soft sound of the spoon stirring. I curl my fingers around the mug and carry it back to bed, sinking into the soft pillows. Taking a sip, I let out a slow breath, feeling the warmth spread through me. The world outside feels distant, and for the first time in a long time, I don't feel restless. Instead, there is a sense of quiet contentment settling in my bones.

Lying back against the pillows, I let my mind wander. Tomorrow will be a fresh start, a new chapter. Working at the bridal store wasn't the dream career I had once imagined for myself, but maybe that's okay. Maybe dreams can change. Maybe this is exactly where I was meant to be. My phone buzzes again, but this time, I don't check it right away. Instead, I close my eyes for a moment, savouring the feeling of peace. I have spent so long chasing happiness, searching for something just out of reach. But tonight, with the memory of Sam's voice in my mind and the taste of chocolate still on my lips, I realise that happiness isn't always something to chase. Sometimes, it is something you allow yourself to feel. I finish the last sip of my drink and set the mug on the nightstand. Curling under the covers, I let out a soft sigh. The apartment still feels new, still a little empty – but it doesn't feel lonely. And that, I think, as sleep slowly pulls me under, is enough.

Sam

The cab ride home feels like a blur, my mind still lingering on the events of the night, on her. Aimee. I can still feel the warmth of her hand in mine, the soft press of her lips when I finally kissed her by the river. It hadn't been planned, not really. We had just been standing there, the moonlight making everything feel like perfection, and then she looked at me with those eyes – like she was waiting for something. So I kissed her. And damn, it felt right. I have never done anything so outlandish, but for her, I would. She has awakened something in me that has been dormant for what feels like centuries.

The cab pulls up outside my place, and I pay the driver without thinking, my body moving on autopilot while my mind stays back with her. The second I step inside, I let out a long breath, raking a hand through my hair. The apartment is dark except for the soft glow from the streetlights filtering through the window. It feels empty, but I am not in the mood to turn on the TV or find something to do. I just stand there for a moment, my fingers brushing over my lips like I could still feel her there. The guys will say I'm moving too fast. I can already hear it – Josh giving me that look, raising an eyebrow before shaking his head. "You just met her, man," he will say. And he wouldn't be wrong. But there was something about Aimee that made me want to let my guard down, to not think so damn much for once. I sit on the edge of my couch, pulling out my phone and staring at the screen. No new messages. I wonder if she is asleep already or if she is lying in bed thinking about me the way I am thinking about her. She's planning the next date – that had been my idea. It means the world she wants to see me again, and I hope she doesn't keep me waiting too long.

Before I could talk myself out of it, I open the group chat with the guys and start typing.

> **Sam:** Hey guys, Just got back. The date was… something else. Feels different.

Then I hit send and wait.

> **Josh:** That good, huh?

> **Steven:** Or is that bad?

> **Sam:** Good. Better than good, she's planning the next one…

Josh was the first to respond, then Steven; I roll my eyes, already knowing where this was going.

Josh sends a gif of someone slow-clapping, followed by,

> **Josh:** Our boy is falling fast boys!

Maybe I am. But for once, I don't want to overanalyse it.

Aimee starts her new job tomorrow, I remembered how she talked about it over dinner, a mix of excitement and nerves in her voice. She had left New York to start afresh, and now she was actually doing it. That took guts. I grab my phone again and type out a quick message. I stare at it for a second before pressing send. I have the day off, which means I can sleep in, my car is still at the restaurant, and I need to pick it up. I shoot a message to Josh, knowing he'll be up early.

> **Sam:** @Josh, Can you pick me up in the morning? Need to grab my car?

He replies almost instantly.

Josh: @Sam, You owe me coffee, be ready for 9.

Tossing my phone onto the nightstand, I peel off my jacket and head to the shower. The water is hot, almost too hot, but I let it run over my skin, hoping it would clear my head. It doesn't. All I could think about was the way she had looked tonight, the way she had laughed, the way her fingers had brushed against mine like she was testing the waters.

I dry off, climb into bed, and turn off the light, but sleep doesn't come easy. I roll onto my side, then onto my back, staring at the ceiling. My mind replays every moment of the night – the way she had switched into her flats before we walked by the river, the way the moon had caught in her hair, the way she had hesitated just a second before kissing me back, like she wanted to make sure it was real. I check my phone again, even though I knew there wouldn't be another message. Aimee is probably asleep by now, resting up for her first day. I should be sleeping too, but instead, I lie there, restless, my body exhausted but my mind is wide awake. I try to convince myself to stop thinking about her, to just let it be, but it is useless. I want to see her again. Soon. I want to know what she might plan for our next date, what she would look like when she saw me again. I close my eyes and let out a slow breath, forcing myself to relax. The room is silent except for the occasional hum of a car passing outside, and yet, it feels like something has shifted tonight.

Maybe the guys were right. Maybe I was falling too fast. But for once, I didn't care.

As I slowly enter sleep, I let the pillow and the mattress swallow my body as I doze off, it's different, tonight; I go to sleep with a smile on my face, which hasn't been my routine for at least five years. I'm embarking on a new journey, and I for one can't wait to see what unfolds.

Aimee

As the dawn draws in on a new day, I find myself tossing and turning, I can hear cars passing the apartment block and the shouts of the nighttime crusade on their way home from a night out. I glance at the window; the moonlight streaming through the linen curtains in my bedroom, the reflection bouncing from the mirror on my dresser. I keep wracking my brain, is it new job day nerves? Is it Sam? Could be a mix of the two. I rise from the bed and walk along the hallway, the flooring is cold on my feet, slight creaks fill my ears as I walk to the kitchen to get a glass of water. As I open the cupboard, I hear the rain hitting the windows, it's a relaxing noise. I hold the glass of water and listen to the rhythm of the rain, I bring the glass of water to my lips and my body sways with the rain, all of a sudden I feel tired again. I set the water on the side and close my eyes, listening to the rain, letting the noise take my mind away somewhere else, somewhere comforting; my mind needs an escape sometimes.

I am morphed out of my current state as I hear a speeding car pass the apartment building and it starts frantically beeping its horn. It's like I have had an out of body experience and I am now in the kitchen, it's pitch black, and I'm staring at my living room, no recollection of getting there. *Am I sleep walking?* I mutter under my breath to myself. Deciding that this is too much for me this time in the morning, I run to bed and startle myself in the process, I throw back my comforter and collapse in my bed and let my mind rest some more before the shrill of my alarm.

When my alarm finally goes off a few hours later, I groan, feeling like I have barely closed my eyes. Still, I force myself up, knowing I need to get moving as I want to make a good first impression. The shower was hot, the steam waking me up as I let the water run over my shoulders. As I stand there, I think about Sam – about his message last night wishing me luck. A small smile creeps onto my lips before I shake my head, refocusing on the day ahead. After wrapping myself in a towel, I plug in my blow dryer and run a brush through my damp hair, willing it into something presentable. First impressions matter, and I want to look professional. I had picked out a sleek navy-blue suit the night before I met Sam – simple, elegant, and perfect for my first day. Slipping into it, I give myself one last look in the mirror. *You've got this*, I tell myself.

I don't have time for a sit-down breakfast, so I grab something on the go. The city is already buzzing with life as I walk to the café on the corner, ordering a croissant and a coffee to take with me. The familiar scent of espresso fills the air, momentarily grounding me. This is different from my usual New York routine, but in some ways, it feels the same – rushing, moving, figuring things out as I go. When I step onto the kerb, I instinctively lift my hand to hail a cab – only to realise a second later that I am not in New York anymore. No endless streams of yellow taxis line the street, ready to whisk me away. Instead, a few cars roll past, indifferent to my outstretched arm. I sigh, feeling ridiculous, and pull out my phone to call for a ride. After a few minutes, I manage to flag down a cab the old-fashioned way, waving awkwardly until the driver pulls over.

The ride to the boutique is a mix of nerves and excitement. I watch the city pass by, taking in the smaller streets, the charming storefronts, the slower pace. This is my new life now. I am not rushing between skyscrapers or pushing through crowded subway stations. I am here, starting afresh, in a place that feels unfamiliar but full of possibility. When I pull up outside the bridal boutique, I take a deep breath before stepping out of the cab. The shop is beautiful, with large glass windows displaying elegant wedding gowns on mannequins. It looks exactly like the kind of place where someone's dream dress would be found. I adjust my blazer, smooth my hair, and push open the door.

Inside, the boutique smells of fresh flowers and vanilla, a soft, welcoming scent. The space is bright and airy, with rows of delicate gowns hanging neatly on display. I barely have time to take it all in before a warm voice calls out, "You must be Aimee!"

I turn to see a woman in her fifties, stylish and poised, walking toward me with a friendly smile. Fiona – Sacha's aunt. I had heard about her, but meeting her in person, I can tell right away she has that effortless elegance some people just naturally carry.

"It's so lovely to finally meet you," she says, shaking my hand. "Sacha has told me wonderful things. Are you ready for your first day?"

I smile, feeling some of my nerves fade. "Absolutely." And in that moment, I realise – I really am.

Fiona then takes me to her office, it's just as stylish as the front of the store, she has elegant taste, I can tell that already and I have only met her for five minutes. Her office is large, there's bridal catalogues, different swatch books of wedding dress fabrics, and articles plastered all over the wall of her achievements with her store. She invites me to sit down.

"So, how are you finding Boston so far?" she asks excitedly.

"I am really enjoying it, to be honest, it's much more slow paced than New York," I tell her.

"Sacha says you guys have been friends for such a long time, I trust her judgement on hiring you, I'm sure you will be an asset to our family here. Today my staff will show you around, show you the ropes and get you settled." She pulls an employee handbook from her top drawer and slides it to me at the other end of the desk. I take it and put it in my bag. She pours a new hot cup of coffee for us both and we sit in her office just getting acquainted and it is such a lovely way to start.

She then pours us both another hot cup of coffee from her coffee machine that's in her office, obviously. She goes on to tell me about the operating hours. "So, on Fridays we have a half day, we typically take appointments up until 11.30, then we can go and start our weekends early! I trust that it's okay for you?"

I nod ecstatically and I take this opportunity to plan my next date with Sam on Friday, if he's not busy. I stand up and ask her where the toilets are. She gestures me to the hallway and as I turn to look over my shoulder, she tells me, "just come back into my office when you are ready".

"No problem at all," I say back to her, scurrying to the toilets. As I push the door open I pull out my phone and write a message to Sam.

> **Me:** Hey Sam, I hope you are ok! I'm at work and they have told me I get half days on a Friday. Wanna meet up then? xx

I wait for a response, but one doesn't come. I wash my hands and head back to the office where Fiona is sitting behind her desk with a pile of papers to her left.

"Thank you so much for giving me the opportunity to do this." I smile.

She sits back in her chair and goes on: "We have these forms to fill out for you, social security and the normal other things that are required. I hope you are happy here, the role is for six months; however, everything going well we would be happy to make the role permanent, I am looking to expand the business so I won't be here very often which is why I need another pair of hands to help run the place."

I am nodding my head and I can hear what she is saying, my mind keeps drifting back to Sam, *he still hasn't replied.* The doubts are setting in, my anxiety rearing its ugly head when I should be focusing on my future, there it is: trying to pull me back. I hate this disorder, only I can move to a new location, have a lovely evening with someone and start an amazing new job and still find the time to dampen the happy thoughts and be constantly wondering about something bad happening, sucking the joy out of me like a lifeless corpse.

Walking onto the shop floor, I take a deep breath, forcing a smile as I approach the group of consultants chatting by the fitting rooms. My stomach tightens – not just from the nerves of starting the new job but from the gnawing worry that Sam still hasn't texted back. Two hours. It's not that long, right? But it feels like a lifetime. I shake the thought away as one of the women – tall, blonde, with a bright pink measuring tape around her neck – turns to greet me.

"Hey! You must be Aimee," she says, her voice warm but professional. "I'm Laura. Welcome to the madness!"

The others laugh, and I manage a small chuckle, though my mind is only half in the moment. I introduce myself, shaking hands with each of them – Sophie, Priya, and Ellie. They all seem friendly enough, but I can't shake the feeling of being the new girl, the outsider trying to fit in.

Laura takes the lead, giving me a quick rundown of how things work. "The fitting rooms get chaotic, especially mid mornings. Brides can bring up to three guests, but sometimes they turn up with an entire entourage." She rolls her eyes playfully, and the others nod in agreement. "Your job today is just to observe, get a feel for things."

I nod along, pretending to focus, but my mind keeps drifting to my phone, tucked away in my pocket. Maybe it's on silent. Maybe I missed the notification. The urge to check it is overwhelming, but I resist. I don't want to look rude on my first day. Still, the anxiety creeps up my spine, tightening my chest. Did I come on too strong? Was last night a mistake? Sophie starts showing me around, explaining where the dresses are stored and how appointments are scheduled. "Some brides know exactly what they want. Others… not so much. That's where we come in," she says with a wink.

I nod, trying to engage, but my mind is looping back to Sam. I replay our last conversation in my head, searching for something – anything – that might explain why he hasn't replied.

The minutes drag. I watch as Priya helps a bride into a fitted lace gown, her friends gasping in delight. The energy in the shop is lively, full of excitement and dreamy anticipation. It's a world I want to be part of, a fresh start. But my stomach twists with doubt. If

Sam isn't replying, is it because he's already losing interest? I finally allow myself a quick glance at my phone when no one is looking. Nothing. No message. I swallow hard, forcing myself to stay present in the moment, I'm witnessing moments a bride will never forget, the day she picks her wedding dress. My mind goes back into overdrive, I barely know him – we've only been on one date. But last night felt different, special. Was I wrong? Was I moving too fast?

Ellie nudges me playfully. "First day nerves?" she asks, mistaking my distracted expression for job anxiety.

I force a laugh. "Yeah, something like that."

She grins. "Don't worry, you'll get the hang of it. Just wait until you have your first 'Say Yes to the Dress' moment. It's addictive."

I nod, determined to push my worries aside. This is my job now, a new beginning. Whatever happens with Sam, I can't let it define my day. But as I help Laura straighten a row of gowns, my phone burns in my pocket like a tiny, silent reminder that I might be hoping for something that isn't meant to last.

Dinnertime has quickly descended on my day and I make my way to the breakroom; the girls kindly asked if I wanted anything as they were going out for lunch, I politely declined as I prepared something last night. As I open the door to the break room I check my phone instantly, like a schoolgirl awaiting a text from her high school crush. As I skim through the notifications, it's like a weight has been lifted from my shoulders, he has finally messaged me back...

> **Sam:** Good Afternoon, SO SORRY, Today has been pretty hectic, Josh came to pick me up this morning to pick the car up and I have had a few drinks with him, I hope the new job is going well, and yes 100% I will check my shifts for you! xx

The first thought in my head is, *it's 1.30 – how long has he been drinking for?* Instead of being happy and elevated he's not lost interest, I yet again find something to pick at. I now need to try and plan something for us to do in a city I know nothing about. I write a message to him in double time.

> **Me:** Oh yes! I totally forgot about that! How you feeling today? Let me know what shift you are on that day and let me know, enjoy your day xx

I can see the three dots appearing on my screen instantly.

> **Sam:** Yeah he picked me up at 9am, then we just hung out for a while and decided to go for brunch and catch up. I am looking forward to Friday! I will message you soon, enjoy the rest of your day! You got this! xxx

The relief hits me like a wave the moment I see Sam's name repeatedly light up my screen. I exhale, letting go of the breath I didn't even realise I was holding. Just like that, the anxiety I've been wrestling with all morning melts away. He still wants to see me. I'm not moving too fast. I tuck my phone back into my pocket, a small smile playing on my lips as I rejoin the shop floor.

The afternoon picks up pace quickly. A bride has just found her dream dress, and the whole shop bursts into cheers as she dabs at happy tears. Laura hands me a bell to ring – apparently, it's a tradition when someone says yes to the dress. I give it a shake since I am the newbie on the block, and the sound is met with a chorus of applause from the bridal party. For the first time today, I feel like I belong here.

Between appointments, I steal a few moments to think about Friday. I barely know this city, and the idea of planning a date here is daunting. Do I go fancy? Casual? What's too much? What's too little? I type and delete three different messages before finally settling on "No worries". I send it before I can overthink, then shove my phone away before I spiral into another cycle of second-guessing. Priya catches me grinning at my screen and smirks. "Someone's got good news."

I shrug, trying to play it cool. "Just making plans for Friday."

She raises an eyebrow but doesn't pry. Instead, she hands me a clipboard. "Come help me check in the new stock. It's more fun than it sounds, promise."

I follow her to the back, letting myself get caught up in the rhythm of work, enjoying the distraction.

By the time 4:30 rolls around, I feel lighter. I survived my first day, and now I have a date to look forward to. As I grab my bag and step outside, the crisp afternoon air feels refreshing. The city hums around me, full of life and possibility. This morning, I felt uncertain – about the job, about Sam, about everything. But now? Now, I feel empowered. As I walk home, I pull up Google Maps, searching for date ideas. There's a rooftop bar that looks nice, but is that too much for a second date? A cosy little wine bar? Or maybe something different – an arcade bar? I make a mental note to ask Sam what he's in the mood for. I like the idea of planning something fun, something that shows I put thought into it.

The streets are still unfamiliar, but they don't feel intimidating anymore. I take a different route home just to explore, weaving through back streets and side alleys, discovering cute cafés and bookstores along the way. Maybe I don't know this city well yet, but I will. This is my fresh start, and I can shape it however I want. By the time I get to my apartment, I feel like I've shed a layer of doubt. I'm doing this – building a new life, a new routine, and maybe even something new with Sam. I kick off my shoes, make a cup of tea, and settle onto the couch, scrolling through places to go. I want Friday to be special, not just for him, but for me too – I deserve this.

After my shower, I clam up on the sofa and throw a blanket over me and reach for my phone.

> **Me:** Hey Sam, I have been thinking... How about that roof top bar by the river? I have checked Google and it says the view is amazing :D I still don't know the best places yet!

I close my phone and I remember I am meant to Facetime the girls back in New York. An incoming call comes through and it's Sam; I'm scared to answer it as we haven't spoken on the phone yet to each other, but I quickly press accept.

I say awkwardly "Hello?", and Sam begins to speak slightly slurred. "Heyyy, Aimee."

I begin to laugh at his voice. "Hey, you. You okay? You sound... different." Hoping he doesn't take that the wrong way.

He replies, "Different? Nah, just had a couple of drinks with the boys. Thought I'd check in – see how your first day went."

I retort, "A couple? Right. My day was good! Kinda overwhelming, but the team is so nice. A bride said yes to a dress, so I got to ring the little celebratory bell, which was fun."

I wait for a response from him, I think we may be on a slight delay.

"Oh, fancy. Bet you looked cute doing it. But seriously, that's cool. You feeling good about it?"

I take a sharp breath and think about what I'm about to say. "Yeah, I think so. It's a lot to take in, but I didn't hate it, which is a good start. Are you sure you're okay?" I reply in a soft tone to him. He sounds so different on the phone to what he does when you speak to him in real life.

He chuckles. "I'm fine. Just wish it wasn't, like, forever until Friday."

I laugh as I feel the same, but I'm not going to say anything. "It's literally four days, Sam." I'm trying to play this cool even though I feel the same way.

He replies and it makes my cheeks flush. "That's three days too long."

I go quiet, I haven't heard anyone say anything like that to me in such a long time, the butterflies are fluttering in my stomach again.

"Wow, you must really miss me. I must have made a really good impression then, eh?" I say in a cheeky tone.

They say you can always tell when someone is smiling on the phone, and I can hear it in his voice as he replies "maybe". As he says that a cheshire cat smile appears on my face. "Well, Friday will be worth the wait. I have looked at that nice bar and I have booked us a table for seven just in case you're at work – it looks amazing."

He goes quiet. "Mm, yeah. Good drinks, good view. And good company, obviously."

"Obviously," I say instantly.

The background goes quiet and he sounds serious. "But seriously, you're happy there? With the job? I know you were nervous."

"I am. I mean, it's early days, but I think I could really like it. Feels like the fresh start I needed."

"Good. You deserve that."

He's so lovely. I say back in a voice that's lowered, "Thanks, Sam. So, how bad was your hangover this morning?"

He groans, "Oh my God, brutal. I don't know why I do this to myself. I needed to be up for 9.30 as Josh came for me and dropped me off to get the car, pretty sure if I got pulled over I would have been charged with DUI."

A loud laugh escapes me. "Sounds productive."

"Extremely. Then I ate the greasiest burger known to mankind and somehow survived, I had that when we went for brunch, I needed food!"

"Classic."

He asks me, "You ever get those hangovers where you just, like, fear life?"

I am smiling from ear to ear, he is so funny. I do have a feeling he is drunk; however, I blurt out, "One hundred percent. The kind where you wake up and immediately check your phone in case you texted something embarrassing."

He beings to mock me straight away and gasps, "Aimee... are you saying you've drunk-texted people before?"

I try and get myself out of the hole I am digging myself. "Never. I am a picture of grace and dignity at all times." Hoping that clears me from him thinking I do that often.

"Uh-huh. I believe that."

As he snickers. I decide to play him at his own game. "You better."

There's a slight pause after that and he yawns. "Ugh, I should probably sleep. But now I'm just thinking about Friday again."

"Me too, Sam."

He then takes a deep breath. "Alright, get some rest, superstar. Dream of wedding dresses or whatever it is you bridal consultants do."

"Will do. Night, Sam." As my voice is lowered a couple of octaves.

"Night, Aimee. Can't wait to see you."

There's those butterflies again. I check the clock on my phone and it's now 6.30, I have an hour to kill before the carnage of the girls comes through my apartment like a whirlwind, I feel like I should have questions and answers prepared.

To say I am tired is an understatement. I am mentally drained after my first day. So much new information to take in and to process; however, as the days go by I feel part of the fabric of the city, not so much as an outsider now. It's a process, but I feel content in how my path is being paved.

Today started with uncertainty, but it's ending with confidence. I've got a job I think I'll love, a date to look forward to, and a whole city waiting to be explored. And for the first time in a long time, I feel like I'm exactly where I'm meant to be.

Sam

I wake up with a groan, my head pounding like a jackhammer. The two bottles of Merlot from last night are waging war against my brain, and my mouth feels like I swallowed a handful of cotton balls. I crack one eye open, immediately regretting it as the morning light streams in through the half-open blinds. Bad idea. I roll over, trying to escape the brightness, but the movement only makes my stomach churn. With a deep sigh, I force myself to reach for my phone on the nightstand. The screen is way too bright, but I squint through the pain and see a notification.

> **Josh 09.00:** I'm outside. Get up.

I blink at the time. Nine o'clock, Way too early for human interaction, but Josh was already here to take me to pick up my car. I let my head fall back onto the pillow. Maybe if I ignore him, he'll go away.

> **Josh:** Don't make me
> come up there…

Another buzz vibrates through my night stand five minutes later.

I groan again, dragging myself upright. The room spins for a second before settling. This is my own fault. I had no business finishing off two bottles of wine, but the conversation with Aimee had been so easy, so effortless, that the drinks kept flowing. I smile to myself, remembering the way she'd laughed at my terrible impression of her New York accent.

I stumble out of bed, throw on the first clean clothes I can find, and run a hand through my mess of hair. I look like hell, but Josh will survive. As I step outside, he is already leaning against his car, arms crossed, looking unimpressed.

"Jesus, Sam," he says, eyeing me up and down. "You look like you got hit by a truck."

I smirk as I agree; I look like crap; however, the night was worth it, I retort. "Feel like it too," I mutter, sliding into the passenger seat.

He gets in the driver's seat and starts driving before glancing at me. "So? How was it?"

A long pause fills the car, I am in no mood to be made fun of. I rub my temples. "Loud. Expensive. Aimee looked amazing. And we drank way too much wine."

Josh smirks. "So, a success, then?"

I exhale, thinking about it. "Yeah. I think so."

He nods, drumming his fingers on the steering wheel. "So you think she had fun?"

"She texted me when she got home, said she had a great time."

Josh raised an eyebrow. "And?"

I genuinely feel like I'm being interviewed by a CIA agent. *Christ, what's with all the questions?* I mutter to myself, my patience is not to be mocked today, I am in no mood. I decide to be brave and throw the cat amongst the pigeons to make the journey more eventful "And... I think I really like her," I admit, which immediately feels dangerous to say out loud as soon as the last syllable has left my lips.

Josh shoots me a look. "Dude, you just met her. You're already acting like this?"

I sigh. "I know. I know. I just–" I pause, trying to find the right words. "She's different. It didn't feel forced or awkward. It felt... easy."

Josh shakes his head. "Man, you fall fast."

I don't argue, because he isn't wrong. But something about Aimee made me want to fall. She is so outgoing but yet, so vulnerable, so vibrant but yet so reserved; she is a true enigma.

By the time we get to the restaurant where I've left my car, my headache has eased slightly, though my stomach still feels unsettled. I climb out of Josh's car and give him a nod as I turn my head over my right shoulder. "Brunch?"

He grins. "Thought you'd never ask." He drives off and I already know where I am meeting him.

We meet at our usual spot, a small café with strong coffee and the best breakfast sandwiches in town. I sip my black coffee like it is a lifeline while Josh scrolls through his phone. "So," he says eventually, setting his phone down, "what makes her different?"

What is his problem? I don't get the sudden change in his demeanour. I hesitate, then shrug. "I don't know. She's smart, funny. She actually listens when I talk, you know? And she doesn't try too hard – she's just herself."

Josh studies me for a moment before shaking his head. "You've got it bad."

I laugh, but there is a nervous edge to it. "Maybe."

"Look, man," he says, leaning forward. "I get it. But don't rush into this. You barely know her."

I feel like I'm fifteen and having a conversation with my dad about a girl in school I have crush on, not in my thirties. "I'm not rushing, Josh," I argue. "I'm just... excited."

He raises an eyebrow. "Excited is fine. Just don't lose your shit over this girl before you even know if she's worth it."

I want to tell him he is wrong, that this wasn't just another passing thing. But a part of me wonders if he has a point.

Was I wrong to be feeling these feelings? Or is it just socially unacceptable to let myself be so vulnerable so early on? Should I feel bad? No. I can't help it, I'm being swept away in a riptide and I can't help it, It's swallowing me whole, I want to let whatever it is banging at my door succumb to me, let me sink it in. It's her, she makes me feel like no other, makes me feel like I contribute to something. *What's she doing to me? This needs to stop.*

We continue with our brunch boys date, and to my surprise the conversation gets somewhat lighter. Boy Brunch is supposed to be my escape from all that, but somehow, I can't shake the image of Aimee in my mind. I try to focus on Josh as he grins across from me, the usual mischief in his eyes, but all I can think about is how fast things are moving with her. Josh starts rambling about his latest obsession – some podcast he's been listening to about conspiracy theories – and for a moment, it works. I tune in, nodding along and pretending like I don't have this knot of anxiety sitting heavy in my chest.

"So, you're telling me the moon landing was faked? Seriously?" I ask, raising an eyebrow.

Josh chuckles, clearly enjoying the distraction. "Exactly." Josh leans in like he is about to drop some earth-shattering truth. "The whole thing was staged. It's all about the government hiding the real agenda – there's some deep state stuff going on with the moon." His grin is mischievous, and for a moment, I almost believe him. Almost. But then, just as quickly, my thoughts flicker back to Aimee.

I've seen her once this week, it feels like the feeling is shifting – like we are building something, or at least trying to. But am I moving too fast? Is it too much, too soon? I don't want to scare her off, but the more I think about her, the more I realise how much I am putting myself out there. What if she doesn't feel the same way? Josh is still talking, but his words feel distant. It is hard to focus on the conversation when all I can hear is the echo of my own doubts. I wasn't used to being this open with someone – at least not so quickly. Usually, I took things slow, measured. But with Aimee, I felt like I was diving headfirst, and I couldn't tell if I was sinking or swimming.

"Sam, are you even listening?" Josh's voice cuts through my spiralling thoughts, and I blink, realising I've been staring at my cocktail cup for a little too long. He is eyeing me with a raised eyebrow, his expression shifting from teasing to concerned. "Come on, what's going on in that brain of yours?"

I hesitate, then sigh. "It's just... Aimee, man." My voice is quiet, almost as if I don't want to admit how much I am thinking about her. "Things are moving fast, and I don't know if I'm rushing it or if I'm just being a little too... vulnerable."

Josh leans back in his seat, considering my words. "Well, first off, you're not alone in that," he says slowly. "I mean, look at me. I've been in this weird mess of a relationship for months, and half the time I can't figure out if we're even on the same page." His tone is light, but there is a real bitterness to it. "It's complicated."

I blink, a little taken aback by the sudden shift in his mood. "Wait, what's going on with you?" I ask, feeling the weight of his words sink in. I wasn't used to hearing Josh talk about relationships seriously – he was usually the one offering me advice, not the one needing it.

Josh shrugs, pushing his plate aside and running a hand through his hair. "It's just… things aren't as great as they seem, you know? My job is a mess, I'm not sure where I stand with the person I'm seeing, and everything feels like it's on the verge of falling apart. But hey, at least I've got French toast to distract me." He lets out a humourless laugh, looking down at his plate, his mood clearly darkening.

I don't know what to say at first. Josh always seems like the guy who has it together – like nothing ever gets to him – but this moment feels different. "Man, that sucks. You know I've got your back, right?" I say, offering him a supportive smile. It feels good, in some way, to turn the focus off me for a minute and be there for him. It also gives me the distance I need to calm down about Aimee for a second.

Josh nods, looking a little more relaxed, though still distant. "I know, man. I appreciate it." Then he pauses for a beat, as if considering something, before giving me a knowing look. "But you should stop second-guessing yourself with Aimee. If you like her, just go for it. Don't let your brain talk you out of it." His words are simple but heavy.

I meet his gaze, feeling a strange mix of relief and uncertainty. Maybe he is right. Maybe I am overcomplicating things. But then again, am I really ready to let go of my guard? It feels like a risk –

one I'm not sure I am ready to take, but maybe that's what I need. I don't know for sure, but as the conversation shifts back to Josh's latest life crisis, I can't help but wonder: was it worth it to make myself this vulnerable with Aimee? Or was I just setting myself up for heartbreak? I feel the whole conversation with Josh has been a double edged sword, the start of the conversation felt like I was in an interrogation, now after some thought I feel he's a lot more subdued, perhaps looking at his own life has made him understand not to question mine so much. I hear my phone vibrate in my back pocket and it's Aimee, bringing me back to my present. She started her new job and she's delivering good news; I get to see her sooner than I thought which is always a bonus. I glance at my phone looking bewildered,

Aimee starts messaging me about her day and as normal, the sight of her name on my screen gives me butterflies. How on earth is this going to play out, I wish I had a fast forward button, but then again do I? Her day at work is going as good as I thought, there's not a lot you can determine about a new job, it's so new and feels exciting; she will boss it, I have no doubt. As the day carries on, a few messages are passed back and forth with Aimee, my brunch idea with Josh is starting to get messy. The cocktails are flowing as quick as the time was passing by.

Brunch has turned into an all-day affair, and now, at 9:30 pm, Josh and I are still at it. The restaurant has long since emptied out its midday crowd, and the servers are giving us that look – the one that says we are slowly becoming those guys who never leave. My head feels light, the warmth of too many cocktails settling in my chest. I glance at my phone again – another message from Aimee. "Still out?"

Josh smirks as he catches me reading the screen. "She checking up on you?" he teases, sipping his old fashioned. He'd switched to whiskey a while ago, while I was still nursing my gin and tonic.

"Not checking up, just chatting," I mutter, typing back. "Yeah, still here. Feeling it now, though."

She replies instantly: "Lightweight." I chuckle.

"She's got you figured out," Josh says, clinking his glass against mine. "Another round?"

I hesitate, then shake my head. "I really shouldn't. Work's going to be hell as it is." But I was comfortable, the world was spinning in a slow, pleasant way, and the idea of standing up feels like a challenge I am not ready for. Conversation had turned lazy, the way it does when the drinks have settled in. We talked about old memories – trips we should've taken, nights out we barely remembered.

"You know, we always talk about going away for a weekend and never do it," Josh points out.

"One day," I say, stretching back in my chair. "Just not tomorrow. Tomorrow, I suffer." We both laugh at the notion.

Another buzz. Aimee again. "You be careful heading home, it's dark out." I exhale, rubbing my eyes. She isn't wrong. The tipsiness has settled into something heavier now, that familiar feeling where I knew if I didn't leave soon, I'd be stuck here until Josh convinced me tequila was a good idea. "Alright," I sigh, pushing my chair back. "I'm calling it."

Josh raises an eyebrow. "For real? You sure you don't want just one more?"

I shake my head, standing a little too quickly. The room sways for a moment before steadying. "Yeah, I'm sure. Before I start texting my boss and saying things I shouldn't."

He laughs. "Good call."

Stepping outside, the cold air hits me hard, making my head spin. I shiver and check my phone again.

"Made it out alive. Walking home now. Will call you soon."

Aimee replies almost immediately. "Bet you're wobbling."

She's not wrong. My steps aren't exactly steady, and the pavement feels weirdly uneven.

The walk home is slow, every streetlight feeling like a checkpoint. My body is heavy, my mind foggy, but I am still grinning, the lingering buzz making everything feel slightly unreal. When I finally reach my apartment, I fumble with my keys for longer than I should before stumbling inside. Collapsing onto my bed, I call Aimee without thinking. She picks up on the second ring.

"Told you you'd regret it," she says, amusement in her voice.

"I don't regret anything," I mumble, pressing my face into my pillow.

"Yet." She laughs.

We talk for a while after I was done with my night, she is such a breath of fresh air, compared to some the female species I have dealt with in the past. I feel my eyelids slowing down and descending to gravity, she says something that pulls me out of my trance. "Enjoy waking up tomorrow, idiot."

I groan, already feeling the hangover creeping in. "Pray for me."

She chuckles again, and we keep talking, my words getting slower, softer, until sleep pulls me under.

Aimee

I wake up to the soft glow of morning light filtering through my curtains. My phone alarm hums gently on my bedside table, vibrating against the wood. I stretch, feeling the warmth of my duvet against my skin, and let out a sigh before reaching for my phone. A quick glance at the time – 7:15 am. I should get up, but for a moment, I just lie there, my mind drifting to my plans for tomorrow night. Sam.

The thought of him makes my stomach do that little flutter again, the same one it always does when I think about our date. I smirk to myself, knowing he's probably still dead to the world, suffering through the aftermath of last night. I roll onto my side and tap out a message. "Morning, hungover mess. Survived the night?" Then I toss my phone onto the bed and drag myself up.

The shower is the only thing that wakes me up properly. Hot water rushes over my shoulders, loosening the stiffness in my muscles. I let it run over my face for a moment before reaching for my vanilla-scented body wash, the familiar scent wrapping around me like comforter. I linger longer than I should, but the heat is too nice to leave just yet. Eventually, I force myself to step out into the cool air, wrapping a towel around myself before my padding feet pull me back to my bedroom.

Getting ready is second nature now. A swipe of concealer under my eyes, a touch of mascara, a hint of blush to bring some colour into my face. My outfit for the boutique is simple but elegant – cream blouse, fitted black trousers, a delicate gold necklace that catches the sunlight when I move. I spritz on my favourite perfume, something light and floral, then glance at my phone. No reply from Sam yet. Typical.

The sun is already warm when I step outside. The air smells fresh, carrying the scent of blooming flowers and coffee from the café down the street. I slip my sunglasses on and start walking, letting the steady rhythm of my footsteps wake me up fully. The streets are already buzzing with life – dog walkers, early commuters, a couple jogging side by side. I pull my phone out and check for a response, smiling when I see his name flash on the screen.

> **Sam:** Barely alive.
> Everything hurts.

I laugh softly, shaking my head.

> **Me:** Told you so. Hope you're
> functional by tomorrow night

> **Sam:** Wouldn't miss it.

I tuck my phone away, my smile lingering as I weave through the morning crowd. The sun is glaring through the windows, it seems a shame to waste this beautiful weather; I decide to walk to the boutique this morning, clear my mind. It's one of my favourite parts of the day. The city feels different in the morning – cleaner, fresher, like anything is possible. When I step into the boutique, the scent of fresh flowers and expensive perfume greets me. The space is bright and airy, all soft whites and blush pinks, with rows of wedding dresses hanging neatly along the walls. Sophie, my work friend, is already behind the counter, adjusting the display of silk ribbons and lace-trimmed veils.

"Morning," she chirps, glancing up. "Looking extra glowy today."

I roll my eyes, but I can't help but grin. "Just well-rested," I lie, hanging my bag behind the counter. "And maybe a little excited for tomorrow."

She gasps, placing a hand on her heart. "The date! Oh my God, I almost forgot. You better give me every detail afterwards."

"Obviously," I say, laughing as I tie my name tag around my wrist like a bracelet. "But first, we survive today."

The first bride arrives not long after we open the doors for business. She's young, maybe mid-twenties, with her mom and two sisters in tow. She's already wide-eyed at the dresses, her fingers grazing the delicate lace. I guide her through our collection the best I can, trying to remember the names and the particular reasons they have the names, helping her pull a few options. She's nervous, giddy, and I can't help but love this part of my job – seeing that moment when someone finds "the" dress. By midday, the boutique is bustling. Sophie and I barely have a moment to breathe between appointments. We help brides slip into gowns, adjust veils, pin dresses in place, all while their loved ones gasp and whisper. It's a whirlwind, but I love the energy, makes me think if I would ever have this type of day and have my best friends there to share the moment, a part of my heart seems to shrink and my belly contract as I picture them in my mind, I miss them, miss the sound of their voices, their laughs and just having the option to go and see them after work. *I don't have that option now.*

In between appointments, I check my phone again. Sam's sent me a selfie – hair a mess, blanket pulled up to his chin, looking thoroughly miserable. "I blame you for this." I stifle a laugh and reply. "I told you to stop drinking. You didn't listen."

My phone buzzes again – Sam.

"Feeling human again. Still excited for tomorrow?"

I bite my lip, my heart doing that stupid little jump. "Obviously. Can't wait." And deep down, I really, truly can't.

The last bride trying on a stunning A-line gown lifts my mood. She steps onto the pedestal, her hands trembling slightly as she looks at herself in the mirror. Then, slowly, a smile spreads across her face. "This is it," she whispers. And just like that, the exhaustion from the day disappears.

The last bride of the day has just left, and the boutique is finally quiet. Sophie and I are stood in the middle of the shop, taking a moment to breathe. The soft scent of floral perfume and fabric still lingers in the air, and faint marks from shoes dot the plush white carpet where brides have stood on the pedestal, seeing themselves in their dream dresses. I stretch my arms above my head, letting out a tired sigh. "That was a long one," I mutter, glancing at the clock.

Sophie groans, tying her long blonde hair into a messy bun. "Tell me about it. I swear, if I have to untie one more corset today, I might lose my mind." She plops onto the velvet settee near the changing area, rubbing her feet. I laugh, already gathering stray hangers and adjusting a few dresses back into perfect position on the racks. "Well, we survived. And you know what that means?" I shoot her a grin.

"Drinks," she says, immediately perking up. "Lots of them."

We move through our closing routine, tidying the boutique back into its pristine state. Sophie vacuums while I wipe down the mirrors, making sure there aren't any fingerprints left from eager brides touching their reflections. We restock the veil display, fluff the sample gowns, and dim the overhead lights to a soft glow. It always feels satisfying to leave the store looking perfect, ready for a new day of appointments. Once everything is in order, we grab our bags from behind the counter and flip the sign on the door to Closed. The evening air is warm as we step outside, the last golden rays of sunlight stretching over the street. I lock up, double-checking the door before turning to Sophie. "So, where to? I'm still not used to the city so I'm not the best at directions yet."

"There's that little bar around the corner," she says, adjusting her purse over her shoulder.

"The one with the amazing cocktails?" I don't need convincing. "Sold," I say to her. This is the part where I must remember not to go overboard as I am still at work tomorrow; however; it's just a half day so that is a huge benefit.

The walk to the cocktail bar is short, and the moment we step inside, the atmosphere shifts from the soft elegance of the boutique to the low hum of conversation and clinking glasses. The place is cosy, with dim lighting and a long wooden bar lined with bottles of every kind of spirit imaginable. We find a high-top table near the window, and I sink into my seat with a sigh of relief.

Sophie waves a bartender over and immediately orders us both espresso martinis. "We need the energy," she reasons, winking at me. "Plus, they make the best ones here."

I don't argue. After a long day of running around, a little caffeine with my alcohol sounds like the perfect combination.

As we sip our drinks, the exhaustion of the day melts away. We laugh about the picky mother-of-the-bride who spent twenty minutes critiquing every dress, and gush over the bride who had found her gown in an instant. It feels good to unwind, to sit with a friend and let the day go. And for a little while, work doesn't matter – just the drinks, the conversation, and the comfortable buzz settling in.

As Sophie lies back in her chair, I can tell she's getting comfortable – I feel a round of questions coming. Sophie leans forward, resting her elbows on the table, her fingers wrapped around the stem of her glass. "Alright," she says, narrowing her eyes at me playfully. "Let's talk about Sam."

I roll my eyes, but I can't help the small smile that has crept onto my lips. "What about him?" I take a sip of my espresso martini, the smooth mix of coffee and vodka warming my chest.

"What do you know about him?" she says, pointing a perfectly manicured finger at me. "Who is this mystery man? How did you even meet him? Because one minute, you're focused on work, and the next, you're grinning at your phone like a lovesick teenager."

She's only known me for a matter of days, do I really give off that impression? I laugh, shaking my head. "It's not that dramatic. I was single in New York before I moved here, and I still am single."

"Uh, it is that dramatic," Sophie counters as she emphasises the 'that', lifting her glass. "Now spill. Where did you even meet this guy?"

I exhale, tucking a strand of hair behind my ear. "Okay, so – this is kind of random – but I first saw him in the park. I was just sitting on the bench, and he was on his morning jog. I didn't even talk to him that day, but I remember thinking he looked... I don't know. Familiar, somehow." I pause, swirling my drink. "And then, like a couple of days later, I walked into this Antique store just browsing for some ornaments for my new apartment, and there he was. Turns out, he works there."

Sophie's eyes widen. "Shut up. That's fate."

"Or just weird coincidence," I say, though deep down, I liked the idea of fate a little better. "But yeah, we got talking, and I don't know – there was just something about him. We went on a date last weekend." "Only one?" Sophie raises an eyebrow. "I feel like you've been talking about him for ages."

I shrug, smiling into my drink. "Yeah, just one so far. But he feels different, you know? Like, I don't have to try so hard. It's easy with him."

Sophie smirks. "Oh, you've got it bad, trust me, I know the signs and you have it bad."

I groan, covering my face with my hands. "I do not." Knowing secretly, I am starting to feel for who he is, do I even know who he is? We have only met a handful of times, not even that. Can you tell?

"You so do," she teases. "And I love it. When's the next date again?"

"Tomorrow," I admit, biting my lip. And deep down, I can't wait.

My phone is placed face down on the table and it vibrates all of a sudden, I smile when I see it's him.

> **Sam:** Good Evening Amz, how has you're day been?

It's now 6.30 and I'm starting to feel slightly hungry, no point in me going back to an empty, desolate apartment. I smirk and write back to him.

> **Me:** Hey! Today has been crazy, I am just out with Sophie at the moment having some drinks and food. Do you want me to call you on my way home? xxx

As I wait for him to message me back, Sophie and I check out the menu, so many delicious things; because it's tea time, I decide to go for a mozzarella, basil, parma ham pizza with a side of fries in my mind. I watch as Sophie studies the menu, her fingers tapping lightly against the edge of the page. She's always taken her time deciding, weighing up every option as if it were a life-changing decision. I, on the other hand, have already made up my mind. "I'm getting the Mozzarella and Basil Pizza," I announce, setting my menu down. "Easy choice."

Sophie glances up at me and smirks. "Pizza is such a go-to" She isn't wrong. There is just something about a simple, fresh pizza that always hits the spot.

I shrug, unapologetic. "At least I know what I like," I say, taking a sip of my drink.

After a few more minutes of deliberation, Sophie finally makes her choice. "I think I'll go for the lemon and herb chicken with roasted vegetables," she says, closing her menu decisively. "That sounds good, right?"

"Very sophisticated," I tease, raising my glass toward her. "To good food and good company."

She clinks her glass against mine, and we both take a sip, already feeling the warmth of the drinks settling in. As we wait for our meals, my phone buzzes on the table. I glance down to see Sam's name flashing on the screen. "I'll call you when you're on your way home." I smile at the message, feeling a small flutter in my chest.

Sophie notices. "Sam?" she asks knowingly, raising an eyebrow.

I nod, locking my phone and setting it aside. "He just said he'd call me later."

She grins. "Cute. You two seem to be doing well."

I can hear the genuine happiness in her voice, and it makes me smile. "Yeah, we are," I admit. "It's nice, it's very new, super new, but I am happy with where things are going, there's promise with him, we shall see."

After a pause, Sophie leans in slightly. "And what about the job? Are you enjoying it?" She looks at me with curiosity, her voice warm and encouraging.

I exhale, thinking about it for a moment. "It's been a big change, moving to a new city and starting afresh. But I like it. The job is challenging in a good way, and I'm starting to find my rhythm."

"I'm proud of you," Sophie says, her voice sincere. "I can only imagine how scary it was for you to move, but you're handling it so well."

I feel a rush of gratitude for her support. As our meals arrive, I realise just how much I have missed these moments – good food, good conversation, and the comfort of a friend who always knows exactly what to say. It reminds me I must catch up with the girls soon, I feel like I have somewhat neglected them. As I take my first bite of the pizza, the warm cheese stretches slightly before melting in my mouth. The basil adds a fresh, slightly peppery taste that balances the rich, tangy tomato sauce. The crust is crisp on the outside but soft and chewy in the middle – exactly how I like it. I let out a small sigh of satisfaction. "This is so good," I say, reaching for another slice.

Sophie nods in agreement as she cuts into her lemon and herb chicken. "Mine too," she says, taking a bite. "The seasoning is perfect. It's got that zesty lemon kick but with this really nice, garlicky depth." She stabs a roasted carrot with her fork and adds, "And these veggies are roasted just right – soft but still with a little bite." We eat for a few moments in comfortable silence, occasionally making small sounds of approval as we enjoy our food. The drinks continue to flow, and I can feel the warmth of the wine settling in. Sophie reaches for her glass and takes a slow sip before turning to me with a curious expression. "So, tell me," she says. "How are you adjusting to Boston?"

I lean back slightly, wiping my fingers on a napkin. "It's been an adjustment for sure," I admit. "The city is so different to New York. It's brimming full of people but it's quiet at the same time, but I kind of love that. There's always something happening – live music, new restaurants to try, festivals. It's never boring."

Sophie smiles. "That's the best part about Boston. The energy is infectious. Have you gotten into any of the local traditions yet?" she asks me, raising an eyebrow.

I laugh out loud. "Well, I had my first real lobster roll last weekend. That felt like a Boston rite of passage." The memory of the buttery, perfectly seasoned lobster still lingers in my mind. "Oh, and I finally tried a proper clam chowder."

Sophie's eyes widen in approval. "Now that's what I'm talking about. Did you eat it in a bread bowl?"

"Of course," I say, grinning. "It was incredible. The soup was thick and creamy, and the bread soaked up just the right amount. I could probably live off that stuff if I was being honest."

She nodded knowingly. "Wait until you experience Marathon Monday. The whole city comes alive – it's not just about the race. The atmosphere is like one giant celebration."

I feel a little rush of excitement at the thought. "I can't wait for that," I say, finishing off the last bite of my pizza. "Honestly, I love how much pride people have in this city. It already feels like home in a weird way."

Sophie smiles, raising her glass. "To Boston, new traditions, and good food."

I clink my glass against hers, feeling grateful for this moment, for this meal, and for a friendship that makes a new city feel a little less overwhelming. The night goes on and we have more conversations about family, hobbies and I learn a lot about Sophie – and she would say the same about me. It's been an evening filled with contentment; however I now feel like I must leave as time is waiting for no one. We both gather our coats and pay the bill. As we walk outside the cold Boston air hits the back of our eyes and the cocktails we were drinking start to take effect as my vision doubles. As we say our farewells, Sophie and I exchange warm embraces and I watch her turn back and head to the opposite side of the street from where I need to be, I take this opportunity to call Sam, and check in,

As I walk home, the cool night air is refreshing after the warmth of the restaurant. My stomach is full, and I still have the lingering taste of mozzarella and basil on my tongue. I pull out my phone and diall Sam's number, smiling as I listen to the ringing.

He picks up after a couple of seconds. "Hey, you," he says, his voice slightly groggy. "How was dinner?"

"Really good," I say, tucking my free hand into my coat pocket. "Had the best pizza. Sophie's meal looked great too, but I regret nothing." I hear him chuckle on the other end.

"You and pizza," he teases. "You're predictable."

"Excuse me," I say, feigning offence. "Pizza is a perfectly respectable choice." Then I smirk. "Anyway, how's your day been? Are you feeling any less like death?"

Sam groans dramatically. "Barely. Still paying for last night. I think I've spent half my day just lying on my couch, contemplating my life choices."

I laugh. "Serves you right. How many did you even have?"

"Too many," he admits. "But I swear, I'll be fully recovered for tomorrow."

"Oh yeah, our big date," I say, a little teasingly. "Looking forward to it?"

"Of course," he says, and I can hear the smile in his voice. "What have you got planned for the rest of your night?"

I glance up at the city lights ahead as I am walking home. "Honestly, just heading home and probably getting into bed early. Maybe I'll put on a movie."

"Solid plan," he says. "Well, get some rest. You'll need your energy for tomorrow."

I smile to myself. "I'll see you at 5.30. I will message you tomorrow." As we disconnect from hearing each other's voices, I see my apartment building becoming closer into my vision. I let out a sigh as my thoughts keep drifting back to the girls, I decide in my mind to call them after I have showered and sorted my outfit for tomorrow. Boston life is getting somewhat busier than I expected and I feel like a terrible friend to be honest, I'm sure the girls are fine; however, I just need to speak with them.

As I unlock my apartment door and step inside, I let out a long breath, finally allowing myself to relax. The night air has been refreshing, but now that I am home, all I want is a hot shower to wash away the day. I kick off my shoes by the door and toss my coat over the back of a chair, already mentally preparing for the warmth of the water against my skin. Walking through my apartment, I make my way straight to the bathroom, flipping on the light. The mirror is still slightly fogged from the shower I'd taken that morning, but I barely glance at it as I turn on the water. As steam starts to fill the small space, I peel off my clothes, feeling the slight ache in my shoulders from the long day.

Stepping under the hot stream, I close my eyes and sigh as the warmth spreads across my back. The tension in my muscles slowly begins to melt away, and I let myself just stand there for a moment, enjoying the sensation. The sound of the water is comforting, drowning out everything else as I let my thoughts drift. I reach for my shampoo, squeezing a generous amount into my palm before working it through my hair. The scent of coconut and vanilla fills the air, instantly soothing me. As I massage my scalp, I feel some of the stress from the past few days slip away. Starting a new job, balancing my social life – it is a lot. But in moments like this, I remind myself that I am handling it. After rinsing out the shampoo, I apply conditioner, letting it sit as I scrub the rest of my body. The warmth of the water, the smell of my soap, and the quiet solitude of my bathroom makes me feel more at ease than I have all day. By the time I step out, wrapping myself in a soft towel, I feel lighter.

With my hair wrapped in another towel, I pad my way into my bedroom and pull open my closet. Tomorrow's date with Sam is suddenly at the forefront of my mind, and I want to find the perfect outfit. Something casual but cute, comfortable but just the right amount of flirty. I sift through my clothes, pulling out a few options and laying them on the bed.

After some debating, I settle on a fitted black top with a square neckline and a pair of high-waisted jeans. It is simple but flattering, something I feel good in. I set the outfit aside, glancing around my room. It is a bit of a mess – clothes draped over chairs, a few empty glasses on my nightstand, and my makeup bag half-open on my dresser. I sigh. It's now Time to tidy up. I move quickly, putting clothes back in my closet, tossing laundry into the hamper, and wiping down surfaces. The act of cleaning is oddly therapeutic, giving me something productive to focus on. By the time I finish, my room looks much better, and I feel a small sense of accomplishment.

Feeling satisfied, I grab my phone and flop onto my bed, scrolling through my messages. I decide to call Sacha, Holly, and Hope – our little group chat has been quieter than usual today, and I missed hearing their voices. As soon as the call connects, Holly is the first to answer. "Aimee! We were just talking about you."

I smile. "Hopefully only good things."

"Obviously," Hope chimes in. "How was dinner?"

"Really nice," I say, leaning back against my pillows. "Good food, good conversation. And now I'm just getting ready for my date with Sam tomorrow."

"Ooooh," Holly teases. "Exciting! Do we get outfit details?"

I laugh. "Black top, jeans, keeping it simple."

"Classic Aimee," Hope says approvingly. "You'll look great."

As the conversation continues, I can't help but notice that Sacha is quieter than usual. Normally, she is the loudest of us, always jumping in with some dramatic comment or joke. But tonight, she is barely saying anything.

"Sacha, you okay?" I finally ask, frowning slightly.

There is a pause before she answers. "Yeah, just tired," she says, but her voice lacks its usual energy.

Holly and Hope must have noticed it too, because the mood shifts slightly. "You sure?" Holly asks gently. "You sound...off."

Sacha sighs. "I don't know. It's just been a long day. I'll be fine."

I exchange a glance with Hope through the screen, both of us sensing that there is more to it. But we don't push. Instead, we spend the next few minutes keeping things light, telling funny stories and reminiscing about old times.

By the time we hang up, I feel happy but also a little concerned. Sacha is usually the one lifting everyone else up – maybe it is time for us to return the favour. As I set my phone down, I make a mental note to check in on her tomorrow. For now, though, I need sleep. I have a big day ahead of me, and something tells me it is going to be an important one. I decide to slump over to my bedside table and take the remote, I am in the mood for a murder documentary. I slide under the bedsheets and take a deep sigh, I can't accept the fact that Sacha is happy – she seems off, something has happened that she's not telling me; none of the girls are. As the documentary starts to fill my ears with thoughts of dread and doubt, I snatch the TV remote from my bed and turn the TV off, sleep beckons me and I need it.

Sam

I wake up to the soft hum of the city outside my window. The early morning light seeps through the curtains, casting a warm glow over my room. I blink a few times, stretching my arms above my head before glancing at my phone. No new messages. Aimee hasn't texted yet, but that's okay – I remind myself not to overthink it. I seem to have a flashback from Josh and our bros' brunch date, him telling me I'm falling too quickly. I shake the thought from my head, letting other people's opinions affect me and influence my outlook on life is a trait that I am eager to change. One day at a time.

Sliding out of bed, I rub my eyes and head toward the bathroom. The cool tiles under my feet send a slight shiver up my spine, but the promise of a warm shower is enough to keep me moving. I turn on the water, letting the steam rise as I step in, the heat waking me up properly. As the water runs over me, my mind wanders to the evening ahead. It's my second date with Aimee. The first one had gone surprisingly well, filled with easy conversation and shared laughter. But second dates feel different – there's more expectation, more weight behind every moment. I feel both excitement and a tinge of nervousness building inside me. I try and force the thoughts to the back of my mind; I need to get through my day at work before I can let loose and enjoy my weekend. It's finally Friday, another week boxed off, another week of endless possibilities, I am very accepting of what's on its way.

Stepping out of the shower, I grab a towel and dry off quickly. The mirror is fogged up, and I swipe a hand across it to get a clearer look at my reflection. I run a hand through my damp hair, debating whether I should style it differently tonight. Maybe something a little more put-together than my usual look? I throw on a casual shirt and jeans, something simple for the morning, and head into the kitchen. My stomach growls, but I don't have time for a proper breakfast. Instead, I grab my car keys – I will pick up my coffee on the way to work; the last thought that crosses my busy mind this morning.

The air outside is changing. I can feel it immediately. The winter chill is fading, replaced by a mild warmth that hints at spring. It's subtle, but noticeable. I take a deep breath, inhaling the fresh morning air as I slide into my car. The drive to work is smooth, the streets not too busy yet. I pull up to my usual coffee shop, parking in my usual spot. It's funny how certain routines become second nature. Stepping inside, I'm greeted by the familiar scent of roasted coffee beans and the quiet chatter of early risers. Coffee shops in the city are such a buzz in the morning, filled with constant chatter and people gearing up to join the rat race.

I order my usual – a black coffee, no sugar. As I wait, I pull out my phone and check the time. Aimee should be finishing her morning shift soon. I wonder if she's thinking about tonight as much as I am. As I sip my coffee, I start mentally going through outfit choices. Should I go for something more formal or stick with a relaxed vibe? I don't want to seem like I'm trying too hard, but I also want to make a good impression.

Back in the car, I tap my fingers against the steering wheel as I think about where the evening might lead. Will it be another long conversation over dinner? Maybe we'll go for a walk afterward, like we did last time. My phone buzzes just as I pull into the parking lot of the antique store. I glance at the screen – it's a text from my mom.

> **Mom:** Hey Sam! We were thinking of coming to visit in two weeks. Let us know if that works for you!

I smile to myself. It's been a while since I last saw my family. Having them here will be nice, though I'll have to make sure my apartment is in decent shape before they arrive, not like the last time when I had the boys round the night before to watch the Red Sox playing – my mom walked through the apartment to find us all sleeping still. I had a constant lecture that full weekend after they had left, she was worried I had turned to a life of alcohol and god knows what else. I say out loud a quick reply, letting her know that sounds great. As I command the car to send the text, I wonder if I should mention Aimee to them yet. It's still early, but part of me wants to share the excitement. Can I bring her up? Will it lead to more questions? More than likely.

The drive to work is as humbling as always, plants are starting to bloom since spring is slowly awakening. The cloud making breathtaking formations, the birds are flying around in the atmosphere, it feels like its Earth's special time and time is moving as it should be.

Stepping into the antique store, I'm greeted by the familiar scent of aged wood and polished brass. The place has a certain charm, a quiet kind of history in every corner. I clock in, ready to start my shift, but my mind keeps drifting back to tonight. Aimee's only working a half-day, which means she'll have more time to get ready. I wonder if she's thinking about her outfit too, if she's feeling the same mix of excitement and nerves that I am.

I spend the morning arranging a new collection of vintage watches in the display case. As I work, I catch my reflection in the glass. I look calm, collected – but inside, my thoughts are racing. Lunchtime comes and goes, and I finally allow myself to check my phone again. Still no message from Aimee. I tell myself not to read too much into it – she's probably just busy.

A customer comes in, an older gentleman looking for a gift for his wife. I help him pick out a delicate silver locket, and he leaves with a grateful smile. Moments like this make me appreciate my job. The afternoon drags on, but eventually, my shift comes to an end. I lock up the store, step outside, and feel that same warm breeze from the morning. It's the kind of evening that feels full of possibility. Sliding into my car, I pull out my phone and, finally, a message from Aimee.

> **Amiee:** Looking forward to tonight! Hope work wasn't too boring.

A grin spreads across my face. I type out a quick response.

> **Sam:** Can't wait. I'll pick you up at seven.

As I drive home, my nerves start to settle. Tonight is going to be good – I can feel it.

Pulling out of the gravel car park, I take a deep exhale and as my hands turn the steering wheel, I feel the tendons in my arms starting to shake, the nerves are kicking in. Shaking this feeling is somewhat bittersweet, I haven't felt like this in such a long time; however, I feel I'm in a shouting match between my head and my heart, who do I trust? Who do I let prevail in the end?

As I travel through the city traffic on a Friday afternoon, I am reminded that the human race never stops. People in crowds scurrying different directions of the pavements, like ants almost. I smile as the sun begins to set on the horizon, it gets me thinking how good my life is now, I'm happy. Everything in my life at the moment seems to be going in the right direction; I love my job, even though my mom and dad were not happy about the choice, my friends and I are starting to rekindle our closeness after I fell adrift a couple of years back; it has taken time, but I suppose all the most meaningful things do.

As I take a different route to my apartment, I drive past the park where I go jogging, it's my own piece of heaven, where I get to put in my headphones and escape the real world for forty-five minutes, to truly drift into the background.

As I pull up in front of my apartment block, I take a deep breath. I turn off the engine and sit there for a moment, running a hand through my hair. I need to get ready, but I also want to savour this feeling – this anticipation buzzing under my skin. Finally, I grab my keys, step out of the car, and shut the door behind me with a satisfying click. The evening air is crisp, and I take a moment to stretch, rolling my shoulders before heading toward the stairs.

The stairwell smells like someone's been cooking something spicy, and my stomach growls, but I ignore it. I take the steps two at a time, my mind still racing ahead to tonight. What if she's as excited as I am? What if this is the night everything shifts, and we go from casual dating to something more? I shake my head, laughing at myself. No need to overthink it. Just enjoy the night.

When I unlock the door to my apartment, I immediately kick off my shoes and head straight for the bathroom. A hot shower is exactly what I need to clear my head and shake off the workday. As the warm water rushes over me, I close my eyes and take a deep breath. Aimee and I have had great chemistry on the occasions we have seen each other, but I want to make sure tonight is special. I let the steam loosen my muscles as I go over what I know about her favourite foods, the kind of music she likes, the little details that make her unique.

After my shower, I towel off quickly, checking my reflection in the mirror. My hair is still damp, curling slightly at the ends. I run my fingers through it, debating whether to style it or just leave it as it is. Casual but put-together – that's the vibe I'm going for. I don't want to look like I tried too hard, but I also don't want to look like I just threw something on.

I step into my bedroom and open my closet, scanning through my options. Aimee had mentioned she liked it when I wore dark colours, so I pull out a navy button-down and hold it up against me. Simple but nice. Paired with my best jeans and a good pair of shoes, it should be just right. I smirk at my own reflection, amused at how much effort I'm putting into this. But hey, when someone like Aimee is involved, it's worth it.

Once I have my outfit laid out, I check my phone for the time. Still a little early, but that's good. I don't want to rush through anything. I send Aimee a quick text – something light and teasing – just to let her know I'm thinking about her. Almost instantly, she replies with a winking emoji, and I grin. She's just as excited as I am.

I take one last deep breath, centring myself. The nerves are still there, but they're the good kind – the kind that means something important is about to happen. Tonight is going to be great. I can feel it. I finish getting dressed, making sure everything looks just right. A final spritz of cologne, a last glance in the mirror, and I'm ready.

As I grab my keys and head toward the door, I feel a rush of confidence. No matter what happens tonight, as I run through my apartment glancing that it is clean, as I can feel the hangover tomorrow already wearing its head from the wings. My apartment is in shipshape and I smile because the apartment is the only place where I can be myself; where I can escape the shackles of life and truly just dissociating from my body.

Aimee

The cool afternoon breeze brushes against my skin as I walk home from my half-day shift, the sun peeking through the soft clouds above. It's one of those days where everything feels light, where the weight of the world doesn't press down as hard. My steps are slow, savouring the time I have to myself. I close my eyes briefly, inhaling the fresh air, letting it fill my lungs before exhaling in a sigh of quiet contentment. Taking as much vitamin D from the sun as I physically can, letting the rays bounce off my face.

The familiar sight of my apartment complex comes into view, and a sense of comfort washes over me. Pushing open the door, I step inside, shutting the world out behind me. The air inside is still, untouched since I left this morning. I reach for the lighter on the entryway table and light my favourite candle, watching the soft glow flicker to life. The scent of vanilla and amber fills the room, instantly making everything feel warmer, softer.

With a deep breath, I make my way to the bathroom, shedding my work clothes as I go. The shower is warm, the steam curling around me as the water cascades down my back. It's a moment of peace, of cleansing, of letting go of the stress that clung to me throughout the morning. I close my eyes and let the warmth sink into my muscles before finally stepping out, wrapping myself in a plush towel.

As my feet slap the floorboards when I'm walking down the hallway, my damp feet press against the cool hardwood floor as I make my way to the kitchen. I reach for the radio, turning the dial until an upbeat song fills the room, vibrating through my chest. The music lifts my mood, makes me sway my hips as I open the fridge to grab a quick drink. It feels good to be home, to have this time to myself.

I move to the mirror, running my fingers through my long, damp strands. My hair has grown so much these past few years, falling in thick waves down my back. It's a reminder of time passing, of how things change even when we don't always notice. I reach for my blow dryer, letting the heat work its magic as I start to style it, making sure each strand falls just right. I have spent the past two years trying to let my hair grow out, I used to dye my hair repeatedly as a young adult and let's just say by age twenty-six, it was starting to show.

Next task in line is my makeup. I've been experimenting with contouring lately, though it's been a slow learning process. I pick up my brush, carefully blending the product into the hollows of my cheeks, trying to create that sculpted, effortless look. The process takes longer than I expect, as it always does, but I don't mind. This is time for me – to create, to enhance, to feel beautiful.

Once I'm satisfied, I step into my bedroom, my heart thrumming with quiet excitement. The red satin dress hangs on the back of my closet door, waiting for me. I reach for it, the fabric smooth and luxurious beneath my fingertips. It was expensive, but I deserved it. After everything I've been through these past few months, it was a treat from me to myself – the sleepless nights, the emotional battles, the way my body and mind have been tested – I owed myself this. Slipping it over my head, I let the fabric cascade down, moulding to my curves like it was made for me. I turn to the mirror, running my hands down the sides, admiring the way it hugs my figure. I smile. I feel good. I feel like myself again.

For a long time, I didn't think I would get here – to a place where I could look in the mirror and recognise the woman staring back at me. There were days I felt lost, as though the version of me I once knew had disappeared. But standing here, in this dress, in this moment, I see her again. She has been a miss, a missing piece. She's been hidden almost; I kept trying the past few years to find her, she was nowhere to be found, when I was close to finding her, she vanished again; except for now, now she's staying.

I step back, twirling slightly, watching the fabric move with me. The way the satin shimmers under the soft glow of the candlelight makes me feel like I'm wrapped in something magical. I close my eyes, breathing in the scent of vanilla and amber, grounding myself in this feeling of self-appreciation. The music still plays in the background, a steady rhythm that keeps my energy lifted. I hum along to the melody, adjusting the straps of my dress, making sure everything is perfect. Tonight isn't about anyone else – it's about me. About feeling good in my own skin, about celebrating the small victories.

I reach for my perfume, spritzing a bit onto my wrists and collarbone, the familiar floral scent wrapping around me. It's a scent I've always loved, one that makes me feel confident, powerful. As it settles, I take one last look in the mirror, letting the image of myself in this dress, in this moment, sink in. I take a photo and send it to the group chat the girls are in, I know it's their movie night tonight; I don't expect a reply so quickly. A quiet, satisfied smile spreads across my lips. After everything, I'm still here. Still standing. Still finding ways to love myself. And tonight, that's more than enough. I glide over to one of my boxes to find a handbag that would look perfect with this outfit and I stumble across my old diary – *why have I packed this?*

I sit down, my diary in one hand and my glass of wine in the other. The pages are old, they are delicate, five years can really do its damage. The pages are crinkled, the diary has been used over and over again, perhaps me in my past self, trying to rack my brain about the words on the paper, hoping to read the writing on the page and maybe, just maybe it may make more sense and move into my brain quicker. I scan the pages with intent, and begin to read the pages that fall beneath my eyes of the words of a lonely girl who had no one at the loneliest time of her life, pretty sad really. I feel like I'm transported back…

Dear diary...

I can't believe I am writing this, I have in the past 24 hours, lost my mom. Her long battle with her illness has finally taken the most important person in my life away from me.

I am sat in my old room, in this house I used to share with her, I am surrounded by photos, clothing and smells that remind me of her, my aunt Clara is in the living room shreiking at the loss of her sister. I have been crying into my pillow the past 2 hours, I am shaking, my heart feels like its beating 200 beats per second. I can't move, I can't sleep, I can't pull myself from my bed, from this space. How do I continue? Where do I go from here? how can i GET HER BACK

I slump back into my sofa, like an unforgiving force is pushing me ever so backwards, its leaning on my torso and not letting me come up for air, its suffocating, my lungs can't keep the air compacted anymore, I need to breathe; I need to decompress the heaviness for my body and my mind. It's like a constant reminder that wherever I go the memory will always be there to weigh me down like a stone.

I need to control these feelings, this happens every time something happy happens in my life, a force from out of nowhere decides to take hold, it grips me between its thin, bony fingers and clutches me to the very brink of living. I can't breathe, I can't see anything but darkness, my body feels limp and I can't move. I try and prise my eyes open and nothing seems to work. I feel like there is a poltergeist at work and I can't gravitate from the emotions pulling me down, *how I do I escape from this?* Why does this happen to me? What do I need to do to escape from this? I flick my wrists to try and make the entity from where ever it has come from to stop holding me down – I'm pinned down, I can't feel my body, my presence. Anything. Something to separate me from the world beyond and what's happening now, something to puncture the veil to wake me up and to get me out of this trance. *Please, let me go, whatever it is, let me go.* I hear myself whisper, my brain trying to decipher what's real and what isn't. My newly painted nails gripping the nearest surface as a support aid to get me through this phase.

Fifteen minutes goes by, I'm still in the same place, my mind dragging back to the time and more than well aware I am more than likely going to be late for my date with Sam. *Fuck.* Trying to focus, close my eyes, breathe, get this episode over and done with, why does this always happen when I'm happy and heading somewhere in my life? Why does it feel like there's always someone or something waiting in the shadows to pounce on me and to drag me to the darkness. I hear high pitched ringing in my ears, within minutes, it seems to subside. My eyes crack open and flicker at the light in the room, I'm shaking, all goosebumps, and I feel cold. As I try and find my feet, I gather my surroundings, check where I am, I know I am at my apartment; however, the past fifteen minutes I have no clue where I have been. It doesn't feel like I have been present in my body at all. Gathering my thoughts, I pour myself a glass of water; as quickly at the water is transported into the glass from under the faucet, the shakes begin and I struggle to hold the weight of the glass. Within moments, it falls. Wrestling with the ringing in my ears, I feel shards of glass in the crevasse of my wrists and hands, the scene of the crimson blood in the sink whips me back into the present. *Jesus Christ,* I scream, holding my bloodied hands in front of my face, shrieking.

My phone rings, I run to my bag on the sofa and whip it from there and I see it's Sam. *Shit.* My head turns and looks at the clock, I am thirty minutes late, as the tears fall I answer.

"Hey, Aimee. Where are you? I've been waiting for half an hour... Are you okay?" He sounds subdued.

I begin to pant and let out a sob. "Sam... I – I'm so sorry. I... I had a bad moment, I'm really not okay right now."

"What do you mean? Where are you? Do you need me to come get you?" He sounds panicked now.

"I – I can't. I don't want you to see me like this. I – my hands... I messed up, Sam. I messed up bad. It was an accident–" expecting him to hang up at any moment; he doesn't.

"Aimee... What happened? Did you hurt yourself?"

As my voice is shaking I piece the words together, knowing the night is now ruined. "Yeah... I – It got too much. My head wouldn't stop, and I – I didn't know what else to do. It just happened, and now it won't stop bleeding, and I–"

"Okay, okay, listen to me. It's going to be okay. Where are you right now?" he asks, worry and grief are well and truly present in his voice now.

"At home. In the kitchen. I wrapped them up, but it's bad, Sam. I don't know what to do."

"I'm coming over. Right now."

"No, please, I don't want you to see me like this. I ruined everything."

"You didn't ruin anything, Aimee. You're hurting. That's not ruining anything, that's just... needing help. Please, let me be there for you. What's your apartment number?"

I whisper quietly, "I don't deserve it..."

"You do. You always have done. I'll be there soon, okay? Just keep pressure on your hands. I promise, we will sort this."

As I slowly start to descend into total madness, streams of tears are now moving full force down my cheeks. I say back, "Okay." I sound defeated, like I have given up, everything going well the past few weeks, evaporated. The trauma coming back to me like a tidal wave, the loss and sheer devastation from losing my mom. I fall to the floor in my kitchen and lie in the foetal position; I just wish this ground would eat me up and swallow me whole.

Twenty minutes later and I hear a knock at the door; obviously he doesn't have a key so I need to muster the strength to pull myself off the floor. "I'm coming, hold on," I shout, my nails pull me along with my bandaged hands, as I manage to cling onto my kitchen chairs and use them to pull me up, I get to the door and I can hear Sam breathing outside the door – he must have ran up the stairs. As I open the door I take a deep breath and slowly walk, my hands shaking as I grip the doorknob. I can feel my heart pounding in my chest as I hear his footsteps outside. I wasn't ready, not by a long shot, b\ut I knew I couldn't keep him waiting any longer. The lock clicks, and the door opens just as Sam's face appears. His expression softens when he sees me, but then his eyes go straight to my hands, the blood-soaked bandages still visible through the fabric. Before I can even speak, he pushes the door open the rest of the way, his arms wrap around me, pulling me into him with a force that nearly knocks the air out of my lungs.

His hands cup my face gently, lifting my chin so he can look into my eyes. His stare is intense, full of worry, but it is also comforting in a way I didn't know I needed. It feels like he is trying to read me, trying to figure out if I am going to fall apart. And in that moment, I feel like I might. My breath catches in my throat, and I can feel my body trembling under his touch. His thumb traces the curve of my jaw, and I can't stop the tear that slips down my cheek.

Sam's gaze flicks to my hands, and I feel a sudden weight in the room as he gently pulls them from my sides. He holds them with such care, like he is afraid that even the smallest touch might break something inside of me. His brow furrows in concern, and I see the way his lips press into a thin line, like he is holding back everything he wants to say. But he doesn't say anything right away. He just holds my hands, as though the simple act of doing so is enough to communicate everything he needs to.

"Talk to me," he whispers, his voice barely above a breath, but it cuts through the silence like a sharp knife. His eyes lock onto mine, and I feel like he is waiting for me to fall apart, but not in a way that is threatening. He isn't trying to rush me, just offering me the space to speak or not. I close my eyes for a second, feeling the weight of everything pressing in on me, and then let out a shaky breath. Before I can say anything, Sam pulls me closer, his arms wrapping around me in the warmest embrace I could imagine. His lips press gently against my forehead, and I close my eyes, sinking into the feeling of safety that I hadn't realised I had needed so badly. His presence, so solid and reassuring, is like a blanket that wraps around me, keeping the chaos at bay. I lean into him, my head resting against his chest, and for a brief moment, I feel like I am not falling apart. I am not alone in it.

His voice is quiet as he pulls back slightly, his hands gently resting on my shoulders. "What happened, Aimee?" he asks, the question carrying more weight than just curiosity. It is laced with care, with concern, and I can hear the tightness in his voice that makes it clear he was afraid for me. His eyes never leave mine as he waits for me to answer, his brow furrowing ever so slightly. But still, I can't bring myself to tell him the whole truth.

"Just had an accident, that's all," I whisper, my voice so small that it barely seems to carry the weight of the situation. I can feel the way my words hang in the air, thick and fragile, and for a moment, I wish I could take them back. I want to be strong for him, to tell him that everything will be fine, but I knew I wasn't there yet.

Sam doesn't seem convinced, though. He doesn't say anything more, but I can feel his gaze on me as he steps inside, guiding me gently by the hand, pulling me with him. His touch is tender but firm, like he is grounding me, making sure I don't slip away into the darkness I'd been hiding in for the past hour. He leads me to the couch, sitting down first, then pulling me down beside him. His arms wrap around me again, this time holding me so close I can feel his heartbeat. It is like he is holding all the broken pieces of me together, willing me to stay whole.

The room feels heavy, filled with the weight of everything that has just happened. I can hear Sam's breath, steady and calming, as he just holds me. I close my eyes and let the silence wash over me, letting it settle before I have to say anything. I knew we needed to talk, to make sense of the night, but I wasn't ready for it yet. Not fully. Still, Sam waits. He wasn't pushing, just holding me, making sure I knew he wasn't going anywhere.

Eventually, I let out a deep breath and speak, my voice barely more than a whisper. "I don't know what happened, Sam. I just... I couldn't breathe, and it all just got to be too much. My head was so loud, and I didn't know how to make it stop. I–" My voice cracks as I choke on the words. "I hurt myself by accident... I couldn't think of any other way to get it to stop."

Sam's arms tighten around me as if he could shield me from everything. His touch is gentle, but I can feel the weight of his sorrow in the way he holds me. I can hear the soft hitch in his breath, and I know it is because of how much he cares. He doesn't speak right away, just lets my words sink in, before softly replying, "I'm so sorry, Aimee. You don't have to go through this alone. Not ever again."

I nod, the tears falling freely now as I let the floodgates open. I know the road ahead isn't going to be easy, but in this moment, with Sam's arms around me, it feels like maybe – just maybe – I can find a way through it. We spend half an hour wrapped in each other's arms, the tears just constantly stream down my face. If tonight proves anything it proves I haven't dealt with my trauma as successfully as I might have thought. I glance over at Sam and see he is all suited and booted, he is dressed in a full get up, it makes me want to cry more. "You look so lovely by the way, Sam."

He looks at me and his lips thin. "You do too, you look stunning, how about tonight we just chill here once we get you cleaned up?"

I release a deep breath as I am so devastated our date wasn't meant to be; however, it meant spending some alone time in each other's company, with just ourselves.

Sam

As I gently lead Aimee to the bathroom, her steps are hesitant, like she's unsure if she can keep her balance. She seems so fragile, and I can't help but feel protective over her. My hand on her back steadies her as I guide her through the doorway. The bathroom is dimly lit, the scent of lavender soap lingering in the air. It's the kind of calm, quiet space where she should feel safe to recover. I turn the knob and slowly push the door open, making sure it doesn't creak too loudly.

Once we're inside, I keep my arm around her waist, feeling her light, uneven breathing as she leans into me. Her legs seem a little weak, and I can sense the exhaustion in the way she's holding herself together. I lead her closer to the sink, placing her hands there gently. The coolness of the countertop seems to ground her for a moment, offering a sense of stability. I glance down at her hands and unwrap the towels she had used earlier, noticing that they're stained with a mixture of dark red and pale pink.

I turn the faucet clockwise, allowing the water to flow into the sink. As the water runs, it changes colour from clear to a faint shade of crimson. The sight of it almost stops my breath. I take a moment to examine her hands more closely, my fingers grazing the surface of her skin. Her scars are a map of past pain, but they're not as bad as I feared. The good news is that, with the right care, these wounds can be cleaned without much discomfort. Still, I can see the fatigue in her eyes, and I know this will take more than just a quick fix.

Her skin is tender, and I'm careful with each movement. I place a soft cloth in the water and gently start to clean her hands. I can feel the texture of the fabric against her skin, and as I work, I try to be mindful of every little touch. It's almost like I can feel her heart beating through my fingertips, and I can't help but catch my breath when I notice the way her eyes are watching me. There's something in her gaze, something that flickers like a quiet spark, a moment of connection. It's enough to make me pause for just a second.

Her eyes are bright despite the pain, and I can tell she's trying to hold it together. The water turns a darker shade as I continue cleaning, the stains on her hands slowly fading. I glance up at her face, her features soft and vulnerable. I can't help but feel an overwhelming urge to protect her, to make sure she's okay. Every movement feels deliberate, but at the same time, I don't want to rush this. As I rinse the cloth and continue cleaning, I notice the way she's still trembling slightly, like the whole ordeal has left her unsettled. It makes me ache inside, but I push it aside. For now, all that matters is getting her cleaned up and making sure she's comfortable. I take a moment to adjust the temperature of the water, careful to avoid any sharp changes that might hurt her. The last thing I want is for her to feel more discomfort. When I finally finish with her hands, I take a step back and look at her, gauging her reaction. She's quiet now, but her eyes tell me everything. They're tired but grateful, and there's a slight relief in the way she's holding herself, as if the pain is a little more bearable now. I give her a soft smile, trying to reassure her even though I'm not sure how much comfort my expression can offer. I can tell she needs more than just this moment of care; she needs time.

"Where's your first aid box?" I ask gently, my voice barely above a whisper. I don't want to push her too hard, but I know we need to make sure she's taken care of properly. Her eyes flicker away for a moment, and then she points toward the cabinet under the sink. She's still so composed, even in her fragile state. I can't help but admire her strength, even if she doesn't see it herself. I open the cabinet and pull out the first aid kit, setting it on the counter. As I begin to open it, I glance back at her to make sure she's okay. Her gaze is distant now, like she's lost in thought, and I wonder if she's replaying everything that happened. I take a deep breath, focusing on the task at hand. She doesn't need me to be distracted right now. She needs me to be here, fully present, to help her get through this. As I grab what I need from the first aid box, I pull out bandages and the antiseptic cream with some tape, as I glance over my shoulder, she is subdued, but I feel she's coming back down to earth now, her pupils don't seem as dilated. As I kneel down in front of Aimee, my hands steady as I reach for the antiseptic cream. The bathroom is quiet, save for the soft hum of the bathroom fan, and the steady sound of water dripping from the faucet. I know she's in pain, but I have to do this. She needs to be taken care of. I open the tube, and the cool cream squeezes out into my palm. My eyes glance up at her, seeking some sign that she's okay. She's looking down at her hands, but I can tell by the way her fingers curl slightly that she's still feeling the burn of the wounds.

I gently start applying the cream to her hands, taking my time to cover the bruises and cuts. As soon as it makes contact with her skin, she hisses sharply, her body stiffening. I feel the tension in her, the way her muscles lock up in response to the sting. My heart aches for her, but I push the feeling aside. She needs me to stay composed, to stay strong for her. I try to focus on my breathing, forcing my hands not to shake as I gently rub the cream in.

Her lips press together in a tight line, and I watch her face for any signs of pain. She flinches as I press down just a little harder, and I immediately feel the ache in my chest. It's so hard to see her in pain, especially when she's doing everything she can to stay strong. But I have to be brave. For her. I can't let her see how much this hurts me, too. She needs me to be calm, to make this easier for her, even when I feel like the world is crashing down around me not knowing what's going on in her mind.

After a moment, she stops flinching, but I can still feel the tension in her hands. I try to be as gentle as I can, massaging the cream into the cuts, trying to make sure it's absorbed properly. I glance up at her, meeting her eyes. There's a certain quiet understanding between us, something unspoken. She doesn't have to say it, but I can see the gratitude in her eyes. Even through the pain, I know she's thankful for my care, and that's all that matters. I finish applying the cream, my movements slow and deliberate, making sure I haven't missed any areas. When the worst is over, I sit back on my heels and take a deep breath. I've done what I can, but I know she still needs more. Aimee looks at me with a tired, half-smile, and I try to return the gesture, though it feels more like a nervous twitch. I stand up, offering her my hand. "Let's get you to your room," I say softly, trying to keep my voice steady despite the emotions that keep bubbling up inside of me. I want to do more for her, but for now, all I can do is help her to her bedroom.

Aimee nods, her movements slow and shaky as she stands with my help. I wrap my arm around her waist, supporting her as we walk out of the bathroom. The house is quiet, the only sound the soft shuffle of our feet on the floor. When we reach her bedroom,

I stop for a moment, letting her catch her breath. "Do you want to get something more comfortable on?" I ask, keeping my voice soft, respectful. I want to make sure she feels at ease, even if she's still hurting.

She glances up at me, her eyes a little glassy from the pain, but she nods again. "Yeah, that sounds good," she whispers.

I give her a reassuring smile before gently guiding her toward the bed. I help her sit down, my hand resting briefly on her shoulder to steady her. "I'll wait outside," I tell her, stepping back toward the door. I don't want to make her feel uncomfortable. She needs space, and I need to give it to her.

As I close the door behind me, I take a deep breath, letting the silence settle around me. The house feels oddly still now, and I find myself standing in the hallway, waiting for her. I can't help but feel like I should be doing something more, something that would make her feel better faster. But I know she needs time. She needs to recover, even if it's just for a few minutes. I lean against the wall, my hands in my pockets, trying to keep my thoughts from racing. Time passes slowly, and I catch myself glancing up at the door more often than I should. I hear the rustling of fabric inside, the soft sound of Aimee moving around. I hope she's doing okay in there, though I can't help but wonder if she's still hurting. My fingers tap lightly against my side as I try to keep myself calm. I want to be there for her, but I also want her to have the space she needs. When the door finally opens, I'm a little startled. Aimee stands in the doorway, now dressed in something more comfortable – loose, soft clothes that look like they belong to her. She looks a little more at ease now, though still fragile. She meets my gaze, her eyes soft, and I feel a rush of relief wash over me. She's okay. At least, she's doing better than she was. She gives me a small smile, and I can't help but return it, my chest easing just a little. "Feel better?" I ask gently, my voice carrying a quiet concern. It's hard to read her right now, but I'm hoping the calm in her expression means that the worst of the pain is behind her. She nods slowly, though I can tell it's not a full recovery. There's still some lingering discomfort, but for now, I'll take whatever small victories I can get. It's a start, and that's all I need to know.

I guide Aimee carefully toward the living room, supporting her as we walk. She's moving a little more steadily now, but I can still feel her weight against me, like she's holding herself together with every step. The couch looks inviting, a place where she can finally relax and let the tension slip from her muscles. As we reach it, I gently help her settle onto the soft cushions, making sure the blanket is wrapped snugly around her. I want her to feel warm, safe, like she can breathe easy for a while.

I give her a soft smile as I tuck the blanket around her, adjusting it just so, and then stand up to make her some soup. The kitchen is quiet, and the sound of the stove turning on is oddly calming. I grab a pot, my movements smooth, almost automatic, as I pour some broth into it. The warmth of the kitchen contrasts with the coolness of the bathroom, and I find myself focusing on the task in front of me – something to keep my mind occupied while I figure out what comes next. She's in good hands now, but I can't shake the feeling that there's more I should be doing. I turn the heat down low and let the soup simmer for a bit. As I clean the sink of the glass, wiping down the counter, I make sure to pick up any remnants of the mess from earlier. The floor is clean too, no signs of the chaos that had filled the kitchen just a little while ago. I'm careful, methodical. I don't want her to have to worry about anything. Not now. She's been through enough.

Once I've done all I can, I turn back toward the living room and find her sitting there, looking so small and fragile beneath the blanket. The way she's curled up, her face soft but tired, makes my heart ache. She's been through so much, and yet she's still here. I walk toward her, my hands slightly trembling, though I'm trying to keep it together. "You really done a number on yourself tonight," I say, my voice gentle but laced with concern. "I'll make you this soup, and I'm going to shoot, okay?" I'm trying to keep it light, trying to hide how worried I really am. But it's hard, and I know she can probably feel it in the way I'm speaking.

The kitchen is quiet now, but I feel it. Her gaze on me. I can feel it burning the back of my head, even before I turn. My movements slow, and when I finally look at her, I see something in her eyes – something fragile and uncertain. There's a kind of vulnerability in her that makes my chest tighten. I want to do more for her, but I don't know how. She's already been through so much, and I feel so helpless at times, just wanting to make it all go away.

"Please don't go," she whispers, and the words hit me like a wave. My heart skips a beat, and for a moment, I freeze. I can't even form words. It's not like I want to leave, but hearing her say it, seeing the pleading look in her eyes... it makes everything in me want to stay, to be right there beside her, to never let her go through anything alone again. I walk back over to her, my steps slower now, my heart in my throat. I sit down beside her, the weight of her gaze never leaving me. Without saying anything, I reach out and gently take her hand, the warmth of her skin grounding me, reminding me that she's still here, still with me. I stay there for a moment, just holding her hand, letting the silence settle around us.

"I don't know what I'm going to wear; however, Aimee; I'm not going anywhere," I finally say, my voice low, as steady as I can make it. I want her to believe me. I want her to know that I'm not going to leave her alone, not now, not when she needs someone. My fingers gently brush the back of her hand, and I feel the delicate tremble in her grip. It's like she's holding on to me, but also to the comfort that comes with knowing she's not alone.

The soup is simmering, but for now, it can wait. Aimee needs me here, and I need her to know that. I stay right where I am, my presence a quiet promise that she doesn't have to face this alone. She's been through enough already, and I won't let her go through anything else by herself. I sit with her, my heart beating just a little faster, but I know this is where I'm supposed to be. Right beside her.

"I might have something you can wear, if you want me to look?" She rushes out with a mouth full of soup.

I laugh, I can't help it. "I have just cleaned up two messes and you're making a third," I giggle to her.

She grabs my arm and lies her face on the side of my chest. This now feels like true safety, and it's addictive. She gives me the tray shakily with her injured hands, she throws herself off the sofa and goes in the hunt for the boxes lying dormant in the corner of the room, I can hear her whispering.

"You okay?" I ask her.

"Yeah, I just don't know why my best friend thought I needed these" as she pulls out two large t shirts. "I mean they will do, it's just so I'm in more comfortable clothing, this suit is starting to get on my last nerve" She smiles and walks over, her feet seem to land with more force on the floor as she walks over now, I think the food helped her.

As Aimee hands me the large T-shirt, I can't help but notice how much care went into the little things she's done for herself tonight. Her best friend must have packed this for her, and it's clear that someone took the time to consider what she'd need. The fabric is soft, slightly oversized, and I can already imagine how comfortable it will be on her. I take the shirt from her, feeling the weight of it in my hands, and then I look up at her. "I'm going to the bathroom to get changed," I say, trying to keep the mood light. I don't want to make a big deal out of it, but I need a moment to clear my head, to shift the focus off of everything that's happened tonight.

"Not a problem," she replies softly, her voice quieter than usual. "Thank you so much for not bailing on me. I know tonight's been pretty rough."

Her words catch me off guard. I can see the vulnerability in her eyes, the rawness that comes with the kind of trauma she's been through. And it's in that moment that I realise just how much I've wanted to stay by her side, even when things got complicated, even when I didn't know how to help.

"I do care about you, Aimee," I say, the words coming out without hesitation. It's true. I care about her more than I think I've let on, but I don't want to make things uncomfortable. I just want her to know that I'm here. I turn my back to her, feeling the weight of the moment hanging in the air. I walk toward the hallway, my steps slower than usual as I head for the bathroom. My heart beats a little faster than I expected. I need a minute to myself, to gather my thoughts and figure out how to move forward in a way that makes sense. Inside the bathroom, I shut the door behind me and set the T-shirt on the counter. I take a deep breath, looking at myself in the mirror for a moment. The quietness is a relief, but I can't shake the feeling of the evening lingering. There's a part of me that wants to get everything right, to make sure Aimee feels okay, even if I don't have all the answers. I change into the oversized T-shirt, the soft cotton material feeling like a small comfort in the midst of everything.

As I finish getting changed, an idea comes to me. Aimee needs something to take her mind off of the events of the night, and I need a way to relax, too. I pull my phone out and decide to order takeout for us. She hasn't had TV services set up yet, and I know she's probably feeling a little isolated without her usual distractions. We might not have much, but there's a pack of DVDs that came with her apartment. It's not the most ideal situation, but it'll work. When I return to the living room, I feel a little lighter, and I can tell she's ready for a break, too. The tension in the air has loosened just a bit. We settle in on the couch, each of us tucked under a blanket, the comfort of being in this space together more than enough for now. I press play on the DVD player, and the opening credits of a random movie fill the screen. As the night goes on, we find ourselves laughing, joking about the absurdity of the plot, and I realise how easy it is to be with her.

There are moments when our hands brush, our legs touch, and it feels like we're not just two people sharing a space, but two people connected in a way that makes everything feel natural. In those moments, we're not weighed down by what happened earlier. We're just... us. I glance at her more than I should, catching glimpses of her beauty in the soft glow of the TV. There's something about her that captivates me. Even in the midst of the trauma she's been through, she carries it with so much grace. It scares me how effortlessly she does it, how she wears her pain like it's just another part of her, a part that doesn't diminish her in any way. I've never met anyone like her before. Her strength, her vulnerability – it's like they're two sides of the same coin, and they make her shine brighter than I could ever have imagined. As she laughs at something I said, I can't help but feel a lump in my throat, the weight of my feelings catching me off guard.

As the night drags on, I find myself glancing over at the clock in her kitchen. The numbers on the digital face tell me it's almost midnight. Time really does have a way of slipping away when you're lost in the moments. Aimee has drifted off on the sofa beside me, her breathing even and soft, but there's a slight tension in her body that tells me she's still hanging on to the night, even if her eyes are closed. It's been a long day for both of us, and I can tell she's exhausted. I'm not sure how much longer I can keep my own eyes open, but I know I should let her rest. "You can go to sleep if you want, Aimee," I say softly, my voice a little more tired than I meant. "I'll lie on the couch."

I thought it was a simple offer, but the way she stares at me – her eyes wide, the expression on her face slightly shocked – immediately tells me I've said something wrong. I can't read her expression at first, but then the realisation hits me like a wave. It's not just about sleep. I can feel the tension in the air, a subtle shift that makes me second-guess my words.

"It's fine, Sam," she says, her voice surprisingly steady, though there's an undercurrent of something I can't quite place. "Just stay in my room with me. We aren't kids."

My mind stumbles for a moment, and I feel the heat rise to my face. It's been at least four years since I've slept in the same room as another woman, and the thought of it catches me off guard, makes me slightly uncomfortable. It's not that I don't want to be with her, it's just... I haven't shared a bed in so long. I've kept my distance from that kind of closeness, and now, with Aimee, everything feels different. I stare at her, unsure of what to say. "I don't mind," I say, trying to downplay the sudden awkwardness in my chest. "Sofas are comfy in their own way."

She glares at me, and I can tell she's tired. Her patience is running thin, and the last thing I want is for her to feel uncomfortable with my offer. She's been through too much tonight, and I don't want to make this harder for her than it needs to be. "Sam, please," she says, and there's a softness in her voice now, almost pleading.

The way she says it, so vulnerable, makes my heart ache a little. It's not an invitation; it's a request – one I know I can't refuse. I swallow hard, a mixture of relief and something else pooling in my chest. I know I need to be there for her, to be close to her. There's no reason to be distant, no reason to hold back, especially when she's asking for something so simple. I nod, and a small, almost imperceptible smile forms on my lips.

"Okay. I'll stay," I say, moving to stand up. My body feels heavy with fatigue, but there's something comforting about the idea of being there, in the same room with her. "Lead the way." I follow her down the hallway, my mind still a little hazy from the whirlwind of the evening, but the thought of lying down beside her feels right. There's a quiet peace in her request, something that tells me she's not just tired, she's seeking a kind of comfort that only another person can offer. I'm not sure what this means, what this connection between us is, but in this moment, it doesn't matter.

When we reach her room, she slips into the bed, pulling the covers back slightly to make space for me. It's an easy gesture, but it's one that carries a weight – an unspoken invitation. I hesitate for just a moment before slipping under the covers beside her. The warmth of her body, the softness of the sheets, and the simple fact that we're here together, gives me a sense of calm that I didn't know I needed. I settle in beside her, careful not to crowd her, but close enough to feel the quiet rhythm of her breathing. The room is dark except for the faint light from the hallway, but the darkness doesn't feel heavy. Instead, it feels like a cocoon – safe and secure. As I lie there, I can't help but notice how natural this feels, even if it's a little unfamiliar. The night has turned into something unexpectedly simple and comforting, and in this small space, it feels like we've found something real, something worth holding on to. Before I can say good night to her, I hear very small snores from her side and I decide that I myself need to call this a night. I pull her closer to me so I can protect her in her dreams as well as the reality. I kiss her on her forehead and whisper sweet dreams into her ears and I see a small smile fill her face and I can tell from that display of emotion she's content.

Aimee

I wake up slowly, the soft morning light filtering through the window, casting a warm glow on everything in the room. For a moment, I just lie there, letting the peace wash over me. It's strange, but for the first time in a long while, I feel at ease, like I'm not carrying the weight of the world on my shoulders. As I shift slightly, I realise that Sam's arms are wrapped around me, holding me close, and it's comforting. His presence feels like a safety net, something solid and real. My body reacts without thinking, instinctively, relaxing into his embrace. I can feel the steady rhythm of his breathing against my skin, the rise and fall of his chest, and I realise how much I've missed this – how much I've missed feeling cared for, feeling safe. It's all so simple, yet so foreign to me. For a moment, I just let myself enjoy it, letting my eyes close again and soaking in the feeling of his warmth. This is what peace feels like, and I wish I could just stay here forever.

As I slowly start to stir, my eyes flicker open and fall on my hands. The sunlight catches on them, and I immediately wince as I take in the damage. The cuts from last night are still raw, and the bruises are a dark purple, almost black in some places. The memory of the accident, of everything that happened in the kitchen, comes rushing back, and I can't help but let out a soft sigh. *This is going to be fun to explain to the girls on Monday*, I think to myself with a bitter chuckle. *Not.*

But as much as the injuries are there, visible reminders of the chaos I've been through, there's something about this moment that feels different. The pain doesn't feel as sharp now. Maybe it's because of Sam, the way he's holding me, the way I feel like I'm not alone in this. It's a strange mix of emotions, and I can't seem to untangle them. I turn my head, carefully, and look at Sam. His face is so relaxed, so peaceful in sleep. His cheekbones are high, his jaw strong, and there's a softness to his skin that I can't help but marvel at. His eyelashes are impossibly long, and for some reason, I can't stop looking at them. I've never noticed details like that before – never had the time or the space to appreciate them – but now, they seem so important, so real. Last night was a revelation. In a way, it was a turning point for me. Sam stayed. He didn't run away when things got tough, when they got messy. He didn't look at me with pity or disgust like some people would have. He stayed, and that means more to me than I could ever put into words.

I think about Sebastian for a moment – my ex, the one who used to give me so much crap and treat me horribly. The one who made me feel worthless for so many years. He used to tear me down, piece by piece, until I wasn't sure who I was anymore. So many things happened that I kept to myself, things I've never told a soul. The emotional scars are just as deep as the physical ones, but no one knew. No one ever knew the extent of it, because I hid it all so well.

But Sam – Sam is different. He's not like Sebastian. He's not like the others who have tried to control me or diminish me. He doesn't look at me with judgment. He doesn't make me feel small. In fact, he makes me feel like I matter. He sees me, the real me, and that scares the hell out of me because it's something I've never experienced before. But it also feels right, like it's supposed to be this way. The universe, for all its flaws and chaos, has brought me to this moment with Sam, and I don't want to mess it up. I don't want to let my past dictate how I move forward, especially not with someone who has already proven himself to be a guardian of my heart. I can't screw this up with Sam. He's too important.

I shift a little closer to him, my heart racing with a mix of nervousness and excitement. He's still asleep, but I can't stop myself from wanting to reach out, to show him how much I appreciate him being here, how much he means to me already. As I watch him, so unaware, I lean in just enough to press a soft kiss to the tip of his nose. Our faces are nearly touching, and I linger there for a moment, breathing in the warmth of the moment. It's a small gesture, but it feels huge to me. It's a promise, a sign of what could be, of what I want to have with him.

I pull back slightly, my heart fluttering, but I stay close. I don't want to let go of this feeling, of him, of everything that's just starting to bloom between us. I know it's fragile, and I know it won't be easy. But for now, in this quiet moment, I just want to hold on to it. I want to hold on to him.

As I shift my weight to get out of bed, I feel Sam's hands at my waist, pulling me back toward him. It's as if he knows I'm trying to leave, but he doesn't want to let me go just yet. I'm not sure what's going on between us – this strange, unspoken connection. My heart beats faster, unsure of whether it's the closeness, the intensity of the moment, or maybe both. Everything feels heightened. His touch sends a ripple through me, something warm and comforting, yet exciting, almost like we're both caught in a moment that neither of us can quite define.

We're locked in this gaze now, eyes meeting with a kind of intensity that makes the world outside of this space feel distant, like it doesn't matter. I can't look away, and neither can he. It's as if time slows down. I study his face, every little detail of it – his eyes, the curve of his lips, the way his brow furrows slightly in concentration, as if he's trying to figure out what I'm thinking. He reaches out to tuck a strand of my hair behind my ear, and that simple act feels like it holds so much meaning.

The quiet between us is full of unspoken words, feelings too complex for language to capture. We're just here, in this shared moment of intimacy, where everything else falls away. I can feel the warmth of his body close to mine, the steady rhythm of his breath matching my own. It's almost like we're both holding our breath, unsure of what will happen next but not wanting to break the spell that's enveloped us. A part of me wants to pull away, to regain control of the situation, but another part, the part that feels safe and connected to him, wants to stay exactly where I am.

As if reading my mind, Sam gently tightens his hold around me, pulling me even closer. The feeling is comforting, protective. The kind of embrace that makes you feel like everything is going to be okay, even when you don't have all the answers. I find myself laughing softly, a quiet giggle that escapes me without warning. I can't help it – there's something about this moment, about the way we're tangled up together, that makes everything feel lighter, easier. The way he's holding me, the way we fit together so naturally, makes me feel like I'm exactly where I'm supposed to be.

I reach up to touch his face, tracing the lines of his jaw, the stubble that's starting to grow in. My fingers graze his skin, and it sends a wave of warmth through me. We both pause, just taking each other in for a few moments longer. The room feels like it's shrinking around us, and yet, in his arms, I feel like I'm in the safest place I've ever been. The butterflies in my stomach stir again, this time with a stronger, more exhilarating intensity. It's as if my body is reminding me that something is changing, that something deeper is blooming between us.

I never want this moment to end. The laughter, the closeness, the feeling of being completely seen and held without fear of judgment – it's all so new, so overwhelming in the best way possible. I find myself melting into him more, letting go of the tension I didn't even realise I was holding. Sam's presence is all-consuming in the most gentle way, and as we continue to embrace, I realise that no matter where this strange, beautiful journey takes us, I never want him to leave. The butterflies are no longer just a fluttering in my stomach; they've taken flight, spreading out and filling me with something indescribable. Something that feels like home.

"Good morning, darling" he says to me as I'm in a state of euphoric closeness.

I try and find the words to match his affections but they don't come. I'm spellbound by this man, in such a short space of time, he has become such an important person in my life. "Did you sleep well?" I ask him as our fingers are intertwined.

His green and brown eyes are spectacles in themselves, he is gorgeous, his arms wrapping around my waist, pulling me back toward him. I giggle softly, playfully trying to wiggle free, but he holds me tighter, not letting me go so easily. We both laugh, tangled in the sheets, and I finally give in, resting my head against his chest.

"Come on, we should get up," I say with a smile, feeling the warmth of his embrace still lingering on my skin.

After a few more moments of teasing, we finally stagger out of bed. The morning is slow, filled with sleepy energy as we make our way down the hall, still wrapped in the comfortable haze of the night we just shared. Sam is the first to suggest making breakfast.

"I'm making us something," he says, a mischievous grin on his face. He's always had a knack for cooking, and honestly, I don't think I could turn down a single offer to let him do his thing in the kitchen.

I make my way to the island and settle in, watching him move around the kitchen with ease. It's funny – he's so comfortable here, even though it's not his kitchen. There's a fluidity in the way he moves, like he's done this a thousand times before. I lean back on the counter, resting my chin in my hand, watching the way he operates, completely absorbed in the task at hand. The warmth of the morning fades a little as my mind shifts, and suddenly the room feels a little heavier. I can't shake off the thoughts from last night. The way things got out of control, how unexpected everything felt.

Sam turns around and catches my eye, his expression softening when he sees the change in my mood. "Hey," he says gently.

I decide to voice my apology. "I can't thank you enough for last night. I don't want you to think bad of me with what happened... it was a genuine accident."

He blinks, taken aback by my words, and my stomach tightens. "Aimee..." he starts, but my voice catches in my throat, unsure of how to respond. His concern is genuine, and I know he's just trying to make sense of everything, to make me feel at ease. But I don't know how to explain what happened, or even why it affected me the way it did.

Sam takes a step closer, pausing in the middle of his task, his hands resting on the counter as he leans toward me. His eyes lock with mine, serious but kind. "Aimee, will you tell me what happened? The full story?" His voice is soft, patient. It's clear he's not rushing me, not pressuring me for answers, just giving me space to speak.

I look down at my feet, my fingers fidgeting with the hem of my shirt. I can feel the weight of his gaze on me, but I'm not sure if I'm ready to open up completely. The silence stretches between us, and I know I owe him some honesty, but my heart feels heavy. Finally,

I speak, my voice quiet but steady. "I was ready to come and meet you, Sam. I was looking through the box for something, a bag, I think? And I came across an old diary. I decided to read some pages and there was one page… that made me over-emotional. Triggered, so to say."

Sam doesn't interrupt. He just stands there, listening, his eyes never leaving mine. He waits, patiently, for me to continue, and I feel like he's holding space for me, not trying to rush me to some conclusion. His presence is comforting, and it makes the words flow a little easier.

"I lost my mom a few years ago, Sam," I say, my voice trembling slightly. "It was awful. I thought I had dealt with the trauma, but after last night's display, I guess I haven't handled it as well as I thought." My chest tightens as I speak, the grief creeping back in, threatening to overwhelm me. "I went to the sink to get a glass of water, and I dropped the glass," I add softly. "I just lost it. I didn't mean for it to happen. It just… it just came out of nowhere."

Sam's expression softens further, and I can see the empathy in his eyes. He doesn't try to fix it. He doesn't say anything about how I should feel or what I should've done differently. He just listens. I appreciate that more than I can put into words. "It's okay," he says finally, his voice low and reassuring. "You don't have to explain it to me if you're not ready. I just… I just wanted you to know that I'm here, okay?" He steps closer, placing a hand on my shoulder, giving it a gentle squeeze. "Whatever you need, I've got you."

I nod, feeling the weight of his words settle in my chest. There's something so comforting about knowing that Sam doesn't judge me for my vulnerability. He's not trying to push me to heal faster or get over it – it's just about being there, right now, in this moment. I feel a little lighter just knowing that.

After a few moments of quiet, Sam changes the subject, his tone lightening as he stands up straight again. "So," he says, smiling. "How about we make the most of today? I was thinking, if you're up for it, we could go for a walk in the park, clear our heads a bit." His suggestion feels like a much-needed breath of fresh air, a way to move past the heavy conversation and ease into something lighter. I smile at him, the weight of the conversation starting to fade. "I'd love that," I reply, my voice a little steadier. "A walk sounds perfect."

After a quick shower to shake off the remnants of last night, we get ready to head out. We grab a cab to Sam's apartment so he can get a change of clothes. It's the first time I've been there, and I'm both excited and nervous to see where he lives, the space he calls his own. The ride is quiet but comfortable, and I can feel the tension from before slowly melting away as we sit next to each other. Sam's apartment is cosy, with soft lighting and a warm, lived-in feel. There's a collection of books scattered across a shelf, and a few photos hang on the walls, some of him with friends, others of family. I take it all in as he moves around, gathering the clothes he needs, and I feel a little like I'm stepping into a new chapter of our connection, one that feels more real and grounded.

"This is nice," I say, my voice soft as I glance around. "It feels... like you." I'm not sure if that makes sense, but it feels true.

Sam chuckles, clearly pleased. "I'm glad you think so. It's small, but it works for me." He pulls a shirt from his closet and holds it up, looking for my opinion. "What do you think?"

I smile and nod. "I think it's perfect." It's an easy moment, comfortable, just the two of us. It feels like we're already settling into something deeper, something more familiar.

As we head out again, I can't help but feel a little more hopeful. The day ahead is wide open, and with Sam by my side, it feels like we're on the brink of something new, something worth exploring. I am intrigued with his book collection; so many first editions, he seems to be into his history novels, makes sense though, him working in an antique shop and being interested in past revelations. I come across a family photo, it looks like him as a boy, his mom and dad, he has a brother? *I don't think I have ever heard him mention that.*

"Is this your family?" I ask, gesturing to the photograph on the bookcase.

He walks over and places his hand to the bottom of my back, he stares at the photo. "Yeah, that's my mom, my dad and my brother Seb. I think this was in Connecticut to be honest, we used to spend our vacations there."

I smile knowing that he has happy memories of his childhood. "You never mentioned you have a brother, are you not close?"

His lips thin and I can feel the atmosphere changing. "He moved away roughly the same time I did to be honest, we message on and off, but there's no genuine connection there."

I try and stare at his features to see if I can detect any deceit; I can't so I just smile at him and change the topic entirely. "So, do you want to stay at my place for the weekend? It was so nice having you last night."

He smirks, he wraps his arms around my waist and pulls me in. "Are you sure? I don't want to rush things, Aimee, please do not think I'm saying no but I don't want you to feel you have to."

I chuckle. "Nothing like that, Sam, I genuinely love spending time with you and you are my knight in shining armour."

Sam's lips gently meet mine in a soft, sweet kiss, just a brief touch that sends a flutter through my chest. It's so simple, yet everything about it feels meaningful. As his lips pull away, I catch a hint of his scent – Chanel Men, subtle but intoxicating – and it mixes with the fresh, clean smell of his skin. It's the kind of fragrance that makes me feel safe and completely at ease, like everything is in its right place. I close my eyes for a moment, taking in the warmth of his embrace, feeling a sense of calm wash over me. His closeness, even in this small gesture, feels like home. There's a softness in his touch, a tenderness in the way he holds me, and I can't help but smile. The warmth of his arms around me is comforting, and his fresh scent lingers in the air, making me wish I could stay in this moment forever. The brief kiss, though fleeting, leaves me with a sense of peace and connection, like he's left a part of himself with me. I find myself wanting more of that closeness, more of the feeling of his skin against mine, but for now, I let myself savour this quiet, perfect moment.

Before I know it, my phone starts buzzing and I can see it's Sacha. I am tempted to just message her to tell her I will call her later; however, judging by her attitude on the group call a few nights ago, I need to pick up. "Sam, can I take this somewhere please? It's my friend from New York."

He points down the hallway. "Sure, my bedroom is the second on the right, head in there."

I mouth thank you and walk down the hallway and press Answer.

The phone rings, and I feel a strange sense of unease when I see Sacha's name on the screen. It's been a while since we last spoke, and lately, she's been distant, almost as if there's something heavy weighing on her. I answer quickly, my voice tentative.

"Sacha? Hey, it's been a while. Are you okay?" I ask, trying to sound casual, though I can tell something's off.

There's a long pause before she speaks, her voice cracking slightly. "I... I don't know, Aimee. I don't know how to say this."

I sit up straighter, suddenly concerned. "What happened? You're scaring me." My heart races as a knot starts to form in my stomach. I can hear her breathing heavily on the other end of the line, like she's trying to hold it together.

"I don't know how to start..." Sacha's voice breaks, and the words come out in a rush. "Your apartment was burgled, Aimee. Some personal things were taken. The police were called. The person who did it, they must have been watching the apartment. They knew the days and nights I wasn't there."

I freeze, my breath caught in my throat. My chest tightens, and I feel like I can't breathe. "What?" I gasp, my heart thundering in my chest like a bear wanting to escape its cage. "Why am I only being told this now, Sacha? What the fuck?"

She sobs harder, the sound of her crying ripping through me. "I... I didn't know how to tell you. I didn't want to make it worse, Aimee."

I start to breathe heavily. "When did this happen?" I retort.

"Five days ago," she exclaims.

I'm pacing the floor in Sam's bedroom now, my mind spinning, trying to process what she's saying. "You should've told me sooner! I would've helped!"

Then, Sacha's voice shakes even more, and she adds, "There's something else, Aimee."

I freeze mid-step, my pulse quickening. I take a deep breath, trying to steady myself, and sit on the edge of Sam's bed. "What is it? Please, just tell me." I lean forward, my fingers gripping the sheets, waiting for the next bombshell.

"I think it's... Sebastian, he's been reported as missing, Aimee," she whispers, her voice barely audible.

I feel my body stiffen, a confused look spreading across my face. "Why is that my problem?" I ask, though I can't shake the strange feeling creeping up my spine.

"I don't know, Aimee. But the police took prints from the apartment, and his were found there. I think... I think he's looking for you." Her voice cracks again, and I can hear her boyfriend in the background, comforting her.

I sit still, trying to process what I've just heard. "What? Sebastian? But... why would he be looking for me?" I shake my head, trying to make sense of it all.

"I've been to his work every day for the past five days. He hasn't been in. I don't know where he is. But, Aimee, I just... I have this gut feeling that he's connected to it all."

The weight of her words sinks into me, like an anchor pulling me down. I feel a cold shiver run through me as the reality of the situation hits. "What are you saying? That he's–"

"I don't know, Aimee. But something's not right, and I can't shake this feeling that he's involved somehow." Sacha's voice trembles, and the fear in it sends a chill down my spine.

What does he want with me? I whisper to myself. I can't move on Sam's bed, I'm frozen. I'm scared. "What does he want with me, Sacha?" I shout at her.

"Aimee, I don't know, I think you rejecting his proposal of getting back together has tipped him over the edge, I think he could be, or already be in Boston."

Fuck.

I hear the hallway floorboard creak outside: Sam. "Is everything okay in there?" he asks.

"Who's that?" Sacha asks.

"It's Sam, I'm at his place. I will be out soon, Sam," I say back to him, hoping he doesn't enter.

"Aimee, I think you need to tell Sam what's going on and get him to stay with you for a while maybe?"

I hiss at her. "Sacha, we have literally just started seeing how things go, I had an episode last night that he had to save me from and now this – he will run for the hills."

She begins to raise her voice, perhaps she's matching my energy. "What do you mean, an episode?" she asks.

"You know those nights a couple of years ago when you would come around and I would be lying on the floor and you couldn't get any sense out of me? One of those. Where I feel my soul has descended away from my body. Not a great thing to happen when you are trying to get to know someone."

She goes silent for a few seconds. "Why didn't you call me, Aimee?"

I can see where this is going and I am not going to start with the arguments. I decide that this conversation needs to be put to bed, I can't take anymore. "Sacha, I'm going to go, okay, I have been on this phone for twenty minutes now and I can't handle it. I will call you tomorrow okay, I love you. I hope you are okay with all of this, don't go back to the apartment by yourself."

She starts to sob again, and I feel so deflated, this morning, I woke up feeling ten feet tall and now I feel like I can't be dragged any lower. "Aimee, please. Look after yourself, Sebastian could be there looking for you. I would never want anyone to hurt you, please just ask Sam or someone to stay with you? For me? Please?"

I rub my temples as I am in total disbelief at what is happening. "I will certainly ask. I just don't know what he wants with me, I'm scared now, Sacha."

"Just be alert, Aimee, don't do anything by yourself, don't go out in the dark on your own. Please. Something in him has snapped and I will keep you posted if we find him."

I start to feel the wetness of tears on my face. "Bye, Sash, I will call you tomorrow."

As we both say our goodbyes I stare at the Boston skyline from Sam's bedroom, the city I was falling in love with; now in my mind, that sky has turned a crimson red, and I look out at the buildings and mutter to myself *where are you?* I then hear a knock at the door and Sam peers his head around the door.

"Are you okay?"

I shrug my shoulders, not knowing how to answer that question. Sam walks over to me and straight away, he can tell that something is wrong. "What's happening, Aimee?"

The tears are well on their way now and my face is bright red with the reaction to my skin. "Sam, my life is just up in the air at the moment, I think we need to press pause on this."

I can see his face change from concerned to upset. "Is it something I have done?" he asks.

"No, please don't think that, Sam, My ex has gone missing and my best friend seems to think that he is looking for me, my apartment in New York was burgled five days ago and his prints were found at the scene. I know this sounds crazy and I don't expect you to stay when all of this is going on. I am scared, I don't know what he wants, I don't know what he has taken." I look at his face and I can tell he feels out of his depth – wouldn't you? I silently sob, expecting him to show me the door.

"Come on, let's go to your place, you're going to stay here for a while, okay? No questions asked, I am not allowing you to be by yourself in your place if someone like that is on the hunt for you."

A mass wave of relief succumbs me, *where on earth has he been all my life?*

He wraps his arms around me and an earthquake of emotions erupt from my chest; as I fall into him, he exclaims, "You're going to be safe here, I will make sure of it." I return the affection and look into those gentle eyes, he smiles at me and advances to say, "Let's go to your place and get some things, huh? My car's parked out back, we will walk down together."

He locks his door to his apartment. As the click of the latch sounds, we both turn and make our way to the garage on the first floor, he grabs my hand, my cheeks start to blush as I return the gesture to him, as we approach the Jaguar I – Pace car I can't get over how beautiful it is, inside is just as stunning.

"Your job must pay well for a car like this! I never realised how gorgeous it was the previous time I was in this," I say to him, rubbing my hands over the smooth interior.

Sam chuckles. "I got a great bonus when I first started at the antique store, so I decided to treat myself, I used to get the bus when I first moved here; however, times of the buses were a nightmare. She's smart, isn't she?"

"She?" I question, thinking who is he talking about.

"I am sadly one of those guys who gives his car a gender, I do have some flaws–" as he holds his hands up.

I smile because he does have flaws, but as this point in time, he is accepting all of mine.

The car ride to my apartment feels like an eternity, the silence stretching between us as I try to hold myself together. Sam, always so steady, is focused on the road, his hand occasionally brushing against mine. I can feel the warmth of the seat beneath me, a small comfort in the midst of this chaos, but the knot in my stomach refuses to loosen. Sebastian. His name keeps swirling around in my head like a dark cloud. I have no idea what he wants or why he's doing this, but the thought of him looking for me sends chills down my spine. I don't know what his intentions are, but I can't shake the feeling that things are only going to get worse. Lauv's "There's No Way" plays softly on the radio, its calming melody doing little to soothe my racing thoughts. I glance over at Sam, his eyes steady on the road. He's the rock I need right now, the one person who isn't panicking, but I can't help but feel guilty. This whole mess is pulling him into a world I don't want him to be part of. He didn't ask for this, and now he's caught in the middle. I don't want to burden him any more than I already have, but right now, I need him more than I ever have before.

"So, how do you think they are going to catch your ex then?" Sam's voice breaks through my thoughts, and I sigh, rolling my eyes.

"I have no idea," I mutter, the frustration in my voice clear. "I don't know what he wants. I don't know why he wants me. I know nothing… just kept well and truly in the dark as usual." I laugh bitterly at myself. Sebastian has always been a mystery to me, a riddle I couldn't solve, and now it feels like I'm living in the aftermath of his twisted games.

Sam nods, his grip tightening on the wheel. "What is his name?" he asks, his tone curious but not judgmental.

I shudder at the thought of saying it aloud, the weight of his name feeling like a stone in my chest. "His name is Sebastian," I whisper, barely able to keep the disgust from my voice. "And he's a total narcissist. Did a lot of damage when we were together, and he wanted me back before I came out here. I rejected him." The words taste bitter as they leave my mouth, like the remnants of something poisonous.

Sam glances at me, his eyes flicking from the road to my face. "He might be the type of guy who doesn't take rejection well, you know?"

His words hang in the air, heavy with meaning, and I feel a cold chill run through me. I don't respond immediately, the fear settling deeper in my chest. I can't stop thinking about Sebastian's reaction when I rejected him, the anger that flared in his eyes. He's never been good with rejection, and I'm afraid that this time, his obsession with me might have gone too far.

The car slows as we approach my apartment building, and my heart starts to race. I glance out the window, my stomach turning as I see the familiar structure loom ahead. I haven't been back here in what feels like forever and it's been a matter of hours, and now it's just a reminder of everything I've been trying to escape. Sam pulls into the parking space and puts the car in park. Before I can even move, he opens his door and comes around to mine, gently pulling it open for me. The gesture is small, but it makes me feel a little bit safer, a little bit less alone. He holds out his hand, and I take it without thinking, letting him guide me out of the car. We both stand there for a moment, looking up at my apartment window. The sight of it makes my stomach flip. I feel exposed, vulnerable, as if Sebastian could be watching from somewhere, waiting for the perfect moment to strike. Sam stands beside me, his presence a quiet strength.

"Come on," he says, his voice calm but firm. "The sooner we go in and grab some things for you, the faster we can get out."

I nod, my legs feeling heavy as I start walking toward the entrance. Every step feels like it takes me further into the unknown, deeper into a situation I don't know how to fix. I'm terrified, but I can't show it. Sam is here, and for now, that's all I have. I just hope it's enough to get me through this.

As Sam and I walk up the stairs to the third floor, I can feel the tension building with each step. We keep exchanging glances, but they're not the same. Sam's glances are filled with concern, the furrowed brow and tight jawline giving him away even when he tries to mask it. I, on the other hand, can't help but look at him with admiration. He's holding it together for me, walking beside me as if everything will be okay – even when I'm not so sure it will. There's something incredibly grounding about his presence, like the steady beat of a drum that keeps me moving forward, even when I want to turn back.

We finally reach my apartment door, and I feel my stomach twist. I can't put it off any longer. Sam stands behind me, his hand gently resting on my shoulder, as I turn the lock. The familiar click of the latch seems deafening in the silence, and I push open the door. Everything looks... normal. Everything is where it should be. Nothing seems out of place. For a moment, I almost feel relieved, like maybe my mind is overreacting, that nothing is wrong.

But the moment we step inside, the air feels heavy, the weight of it pressing down on me. The old floorboards creak under our weight as we move through the space. I can't help but notice the way the apartment feels smaller now, emptier in a way I can't explain. I can hear Sam moving around behind me, his steady footsteps echoing as he checks each room. I rush into my bedroom, the door slamming behind me as I quickly pull out a large duffel bag. My hands shake as I start tossing clothes and other things into it, not even thinking about what I'm grabbing. I just need to get out. I need to leave this place behind, as fast as possible. I hear Sam moving through the apartment, checking cupboards, looking under piles of junk, doing his best to make sure no one is hiding in the shadows. It's almost like he's trying to protect me from something that might still be lurking in this place. I appreciate it, but I can't shake the unease that's building in my chest. There's something off about this place, something that feels... wrong. Suddenly, something catches my eye out of the corner of my vision. A shift, a movement, so slight that I almost convince myself it's nothing. But then it happens again. This time, I'm sure of it. A figure, just a blur, darting across the room. My heart stops, and my breath catches in my throat. The fear is instant and overwhelming. Before I even realise what's happening, I scream. I scream with all the force in my lungs, the sound reverberating through the walls.

"Sam!" I manage to gasp out, but I'm too paralysed with fear to move. My mind is racing, trying to make sense of what I saw. Was it just my imagination? Did I see something that isn't there? My chest tightens, my breath coming in short, frantic bursts.

And then, in an instant, Sam is bursting through the bedroom door, his face filled with alarm. "What's up?" His voice is urgent, but I can't speak. My mind is still trying to catch up with my body, my heart hammering in my chest. I try to take a deep breath, but the air feels thick and suffocating.

"I – I don't know," I stammer, my hands shaking as I try to compose myself. "I don't know what I saw. It... it was just a flash, but–" My voice breaks, and I can barely find the words. I don't know if it was real or if I'm just losing my mind.

Sam steps closer, his hand on my arm now, grounding me. "Aimee, calm down," he says softly, though there's a sharp edge of concern in his voice. He's trying to make sense of it too, but I can see in his eyes that he's as unsettled as I am.

"I need to get away from here," I whisper, my voice low but full of urgency. "Let's go. Please, Sam. Let's just leave." I don't know what I saw, and I don't know if it's connected to Sebastian, but I don't want to take any chances. This apartment, my home – this place that's supposed to be safe – feels like it's suffocating me. I can't stay here. Not now. Not with this fear crawling up my spine. The thoughts I once felt for Sebastian, he was once safe, like home, now I know, he's out for blood.

Sam doesn't hesitate. He nods once, his eyes scanning the room like he's checking for any threat. "Okay. Let's go. We'll figure this out. Just – just take a deep breath, Aimee."

His voice is calm, but I can feel the tension in the way he holds me, like he's ready to get us out of here as quickly as possible. We move toward the door, my duffel bag slung over my shoulder, but I can't shake the feeling that something is following us, something watching from the shadows. My heart is racing, and every little noise in the apartment makes me jump. Sam walks in front of me, his back to the door, scanning the space one last time before stepping out into the hall.

As we leave the apartment behind, I can't help but feel like we're leaving more than just a building. We're leaving a piece of my meant-to-be-future, and maybe – just maybe – it's something I'll never be able to go back to. But for now, all I care about is getting out. Getting away from the fear. From the uncertainty. And with Sam by my side, I feel a flicker of hope, even if it's small. At least for now, I don't have to face this alone.

Sam

I don't know what the fuck is going on. This whole situation feels like I'm trapped in some messed-up plot that someone else wrote, but I'm stuck in the middle of it. Aimee's at her wits' end, and I can't stand the thought of her being alone right now. She's already far from home in a city she doesn't know very well, and I'm not about to let her handle any of this by herself. It's not even a choice anymore – she needs me, and I'm not leaving her when things are this bad. Not now. Not ever.

We finally make it to the car, and Aimee's still visibly shaken, the way she was clutching at that duffel bag like it's the only thing keeping her grounded. I take it from her, feeling the weight of it in my hands, and open the large boot of the car, tossing it in with a bit more force than necessary. I'm trying to focus on getting her settled in, getting her out of here as quickly as possible.

"Come on, get yourself in," I say, my voice soft but firm as I lift her into the car. The door slams behind me, and for the first time today, I feel a little bit of relief. We're in the car now, at least. For now, we're safe. I let out a long sigh, trying to shake off some of the tension that's built up in my shoulders. I glance over at Aimee, and I can see it – the guilt written all over her face. I know she feels like she's putting a lot on me, but she doesn't have to. I'm here, and I'm not going anywhere.

"Wow, been a hell of a day, hasn't it?" I say, trying to lighten the mood. I keep my tone casual, though I can hear the underlying concern in my voice. She looks pretty down, her eyes distant, but she offers me a small smile. I reach over, my hand resting gently on her knee, a subtle reminder that I'm not going anywhere anytime soon. I want her to know that she's not alone in this. She needs to feel safe, and if that means being here with her, making sure she's okay, then that's exactly what I'm going to do. Her smile widens just a bit, and for the briefest moment, I can see some of the tension leave her body.

"Let's go for some food?" I suggest. "We haven't had anything since breakfast, and you need to keep your strength up."

She nods, my stomach growling in agreement. The thought of food feels like a distraction, something to take our minds off everything. Plus, I know she's probably not been eating well with everything that's been going on, and I want to make sure she's taking care of herself too. "Sounds good to me. Let's get some real food."

We drive out of the city, the noise of it fading as we head further into quieter streets. About forty minutes later, we pull up to a small Italian restaurant nestled in a charming part of town. The cobbled streets give it an old-world feel, and the buildings are draped in ivy, climbing up the sides like they've been there forever. It's the kind of place that makes you forget about everything else, if only for a little while. The warm glow from the restaurant windows invites us in, and I feel like a weight lifts off my shoulders as I hold the door open for Aimee.

The place is cosy, intimate even. The scent of garlic and fresh basil fills the air, and it's like a reminder of normal life, something simple and good. We're seated by the window, the flickering candlelight between us casting soft shadows. I can feel Aimee relaxing a little bit, the tension in her shoulders easing as she takes in the ambience. We order some antipasti to start – crispy bread with a bit of olive oil, some salami, and mozzarella that melts in your mouth. Aimee picks at it, her fingers tracing the edge of the plate before she takes a bite. I watch her closely, knowing how hard it's been for her today, and I'm glad to see her eating, even if it's just a little. I also spy some of the cuts on her hands, I will check these over when we get home.

As the night goes on, the conversation starts to flow a little easier. She asks me about my past, about working different places, and I tell her the mundane details to try and distract her from the weight of everything that's happened. Her laughter comes in small bursts, but it's enough to make me feel like she's still with me, like there's a part of her that hasn't been swallowed up by the chaos. When the main course arrives, we dive into it. I've got a bowl of pasta with truffle oil and wild mushrooms, and she's opted for the classic spaghetti carbonara. We share bites between us, the flavours comforting and rich, everything warm and satisfying in a way that makes me forget about the world outside for a little while.

"I think I needed this," Aimee says, her voice softer now. She takes a long sip of her wine, the tension slowly melting away as she leans back in her chair. "Not just the food... but this. Being here with you." Her eyes meet mine, and there's something there – something unspoken, but real.

I smile at her, setting down my fork. "I'm glad you're here. You don't have to go through this alone, Aimee. I'm here for however long you need."

She smiles, the warmth returning to her eyes, and for the first time today, I see a little bit of hope in her expression. Maybe it's just a flicker, but it's enough to make me feel like, for tonight, we've found a small piece of peace. And that's enough.

Considering the day has been mentally draining for us both, the night was a success. We left the restaurant revived and more alive, I strongly believe she can get through this, she doesn't give herself credit for what she's been through. The journey back to my place is pleasant enough, Lizzy McAlpine – Ceilings plays on the soundwaves, this seems to mellow Aimee out. I can see that she is tired as her face is resting on the window. The skyline of Boston now coming into view, the lights adorning the sidewalks; people are now emerging from their jobs to join in on the night life. As we pull up to my apartment, I decide to park my car in the secure garage on the ground floor, just in case. The car is stationary in the car park and I glance over to her, I think she's asleep; I stroke her hair to try and wake her calmly; as I do that she flinches awake. "It's just me, Aimee, you're good. We're home."

She looks over her left shoulder at me and I can tell she is tired, her eyes have gone all glassy and heavy. I grab her hand and pull ever so slightly to engage with her that we need to get out of the car. Aimee takes her seatbelt off and exhales a large sigh as she opens the side door to exit. I walk to the back of the car and open the boot to retrieve her duffel bag and throw it over my shoulder.

Putting my key into the lock of the front door with Aimee by my side is very surreal, I was not expecting things to take this turn so quickly, her practically living with me now for the foreseeable future. I can't say I'm unhappy about it though, least this will test our relationship to the max.

As we both enter the apartment, we're immediately hit with the scent of orange and bergamot. It's an unexpected but welcome greeting, filling the air in every room. The sharp citrus notes mingle with the calming warmth of the bergamot, creating an atmosphere that feels almost... safe. Like a little oasis in the middle of everything else. I inhale deeply, hoping the scent will help both of us settle, to ease some of the tension from the day's madness. Maybe it's a small comfort, but it's one I'm grateful for.

I take the duffel bag to my bedroom and set it down on the bed, trying to make some room for Aimee in my space. "You can unpack your things here," I tell her, gesturing to the now-empty drawers and closet. "I'll make some room for you." It feels like a little thing, but I can't help but think about how soon all of this is happening. How quickly our lives are shifting.

"Didn't expect to be doing this so soon," I say, trying to lighten the mood, but I can see in her eyes that she's too exhausted to even crack a smile. I think she finds it funny, but her body is just too drained. The day's emotional toll is written all over her face.

She nods, but there's a sadness behind her eyes. "I guess everything happens for a reason, so they say," she says, her voice soft. It's like she's speaking more to herself than to me, and I can tell she's processing things in her own quiet way.

I don't push her to talk, though. I just let her be. "You're looking tired," I say, sitting next to her on the bed. "Do you want to settle down for the night and unpack tomorrow?" Her eyes are already heavy, and I can see the weight of the day pressing down on her.

"That sounds perfect, Sam," she whispers, and I can see the exhaustion pulling her under.

I smile softly, knowing she needs this – rest, peace, a break from the chaos that's been following her around.

"Okay, you get yourself to bed, I'm going to watch some TV for a bit, alright?" I tell her as I start to stand. But before I can leave the room, she looks at me. Her gaze is full of gratitude, and for a moment, I just stand there, frozen.

"Thank you, Sam," she says, her voice barely above a whisper. "I really mean that. From the bottom of my heart, I do."

I smile back, feeling a little warmth in my chest. The situation is shit, but there's something nice about having her here. It's comforting, in a way. The silence between us isn't awkward, but peaceful. It feels like the right thing to do, having her here, taking care of her in the middle of everything.

As I nearly exit the room, I hear my phone vibrating in my pocket. It's Josh, and I can see his name lighting up the screen. I step out of the room and into the hallway before answering.

"Hey, man," I say, trying to keep my voice casual.

"Sam! It's been a minute, how's everything going?" Josh responds, his voice upbeat as usual. But I can hear the curiosity in his tone, like he's waiting for me to fill him in.

I take a deep breath before speaking, glancing back toward the bedroom where Aimee's now lying down. "Actually, Josh, I've got some stuff going on. Aimee's staying with me for a while."

Josh's voice goes quiet for a second. "Wait, Aimee? As in, your new friend Aimee?"

"Yeah, she's here. Her ex from New York – well, let's just say he's making things complicated. The guy's... unstable. He's been looking for her, and she's in a pretty bad place right now." I run a hand through my hair, feeling the weight of the situation settle in again.

"Shit, that's rough," Josh says, his tone now serious. "What happened?"

"Her ex is a real piece of work," I explain, trying to keep it short. "He's been keeping tabs on her, showing up at her old apartment and he broke in! And she's afraid he might be trying to find her again. The police are involved, but who knows how long it'll take for them to catch him."

Josh is silent for a moment, clearly processing everything. "Jesus, man. That sounds terrifying. But you're sure she's safe, right? I mean, are you safe?"

"I'm doing my best to keep her safe," I reply, glancing over at the bedroom door. "She's staying with me for the time being. I'm not letting her handle this alone."

"Good call, Sam," Josh says. "I'm glad you're there for her. If you need anything, you know I've got your back, right?"

I appreciate the offer. "Thanks, Josh. It means a lot. But for now, I've got it covered. I'm just making sure she's okay."

"Alright, man. Just wanted to check in. You guys take care of yourselves, okay?"

"We will. Thanks again, Josh." I hang up the phone, pocketing it as I stand still in the hallway for a second. The weight of everything is finally starting to hit me – Aimee staying here, her ex on the loose, and the uncertainty hanging over us. But I know I can't let it consume me. Not while she's under my roof, safe for now.

I walk back to the bedroom, taking a deep breath before entering. I can't help but feel a sense of responsibility, of wanting to protect her even when things feel completely out of my control. It's like everything in my life just shifted, and now I'm stepping up in a way I never thought I would.

I glance at Aimee, already asleep. She's finally found some peace, even if just for a moment, and I'm here to make sure that peace lasts. The world can be chaotic and unpredictable, but right now, all I need to focus on is making sure she's okay.

I step into the bathroom, trying to keep my movements slow and quiet, not wanting to wake Aimee. She's already fast asleep in my bed, her breathing steady and peaceful after everything that's happened today. I wash my face, feeling the cool water splash against my skin, trying to shake off the weight of the day. I'm exhausted, but there's a knot in my chest that keeps me from fully relaxing. I know Aimee's been through hell, and it's hard to shake the feeling that I can't do enough to help her. The situation just feels so out of control, and all I want is to make her feel safe again. After I get changed into some comfortable clothes, I make sure to be as quiet as possible as I slip into the bedroom. The soft glow of the bedside lamp is the only light in the room, casting a warm hue over everything. I glance at the bed and see Aimee lying there, curled up beneath the covers. Her face is peaceful now, but I know she's probably not going to get much rest with everything that's been going on. I feel guilty, knowing that she's had to go through all of this. I tiptoe over to my side of the bed, careful not to disturb her. The last thing I want is for her to wake up in the middle of the night and start reliving all the chaos. I pull the covers back slowly and slide in next to her, positioning myself on my side of the bed. I try not to make a sound, even though I can't help but feel a bit of a sense of relief as I finally settle in. It's strange to feel this sense of calm with everything that's going on, but there's a quiet comfort in just being here with her.

The first few moments are peaceful, but soon I feel myself starting to shift. I can't get comfortable. My mind keeps racing with thoughts of Aimee's ex, of everything that's happened and everything that could happen next. I glance over at her, her face relaxed in sleep. She looks so vulnerable, and it hits me harder than I expected. I toss and turn, unable to get the thought of her safety out of my head. Every time I close my eyes, I see flashes of the fear she's been carrying. I can't stop thinking about how this all could have been avoided, how I wish I could've been there for her sooner. I stare at Aimee again, and for a moment, I just watch her. Her face is peaceful, but I know it's only temporary. Tomorrow is Sunday, and both of us have work on Monday. I know we can't avoid life for long, but I don't want her going anywhere alone. Not now, not when she's still so shaken. I think about the commute, the busy streets, and all the uncertainty she'll face as soon as she steps outside. I don't want to make her feel like she's a prisoner in my apartment, but I can't shake the thought that her safety has to come first. I don't want to crowd her, but I also can't ignore the fact that she's been through enough already. She's my priority now, and I'll do whatever it takes to keep her safe, even if that means adjusting my routine to accommodate hers. I don't want her to feel like she's being smothered, though. I know how independent she is, and I don't want to make her feel like she has to rely on me for everything. But with everything going on with her ex, I'm just not comfortable letting her go anywhere alone. I start making a mental list of all the little ways I can make sure she feels supported without overwhelming her.

I shift again, the bed creaking beneath me as I adjust my position. I wish I could fall asleep, but my mind is racing. I look over at Aimee once more, watching her breathe softly in her sleep. She's so brave, and I admire her strength even if she doesn't see it. She's been through so much, and I hate that her ex is still a threat. I wish there was more I could do. As I continue to lie there, I finally start to feel the weight of sleep pulling at my eyelids. I try to let go of all the worries, to quiet my thoughts just enough to get some rest. Tomorrow will come with its own challenges, but for tonight, I just need to be here. To be present for her. I hope that, in the morning, we can take one step closer to feeling like ourselves again, even if just for a little while.

Eventually, I manage to drift off, though my mind still lingers on Aimee and everything we have to face. But as long as I'm here, as long as I can keep her safe, I'll be alright. For tonight, that's all I need to focus on.

THREE DAYS LATER...

the past three days have been a whirlwind. A mix of challenges and unexpected moments of peace. I think it all started on Sunday when Aimee and I sat down to talk about travelling to and from work. We both agreed that it wouldn't be healthy for me to shadow her, but I couldn't ignore the fact that she needed someone looking out for her. So, we came up with a plan – me taking her to work in the mornings, then dropping her off in the evenings at my place, and just making sure she wasn't alone at any point. It's been tough on her, I can tell, but Aimee has been a trooper, handling everything with a strength that continuously takes me by surprise.

That night, Sacha called with some troubling news. She sounded shaken, which immediately made me uneasy. The police had reached out to her, letting her know that Aimee's ex, Sebastian, he had used his card at the New York Station. They'd traced it to a ticket for Boston, purchased just a day ago. It was the confirmation we dreaded: Sebastian was on his way here, or maybe he was already here. I could hear the tension in Sacha's voice, and for the first time, I felt a real wave of fear wash over me. This wasn't just an inconvenience anymore. This was serious.

The next morning, I tried to mask the unease as we continued our routine. Aimee went to work, still determined to keep things as normal as possible, and I was there to make sure she wasn't alone in the process. I picked her up, dropped her off, and tried not to hover too much. I knew she appreciated the support, but I also knew she needed her space. It's strange, feeling so protective, but also trying not to smother her. It's a delicate balance, and one I don't always know how to navigate.

On Monday, I decided to head to the bridal boutique where Aimee worked. I didn't expect it to be the way it turned out. I wanted to talk to her boss, see if there was anything I could do to make her feel more secure during the day. I spoke to the owner about Aimee's situation, and how I was picking her up, but I wanted to see if someone could wait with her at the end of the day until I could get there. It was then that I learned her boss was none other than Sacha's aunt. The irony wasn't lost on me. Of all the places Aimee could work, of course, it had to be with family.

It made me feel slightly better, though. At least Sacha's aunt would know what was going on and could keep an eye out for Aimee at the end of the day. The more people looking out for her, the better. I didn't realise how much I needed that reassurance until it was offered so freely. The thought of Aimee being vulnerable and alone at work, without anyone noticing, made my stomach churn. But outside of the stress, I have to admit, the last few days have also been unexpectedly comforting. Having Aimee here, sharing our evenings together, it's been a kind of peace that I didn't know I needed. We've started cooking together – nothing fancy, just simple meals, but it's become one of my favourite parts of the day. We laugh, we talk about whatever's on our minds, and for a few hours, the world feels normal again.

It's been bittersweet, though. On the one hand, I get to spend so much time with her, and that's been nothing short of amazing. But on the other, I can't stop worrying about her. I can't stop worrying about what Sebastian is going to do next. I feel like a piece of my life has shifted in ways I can't fully control, but the strange thing is... I don't mind it. Not really. As the days have passed, I find myself more and more attached to her. There's something about having her here, in my space, that has made me realise how much I've grown to care for her. I don't want to admit it to myself yet – don't want to acknowledge that I'm falling for her – but I know it's happening. It's happening with every moment we share, every laugh, every conversation we have over dinner, every walk we take in the park.

I catch myself staring at her sometimes. Just watching the way her lips curl into a smile, how her eyes light up when she talks about something she loves. I've always admired Aimee from afar, but now that I'm seeing her every day, I'm realising just how much she's truly captured my heart. I can't deny it. I've already fallen for her, and it scares me to think about what that could mean. What happens when things settle down? Will I just go back to being her friend, her protector, or will this turn into something more?

The walks in the park after dinner have been our new routine. It's something simple, but it's become one of the highlights of my day. There's something about the quiet calm of the evening, the cool air, the way the city fades away as we walk together. We don't have to talk the whole time; sometimes, it's just the presence of each other that makes everything feel a little lighter.

Aimee's been keeping her head held high, and I admire her for it. She's still going to work, still putting in the effort to keep everything as normal as possible. But I know it's not easy. I can see the way her shoulders tense when she hears a strange noise, or the way she flinches when someone walks too closely behind her. She's carrying the weight of all this fear and uncertainty, but she's doing it with grace, and I'm constantly in awe of her resilience. At night, when we're finally able to sit down, eat dinner, and just enjoy each other's company, I feel a sense of peace that I haven't felt in a long time. I know there's still danger, still uncertainty, but for those few hours, it feels like we're just two people trying to make it through. And that's enough for me, at least for now.

But the thoughts always creep back in. What if Sebastian finds her? What if he's closer than we think? What if tomorrow brings something worse than we expect? These thoughts don't go away, no matter how many times I try to push them out. But for tonight, I'll just enjoy this quiet moment with Aimee. I'll savour these little pieces of happiness while I can. Because in the midst of all the chaos, that's what matters.

Aimee

I have just finished a meeting in the office with my manager going over the new dresses for the new spring season coming in. Some of the gowns are so intricate and they look like they have been crafted by black widows, the lace is like a spider's web, so stunning. Sacha's aunt has been a guardian angel for me when I have been at work, she has brought out a new policy where people now need to book appointments, walk ins are no longer allowed in the store in case Sebastian walks in. I know the measures seem over the top; however, we did have it confirmed via the police that he is coming here. *Typical of my Aunt Clara, not keeping her mouth shut.* Being at Sam's apartment has been so blissful, he has been the ideal partner, haven't declared ourselves as anything yet; however, I know the feelings are there; he catches me looking at him and I do the same for him. He has done something no man in my life has done, he has stood his ground and shown up when I needed him to. My dad left my mom when I was just three years old and I haven't seen him since, no effort to get to know me or to even meet me, his loss I know.

I'm in the middle of helping a customer when Sophie bursts through the door of the dressing room, practically bouncing off the walls with excitement. She's always had a certain energy about her, but today, it's on another level. I can barely get the words out before she's pulling me aside.

"Aimee, OMG, you will not believe it!" she exclaims, her face lighting up as she grabs both of my arms. "There's a party at my friend's house on Friday night, and we are going! It's going to be so much fun!"

I take a breath, trying to focus on what she's saying. I've had a lot on my mind lately, and the idea of going out and having fun doesn't exactly seem like a priority. In fact, it feels like a distraction I can't afford. "I don't think I can make it, Sophie. I'm not really in the mood," I say, trying to keep things light, but she's having none of it.

She looks at me, and I can see the disappointment flicker in her eyes. "Oh come on, don't let the fact that you're off the market ruin our fun, please!" she pleads, practically begging me with those big, wide eyes. I can tell she means well, but I just don't know if I'm in the right place to go out, especially given everything that's been happening. I can't risk anything happening with Sebastian if he finds me, I'm still trying to figure out how to handle it all, and the idea of letting loose at a party feels like the last thing I should be doing.

But I can't help it. The thought of a night out, the chance to relax and forget everything for just a few hours, is tempting. I've been stuck in a bubble of stress, worrying about Sebastian and how all of this is affecting my life. Maybe a little escape is exactly what I need. "Can I at least bring Sam?" I ask, even though I know that might be a deal-breaker. I'm hoping the idea of him being there will make it more comfortable for me, that it'll feel safer somehow.

Sophie rolls her eyes dramatically, groaning in mock frustration. "No men allowed," she says with a grin, crossing her arms and leaning against the doorframe like she's made the final ruling.

I can't help but laugh at her theatrics, but deep down, I'm still unsure about whether I should even consider going. The girls don't know what's going on as I don't want any questions.

"Okay, okay, I get it," I say, trying to sound nonchalant, but I know I'm already second-guessing myself. My mind is pulling in two different directions. One part of me wants to go, to get out, to feel normal again. The other part is telling me I should be more cautious, that I need to keep my guard up. After all, I don't really know what Sebastian is planning, or if he's even in the city yet.

Still, Sophie's excitement is contagious, and despite the worry that sits heavy in my chest, I can't help but picture myself at that party, even just for a little while. It would be nice to laugh, to be carefree, to forget about everything else. But there's that nagging feeling that maybe I'm not ready to let go of the fear just yet.

As Sophie continues to talk about the party, rattling off all the fun things that are supposed to happen, my thoughts drift back to Sam. He's been amazing throughout all of this, always there when I need him, always making sure I'm okay. I wonder how he would feel about me going out, whether he would be worried, or if he would even encourage it. I wish I could ask him, but at the same time, I know he's been working just as hard to keep things together for both of us. I stand there, caught between the pull of wanting a night out and the reality of the life I'm currently living. I know I need to make a decision, but for now, I just let Sophie's excitement wash over me. Maybe I will go. Maybe I won't. For now, though, I have the rest of the day to figure it out.

By the time 4 pm finally rolls around, I can't help but feel a little bit of relief. It's been a long day at the bridal boutique, full of trying to help frantic brides-to-be and running around to organise the gowns. But now, the dresses are all back in their rightful places, hanging neatly on their racks, and the shop is quiet. The other girls have already left for the day, which leaves just me and Fiona, both of us standing outside, waiting for Sam to pull up. The sun is starting to dip low in the sky, and I can't wait to get home.

As I stand there with Fiona, the minutes seem to stretch on. Ten minutes feel like an eternity, but then, I finally see Sam's car pulling down the street. My heart picks up speed as I watch him carefully navigate the road, turn the corner, and mount the kerb. He parks, and Fiona wraps her arms around me for a hug, her excitement and joy for me clear in the way she squeezes me tight. I feel grateful for her support, but a little sad too. I wish I could just go home and relax without any weight on my shoulders.

I give Fiona a long wave as I climb into the car, the door clicking shut behind me. The sound of the car door closing brings a sense of finality, and it's a relief to be leaving the boutique behind. I turn to look at Sam, and as always, he's smiling at me. That smile that makes my heart flutter, even on the rough days. Without thinking, I lean in and kiss him. It's a soft kiss, but it says everything I need it to. I've missed him today. Sam doesn't pull away, his hand resting on my knee as he smiles against my lips. The tension I've been holding onto all day starts to melt away. As he pulls back, his eyes meet mine, warm and understanding.

"So, how has your day been then?" he asks, his voice calm.

"Been super busy," I reply, sinking into the comfort of the seat. "Fiona has stopped walk-ins now, though. So you need an appointment to even get into the store. I feel bad."

He shifts gears and glances over at me. "Never feel bad for someone taking your safety seriously," he says with a sincerity that makes me smile. That's Sam for you – always thinking ahead, always protecting me. "I know you have a good heart. You care about everyone around you. But your safety should always come first."

I can't help but feel a sense of gratitude toward him. He's been my rock, truly. I lean back and let his words sink in before asking,

"So, Sophie has a party on Friday night. She invited me to go. What do you think?"

Sam's face turns serious as he concentrates on the road. "Do you think it's wise, going to a party with people you hardly know, when your ex is more than likely in the same city looking for you?"

His words make me pause, and I feel a tightness in my chest. I can feel the weight of his concern, and it's hard not to let the defensiveness creep in. But I don't want to fight with him. I've never wanted to feel like I need permission to do something.

"Why do I feel like I need to ask you?" I ask him, my voice barely above a whisper. It's a genuine question.

"Aimee, you never need to ask me to do anything," Sam says, his voice gentle yet firm. "You are your own woman. I trust you. I just want to make sure that you're safe. I don't want to keep you locked away, but I also don't want you in danger. I think going to a party with people you hardly know, with everything going on, is asking for trouble. He could easily know where you work by now. He might be talking to one of the girls there already. You just don't know. Please don't take this as me being controlling. I just want your safety. Once alcohol is involved, you won't know anyone there if you need help."

I take in a deep breath, trying to keep my emotions in check. Sam's words make sense. I know they do. But a part of me wants to feel normal again. I want to have a night out, a few hours to forget everything. "I understand that, Sam," I say, my voice soft. "But it's just a couple of hours, max. I just want to let my hair down. I shouldn't have to explain myself, though."

Sam pulls over at the apartment building, the engine purring softly. "Aimee, I'm not telling you what to do. If you want to go, I'll do what I've been doing all week. I'll drop you off and pick you up. I just want you to be safe. I wouldn't forgive myself if anything happened to you."

I open the car door with a force I don't mean, grabbing my handbag, my heart suddenly full of frustration. "I just don't want to feel like I need permission to go out, Sam," I mutter, a hint of anger creeping into my words. I walk up to the apartment, leaving Sam behind in the car, the anger simmering inside me. I know he's just trying to protect me, but why does it feel like I have to ask for his approval? When did I start needing someone's permission to live my life? I want to be normal, but with Sebastian still out there, I don't know how much longer I'll feel normal. How long will it take the police to catch him? How long until I can feel safe again?

Once inside the apartment, I head straight for the shower. The hot water feels like it's washing away not just the grime of the day, but all the stress and anger building up inside me. I close my eyes, letting the steam and warmth envelop me, trying to forget the frustration I felt just a few moments ago. I need to clear my head, to feel like I'm in control of something again.

Thirty minutes later, Sam walks in with a takeout bag from our favourite restaurant. He places it on the counter and looks at me, his face softened by concern. "I know we didn't end on the best note earlier, but can we talk about it?"

I nod, sitting down on the couch as he joins me. The food smells amazing, and for a second, it distracts me from the tension still lingering between us. We begin to eat in silence, but the air is thick with unspoken words.

Finally, I break the silence. "I know you're just trying to protect me, Sam, but sometimes it feels like I'm being caged in. I don't want to feel like I can't do anything without asking permission."

"I don't want you to feel like that, Aimee," Sam says softly, reaching over to take my hand. "I just care about you. I want you to be safe. But if you want to go to the party, we can figure it out together."

I look at him, really look at him, and for a moment, I realise he's right. It's not about control; it's about safety. But I also need to remember that I'm my own person. I feel like a spoilt brat who has thrown a tantrum when she has not gotten her own way, this guy has done everything for me, he has given up his home for me, he has changed his schedule for me, he hasn't seen his friends in a week and a half because I don't want to be left on my own; he has given me anything he physically can, and this is how I repay him? *I'm such a dick.*

I take a deep breath, and as I do, my hand reaches for his, guiding it gently to my chest. I want him to feel the rapid beat of my heart, to know just how much I appreciate everything he's done for me. "I am so sorry I acted like that before," I whisper, the words heavy with sincerity. "It was not right, Sam. You've done everything in your power to keep me safe. You've given up your home for me, you've kept me safe, and you've done exactly what you said you would. I'm sorry if I came across as ungrateful. It's not what I want."

His hand rests gently over my heart, and I can feel the warmth of his palm seeping through me, soothing the storm of emotions inside. Sam leans in, his forehead brushing softly against mine, his right hand lifting to stroke through my hair. I close my eyes at the tender touch, letting the calmness of the moment wash over me. The words he says next hit me in a way I wasn't expecting.

"Aimee, I..." Sam hesitates, his voice barely above a whisper.

I pull back slightly, just enough to look him in the eyes. I can see it, the uncertainty, the weight of something unspoken. "What's up?" I ask, my voice soft but laced with confusion. His expression shifts, something brewing behind his eyes, and for a split second, I wonder if I've misread him all this time.

He sighs, running his hand down my hair slowly, almost as if he's trying to steady himself. "I don't know how to say this because it's probably the last thing you want to hear, but..." He pauses, searching for the right words, and I can feel my chest tightening, my heart rate picking up again, but this time it's out of anticipation. "The past few weeks, having you here, have been the best," he continues, his voice soft but filled with so much emotion. "I never want them to end. You are my everything, Aimee, I... I love you."

The world seems to stop, the air thick with the weight of his words. I feel like I'm standing on the edge of something – something beautiful, yet terrifying at the same time. I blink, unsure if I heard him correctly, but when I look into his eyes, I see the raw honesty there. It's not just a passing sentiment; it's real, and it's for me. And for the first time in a long while, I don't feel so alone in this world.

Still reeling from when Sam told me he loved me, everything around me seems to blur. I feel like I am floating, like I am weightless, suspended in this moment of pure emotion. For a split second, I wonder if I am dreaming, if this is some sort of elaborate fantasy I have conjured up in my head. Was I having another episode? My mind races with questions, each one louder than the last. What is happening? Why does everything feel so surreal?

I look into Sam's eyes, searching for any hint of doubt, but all I see is raw, unfiltered emotion. His eyes are filled with love – love for me – and the magnitude of it hits me like a wave. It is overwhelming, in the best way possible. But then, out of nowhere, the ringing in my ears starts again, that familiar buzz that always accompanies the anxiety, the voices in my head that I can't escape. "You always wanted this, Aimee. Why aren't you answering him?" The voice taunts me, questioning me, pushing me further into uncertainty.

I squeeze my eyes shut, trying to shake the ringing, trying to block out the voice that was trying to pull me away from this beautiful moment. I need to be present, to be here with Sam. He is here, right in front of me, and he has just bared his soul. I can't let the voices take this away from me. So, I take a deep breath and focus on Sam, his warmth, his presence, and the way he is looking at me with nothing but kindness and affection.

It is like a jolt back to reality, the way my heart raced when I realised I could feel him so strongly, like my heartstrings were being pulled in every direction. I couldn't just sit there, frozen by the moment and my thoughts. I couldn't waste this chance. I jump up, my arms wrapping around him, pulling him close. I kiss his beautiful face, each soft touch of my lips a desperate promise to him. I want him to be mine, for the world to know that I am not hiding anymore. I want us, together, out in the open.

Sam's hands grip my waist, lifting me effortlessly into his arms, and then his lips on mine, gentle yet full of passion. My heart flutters in my chest, my mind spinning with the intensity of the moment. I feel like a princess, weightless in his embrace, every kiss he places on me sending warmth flooding through my veins. The world around us ceases to exist, and it is just the two of us, caught in this whirlwind of emotion. The energy between us is electric, like something neither of us could control, but neither of us wanted to either. The way Sam holds me, the way he kisses me, it is like he is grounding me, reminding me that everything is going to be okay. That I don't have to fight this anymore. He is here, he loves me, and that is all that mattered.

The room seems to fade away, leaving just the feeling of his arms around me, the softness of his lips, and the overwhelming warmth that fills the space between us. I never want it to end, never want to leave this moment. It is everything I have dreamed of, everything I have longed for. Sam is here with me, and he is mine. His hands slowly caress the sides of my face, his thumb brushing over my cheek in a gentle motion that sends shivers down my spine.

"I love you, Aimee," he murmurs against my lips, his words so soft and filled with sincerity. "I'm not going anywhere. Not ever."

I can hear the depth of his conviction in his voice, and it makes me feel more secure, more cherished than I have ever felt in my life.

My heart is still racing, the emotions swirling around me like a storm I didn't want to escape from. I lean my forehead against his, closing my eyes as I let the feeling wash over me. For the first time in so long, I feel at peace, like everything in the world is right. The fears, the anxieties – they were still there, but in that moment, they didn't matter. All that mattered was Sam, and the way he made me feel. "Sam, I –" My voice cracks slightly as I try to find the words to explain everything I was feeling. "I've never felt like this before. I don't even know how to tell you how much this means to me."

He smiles softly, his hands still gently holding me as if afraid I might disappear. "You don't have to say anything, Aimee. I already know. Just... be with me. That's all I need."

His words are simple, yet they carry a weight of reassurance that I need more than anything. And in that moment, with his arms around me, his lips still pressed against mine, I know that no matter what happens, we would face it together. I don't need to fight this battle on my own anymore. Sam is here, and we are stronger together.

The week has felt like it's lasted a lifetime. Every day has been a blur of uncertainty, with Sebastian's whereabouts hanging over my head like a dark cloud. The paranoia creeps in every moment, gnawing at me when I try to focus on anything else. I can't shake the feeling that something is wrong, that something is happening just outside my reach. But there's a strange sense of comfort in knowing that Sam's been by my side through all of it. As the days go on, he and I have become inseparable in a way I never expected. Our bond has only grown stronger, and I can't help but feel like everything that's happening right now, as chaotic as it is, has brought us closer.

The night we both said our "I love yous" was unlike anything I could have imagined. It was like everything clicked into place, and all the fear and anxiety melted away for just a little while. I had never felt so certain about something, about someone. Yes, it's so soon. No one can deny that. The world keeps reminding me of that. But, despite what anyone else might think or say, I feel like this situation has turned out to be a blessing in disguise. It's as though I was thrown into this mess to see who would step up and face it with me. Sam stepped up. He's been right here, the entire time.

Sitting here in Sam's living room, I still can't help but feel a bit overwhelmed by everything. We've both been through so much in such a short time, and I wonder if things would have progressed so quickly if life hadn't thrown us into this whirlwind. But here we are, and I wouldn't change a thing. Sam is sitting across from me, his eyes focused on mine, as always, and there's this familiar warmth between us that has become my safe place.

"So, about the party tomorrow," I say, breaking the silence. "Are you happy for me to go?" I can see the concern in his eyes. He's worried about me being in a situation where I'm surrounded by people I don't know, and I get it. The uncertainty of everything has him on edge, but I can't let that hold me back. I can't let this situation define me. I need to live.

I look at him for a moment before adding, "Yeah, I want to go. I know it's not ideal, but I can't just hide away forever." The truth is, I'm nervous. The idea of being around so many unfamiliar faces makes my stomach churn. But I know Sam's right – it's about my safety. He's not trying to control me. He's looking out for me, and I appreciate it more than he knows.

"As long as you can promise to keep me updated," he says, his voice serious now. "If you feel at any point it's too much, please call me."

I can tell that this is important to him, to make sure I'm okay no matter what. I give him a soft smile, my heart swelling with gratitude. He's been my rock through all this, and I can't help but feel lucky to have him.

"I will," I promise him, nodding. I mean it. I know he worries, and I don't want him to feel like I'm putting myself in danger just to prove a point. I've seen how much he cares, how deeply he's been affected by all of this, and it's hard not to feel touched by it. "I won't do anything to make you worry more."

Still, my nerves are gnawing at me. The idea of going to a party with a bunch of strangers isn't something I'm used to, especially with everything that's been going on in my life. It's like I've stepped into someone else's life, and I'm just trying to make sense of it all. But Sam's insistence on looking out for me, on making sure I stay connected to him, is enough to ease some of my fear.

Later the next evening, as I start to get ready for the party, I can feel the tension in my chest. I take a deep breath and try to calm myself. Sam's been quietly watching me as I apply my makeup, and I catch his gaze in the mirror. It's like he's not just looking at my face, but at something deeper. His eyes soften when they meet mine, and I can see the pride in them, as if he's proud of me for going through with it, even though he's worried.

I finish applying my makeup slowly, carefully. The soft glow of foundation, the delicate swipe of mascara, the boldness of red lipstick. It's my bit of armour, something to make me feel stronger, more confident. But even as I do it, I can feel Sam's eyes on me, making my movements seem more purposeful, as if I'm not just getting ready for a party, but for something bigger.

"You look amazing," Sam says, his voice quiet but full of admiration.

I glance at him through the mirror, offering him a smile. It's strange, how even in these simple moments, his presence can make me feel like everything is just right. I never thought I'd feel so at home with someone, especially with everything that's happened.

"Thanks," I say, my voice soft. "I'm nervous, but I think I'm ready." There's a flutter in my stomach, the kind that comes before something unknown, something exciting. I take one last look at myself in the mirror before turning to face him. "Are you sure it's okay?" I ask, needing the reassurance. I want to make sure he knows that I'm not just doing this for myself, but for us. I want him to know that I'm willing to take the step forward, even if it scares me.

Sam steps closer, his hand brushing against mine. "It's okay, Aimee. You're going to be fine," he says, his voice steady, like a promise. He leans in, pressing a gentle kiss to my forehead, and I feel a wave of calm wash over me. In this moment, everything feels right. Despite all the uncertainty, despite the worries, we're here together.

As I finish getting ready, I feel a bit more grounded. The nerves haven't fully disappeared, but I know I have Sam's support. He's right there, steady and calm, and in a world that's anything but, that's all I really need. The party still feels like a leap into the unknown, but with Sam by my side – whether physically or in spirit – I'm ready to take it. Whatever happens, we'll face it together.

We head out into the night and the sun is beginning to set in Boston, I have been given the address of the party by Sophie and I plan to meet her there, The conversation in the car seems to be flowing nicely between me and Sam.

"You excited?" he asks me.

I turn to my left and look at his face; he holds his right hand out for me.

"I am yeah, my belly is going crazy for some reason."

He smiles. "It will be because you have been cooped up for a few weeks, human interaction is scary once you have been out of the game for a while, babe, you will be fine," he tells me in a comforting tone.

"What time are you coming for me again?" I ask him.

"I was thinking 10 – 10.30? It's 7pm now so that gives you some time to enjoy yourself."

I feel the motion of his hand rubbing mine as we glide though Boston traffic, my cheeks' heat and those butterflies are fluttering in my stomach again.

As we arrive outside the house where the party is taking place, already grown men and women are falling flat on their faces on the grass outside. Like a typical frat party. Sam narrows his vision to every person, it's like he is scanning their features for him to remember them, like a photographic memory. I can tell he is nervous and I know he would wait outside if he could. I wouldn't expect that from him – he needs his own relaxation time just as much as I do. I grab his hand in reassurance.

"I will be fine, okay?" I kiss him on the cheek as I see Sophie running outside with two cocktails which look like she made them, they look strong.

"Hey guys! How you doing this evening?" She shouts as she makes her way over the to the car.

"I'm good how are you?" Sam exclaims to her, being kind as ever.

"Good, I am ready to let off some steam with this one though," as she points to me.

I kiss him again in front of Sophie and walk in front of the car to take the drink from her. I feel somewhat awkward drinking it in front of Sam, I feel like I'm rubbing this in his face. As we turn our backs to him, he is still scanning the faces of everyone here. I turn around and give him a wave, to signal I am okay and he can leave. He smiles and slowly puts the car into the correct gear, the tyres grip onto the gravel on the road and the traction noises appear. *Off he goes, you got this.*

The party is in full swing when Sophie and I enter, the atmosphere alive with laughter, music, and the clinking of glasses. It is everything I had imagined – loud, chaotic, and undeniably energetic. People are scattered around in groups, some in the kitchen chugging drinks for a dare, others huddled in corners playing drinking games, laughing as they tried to balance the growing chaos around them. It feels like a pressure cooker about to explode, and I can feel my heart rate picking up just from the noise. Despite my nerves, I try to relax and let myself blend into the crowd, but it isn't easy.

Sophie, as always, is the life of the party, moving through the space with ease, her infectious energy drawing people in. She is in her element, laughing, joking, and adding fuel to the fire of the night. Every now and then, I catch a glimpse of her disappearing into another room, phone in hand, texting or talking to someone – someone who isn't exactly at the party. It feels strange. I can't help but notice how she keeps slipping away, and it makes me wonder what is going on.

I try to push it from my mind. After all, we are here to have fun, right? But as I stand there, trying to engage in conversation with a few people, I start to feel the weight of the situation press down on me. The music is so loud that it is like the bass is reverberating in my chest, and the conversations around me become a blur. People kept bumping into me, spilling drinks in their haste to get somewhere. The clink of glass against the floor as someone drops their cup echo in the room, followed by a burst of laughter. I was losing track of everything, the room spinning as I try to steady myself. Maybe Sam was right – I wasn't ready for this kind of social interaction yet.

A guy approaches me, smiling a little too widely, his breath smelling faintly of alcohol. "Hey, you having fun?" he asks, his voice too close.

I shift uncomfortably, trying to take a step back, but it feels like my personal space is shrinking by the second. It is like they can sense my discomfort, and I don't know how to get out of it.

"You should play the next round of beer pong with us," he says, his words slurring together.

I am not sure how to respond, my palms suddenly sweaty. I try to smile, but it feels strained, forced.

The guy doesn't seem to take the hint. He leans in a little closer, and I can feel my heart race. I am starting to panic, the noise of the party pressing in on me from all sides. I don't know anyone well enough to feel comfortable in this crowd, and his attempts to invade my space were only making me feel more isolated. Where was Sophie? Why was she disappearing so often?

I take a deep breath, trying to calm myself down, but my skin is hot, my palms clammy. I could feel the anxiety rising in me. The party was supposed to be fun, a chance to loosen up, but instead, I feel trapped. The walls feel like they are closing in, and all I want is to get out of this room, to breathe. I scan the crowd for Sophie, but she is nowhere to be seen. It is as if she has just vanished, absorbed into the chaos.

A burst of laughter erupts from across the room, followed by the unmistakable sound of a scuffle. Two guys were pushing each other, their voices rising in anger over some silly game they had been playing. It isn't anything major – just a bit of testosterone-fuelled drama – but the tension in the room only adds to the feeling that I don't belong here. I step back from the crowd, trying to put a little distance between myself and the growing spectacle. Maybe I'll just sit in the corner for a while.

I grab a drink from the nearby table, the coldness of it helping to calm my nerves, but it doesn't do much. The more I stood there, the more I felt out of place, like I was just an observer in someone else's world. The music pulsed louder, the people grew rowdier, and I found myself retreating further and further into myself. Was I just overthinking it? Was this how things were supposed to feel at parties? Or was it just that I wasn't cut out for this kind of thing?

I feel my phone vibrate in my pocket, and I pull it out, hoping to find a message from Sam. His text is a simple one: "You okay?" It was enough to make my heart flutter. He always knew when something was off.

I smile, quickly typing back: "Not great, but I'll be fine. Just a little overwhelmed." I couldn't explain it to him in a message – not in the way I wanted to – but it feels good to know that someone cares enough to check in.

Just as I am about to lock my phone, Sophie reappears, her face flushed from the excitement of the party. She seems happy, but there is something about her that is different now. She seems distracted, her mind elsewhere. I don't have the energy to ask her what is going on, not when I am barely holding it together myself. Instead, I give her a small smile, hoping it will be enough to mask how unsettled I feel.

"What up with you?" she asks me.

"Nothing, Sophie, I think I'm gonna leave in thirty minutes, to be honest I feel pretty overwhelmed."

She tuts at me and her brows furrow; she looks different. My eyes are bulging at this point, due to the change in her demeanour.

As the loud music rattles my bones, I stand at the edge of the crowd in Sophie's friend's house. Everyone seems to know each other, laughing, chatting, and drinking. I, on the other hand, feel like an outsider. I'm dressed in a simple outfit – Converse, shorts, and a t-shirt, trying to fit in, but it feels forced. Sophie has already pulled me from room to room after our mini argument, introducing me to more strangers than I can count. I smile and give my name, but before I even have a chance to get comfortable, she's already tugging me away, eager to move on to the next group.

The music pulses, a thumping beat filling the house, and I try to focus on the rhythm, but it only amplifies my unease. I can hear "Roses – Imanbek, SAINt JHN remix" blasting from the speakers, the bass vibrating through the walls, but it doesn't help. I feel like I'm drowning in the noise. I glance around the room, hoping to spot Sophie, but she's nowhere to be seen. Instead, I stand alone, scanning faces I don't recognise, feeling more and more out of place. A knot forms in my stomach, a gnawing feeling of anxiety that only grows the longer I stay here. I can't shake the feeling that there's something off about the whole situation, like I'm being watched, like everyone here knows something I don't. It's suffocating. I can feel my pulse quickening, the overwhelming sense of being in the wrong place at the wrong time taking over. Should I have come here? Was this a mistake? I don't even know what I'm doing here anymore.

The party seems to be in full swing, but I can't handle the noise, the heat, the crowds. My gut tells me I need a break, so I excuse myself from the room, telling myself I'll just find a quiet space for a few minutes. I weave through the mass of people, hoping for a moment of peace, I check my back to see if anyone is following me until I finally find the bathroom at the back of the house. It's small and tucked away, offering the privacy I desperately crave. I close the door behind me, my heart still pounding as I pull my phone from my pocket.

I dial Sam's number quickly, feeling the need to hear his voice. Maybe if I just talk to him for a minute, I can calm down. Maybe I'll feel better. As the phone rings, I lean against the door then decide to look out the window, my breathing coming out in uneven gasps. The music outside is muffled now, and the silence in the bathroom feels too loud. But then, as if I'm being pulled out of the moment, I hear the sound of the door behind me creak open.

I freeze, expecting it to be Sophie, but when I glance at my phone's screen seeing Sam's number still dialling, my stomach drops. I don't know how, but there he is – Sebastian. *Fuck!* His figure looms in the reflection, a dark silhouette that I know all too well. My blood runs cold as a rush of panic washes over me. How the hell did he find me? What does he want? I feel my soul levitating from my body, *this can't be happening, no.*

Before I can fully comprehend what's happening, I spin around to face him, my instincts kicking in. But Sebastian is faster. His hand shoots out, grabbing my hair with an iron grip, and the next thing I know, he's slamming me into the mirror hanging on the wall. My breath is knocked out of me, and pain shoots through my skull as my head connects with the cold surface. I try to struggle, to push him off, but he's too strong, too forceful.

"You're not getting away this time, Aimee," he sneers, his voice low and dangerous and his face is so close to mine I can see the anger in his eyes. I can feel his breath on my face, smell the stale alcohol that clings to him. My body trembles, but I refuse to let the fear take over. I won't let him win. I've been running from this man for far too long, and I won't let him control me anymore.

I attempt to free myself from his grip, but it's useless. He pulls me closer, his hand tightening in my hair as he presses his body against mine.

"You thought you could escape me?" he spits, his eyes wild with fury.

I can barely breathe under his weight, the pain in my head making it hard to focus. But my thoughts race, my mind trying to grasp onto anything that can get me out of this. I can feel blood slowly running down my face. I need to run out of here, people will see that I'm hurt and get help.

My phone is still clutched in my hand, and in a moment of desperation, I manage to raise it just enough to press the emergency button. My thumb trembles as I dial Sam's number again. It's a long shot, but it's all I've got. If I can just get him here, I let the phone dial and slide it across the floor under the bath so Sebastian thinks I have lost it by accident, if I can just get someone to help, maybe I can escape this nightmare.

But Sebastian yanks the phone from underneath the bath, tossing it across the room with a laugh. "You think anyone's coming for you, Aimee?" he taunts. "No one's going to save you."

His words sting, but I refuse to let him see how much they hurt. I won't give him the satisfaction of knowing that he's getting to me. I feel dizzy now, my mind is giving up, my adrenaline is lacking, I feel weak as I need to be strong. I can't.

The door to the bathroom is still shut tight, and it feels like I'm trapped in this small, suffocating space with him. I try to kick my legs, to push him away, but it's like trying to move through quicksand. His grip on me is unyielding, and every time I try to break free, I only end up getting pulled in closer to him. I can't breathe. I can't think. All I can focus on is the fact that I need to get away, I need to escape before it's too late. The sound of the party outside, the laughter, the music – it all seems so far away, like I'm in a different world altogether. In this moment, all that matters is survival.

"Please," I manage to gasp, the word barely audible through the fear. "Please let me go."

But Sebastian's grip only tightens, his eyes narrowing in a cruel smile. "You belong to me, Aimee," he whispers, his voice low and venomous. "And you always will."

Tears well up in my eyes, but I refuse to let them fall. I've come too far to break now. Sam will be here. I have to hold on, I have to fight for my freedom, for my life. Because I know if I don't, I might never get out of this bathroom alive. My vision then goes black, the anxiety, the voices, they haven't helped me here, my brain has cut itself off from reality; I'm as good as dead.

I am no longer present. *Wake up* I hear a voice whisper in my head, I feel like I am in a nightmare, I feel movement, I am going somewhere. I hear Sophie's voice. *Thank God, she must have found me and scared Sebastian away.* My eyes flicker open and I am in an enclosed space, I try and stretch to allow the blood flow to the rest of my body to see if this wakes my lifeless corpse. *Denied.* I don't know how long I've been in this car, but the air feels thick, suffocating. The first thing I notice is that my hands are tied, tightly behind my back. I try to move, to push myself upright, but there's no room to escape, no way out. Panic surges through me. *What's happening?* My thoughts are a blur, a whirlpool of confusion and dread. I can hear voices, faint at first, distant, but as my senses sharpen, I realise it's Sophie. Her voice is soft, but I can't make out the words. Is this real? Is my mind playing tricks on me?

Tears begin to well in my eyes, and suddenly, I can't control them. They spill down my cheeks, hot and uncontrolled. My chest tightens with every sob, and my heart aches in a way I can't even describe. I think of Sam. *I want Sam. I need him.* I feel the weight of the world pressing down on me, suffocating me. I think about the girls – about my friends – and how far away everything seems now. I think of New York, the city that felt so vibrant and full of promise, but now, it feels like a lifetime ago. I want to go back to a time when everything was normal.

And then, my mind drifts to my mom. My throat tightens at the thought of her. "Please, if you're out there, please help me." I whisper the words inside my head, hoping somehow, somewhere, she can hear me. If she's somewhere in the afterlife, watching over me, I need her now more than ever. I need someone to help me. I need something – anything – that will make sense of all this. But no answer comes, just the endless sound of the car rumbling beneath me.

Suddenly, the texture of the road changes. The smooth pavement is gone, replaced by the uneven, jarring rhythm of cobblestones beneath the tyres. The sound of the car shifts as the wheels rattle against the stones, and I feel a sharp jolt in my body. My stomach flips, and the panic grows even stronger. *Where are we? What is going on? Why are we on cobblestones?* I try to calm myself, but the questions continue to swirl in my mind like an endless storm.

The car slows down, and with a sudden, jarring stop, everything falls still. I hear the engine turn off, the silence so heavy it almost suffocates me. *Where am I?* I whisper to myself, unable to shake the fear that's closing in around me. My heart beats so loudly in my chest I'm sure the whole world can hear it. Then, two sets of footsteps approach the car. I freeze, straining to hear every sound, every movement.

The boot of the car suddenly swings open with a loud creak, and light floods in. It blinds me instantly. My eyes squint against the intensity, but I can't cover them. My hands are still tied. The light is unbearable, cutting through the darkness of the car. I feel a chill of dread wash over me as a voice breaks through the silence.

"Hope the ride wasn't too bumpy for you," Sebastian says, his voice low and taunting.

My eyes are still adjusting, and I can't stop the involuntary scowl that forms on my face.

No. No, this can't be happening. I try to speak, to demand answers, but my voice is shaky, weak with fear. "Where have you brought me?" I ask, hoping he'll explain, hoping there's some sort of reason behind all of this.

But Sebastian just chuckles, his tone dripping with amusement. The sound makes my blood run cold. There's something off about this – something twisted that I can't quite grasp. I feel trapped, like a bird in a cage, with no way to escape.

Before I can protest, I feel strong hands grab me, yanking me out of the car. The sudden motion sends pain shooting through my body, and I cry out, kicking and struggling. *Why are they doing this?* My blood is boiling, my body moving on instinct, but the hands that grip me are unyielding. I feel them dragging me across uneven ground. My heart races as panic overtakes me. I can't see much – everything is a blur – but I hear the sound of footsteps pounding the ground. It's not just one person dragging me; there are two, and they're moving fast.

My head swings to the side, and I feel a sharp pain on the right side of my skull where I hit the bathroom mirror. It sends a wave of dizziness through me, and for a moment, I lose my bearings. I try to focus, but it's hard. My thoughts are scattered, and the pain in my head blurs everything. *Where are they taking me?* I try to focus on the sound of the footsteps, to get a sense of where I am, but all I can hear is the pounding of my heart in my ears. They pull me into what feels like a large, open space, and my legs stumble beneath me as they force me into a chair. My body feels weak, my muscles sore from the struggle. I try to make sense of my surroundings, but it's hard with the bright light still blinding me. My vision is fuzzy, and everything feels out of place, distorted. I feel like I'm trapped in some twisted nightmare. And then, as the light gradually adjusts, I see two figures move into my line of sight. My eyes are still struggling to adjust, the brightness searing into my retinas, but I see their shapes clearly now. *No.* The word escapes me before I can stop it. I shake my head in disbelief. *It can't be.* But it is. The person standing in front of me is Sophie. She's here, and yet, she doesn't look the way I remember. There's something off about her, something that sends a shiver down my spine.

"Sophie?" I manage to gasp, my voice barely a whisper, trembling with confusion and fear.

She doesn't answer at first, her eyes narrowed, distant, like she's not really there. The sight of her like this sends a jolt of panic through me. *Why? Why is she here?* The woman I thought I knew, the friend I trusted, is now standing in front of me, and yet something is horribly wrong. "No…" I whisper, shaking my head. "This isn't real. This isn't happening." I can't process it. I can't make sense of anything. The world around me feels like it's spinning out of control, and I have no idea what's going on or why I'm here, tied to a chair in the middle of some cold, abandoned warehouse. I feel like I'm suffocating, like I'm losing myself in the chaos.

Sophie takes a step closer, and I can see the faintest hint of a smirk on her face, but it doesn't reach her eyes. Those eyes are cold, distant. I try to speak, to plead with her, but the words don't come. All I can do is stare, helpless, as the nightmare unfolds around me.

"Hey hon." She has the audacity to wave in front of my bloodied skull and streaming eyes.

"What's going on, Sophie?" I can't help but look at Sebastian in my peripheral vision as he's walking in circles around me, like a predator circling its injured prey before it strikes and kills.

"Have you not put two and two together yet, sweetie?" She glares at me. If my hands weren't tied I would crack her one.

"Well you two obviously know each other."

A guttural chuckle comes from them both, I stare at the floor and before I know it a slap to my face sends blood shooting from my nose. I cry in pain.

"You should have thought twice about hurting my boyfriend, Aimee."

What? Boyfriend? Why the fuck is she helping him kidnap his ex? "Boyfriend? You serious? Him?" I feel the blood rushing to my head, I am so fucking confused.

She walks over to Sebastian and he grabs her as they begin to kiss each other and a part of me retches. "I think we need to explain it for her, babe, she's not getting it."

Sebastian then comes into my vision. " Sophie is the woman who I cheated on you with, Aimee, I was more than happy to forget you, but then, then you left to go to Boston, you fell right into her hands and well, she didn't know who you were – but the words you and your manager were having got out. That was when she called me and I had to come and see you! For old times' sake," he laughs out, gesturing at the craziness of this whole situation.

"You text me in New York, you wanted to try again," I shout to him.

Sophie laughs in a menacing way – she is loving this,

Sebastian then follows. "Nah, I was just seeing if I could get something from you, you then declined. I then spoke to your aunt one day and when she told me you were moving to Boston, where my girlfriend is, I came by to warn you not to mention what happened with us to her; however, the night I went to your apartment it was empty, your things were gone. But when I told Sophie about us she wasn't bothered."

"It was you who broke into my apartment, you asshole."

I feel his hand slap me on the face, the sting, and I hear the ringing in my ears again. I cough, I feel cold. "Why are you both doing this if you are so happy?" I ask them both. I must look a right state. I don't get an answer from them, they must be psychotic, deliberately trying to damage my mental health; more than likely wanting to ruin what I have with Sam.

Sam

Three hours. It's been three fucking hours, and Aimee hasn't answered any of my calls or texts. Not one. Something isn't right, and I can feel it in my bones. I'm pacing my apartment now, the floor creaking beneath my feet as I walk in tight circles. My heart is pounding like it's trying to escape my chest, and every time I try to calm myself, I just feel the anxiety growing. I reach for my phone again, dialling her number without thinking. The phone rings, and rings, and rings… then straight to voicemail. *Fuck.*

I drop the phone onto the couch and run my hands through my hair, breathing heavily. I try to rationalise it. Maybe she's busy. Maybe she just stepped away. But deep down, I know it's not that simple. This isn't like her. She always responds. *Always.* She's reliable, she's grounded, and she wouldn't just vanish for hours on end without a word. I feel this gnawing sensation in my gut, this instinct telling me that something is terribly wrong.

Without thinking, I grab my phone again and call Josh. I'm practically pleading when he picks up. "Hey, Josh, I need your help." I try to keep my voice steady, but it cracks a little, betraying the worry inside me. I'm not sure what's happening, but I can't shake this feeling that Aimee is in trouble.

"Go for it," Josh says casually, the sound of him moving around in the background. I can tell he's not taking me seriously.

"Aimee isn't responding to my calls or texts, Josh. Something doesn't feel right." I can hear the desperation creeping into my voice now. I try to keep my tone even, but I can't help it. I need him to understand. "She's always been reliable. This… this isn't like her."

Josh scoffs, almost like he's dismissing me, and the words that come next make my blood boil. "Do you not think she's just out having a good time?" He sounds almost condescending, like I'm overreacting. "She's probably just with friends, man."

"This isn't like her!" I snap, my voice coming out harsher than I intended. "Something's wrong, damn it! I'm coming to get you, and we're going to the party to see if she's okay."

Josh hesitates for a moment, like he's weighing it all in his head. Then, in that nonchalant tone of his, he says, "Dude, you sure? She might think you're checking up on her."

"Grab your fucking coat," I growl, "I'll be there in ten minutes. We're going."

I hang up before he can say anything else, and in that moment, the weight of the situation hits me harder than before. My chest tightens as I grab my jacket, the cold air of the apartment not even registering. I don't waste time; I'm already out the door and into the car, speeding down the road like a madman. Every light that turns red feels like a betrayal, like time is slipping away, and I don't have enough of it. As I drive, I try calling Aimee again. The phone rings once, twice, three times... then goes straight to voicemail. The pit in my stomach deepens. Something's not right. I can feel it, and the longer this drags on, the harder it is to ignore. I pull up to Josh's place and practically jump out of the car. My legs feel like they're moving on autopilot as I pound on his door, my mind still spinning with worry.

Josh answers, looking a bit confused at my sudden appearance. "Dude, what's up?" he asks.

"I'm not fucking around, Josh," I say, trying to keep my voice calm despite the panic rising in me. "We're going to the party. Aimee's not okay. I know it."

Josh raises an eyebrow but doesn't argue. He grabs his coat and slings it over his shoulder, still looking like he doesn't really get why I'm freaking out. "Alright, man. Let's go."

We get in the car, and I don't waste any time. I slam the door shut, start the engine, and peel out of the driveway. My mind races again, and I can feel the adrenaline pumping through my veins. Josh starts talking, but I can barely hear him over the roar of the engine and the pounding of my own heartbeat.

"You've really fallen for her, huh?" Josh says, his voice almost too casual. He's watching me as I drive, like he's trying to gauge my reaction. "I can see it, man. You're really into her."

I shoot him a quick glance, my grip tightening on the steering wheel. "Shut up, Josh," I mutter, my voice edged with frustration. The last thing I need right now is him psychoanalysing me. I'm not thinking about that. I'm thinking about Aimee. I need to focus. She's out there, and I have no idea where.

Josh presses on, though. "I'm just saying, man. You've got it bad. And if she's out having fun, maybe–"

"Shut. Up," I snap again, louder this time. My patience is wearing thin, and his words aren't helping. "We need to find her, Josh. I'm not leaving this to chance. Something is wrong, and I'm not sitting around doing nothing."

We fight a little more in the car, but eventually, Josh quietens down. The drive to the party feels like it takes forever, but eventually, I pull up outside. The house is alive with the kind of chaos I'm all too familiar with – music blaring, laughter echoing, people spilling out onto the lawn. I don't even think about it. I throw open the car door and march straight for the entrance. Inside, the noise hits me like a wall. I can barely hear myself think over the bass of the music, the laughter, the shouting. I push my way through the crowd, moving quickly, my eyes scanning the sea of faces for any sign of Aimee. But there's no sign. I start asking people, showing them her photo, trying to get any kind of answer. "Have you seen her?" I ask, desperate now. My voice rises above the noise. "She has brown hair and wearing black converse. Have you seen her?"

Most people just look at me like I'm crazy. Some laugh it off, some shake their heads, some just ignore me entirely. I feel like I'm losing it, like the walls are closing in. I move faster, pushing through the throng of bodies, desperation clawing at my throat. Then, finally, a voice – drunk, slurred, and barely audible – cuts through the noise. "Oh, yeah. That blonde chick? She was with some guy, man. They put a brown haired girl in a car like two hours ago. We thought they were just taking her home."

Two hours ago? My heart stops for a second. It feels like someone has punched me in the gut. I stumble forward, almost in shock. "What guy?" I demand, grabbing the drunk guy by the collar and yanking him toward me. I slam him against the wall, my grip tight, my face inches from his. "Where did they take her?" I can feel my blood boiling now, the anger and fear mixing into something wild, something dangerous.

The guy stumbles for words, his eyes wide with panic. "I – I don't know, man. I swear! They were just leaving… they said they were taking her home. That's all I know. I swear."

I tighten my grip on his collar, my voice low and threatening. "Where. Did. They. Take. Her?" I feel sorry for the poor guy. No, really, he has not got a clue what's going on. As Josh grabs the neck of my shirt and tries to pull me off him as he's very close to being thrust into the other room. All I can hear is Josh yelling, it's muffled though; and the brickwork slowly falling to the floor. Crumbling. *Where is she?* I keep wracking my brain to figure out where they have taken her.

"This is getting us nowhere, Sam, let him go!" Josh exclaims, shouting in my right ear.

I thrust my fist into the wall and turn around. Faces are glaring back at me like I have committed a murder, no music is playing, people staring and looking at me as if I am crazy. I can't even remember when the music was turned off, I am struggling to breathe, I look down at my hands, blood. I have cuts on my hands from where my hand connected with the wall, these remind me of Aimee's hands, *what if she's hurt?* The voice in my head is saying to me, my heart thrashing in its cage. This hurts.

Josh drags me outside. "Let's go before the police are called, huh?" As we walk down the stairs of the house to the car, I feel him shove my right shoulder. "What the hell was that all about, Sam? In all the years we have known each other, I have never seen that."

I am panting and tears are forming. "Something isn't right, Josh, she has been taken somewhere, why can't you see this?" I'm now a man on my knees, my knees are on the grass as I repeatedly punch the ground, hoping it opens up and swallows me whole.

"Let's just think about this, Sam, okay?" Josh tries to calm me down; it doesn't work.

I need to remain focused on Aimee, on finding her, finding her alive. I compose myself by getting into my car, Josh follows. As I slam my door shut, I fall back into my seat, rubbing my eyes, the torment is devouring me.

"Where the fuck have they taken her, Josh?" I say to him, hoping he has the answer, which I know deep down he doesn't.

"How do you know anyone has taken her anywhere? She could have left on her own accord, she's been cooped up for weeks, Sam, she is more than likely in a bar or something."

I hiss as he finishes his sentence. I glare at him, the whites of my eyes seeping through him. "Did you not hear what that guy said? He said two people put her in a car, Josh," my hands tightening around the steering wheel, reliving the memory.

He lets out a deep sigh. "So what do you want us to do then? Boston is a huge city, we don't know where she could have been taken."

My head falls into my hands, *why couldn't I have brought someone more useful and less of a pessimistic brute?*

Twenty minutes have flown by, we have contacted the police, driven around the neighbourhood for what feels like five hundred times, no luck still, no lightbulb moment where I can figure out where she is. The police are useless, told me I had to wait twenty-four hours before I could file a missing person's report – in twenty-four hours he could kill her for all I know, I have no idea what that son of a bitch is capable of.

"Does she not have any friends nearby?" Josh asks.

That's it. I remember I don't have Sacha's number, but I do know someone who does have it, her aunt. This is a shot in the dark; however, I need to try something. "Put the name of the bridal shop in your phone and call the number, her manager still might be at work."

As Josh taps the keys on his phone, he looks and me as I hear a dialling tone. "Hello, thank you for calling Boutique Brides, how can I help today?"

A life force runs through me, I need to take advantage of this. "Fiona, is that you?" I shout.

"Who is this please?" she sounds back, being as professional as ever.

"Fiona, it's Sam, Aimee's boyfriend," I let out with a deep ache in my chest.

"Oh yes, dear, are you okay? Has Aimee left something here?" she asks inquisitively.

"Fiona, something's happened!" I exclaim as we both go silent, I can't bring myself to tell her and to say the words but Josh is signalling for me to hurry up and to get straight to the point. "Aimee went to a party with Sophie, and her ex showed up. Apparently, Sophie was helping him put her in the back of a car. I don't know what to do but I need you to give me Sacha's number. Just in case she knows where they would have taken her."

I hear sobs on the other end of the phone. "Sam are you being serious?" she asks me.

I bite my lip at the thought she thinks I would joke about something like that. "I'm being serious, Fiona, she came to this party and she's been taken, she not answering her phone. Sophie has gone too."

I hear her breathing start to slowly increase; *something's wrong.* "Fiona?" I ask, the air around me suddenly feels suffocating, it's sucking the air out of my lungs.

A couple more excruciating moments later, she begins to speak: "I don't know how to tell you this, Sam, I don't know if it's connected or not."

Josh has a concerned look on his face, I know the fear with him is starting to set in.

"Sophie handed her notice in today, that's why I'm here working late. I thought Aimee knew? I was going to have a meeting about it on Monday with her."

The puzzle starts to fit into place – "Did you not want to tell Aimee this today?" I ask her, all of this now pointing to her involvement in this. "Sam, you don't understand, I came in to check a few things and her resignation was on my desk, I haven't actually spoken to her about it."

I am at a loss at what to do, the police won't help me, Fiona knows very little about this whole situation. Josh is, well. Just Josh, he just continues to look at me with this bewildered look on his face.

"We need to go and look for her," I shout.

"Sam, dude; Boston is a huge place, she could be anywhere."

I then hear Fiona on the other end of my mobile – "Sam you need to be careful, the police will do all they can."

"Fiona, how can you say that? She's missing."

Before I can say anything else her phone disconnects.

"We need to go back to the party and ask if anyone knew where they were taking her," I tell Josh, before he even opens his mouth. I am pulling away from the kerb and heading back to the party. Though the drive there is only around twenty-five minutes, it feels like days. I try to keep calling Aimee but voicemail kicks in after one ring – this has not happened before. "Someone is declining those calls, Josh, someone is with her and knows we are trying to call her."

His lips thin as I realise the seriousness of the situation is sinking into his reality. We are passing through Main Street of Boston, people are everywhere, going about their own business, I would normally love to see that sight of my hometown, but people acting normal when Aimee is not safe is very alien to me, it's odd. How dare the human race go on as normal; when my girl is somewhere she shouldn't be.

Aimee

I am a wreck. I am bound to a chair that is thin wood, I can feel every crevasse of my body that sits on it. My face is numb from being smacked, I'm cold, wet from the dampness. I want to give up, my life was going well, had everything – then he shows up; rips it all from me like taking candy from a child. So because he isn't happy – I don't get to be either. I have been here hours, I still don't know what they want. They keep me here like a caged animal, I am scared, my mind is in total disarray. *Is anyone looking for me?* I can smell the dampness in the air, the air is cold, harsh and bitter; it makes me wince every time the wind blows. This place has windows; half of them are broken. I don't know the city very well so I can't determine where I am. My mind is spiralling out of control, not in a good way; I need to be sharp, focused and in control, but I'm not. There's brickwork scattered across the floor, my life somewhat feels like this, crumbling, disturbed; however, some parts of the building are still standing – I need to find the strength to do the same. I close my eyes and try and collect my thoughts together; *you got this,* I hear in my head. I breathe, look around and I can't see anyone. I have no idea where they have gone, there is no clock in here, not that time is moving in this vacuum for me. I manoeuvre my wrists to see how tightly the ropes are wrapped, I don't have a lot of room, but if I find something sharp I can try and do something with that, maybe?

I hear a car coming into the building but it's behind me, I can't rotate my head a whole 180 degrees. My heart begins to beat out of my chest again, the anxiety is setting in again, *come on, not now – you need to be sharp, you need to get out of here.* The lights on the car reflect on the windows, I hear the car doors open and footsteps, something's strange though – I only hear one set. It's him. This is it, has he brought me here to die?

His menacing chuckles wreak havoc in my ears as he circles me like a great white circling its prey. "Well, well, well, Aimee, I never thought we would be together like this again; did you?" His blue eyes piercing through me, so much so that I'm scared to look back into them. They are empty, hollow like a demon possessed.

I try to gather all my confidence of what is left in my shell of my body, but nothing arises. "What do you want, Sebastian?" I murmur, scared of his response.

"Good question actually, it all stems back from New York – seems like so long ago, doesn't it?"

I can tell by his gaze that he is mocking me, I stare right back at him. "Just get to the point, please and let me go," I scream.

A guttural laugh escapes him, he thinks this is a joke, this is the Sebastian I ran away from that night, he's a psychopath, like a spectre from the depths of hell, he shows no remorse for what he has done and how he treated me in the past. "You see, Aimee, we were together a good few years, but there was something that I always wanted from you, even when you were moping around after your mother."

I see red after that cruel statement – how dare he use my mom in his sick motive. "What is the real reason, Sebastian? You have a girlfriend, your life is pretty much made in New York, what is it you want?" I ask, shaking. These ropes are beginning to cut my wrists as I begin to thrash around to try and escape, the adrenaline coursing through my veins, then I remember my hands still have wounds that haven't healed.

He bends over so his face is practically touching mine. "I want you, Aimee, like I told you in New York – you know, before you rejected me."

I feel an overwhelming feeling of courage, I don't know what it is – maybe it's my mom speaking through me, she always knew what Sebastian was like, she never agreed with me and him from the word go, another thing I should have paid attention to. *I wish she was here.* She would have protected me.

"Where does Sophie fit into this?" I ask him. I sit back into my seat scared of the answer he is about to give me, my breathing starts to hitch.

"Sophie… now that is a good question, Aimee, and I am glad you asked! Sophie is the woman who I was seeing behind your back, when you were grieving and wallowing in self-pity, I met her in a bar in New York and we hit it off straight away; however, I can never control her like I could with you."

As the tears roll down my face, I thrash so hard the chair falls over as my body crashes on the floor. Parts of the chair break, in pieces. This is it, my escape. I wriggle on the floor with all my might, kicking repeatedly as he comes after me to lift me up, the leg breaks and I manage to get one leg free, I glance to my left and see the back of the chair, I manage to pick this up with my hands which were made free once the chair was in pieces on the floor, already bruised and cut from the episode a week or so ago. He grabs me and lifts me by the scruff of my neck; I gasp for air, I pull a large piece of wood from behind my back and strike him with it, once, twice and a third time.

As we both scuffle, fists are flying as mine are now bleeding, the wounds Sam tended to have now come apart, the first layer of skin is ruptured and bleeds. I am too in shock to pay attention, too angry, too hurt to give a damn what I do to this man and the years he has stolen from me, the lying, deceit and most importantly the time I have wasted and the time I will never get back. He grabs a fistful of my hair and pulls so hard that I feel some strands tear from my scalp, as I scream and go full for blows with him, he struggles but still has some fight left in him. I now face him as I am straddled over him, I look to his right and spot a pile of old bricks, I reach for one with all my might. He knows what I'm about to do, his eyes follow my movement, I can see the whites of his eyes move and watch my direction. I close my eyes and clench the brick between my hands, the same hands that have struggled, the same hands that held my mom's coffin walk her down the aisle, the same hands that have witnessed his domestic abuse for so long. *It's time,* the voice in my head says. I lift the brick so high into the air I am nearly standing above him, totally free – I'm about to be. As I shriek, I repeatedly strike his torso with it, wanting to cause damage, he wanted to re avenge me for rejecting his advances, this is mine.

"How the tables have turned, Sebastian, huh?" One strike to the head and he's as good as dead. I cry, he's not moving. My hands are quivering as I stare at them and then his lifeless body comes into focus. I decide not to waste any more time, I need to get out of here. I need to find my phone. I check his pockets…nothing. I then stumble to the car limping and there it is on the passenger seat. I grab it and the pain as I do this is excruciating, I barely have the grip to call Sam, but I just about manage. Scared of Sebastian moving I decide to lock myself in the car.

I hit the call button uncontrollably sobbing, is he alive? Have I just committed a crime? There's only one way to find out.

Sam

"I can't believe you are making us look through these abandoned places, Sam, I don't know what you are expecting to find," Josh huffs in my right ear, and the phone rings throughout the car. It's Aimee's phone. When I saw her name flash on my screen, I nearly dropped the phone. I was halfway through tearing apart another empty building, every muscle in my body wound tight.

"Aimee?" I answer on the first ring, heart stuttering in my chest. "Aimee, is that you? Where are you? Are you okay?"

Her voice comes through – shaky, breathless, cracked with panic. "Sam – oh my God – I got out. I fought him. I – I'm in his car, I locked the doors. He's still out there... I think I hurt him. I think I really hurt him."

I stop dead in my tracks, the flashlight trembling in my hand. "Okay, okay. Breathe, babe. You're safe for now. Just breathe for me. You did so good. Just tell me where you are – I need to come get you."

There is a pause, like she is trying to ground herself. Then: "Some kind of warehouse... edge of the docks, I think. There's a broken sign that says 'Crawford Shipping'. It's rusted. The car's parked behind one of the buildings."

I turn on my heel and run, fast. I knew exactly where she was – used to do drop-offs near Crawford back in the day. I throw the flashlight to the ground and jumped into my car, engine roaring to life. "I know it. I'm not far – ten minutes tops. Just hang on. Don't open that door for anything, you hear me? I'm coming."

Her next words gutted me. "I thought I wasn't going to make it, Sam. He was going to kill me. I saw it in his eyes. I thought – I thought I'd never see you again."

My hands clench the wheel until my knuckles turn white. "Don't say that. You're here. You're talking to me. You made it out, Aimee. You're the bravest damn person I know." My throat tightens. "I swear to God, if he touched you–"

"He did," she whispers. Her voice is small, but steady. "He grabbed me, slammed me against the wall. But I fought back. I found a pile of bricks, and I... I hit him. A lot."

Rage burns through my chest like fire, but I swallow it down. "That's my girl. You did what you had to do. You're alive. That's what matters. I'm so damn proud of you." The truck tears down the dark road, my foot heavy on the gas. Every second feels like a year. Then I hear her gasp. A noise on her end – scraping metal, maybe. My heart stops. "Sam – I think he's up. Or someone is. I heard something." Her voice is barely a whisper.

I fight to keep my voice calm. "Don't panic. I'm almost there. Keep low. Don't make a sound. He's not getting near you again. I swear it."

"I'm scared," she says, and I can hear the tears in her throat. "I'm trying to be strong, but I – I need you, Sam. Please. Just get here."

"I'm coming, Aimee," I say, every word a promise carved into steel. "You hold on, alright? I'm not losing you. Not tonight. Not ever."

The second I turn onto the dock road and see the rusted "Crawford Shipping" sign hanging by one bent chain, I kill the headlights. The place is barely lit, shadows crawling across the broken concrete. My eyes scan everything – every movement, every flicker. And then I see it: the black sedan tucked behind a warehouse. Her silhouette in the driver's seat. Motionless. I pull up slow, parking a good distance back so I don't draw attention. Heart hammering, I slip the pistol from the glovebox – not because I wanted to use it, but because if Sebastian laid one more hand on her, there wouldn't be a second chance.

"Dude, are you serious?" Josh asks me.

"Self-defence" I whisper.

"Aimee," I whisper into the phone. "I see you. I'm here."

She gasps. "Sam? Oh my God, I see you – don't come out in the open. I don't know where he is. He was bleeding, but – he just disappeared. Like he vanished."

I crouch low, moving around the side of the warehouse, eyes darting. The air is thick with salt and fear. Every creak of metal sounds like a gunshot. I make it to the passenger side of the car and tap twice, the signal we used back when things were simpler. She flinches at first, then unlocks the door. Her face – God, her face. Bruised, tear-streaked, but alive. Alive. I slip in and immediately and pull her into my arms. She collapses into me like a wave breaking, fingers gripping my jacket, shaking. "I've got you," I whisper into her hair. "You're safe now. I swear to you, he's never touching you again."

"I didn't know if I'd ever feel you again," she cries, voice muffling against my chest. "I was so scared, Sam. I didn't want to die in that place."

"You didn't," I say firmly, pulling back just enough to look into her eyes. "You fought your way out. You did that. I'm just here to take you home."

Suddenly, a metallic clang rings out behind the car. We both freeze. I reach for my weapon instinctively, gently pushing her down in the seat. "Stay down." A shadow moves near the back wall, stumbling. I step out of the car, silent, steady. "Sebastian!" I call into the dark. "It's over. She's not yours to take. Never was."

He staggers into view, clutching at his ribs, blood dark on his shirt. He laughs – a wet, broken sound. "She came to me, you know. In the end, they always come to me."

"You're done," I say, raising the gun. "Get on the ground. Or I'll put you there."

He takes a step forward – I see another shadow behind him, "Aimee, who did he have with him?"

She's crying uncontrollably, I want to comfort her, I'm the one thing that's protecting her right now, life and death situation. "Sophie was with him, but I haven't seen her for a while."

As soon as she finishes the sentence a sense of dread overcomes me, *what if we are outnumbered?* I keep the gun on him, forgetting about the shadow for a moment, I need to take care of this prick first. Out of nowhere, I see a leg of a chair smash across his calves, he falls to the floor and he knocks himself out. I see who it is. "Josh?" I shout into the darkness.

"Sam, you owe me a brunch date after this evening, dude." I chuckle at his comment but in total realisation of the pain Aimee is in. I pull her close to me; she has passed out. I put my hand over her mouth – she's still breathing. "Let's get her to the ER, we need to call the police."

Josh sprints towards me to help with Aimee but I shove him aside. I have let her down, it's the least I can do. I'm overjoyed to have her back,

I carry her in my arms; her hands are worse than they were before. As we head to the car my alertness is piqued, I feel eyes on me but we are at the car. "Open the car door, Josh."

He rushes to be of assistance, as we both get her into the back of the car, I can hear mumbling from her, but to be honest, we just want to get out of here. "Thank you so much for this," I say to Josh, my gratitude holds no bounds for him.

The car is silent except for the low hum of the engine and Aimee's uneven breathing on the back seat. My hands grip the wheel tighter than they should've, knuckles white as I stare down the dark road. Every pothole, every flicker of passing light scrapes at my nerves. She is behind me, alive, but I can't stop looking over every few seconds just to make sure she is still there.

Josh was sat in the back, quiet. I catch his reflection in the rearview mirror – eyes glazed, jaw clenched, like he was replaying the whole thing in his head. Hell, I was too. Sebastian's voice still echoes in my ears. That sick smile. The way Aimee trembled when she was trapped in that car. I could feel the rage still burning low in my chest, but it was buried under something else now. Fear. Guilt. Relief. All tangled together. Aimee was passed out the entire journey to the ER, then she was holding the blanket Josh had wrapped around her like it was the only thing keeping her together. There were bruises on her wrists, a small cut near her temple, and probably more we couldn't see. She was hurting. And I couldn't fix it with words.

"You okay back there?" I ask, voice low, eyes still on the road.

Josh doesn't answer right away. When he finally does, his voice is flat. "Yeah. Just… trying to process. Didn't expect to be part of the takedown squad tonight."

I give a small, humourless chuckle. "You did good, man. You saved us both. I owe you big."

He doesn't respond, but I see him nod in the mirror. That is enough for now. I glance at Aimee. Her lips are parted slightly like she wants to say something but can't figure out how. Her hand moves from the blanket to the space between us, resting on the centre console. I reach over and take it. She doesn't pull away.

"I'm sorry," she whispers. Her voice is raw. "I didn't want to drag you into this. Either of you."

I shook my head, gripping her hand tighter. "You didn't drag us anywhere. He did. And we got you out. That's what matters."

Her eyes meet mine, just for a second, and I could see everything she wasn't saying. The fear. The anger. The exhaustion. But also something else – something like hope, trying to claw its way back in. "We'll get you looked at," I say, more to reassure myself than her. "Hospital's ten minutes out. They'll check you over, patch you up. And then we go home. All of us."

No one says anything after that. But Aimee leans her head on the other seat in my car, and Josh leans back in his seat like the weight of the night is finally catching up with him. The road stretches out ahead, empty and quiet. For the first time in what felt like forever... we were heading somewhere safe.

Josh, and Aimee arrive at the hospital. It's quiet, emotional, and heavy with that in-between feeling – relief that she's alive, and the weight of everything she's just been through.

The ER's automatic doors slide open with a soft hiss as I pull the car to a stop under the overhang. Harsh white lights spill over the cracked pavement, and even though we are finally somewhere safe, my pulse doesn't slow. I cut the engine and look over at Aimee. She hasn't said a word since she leaned her head against the seat in the car. Her eyes are glassy, far away. I didn't want to let go of her, but I had to. Josh is already out of the backseat by the time I open my door. He looked just as wired as I felt – his clothes rumpled, hands twitchy, like his body was still waiting for the next threat. We don't speak. We don't need to. He opens the door for Aimee while I come around the other side to help her out.

Aimee moves slowly, like her limbs don't quite belong to her. She holds onto my arm as I guide her inside, her fingers digging into the fabric of my jacket like it was the only thing anchoring her. I could feel the tremble in her grip, and it made something twist deep in my gut. This wasn't just physical. Sebastian had tried to steal her spirit, too. But she was still here. Still standing. As soon as we step into the lobby, the nurses move fast. One of them – short, sharp-eyed, probably in her forties – comes right over with a wheelchair and a clipboard. "She's with you?" she asks, and I nod. "Name?"

"Aimee Rourke," I say. "She's been through–" I stop, suddenly unsure how much to say in front of her. She squeezes my hand once, as if to tell me she doesn't want me to protect her from the truth. I clear my throat. "She was held against her will. Injured. We need someone to check her over. Immediately."

The nurse's expression doesn't change, but her voice softens. "We'll take good care of her." She gestures toward the wheelchair, and Aimee sits without a word. She still hasn't let go of my hand. The nurse notices. "You can come with her. One person only."

I turn to Josh. "Stay close. I'll be right back."

He gives a nod, eyes scanning the room like he still wasn't convinced we were in the clear. I knew the feeling. It was hard to switch off survival mode when the threat had been so real.

As the nurse wheels Aimee through the triage hallway, I walk beside them, matching her slow, shaky breaths with my own. She hasn't spoken since we entered the building, but every now and then her fingers would tighten around mine, like she needed to make sure I was still there. I wasn't going anywhere. They bring her into a small exam room – curtains, buzzing fluorescent lights, that sharp antiseptic smell. Another nurse comes in with gauze and gloves, asking gentle questions Aimee barely answers. I stand there, feeling useless and raw, watching them patch her up, wishing I could trade places with her for even a second.

When the nurse steps out to get a doctor, Aimee finally looks at me. Her voice is barely above a whisper. "You really came for me."

I lean in, brushing her hair gently away from her face. "Of course I did," I say. "Always."

The fluorescent lights in the hospital hallway buzz, giving everything an artificial, sterile feel. I have to pull myself away from Aimee's side, even though it feels wrong. I tell her I'd be back soon, that she needs to rest, but my mind is already racing ahead, ticking off everything I still have to do.

Josh walks beside me in silence. The weight of what has just happened is still pressing down on both of us. I can tell from the tightness in his jaw and the way he keeps his hands shoved deep into his jacket pockets. Neither of us knows what to say, so we don't say anything at all. The beeping of heart monitors and distant voices fades into a dull hum as we pass a row of rooms. We reach the hospital's small café at the end of the hall. It is quieter than I expected, with only a couple of people slumped over their cups, lost in their own worlds. I glance at Josh. "You want anything?"

Josh runs a hand through his hair, eyes blank. "Coffee. Strong."

I nod and walk up to the counter, getting two cups – black, no sugar – and hand one to Josh when I return. He takes it without looking at me, then takes a slow sip. Neither of us speak again for a moment. The bitter warmth of the coffee helps clear my head, but it doesn't stop the gnawing feeling in my gut.

I stare down at my cup for a second, feeling the weight of everything crashing back in. Aimee. Sebastian. The warehouse.

"I'm calling the police," I say finally, breaking the silence. "We need to get them over to that warehouse. Sebastian's not just going to disappear. They need to know everything."

Josh's eyes lift, his face taut, like he is still reeling from all of it. "Yeah. He's not gone. He's still dangerous." He takes another long sip of his coffee, he looks like he is trying to centre himself. "You think they'll believe us? After everything?"

"I don't care if they believe us," I say, my voice sharper than I meant. "They need to know what's happened. The sooner, the better. I'm done pretending this is just some sick game." I take out my phone and diall, the ringing steady and almost too loud in the quiet café.

The operator picks up on the third ring. "911, what's your emergency?"

I give her the details, trying to sound calm while my chest feels like it is about to burst. "We have information about a kidnapping. The suspect is named Sebastian... and he's still at a warehouse near the docks. We need you to send units there immediately. He's armed, and he's not alone."

"Can I ask what your name is, sir?" the operator asks.

"My name is Sam Thorne."

Josh looks up when I say Sebastian's name. His eyes are locked on mine – sharply, questioningly. I give him a nod. This was it. No more hiding, no more guessing if we were just being paranoid. We weren't. The operator asks me for details. Where had we last seen Sebastian? What did he do? Did I believe he posed an immediate threat? Yes. Yes to all of it. I keep my voice steady as I rattle off the information, but inside, my stomach is churning.

"He knows where we are. He's already shown he's willing to hurt people. Aimee's only here because of him," I say, my voice cracking a little toward the end.

I close my eyes and take a breath. I couldn't lose it now. Josh reaches across the table and puts a hand on my arm. It's a small gesture, but grounding. I open my eyes and give him a faint nod.

This wasn't just about Aimee anymore. This was about all of us getting out of this intact.

The operator says someone would follow up soon. That they'd notify local authorities. That if we feel unsafe, we should go somewhere secure. I hang up, but I don't feel any safer. I feel like I'd just lit a fuse on something I couldn't see the end of. I set my phone down gently and stare into the dark swirl of my coffee. Josh doesn't say anything, just waits. I finally speak. "They're going to do something. At least, they said they would."

He nods, quiet. "You done the right thing." His voice is steady, but there is a tension in it. He is scared too – just better at hiding it.

I look toward the hallway again, where Aimee had disappeared ten minutes ago. "If something happens to her…" I trail off. The thought alone makes my chest ache. Aimee has been through enough. We all have.

Josh follows my gaze. "She's strong. She's got this." He doesn't sound completely convinced, but he is trying. That is more than I can manage right now.

I run a hand through my hair and lean back in the chair. My leg bounces restlessly under the table. Everything feels like it is teetering – like we are standing on the edge of something sharp and uncertain. We sit like that for a while. The sounds of the hospital around us – beeping monitors, footsteps, distant conversations – feel like white noise. I want to run. I want to fight. I want to make this all stop.

But instead, I wait. Wait for the nurse to come back. Wait for the police to call. Wait for the next thing Sebastian might do. And through it all, I hold onto one fragile hope: that we still have a chance to put things right. Before it is too late. The hallway smells like antiseptic and something faintly metallic – maybe blood, maybe just my own nerves playing tricks on me. I stand up too quickly when the nurse calls my name, and the chair behind me scrapes loudly against the floor. Josh looks up but doesn't say anything. I just nod and follow her.

I hate the way she walks. Not because she's done anything wrong, but because she walks too slowly, too carefully. Like she's preparing me for something I'm not going to like. I already don't like it. Her voice is soft, but it's clinical. Practised.

"We've finished examining Aimee. She's stable, but we want to keep her under observation for a while."

I nod, but my brain's lagging behind. Stable is good, right? That should be good. We stop in front of a room. She doesn't open the door yet – just looks at me with a kind of cautious sympathy that makes my stomach twist. "There are some things we need to go over before you see her," she says.

I want to push past her. I want to see Aimee. But something in her eyes stops me. So I nod again and try to keep my breathing even. "She's got a fractured rib on her right side," the nurse begins. "There's bruising across her abdomen and back, some of it consistent with blunt force trauma. She's lucky nothing was ruptured."

Blunt force trauma. The words hit harder than I expect. I grip the edge of the wall just to steady myself, but I don't say anything. I let her keep talking, even though every sentence feels like a punch to the gut.

"There's also a mild concussion. We're monitoring for signs of increased intracranial pressure, but so far, she's responsive. Disoriented, but responsive."

I blink a few times. The lights in the hallway feel too bright now. I didn't realise I'd been holding my breath until my chest starts to ache. "Did she say what happened?"

The nurse hesitates. "She hasn't given a full statement yet, and we're not pushing. But she did mention someone named Sebastian." She watches my face carefully. "Is that the man you called 911 about?"

I nod. "Yeah. That's him." I don't elaborate. I can't – not now. There's too much to say, and none of it feels real when I try to form the words.

She softens a bit at that. "Then you did the right thing. Reporting it, I mean. She's safe now."

Safe. It's such a simple word. It shouldn't sound like a question in my head. I want to believe it. God, I need to believe it. But I've seen what Sebastian is capable of. Safety isn't a room. It's distance. It's time. And we don't have enough of either.

The nurse finally opens the door, but doesn't step inside. "You can see her now. Just… be gentle. She's awake, but she's scared. And she's in pain."

I nod and step into the room. It's quiet – too quiet. Aimee's lying there, hooked up to monitors, her face pale and drawn, but her eyes are open. They meet mine the second I walk in, and for a moment, everything else fades out.

I want to say something strong. Reassuring. I want to tell her it's over, that she's safe now, that I've got her and I'm not going anywhere. But all that comes out is her name, barely a whisper. "Aimee."

She gives me the faintest smile, like she's using every bit of energy just to do it. "Hey, Sam." Her voice is hoarse. Cracked around the edges. But she's alive. She's here. And suddenly, I can breathe again. Not because everything's okay. It's not. But because for now – just for this second – she's still with us. And that's enough. I step closer to her bed, my heart thudding like it's trying to tear out of my chest. I lean down and press my lips gently to her forehead. Her skin is warm, and for the first time in hours, I let the tears fall.

I don't bother to wipe them away. There's no point pretending. I thought I was going to lose her. I thought I was too late. And now, she's here – broken maybe, bruised definitely – but alive. "God, Aimee," I whisper. My voice cracks in the middle of her name. "You scared the hell out of me."

She closes her eyes for a moment, and I can see her swallow hard. "I'm sorry," she murmurs, barely audible. "I didn't think he'd go that far." Her voice is hoarse, brittle, like it hurts to speak.

I pull a chair close to the side of her bed and sit, still holding her hand. It feels too small in mine. Fragile. I squeeze it gently. "How are you feeling? Are you in pain?" I ask, even though I already know the answer.

She nods, just once. "Hurts to breathe," she says, then tries to smile through it. "But I'm still here."

That weak smile nearly breaks me all over again. How the hell does she still have that kind of strength? I shake my head, brushing a strand of hair from her face. "What happened?" My voice is quieter now, more careful. "You don't have to tell me everything right now, but... please, Aimee. I need to know what he did."

She shifts slightly, wincing. "He showed up at the house. I went to the bathroom as I felt strange, like someone was watching me, I pulled out my phone to call you but then I saw his face in the reflection of the mobile phone, but I didn't have time to run." Her hand trembles in mine. "He grabbed me. Threw me against the mirror. Said if I screamed, he'd..." Her voice trails off, her breath hitching. She doesn't finish the sentence, and I don't ask her to.

I can feel the rage boiling in my chest, but I force it down. She doesn't need my anger right now. She needs comfort. Stability. "You don't have to say more," I tell her gently. "I'm so sorry I wasn't there."

Aimee turns her head slightly, meeting my eyes again. "You got me out. That's what matters." Her words are quiet, but there's something unshakable in them. "You didn't give up on me."

I nod, blinking back another wave of tears. "Never. I'd burn the whole damn world to keep you safe." And I mean it. Every word. I lift her hand to my lips, kiss her knuckles softly, and swear to myself that Sebastian won't ever touch her – or any of us – again.

"I wonder what happened to Sophie," she exclaims, and it jars my mind – I totally forgot about her.

"I wouldn't worry, the police have been called, they should be on their way to the warehouse now to arrest him."

Aimee

Everything hurts. That's the first thing I register as I drift awake – an ache that spreads through my body like fire licking at my ribs and shoulders. I try not to move, not yet. I keep my eyes closed and listen to the steady beeping beside me. I know that sound. Hospital. I'm not dead. That surprises me. For a moment, I thought maybe I was. Every time I close my eyes I see myself in that chair of the warehouse, strapped down, cold and trapped. I open my eyes slowly, blinking against the harsh ceiling lights. My head throbs, and it takes a second for everything to come into focus. There's a dull hum around me – machines, footsteps in the hallway, someone breathing close by. I turn my head, just enough to see who's beside me, and the movement sends a sharp, raw pain through my side. I hiss quietly, biting down on the groan that tries to escape. Then I see him. Sam. Sitting there, eyes tired, his hand wrapped gently around mine like he's been holding it forever. "Hey," I whisper, my voice cracked and dry. It barely comes out, but he hears it. He looks up instantly, like the word reached deeper than it should have.

His face shifts – relief, pain, something too big for either of us to name. He leans forward and kisses my forehead, and I feel something wet hit my skin. Tears. Sam's crying. Sam never cries. "You scared the hell out of me," he says, his voice thick and trembling. I've never heard him sound like that. So undone. So human. I try to smile, but it feels crooked.

"I scared myself," I say, and the memory starts to return – flashes of Sebastian's face, the weight of his hand, the floor against my back. My stomach clenches. "I thought... I thought he was going to kill me."

Sam shakes his head, squeezing my hand tighter. "You're safe now," he says. "I've got you."

Tears well up in my eyes before I can stop them. I turn my face away, trying to breathe through it. The pain surges again, sharp and unforgiving in my ribs. "It hurts," I whisper. "Everything hurts."

"I know," he says softly. "You've got a fractured rib. Bruises. A concussion. But you're here, Aimee. That's what matters."

I let out a shaky breath. "He came out of nowhere. but I – I didn't think he'd really…" I stop. It's too much. Saying it out loud makes it feel real again.

"You don't have to explain," Sam says quickly. "Not now. Not ever if you don't want to."

"No," I whisper, forcing myself to continue. "I need to. I need to say it." I turn back to him, meeting his eyes. "He grabbed me. Threw me. I hit the mirror in the bathroom and then the floor. And then I just… I woke up at the warehouse."

His jaw clenches. I can see the guilt in his face, the rage sitting just under the surface. "I'm so sorry," he says. "I should've been there sooner."

I shake my head. "You came. That's all that matters. I heard your voice. I think I passed out, but I remember hearing you say my name."

Sam leans in closer, like he's afraid I'll disappear again. "I'd never stop looking for you, Aimee. I don't care what it takes."

I can barely speak past the knot in my throat. "Thank you," I whisper. It doesn't feel like enough. How do you thank someone for saving your life? I close my eyes, breathing through the ache, the fear, the weight of everything. But for the first time in what feels like forever, I'm not alone. Sam's hand is still in mine, and I know – deep in my bones – that he means it. I'm safe. I'm alive. And that has to be enough for now.

I glance at the clock and it is 5.45am, I arrived at the party for 7.30 last night, I think, from what my brain will allow me to relive. The guys must be shattered; I know the way I'm feeling I could sleep for a week. The pain in my ribs is a constant feeling that I have sharp knives, twisting and turning into my skin. I can't put into words the feeling of admiration I have for Sam, I rack my brain and ask how I met someone so wonderfully selfless.

Sam's hand is still wrapped around mine, and I hold onto that like it's the only thing tethering me to reality, feeling like if I let go I will float away into some sort of oblivion. The pain is still there, sharp and simmering beneath the surface, but I can feel the medication starting to take the edge off. My body is heavy, worn down from everything – what it's endured, what it's survived. I blink slowly, and the light in the room softens around the edges. My grip on consciousness loosens with it. Sam murmurs something I don't quite catch, but I feel the shape of his voice in my chest. Safe. That's all I need to feel.

I don't mean to fall asleep. I want to stay awake, to stay here with him. But my body doesn't give me a choice. The weight of exhaustion is too much. My eyes close, and the room slips away. The last thing I feel is Sam's thumb brushing over the back of my hand, steady and gentle. Like a lullaby I don't want to forget.

When the dream begins, it doesn't start like a nightmare. It's soft. Warm. I'm back in the woods behind my childhood home, where the trees always seemed taller than anything in the world. The sunlight filters through the branches in golden stripes, and the air smells like summer – like pine, dirt, and something sweet I can't quite name. I walk barefoot through the grass, and for a moment, I feel light. Untouched. But the dream shifts. As I walk deeper into the trees, the sunlight fades. The warmth drains from the air, replaced by a slow, creeping cold that sinks into my skin. The trees start to close in – branches that once felt welcoming now look like claws. I start to hear footsteps behind me. Quiet. Precise. I don't turn around. I already know who it is. I try to run, but the ground turns to mud beneath my feet. Every step is slower, heavier. My legs won't move fast enough. I can hear breathing now – ragged and angry. I don't need to see his face. I feel Sebastian in the air itself, like smoke, like poison. He doesn't speak. He never needs to. His silence is louder than any scream.

I break into a clearing and find myself standing in front of a house that looks like my old one – but the windows are shattered, the door swinging open on broken hinges. Inside, everything is wrecked. Torn photographs. Furniture turned over. I see a picture of me and Sam, burnt around the edges, the flame eating away at our faces. I scream, but no sound comes out. My voice is gone. Just like it was that night – when fear stole it from me, when pain pushed it down. The dream has me trapped in a loop. I relive it over and over. The impact. The fall. The helplessness. His shadow always right behind me, just out of reach but never far enough away. Then something shifts again. The air trembles. The light changes. A door creaks open in the ruined house, and suddenly, there's a figure standing in the doorway. Not Sebastian. Not fear. It's Sam. He looks different here – taller, stronger, lit from behind by something golden. He doesn't speak either, but his presence is loud in its own way. Steady. Safe.

He steps toward me, and with each step he takes, the house begins to repair itself. The broken windows knit back together. The flames extinguish. The torn photographs on the floor lift into the air and heal, piece by piece. His hand reaches for mine, and when I take it, the mud beneath my feet vanishes. I can breathe again. In this dream version of Sam, his eyes still hold everything I saw in the hospital – grief, love, fire – but here, he isn't crying. Here, he's a shield. He wraps me in his arms, and suddenly, the world goes quiet. I don't hear the breathing behind me anymore. I don't feel the shadow. It's just him. Just peace.

We sit down together on the forest floor, and the grass starts to bloom beneath us – wildflowers and soft moss wrapping around our legs like nature itself wants to hold us. I rest my head on his shoulder and close my eyes within the dream. I don't want to leave. I know this isn't real, but it's the first time I've felt okay in what feels like forever. But even in this safe place, something inside me trembles. There's still healing to do. The wounds Sebastian left aren't just on the outside. They're stitched into the fabric of my thoughts, my fears. Even here, I feel them. But Sam's dream-voice finally speaks, so soft I barely hear it. "You don't have to carry it alone." When I hear those words, I start to cry. Not the kind of crying that rips you apart. The kind that washes something clean. My hands shake, and I feel warmth on my cheeks again. I'm not sure if I'm still in the dream or if I've woken up. Maybe it's both.

I stir slightly in the hospital bed, not fully awake but not fully asleep either. My body shifts, and I feel the pull of the IV, the weight of the blanket. My eyes flutter open, and I see Sam still there – still holding my hand, his head resting against the bed now. He hasn't moved. He stayed. A single tear escapes down my cheek. This one is real. And this time, I know exactly why it's falling. Because even in a world where darkness feels relentless, someone came for me. Held me through the storm. And right now, as I drift back into sleep, I carry that with me – not as a dream, but as truth.

Sam

I don't want to leave her. Not even for a second. Aimee's face is softer now, her breathing a little steadier. She's deep in sleep, probably still riding the tail end of the painkillers. I sit there, just watching her, memorising the way her fingers twitch ever so slightly in mine. There's a kind of peace in the moment, but it's fragile – like the surface of still water before a storm hits.

The nurse pokes her head into the room, voice low and professional. "Mr Thorne, there are two officers in the main reception asking for you." Her eyes flick to Aimee. "They didn't want to disturb her. They said it wasn't urgent, but it sounded important."

I nod, the weight of those words sitting heavily on my shoulders. Important, but not urgent. That's how they always say it. What they mean is: We need you to relive it. Again. I glance down at Aimee once more and squeeze her hand gently before I let go. It feels wrong, like I'm unplugging from something keeping me sane.

The hallway feels colder now. I step out and close the door quietly behind me. For a moment, I just stand there, staring at the white tiles and the endless neutral tones of the hospital corridor. I'm not ready for this conversation. Not after what I just saw in that room. But I know I can't delay it.

Instead of heading straight to reception, I duck down the corridor to the hospital canteen. I need a breath. A minute. A second to recalibrate before I say her name to strangers in badges and take the story of what happened and reduce it to bullet points and statements. I need Josh. The canteen is half-empty. A woman in scrubs sips coffee at a corner table. A teenage boy stares blankly at a vending machine. I make my way to the back where the noise is thinnest and pull out my phone, scrolling to Josh's name. I hit call and press the phone to my ear, my leg bouncing anxiously under the table. He picks up fast.

"Sam? What's happening? How's Aimee?" His voice is tight, alert. He's been waiting by his phone like I have; I gathered Josh had left to go home after I went into the room to see her. Can't blame him really as we have been out for nearly more than twelve hours.

"She's stable. She's sleeping now," I say quietly. My voice sounds tired to me, like it's dragging a hundred pounds behind every word.

"She was in rough shape, man." Josh swears under his breath on the other end. I hear rustling, like he's grabbing his coat. "Do you need me to come back down?"

I laugh, "No buddy, honestly it's fine, just look after yourself please, until I speak to the police we don't know where he is or if he's even alive.

"The cops are here. They want to talk. I don't know how much I should say without Aimee being there to confirm it, but... it's starting. Everything we were afraid of. It's happening now." There's a pause. I know Josh is thinking through all the implications, just like I am. We've tiptoed around Sebastian's name for weeks, always hoping it wouldn't come to this. But it has. And there's no turning back.

"I'll be there in ten. I have been with you throughout all this so they will want to speak to me as well," Josh says. "Just... don't face them alone, alright? Say what you need to say, but don't let them twist it. You're not the one at fault here."

"I know," I say, but I don't feel it. I still feel like I failed. Like the minute Aimee hit that floor and I wasn't there, I failed her. No matter what anyone says, that's not a feeling that fades. I hang up and sit there for another minute, staring at the old coffee machine across the room. There's a crack in the plastic cover, right over the button that says "Latte". Something about that detail sticks in my head. Nothing's ever untouched. Not people. Not places. Not cheap hospital machines.

When I finally get up, I stretch my shoulders and head toward reception. I can see the two officers standing off to the side, talking quietly. One's older, mid-40s, the other young, fresh out of the academy if I had to guess. The older one's got a notepad out already. That doesn't help my nerves.

They both look up as I approach. "Mr Thorne?" the older one says. His tone is neutral but not unfriendly. "We're with the city department. We got your 911 report regarding a man named Sebastian Hale. We'd like to take a statement from you."

I nod. "Yeah, I can talk. But Aimee – she's the victim. She's resting right now. She'll talk when she can." My voice has more steel than I expected. It surprises even me. I guess being near her, seeing what she's survived, gave me that.

They ask if there's somewhere private we can speak, and I motion toward a small seating alcove down the hall. We walk together, but I feel alone. Every step I take away from her room feels like walking into something colder. But I do it anyway. For her. Because someone has to. As I sit down across from them, I take a deep breath and glance toward the hallway that leads back to Aimee's room. She's resting, dreaming maybe. Healing. And here I am, about to lay everything bare. I owe her that. I owe her the truth – no matter how ugly it is.

283

So I start. "All of this began a few weeks ago, Aimee is from New York originally and has just moved here. Sebastian is her ex and he trespassed on her apartment in New York – luckily she was here; although, once he found out where she was he bought a ticket here to do god knows what. She went to a party with a friend; however, they knew each other and were in cahoots all the time – he assaulted her and took her to the warehouses near the dock and luckily she escaped. You need to find him before he finishes what he started."

The officers don't interrupt me much as I talk. They take notes, ask for specifics – times, places, any texts or photos we might've saved. I do my best to recall it all: the first time Sebastian parked across from Aimee's apartment Sacha sent the footage over to us, and he was just sat there with the engine running, the voicemail she got at 2:13 am with nothing but silence. The way she'd started flinching at shadows, locking the door three times before bed. The younger officer scribbles fast. The older one just watches me carefully, as if weighing my every word for inconsistencies. I don't blame him. It's his job. But it makes my skin crawl. This isn't a script I'm reading from. This is my life. Her life. And it's unravelling right here in a hallway that smells like floor polish and too much waiting.

Then I hear the elevator ding. I turn toward it without even thinking, and there's Josh – walking with purpose, eyes scanning until they land on me. Relief rushes through me like a warm tide. He came. Of course he did.

"Sam," he says, breath slightly short as he reaches us. He gives the officers a nod, polite but wary. "I'm Josh Cartwright. I'm a close friend. I was there during some of the earlier incidents, if you need another statement."

The older officer gestures to the seat beside me. "You're welcome to sit in. We've just started reviewing the timeline. Anything you can add would be helpful."

Josh sits, and I feel a little less alone. A little more anchored. We go over it all again, and I hate that it sounds like a story now – neatly broken into parts, like chapters in a book. The threats. The visits. And we thought maybe it was a coincidence until he texted her that night. Josh takes over when I start losing my voice, filling in details I didn't even remember – how Aimee didn't sleep for three days after that.

At one point, the younger cop asks, "Did she ever file a restraining order?" I feel the heat rise in my chest, but I keep my voice even. "She was going to. However, the tricky thing was that we didn't know where he was, her best friend called to tell us about her apartment, and then a couple of days later the Boston PD had tracked a purchase to a ticket to Boston; she was scared, okay? Sebastian's not some random guy on the street. He knows her. He knows how to manipulate her, when to disappear, when to push. He made her feel like reporting him would make it worse."

Josh leans forward. "And he's smart. Not legally, but tactically. He never leaves enough proof. Just enough pressure. Like he's hunting. And now..." His voice drops. "Now she's in a hospital bed."

The officers share a look. The older one finally puts his pen down and folds his hands. "We take stalking and assault seriously. Especially when there's a pattern. But we'll need her formal statement when she's awake enough to give one. That said... based on what you've told us, we have enough to begin looking for him. If you hear from him – anything at all – you call us. Immediately."

I nod, jaw tight. "You haven't been to the warehouse to look for him?" I don't mean to sound bitter, but I do. I am bitter. We called. We warned. We waited. And now we're picking up the pieces of Aimee's body and mind because no one listened fast enough.

The officers stand. They thank us and walk off toward the administrative wing, leaving silence in their wake. I sit back against the hard plastic of the chair and exhale like I've been holding my breath for the past hour.

Josh runs his hand through his hair. "Jesus, Sam..." He looks over at me, and there's something raw in his eyes. "She's lucky we got there when we did."

I don't answer. The truth is, I don't feel like a hero. I feel like someone who showed up too late and is now trying to play catch-up with a man who's always been three steps ahead.

"I don't know what comes next," I admit quietly. "What if he runs? What if he hides? Or worse – what if he tries again?"

Josh leans forward, elbows on his knees. "Then we stay alert. We stick together. And we make damn sure he doesn't get that close again." His voice is low, firm. "He's not going to touch her. Not now. Not ever."

I nod slowly, but the unease doesn't leave me. Not entirely. I feel like the clock is still ticking, like we've delayed something but haven't stopped it. Aimee might be safe today, but tomorrow? Next week? I don't know. And that unknown is eating at me.

I stand up suddenly, my body restless. "I need to check on her. I just – can't sit here anymore."

Josh follows without question. We walk back through the halls in silence. My mind is full, loud with thoughts I can't silence. But beneath all of that, there's a single thread pulling me forward. Her. When I open the door and see her still sleeping, her chest rising and falling in a steady rhythm, something settles in me. Just for a second. She's alive. She's safe. And whatever happens next – we face it together.

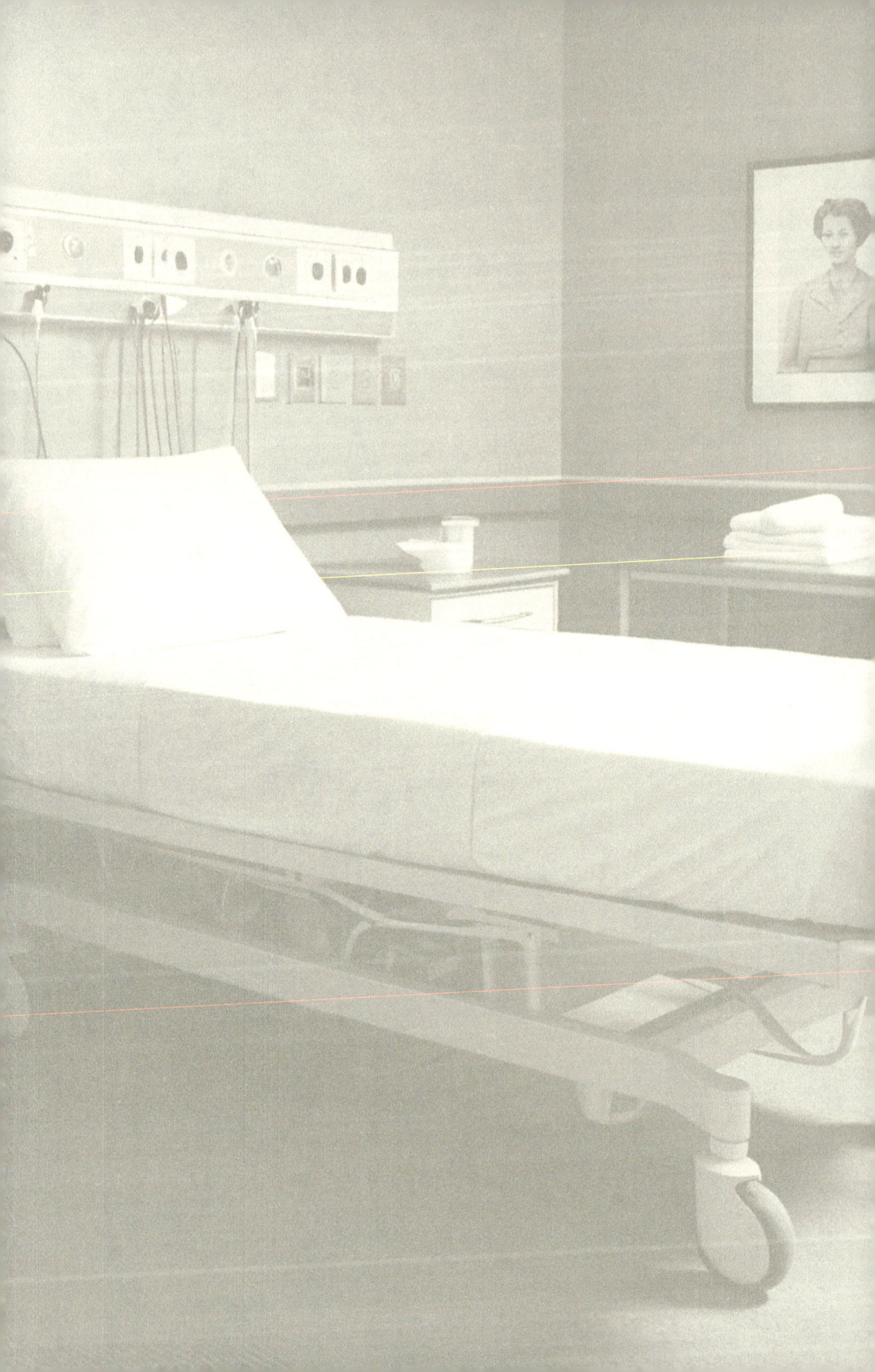

Aimee

The first thing I notice is the sunlight. It's gentler today, slanting in through the blinds in long, golden strips. It feels warmer than the last two mornings, softer. Or maybe I feel softer. Less like a fracture. Less like I'm about to break open again.

I blink up at the ceiling, letting the quiet sink in. The hospital is never truly silent – there's always a beep, a cart being wheeled, a low voice down the hallway – but right now, this room feels like a bubble. Safe. Calm. I exhale slowly and feel the weight of sleep still wrapped around my limbs, but I'm stronger than I was yesterday. I feel stronger. When I turn my head, he's there – of course he's there. Sam's curled awkwardly in the visitor's chair, one arm thrown over his chest, the other hanging down with his fingers just brushing the side of my bed. Like he fell asleep holding me and didn't want to let go, even after I drifted.

"Sam," I say, my voice raspy but clearer than it's been in days. It comes out more like a breath, but his eyes snap open instantly. That familiar green/brown meets mine, and something in his face softens in relief.

"You're awake," he breathes, sitting up fast and reaching for my hand. "God, Aimee – how do you feel?" He looks exhausted but hopeful, like he's been holding himself together with string.

"Sore," I admit. "Tired. But... awake." I squeeze his fingers. "You're still here."

"Every day," he nods, brushing his thumb over the back of my hand. "Wasn't going to be anywhere else." There's a pause, a weight in the space between us. "The police are here. They're waiting to take your statement – but only if you're up for it."

I inhale slowly. I've been expecting this. Dreading it, maybe. But I know it has to happen." I nod, voice quiet. "Okay. Let's do it."

289

Sam steps out to let the nurses know, and within minutes, two officers walk in. One I recognise from the day I was brought in – older, calm, with kind eyes. The other is younger, clipboard in hand, polite but focused. Sam sits beside me again, silent support as they begin.

"Miss Rourke," the older officer begins, giving me a reassuring nod, "first, we're glad to see you're awake and healing. We understand this isn't easy. We'll take our time, and you can stop whenever you need."

I sit up a little straighter, even though it pulls at my side. "I can do this," I say, and I mean it. My voice shakes, but I won't let that stop me.

"Can you walk us through what happened that night?" the younger one asks gently, pen poised over paper. "In your own words."

I nod, swallowing. "He knocked first," I begin. "I went to a party in downtown with a woman I work with…Sophie – she disappeared so I walked to the bathroom to call Sam as I felt like I was being watched. Before I knew it I pulled out my phone and Sebastian was in the reflection. There was a struggle, he smashed me into the mirror and I must have been knocked out because I woke up in the warehouse."

The words start slow, but once they come, they don't stop. I tell them about how he pushed the door open, how his eyes weren't angry at first – just cold. Controlled. That was worse, in a way. It wasn't a rage. It was planned. "He grabbed my arm. Threw me down," I say, staring at my blanket. "I hit the edge of the cabinet, then the floor. He didn't even flinch. Just stood over me. I tried to scream, but he told me if I did, he'd finish it. I believed him." Sam's hand tightens around mine. I can feel his jaw tense even though he's silent. I don't look at him – I can't. Not while I'm trying to hold it together.

"Did he say anything else?" the older officer asks gently. "Anything that might help us track him down?"

I shake my head. "Not really. Just that no one was coming. That he'd been watching. That he knew when Sam wasn't around." I finally glance at Sam then. "He knew our patterns. He waited for the right moment."

The officers exchange a look, and the younger one writes something quickly. The older one speaks again. "We've issued a warrant. We're coordinating with units across state lines. Based on your testimony – and Sam's – we've got what we need to pursue charges."

A weight lifts off my chest. Not completely, but enough. It doesn't undo what happened, but it's a step. A start. "Good," I whisper. "He doesn't get to disappear again."

They thank me. Leave quietly. I watch the door close behind them and lean my head back against the pillows, heart thudding. Sam doesn't speak at first. He just sits with me in the quiet. I don't need words from him – not yet. Just this.

My phone buzzes on the tray next to me. I reach for it and find a message from the girls: "We're on our way, babe. Two more sleeps. Hold on. We love you." I smile, a little broken, a little whole. They're coming. Sam's here. And for the first time in a long time, I believe I'm going to be okay.

THE DAY AFTER...

the doctor smiles when he walks in this morning. It's the kind of smile that doesn't feel rehearsed. Warm. Confident. "You've made remarkable progress, Aimee," he says, flipping through my chart. "We'll be discharging you tomorrow. Just a few final checks today, but everything looks good."

I don't know what I expected to feel when I heard those words. Relief? Maybe. Joy? Definitely not. What I feel is something heavier – like I've been hiding under a blanket and someone's just yanked it off. The real world is out there, waiting. And I have to step into it again.

Sam is already in the room, sitting by the window with a coffee that smells stronger than it has any right to be. He looks up when the doctor leaves, his eyes immediately coming to rest on me. "Tomorrow, huh?" he says softly, almost like he's testing how I'll react.

I nod, picking at the edge of the blanket. "Yeah. Tomorrow." The word feels big in my mouth. Like it belongs to someone braver.

The nurse comes in with a walker. "Let's try standing today," she says gently. "You've been off the IV for twelve hours. We'll take it slow, just around the room, okay?"

I stare at the metal frame like it's some kind of cruel joke. It looks bulky and awkward, nothing like the person I used to be – who ran five miles on Sundays and danced barefoot in kitchens. But I nod. "Okay." My voice is steadier than I expect. Sam is already on his feet, standing close but not too close. He knows me well enough to understand I need to do this on my own, but that he better not be more than an arm's reach away. When I swing my legs over the side of the bed, the floor feels further away than it used to. My body is stiff, sore, but responsive. The nurse steadies the walker in front of me and I push myself up. My legs tremble. My arms ache. But I'm standing. That alone feels like a miracle.

Sam smiles – just a little – but his eyes are glassy. Like he's holding something in. I take a shaky breath, grip the walker, and take one step. Then another. Each one burns, but I don't stop. Around the bed. To the window. Back again. The room spins slightly, but I stay upright.

When I collapse back into the bed, the nurse is beaming. "You're stronger than you think," she says, and leaves me with a glass of water and a wink. I stare at the ceiling, heart pounding, and for the first time in days – I feel proud.

Sam sits down beside me again. "You did it." His voice is so quiet, like he doesn't want to jinx anything. "You really did."

"I hated every second of it," I say honestly, then smirk a little. "But yeah. I did."

My phone buzzes again. A message from Hope this time:

"We land tomorrow night. Get the wine ready, cripple."

I laugh, and it hurts, but I welcome the sting. I text back a middle-finger emoji and type, "I'll be the one drinking tea and wearing a back brace, but sure – wine." It feels normal. The first normal moment in too long.

The rest of the day is slow. I nap. Sam reads next to me. We talk about nothing and everything. He brings me a sandwich from the café downstairs and sneaks me a cookie the nurse definitely wouldn't approve of. I savour it like it's a delicacy. Because today, everything tastes a little better. Before bed, I take one more walk around the room. This time with less help. My legs still shake. My back still aches. But I'm upright. I'm moving. I'm not broken.

That night, I don't dream about Sebastian. I don't see his face or feel his hands or hear his threats. I dream about a beach. One I've never seen before. Endless water. Soft wind. Sam is there, and the girls are laughing in the background. I wake up smiling, the ghost of sand still warm in my mind. Morning comes fast. A new nurse wheels in the discharge papers and the clothes Sam brought from my apartment. My heart thuds as I look at them – jeans, a t-shirt, and a hoodie I stole from Sam's closet weeks ago. I touch the fabric like it might fall apart in my hands.

Getting dressed is a slow process, but I do it. Button by button, inch by inch, I put myself back together. I even pull my hair into a loose braid, shaky fingers catching on tangles. When I look in the mirror, I still see the bruises, still feel the ache – but I also see someone standing. When we walk out of the hospital, the sunlight feels different than it did through the window. It's warmer. Brighter. People pass by me without a second glance, and I cling to Sam's arm not because I'm scared – but because I can. And because I want too. I'm not whole yet. Not by a long shot. But I'm not shattered either. I've taken my first steps. Out of the room. Out of the fear. Out of the place where Sebastian left me broken. And into something that almost feels like healing.

3 MONTHS LATER...

It's hard to believe it's only been 3 months...
So much has changed, and yet parts of it still feel like they happened yesterday. The hospital, the pain, the fear – I don't think those memories will ever fully leave me. But what's surprised me the most is how much light has come after all that darkness.

The day I left the hospital, I expected it to be quiet. Just Sam, maybe the girls on the phone. But instead, he somehow managed to pull off the most beautiful surprise I could've imagined. He worked with Sacha, Hope, Isabella, and Sally – my girls, my absolute lifeline – and they threw this cosy, warm, healing celebration at his place. There were candles everywhere, music playing low in the background, and photos of all of us pinned to twinkle lights across the wall. Fiona, my boss, even showed up, wrapping me in this tight hug that made me cry on the spot. I didn't know how much I needed that until it happened.

And then – because Sam never does anything halfway – he asked me to move in with him. Right there in front of everyone. I said yes, of course. Honestly, I probably would've said yes two weeks earlier if he'd asked. That man has been my rock. He stayed every night at the hospital, brought me back piece by piece when I felt like I couldn't keep going. I don't know where I'd be without him, and I'm not sure I ever want to find out.

But it hasn't all been perfect. Not really. The police still haven't located Sebastian or Sophie. That part weighs on us. The not knowing. The silence. Sometimes I wake up in the middle of the night and check the locks twice, even though we've left Boston behind. Sam and I talked about it – really talked. And we decided it was time for a fresh start, somewhere quieter, somewhere safer. I decided to leave the Bridal Boutique, Boston was an unsettling place for me now and I needed to leave. Fiona understood this and was happy to give me a fantastic reference for my next job, whatever that may be.

His parents, being real estate developers, found a small commercial property in a tiny town in Wisconsin. Honestly, I didn't expect to fall in love with it. But Sam saw something in it, and when he put his hands on it – we spent a good month and a half restoring it, painted walls, restored floors, even hung a crooked little bell over the front door – it became his. Ours, in a way. He runs the shop himself now, and watching him build something from the ground up has been this quiet kind of beautiful.

The girls and I still talk almost every day. Between time zones and work and life, we don't always catch each other live, but the video calls, the messages, the stupid memes – they keep me grounded. Keep me laughing. It doesn't matter where we all are now, we're still us. Still fiercely, messily, unshakably together.

Life is different now. Simpler, slower. Safer, mostly. I'm not naïve enough to think the past won't follow us in some ways. But for the first time in a long time, I'm not just surviving – I'm living. And loving. And healing.

One step at a time.

Aimee

Within the two years of us actually breaking even on the Antique shop, myself and Sam were also in for another surprise, I hadn't been feeling myself for a few weeks and one trip to the doctor later, we found out we were expecting our first child together; emotional as I don't have my mom here to support me, but Sam's mom and dad have been terrific. I am falling in love with him more and more every day, I look back at the woman I once was, scared to book a flight ticket on my own, but, in turn I have catapulted myself into a different life; I couldn't be more proud.

Sam is flourishing day by day, I look at him and I can see him being the most amazing father to our child. I never thought anything like this would happen to me. I remember the night being sat in the diner, drained from my retail job, no social battery to see my friends – closing myself off from the world. Then my crazy ex tilted my world upside down, I fled New York – my city, my home only to be followed. However, when I was followed, I didn't picture life had someone special waiting in the wings for me, someone who was going to charge into my life, sweep me off my feet, this guy just so to be an antique shop assistant – he dealt with old, damaged, delicate and vulnerable trinkets for a job; little did he know I was going to offer him my heart; and he would do the same, take care of it, protect it.

Sam

It's been three and a half years since Aimee walked into my life – more specifically, into my old antique shop with the sun in her hair and curiosity in her eyes. I don't think she meant to change everything.

She just wanted to browse. But from the moment she smiled at me over that dusty glass counter, I was gone. And even now, I still am.

We've been through more than most couples ever will. The kind of trauma that either shatters people or welds them together. We chose to become stronger. Chose each other, again and again, even when it would've been easier to pull away. There's not a day that goes by where I don't thank the stars – or fate, or whatever brought her to me – for that.

Today, our home is full of warmth, laughter, and the soft coos of our son, Aston. He's everything. Truly. A perfect little bundle of sleepy grins, tiny hands that grip your finger with impossible strength, and eyes that look up at the world like it's all brand new. He looks like his mother – which honestly just wrecks me in the best way. Same dark lashes, same smile, even that little wrinkle between his brows when he's thinking hard. Watching Aimee in him is like falling in love with her all over again.

And her? She's a mother now, but she's still every version of herself I've ever loved. Brave, soft, smart, stubborn. I watch her hold Aston to her chest and hum quietly as she rocks him, and I swear, sometimes it brings tears to my eyes. There's a gentleness in her now, layered over steel, and I don't think I've ever admired anyone the way I admire her.

I run the refurbished shop a few blocks from home now – still antiques, still old-world charm, but with a nursery tucked in the back and a photo of Aimee and Aston on the counter where the register used to be. Some days she stops in with him, and we sit on the front steps while the sun goes down, just talking about nothing and everything. That's my favourite time of day.

It's quiet here in Wisconsin. A different life from what we imagined, maybe, but it's ours. The shadows of the past still exist – Sebastian and Sophie were never found, and that mystery still follows us in quiet moments – but it no longer controls us. We've learned to live despite it. To smile and sleep and build something new, something safe.

The girls still call – every week, like clockwork. Aimee lights up when she talks to them, and I love that about her, how she's never lost the people who matter. Family, chosen or not, is sacred to her. And Aston already knows all their names, even if he says "Issa" for Isabella and "Sa-sa" for Sacha. It makes her laugh every time.

Our life isn't always easy. The baby has colic some nights, and sometimes we argue over stupid things like laundry or who left the porch light on. But even in those little moments, I never feel doubt. I never feel distance. Being with Aimee has shown me that love isn't just the high points – it's the consistency, the quiet choosing of each other, day after day, even when life gets messy.

I love her more now than I did yesterday, and I'll love her even more tomorrow. That's the truth. It keeps unfolding, this love. Growing roots. And every time I look at her – holding our son, or curled up on the couch, or dancing barefoot in the kitchen – I still see the girl who stumbled into my shop that day. Only now, I also see my best friend, the mother of my child, and the love of my life.

And somehow… she chose me right back.

In the end, it was all born from coincidence – but what a beautiful story it became.

THE END